The Faces of Anonymity

The Faces of Anonymity: Anonymous and Pseudonymous Publication from the Sixteenth to the Twentieth Century

Edited by
Robert J. Griffin

First published 2003 by
PALGRAVE MACMILLAN™
175 Fifth Avenue, New York, N.Y. 10010 and
Houndmills, Basingstoke, Hampshire, England RG21 6XS
Companies and representatives throughout the world

PALGRAVE MACMILLAN is the global academic imprint of the Palgrave Macmillan division of St. Martin's Press, LLC and of Palgrave Macmillan Ltd. Macmillan® is a registered trademark in the United States, United Kingdom and other countries. Palgrave is a registered trademark in the European Union and other countries.

ISBN 0–312–29530–8 hardback

Library of Congress Cataloging-in-Publication Data
The faces of anonymity: anonymous and pseudonymous publications from the sixteenth to the twentieth century/edited by Robert J. Griffin
    p. cm.
Includes bibliographical references and index.
ISBN 0–312–29530–8
    1. Anonymous writings, English—History and criticism. 2. English literature—History and criticism. 3. Anonyms and pseudonyms, English—History. 4. Authorship—History. I. Griffin, Robert J. (Robert John), 1950–

PR121.F33 2003
820.9—dc21   2002072830

A catalogue record for this book is available from the British Library.

Design by Newgen Imaging Systems (P) Ltd., Chennai, India

First edition: January, 2003
10 9 8 7 6 5 4 3 2 1

Printed in the United States of America.

CONTENTS

PREFACE

My interest in anonymity was first aroused when I noticed that nearly every book or poem I was preparing for teaching in class was originally published anonymously or pseudonymously. When I began to look into it more systematically, it became clear how immense the subject was, for it seemed to take in nearly every author. That realization quickly led to the decision to pursue a track parallel to my plans for a monograph on anonymity and authorship by soliciting scholars in different periods to write essays drawing on their expertise. This volume is the fruit of that initiative.

In the planning stages I received invaluable advice from Josie Dixon and from my colleagues at *Poetics Today*, Meir Sternberg, Brian McHale, and Orly Lubin.

While working on this project, my research was enabled by grants and fellowships from the National Endowment for the Humanities, the Israel Academy of Arts and Sciences, the Huntington Library, the William Andrews Clark Library, the Lewis Walpole Library, and the Folger Library. It is impossible to say how grateful I am for this support. I have also learned much from the staffs of these great libraries.

I have received assistance of all kinds from very many people, more than I can name. Nonetheless, I wish to name a few: Leo Damrosch, Frances Ferguson, Joe Litvak, Helen Deutsch, Sonia Hofkosh, Lars Engle, David Kastan, Ronald Paulson, Annabel Patterson, Ruth Yeazell, Geoffrey Hartman, Margaret Ezell, Paul Fry, Roy Ritchie, Mary Robertson, Anna Malicka, Richard G. Williams, Cyndia Glegg, Werner Sollors, and Charles H. Rowell.

I thank the editors of *New Literary History* for permission to reprint in my Introduction material that first appeared in their journal.

NOTES ON CONTRIBUTORS

Vincent Carretta is Professor of English at the University of Maryland, College Park. His publications include *"The Snarling Muse": Verbal and Visual Satire from Pope to Churchill* (1983); *George III and the Satirists from Hogarth to Byron* (1990); ed., *The Interesting Narrative and Other Writings* by Olaudah Equiano (1995); ed., *Unchained Voices: An Anthology of Black Authors in the English-Speaking World of the Eighteenth Century* (1996); ed., *Letters of the Late Ignatius Sancho, An African* (1998); ed., *Thoughts and Sentiments on the Evil of Slavery and Other Writings* by Quobna Ottobah Cugoano (1999); *The Complete Writings of Phyllis Wheatley* (2001); and coed., with Philip Gould, *Genius in Bondage: Literature of the Early Black Atlantic* (2001).

Susan Eilenberg is an Associate Professor of English at SUNY-Buffalo and the author of *Strange Power of Speech: Wordsworth, Coleridge, and Literary Possession* (Oxford, 1992). She is currently writing on Milton and quantifiability, and is a regular contributor to *The London Review of Books*.

Margaret J. M.'Ezell is the John Paul Abbott Professor of Liberal Arts at Texas A&M University. She is the author of *The Patriarch's Wife: Literary Evidence and the History of the Family* (1987), *Writing Women's Literary History* (1993), *Social Authorship and the Advent of Print* (1999), the editor of *The Poems and Prose of Mary, Lady Chudleigh* (1993), and the co-editor, with Kathleen O'Keeffe, of *Cultural Artifacts and the Production of Meaning* (1994).

Robert J. Griffin is Senior Lecturer in the Department of English at Tel Aviv University, and the Associate Editor of *Poetics Today. Wordsworth's Pope: A Study in Literary Historiography* was published by Cambridge University Press in 1995. He is currently completing a book-length study of the cultural history and poetics of anonymity, 1700–1830.

Kristine Louise Haugen recently completed a dissertation at Princeton on Richard Bentley's philology and criticism, and has published articles on Richard Hurd, Ossian, seventeenth-century Oxford, and on sixteenth-century pedagogy. She has received Mellon, Javits, and Whiting fellowships, and is now a Frances Yates Postdoctoral Research Fellow at the Warburg Institute in London.

Holly A. Laird, Professor and Chair of the Department of English at the University of Tulsa, is Editor of *Tulsa Studies in Women's Literature* and a past president of the Council of Editors of Learned Journals. Her book, *Women Coauthors*, which focuses on late nineteenth-century to contemporary women literary collaborators, was published by the University of Illinois Press in 2000.

Susan S. Lanser is Professor of English and Comparative Literature and Chair of Women's Studies at the Brandeis University. She is the author of *The Narrative Act* (1981), *Fictions of Authority: Women Writers and Narrative Voice* (1992), and the co-editor of *Women Critics: An Anthology 1660–1820* (1995) and the Broadview edition of Helen Maria Williams's *Letter from France* (2001). She is currently at work on a book-length study of changing constructions of sapphism in the long eighteenth century.

Brian McHale is Professor of English at The Ohio State University, and co-editor of *Poetics Today*. He is the author of *Postmodernist Fiction* (1987), *Constructing Postmodernism* (1992), and of numerous articles on twentieth-century fiction, postmodernist poetry, and narratology. He is currently completing a book-length study of the postmodernist long poem.

Marcy L. North is Assistant Professor of English at Florida State University. She has published articles on early modern anonymity, and her book, *The Anonymous Renaissance: Cultures of Discretion in Tudor-Stuart England*, is forthcoming from the University of Chicago Press.

Leah Price is Professor of English at Harvard University. She is the author of *The Anthology and the Rise of the Novel: From Richardson to George Eliot* (2000) and a regular contributor to the *London Review of Books*; she is currently working on two book projects, *Novels and Knowledge in the First Information Age* and *The Secretarial Imagination*, as well as an anthology called *Victorian Readers: A Reader*.

James Raven is Reader in Cultural and Social History in the University of Oxford and Professorial Fellow of Mansfield College, Oxford. He is the author of numerous books and articles on the history of British, European and North American literary, publishing and communications history, including most recently *The English Novel, 1770–1829*, 2 vols., coedited (Oxford University Press, 2000) and *English Books and American Customers* (University of South Carolina Press, 2002).

INTRODUCTION

Robert J. Griffin

This collection of ten original essays is, as far as I am aware, the first book of its kind to address the topic of anonymous and pseudonymous publication. Literary studies exhibit a curious reluctance to acknowledge that most of the literature ever published appeared either without the author's name or under a fictive name. We have very few statistics, but the ones provided by James Raven in his essay for this volume are quite astounding. According to Raven, over 80 percent of all novels published in Britain between 1750 and 1790 were published anonymously. During the 1790s, the amount fell to 62 percent, and to less than 50 percent in the first decade of the nineteenth century. But during the 1820s it rose again to almost 80 percent. Given the sheer amount of unsigned and pseudo-signed publication from antiquity to the present, however, my first realization, as editor, was that no book on this topic could adequately survey such a vast field, for it appears that there are very few authors who did not resort to anonymity or pseudonymity at least once in their careers.[1] The focus on England (with one exception), and primarily on literary texts such as poems, novels, and essays rather than printed matter generally, is therefore purely pragmatic. The chronological field delimited, with concentrations in the seventeenth, eighteenth, and nineteenth centuries, runs parallel to traditional literary history's account of the rise of the professional author. Topics covered are genre, gender, nationalism, authorial cross-dressing, collaboration and co-authorship, ghostwriting, hoaxes, attribution, manuscripts, and problems of reading.

"Anonymous" is generally understood as a text whose author is not identified on the title page. Pseudonymity is therefore a subset of anonymity; the important fact in both cases is that the legal name of the writer is not in evidence. This widespread practice, which cuts across centuries and affects both the production and the reception of written texts, has been under-researched in relation to its ubiquity. Moreover, the critical work that does exist, much of it excellent, confines itself to an author, a genre, or a period.[2] By gathering essays on different periods together in the same volume, this collection serves (at least) two purposes. First, it calls attention to the continuing functions of anonymity in what Coleridge already calls, in *Biographia Literaria*, "an age of personality." Second, although complete coverage even within these centuries is itself impossible, the chronological range reveals significant historical differences, as well as structural continuities.

Michel Foucault established a kind of default position for thinking about the relation between anonymity and authorship in his widely cited essay, "What is an Author?"[3] For Foucault, modern literary authorship is defined by the author-function, by which he means the various ways the *name* of the author functions in discourse. In an earlier period, literary texts were anonymous whereas scientific texts were named until a reversal occurred:

> There was a time when texts that we today call "literary" (narratives, stories, epics, tragedies, comedies) were accepted, put into circulation, and valorized without any question about the identity of the author; their anonymity caused no difficulties since their ancientness, whether real or imagined, was regarded as a sufficient guarantee of their status. On the other hand, those texts that we now would call scientific—those dealing with cosmology and the heavens, medicine and illness, natural sciences and geography— were accepted in the Middle Ages, and accepted as "true," only when marked with the name of the author .... A reversal occurred in the seventeenth or eighteenth century ....[4]

In response to this dating, Roger Chartier showed that the author-function for literature existed in the Middle Ages as well, and indeed, since Foucault provides no evidence but his own authority, there seems to be little reason to assume that readers' or hearers' interest in authors as the originators of works began in what is now referred to as the early modern period.[5] But if naming occurs much earlier, or, rather, appears to exist as far back as we can go, and thus puts in question the neat chronology of the story, it is also the case that anonymity does not simply disappear with the emergence of a commercial culture. While there is certainly much less authorial anonymity today than several centuries ago, we are misled if we assume that it is simply a matter of "reversal." Foucault's narrative can thus be faulted on two important points: first, there is no necessary connection between copyright ownership and the author's name on a title page; and second, there is a very large amount of anonymous publication in the nineteenth century while authors in our own day continue to hide themselves behind masks of all kinds. By looking more deeply into these issues we can begin to rethink the relation between anonymity and authorship in fundamental ways.

The name of the author comes to assume a pivotal role, so the argument goes, because once the manuscript becomes a commodity to be sold rather than a gift to be given away to the fortunate bookseller, as it was under the aristocratic dispensation, and once the author is given formal legal protection as the proprietor of intellectual property, the value of the commodity in the marketplace extends itself back, metonymically as it were, to the author as origin of value. As Mark Rose explains: "The name of the author becomes a kind of brand name, a recognizable sign that the cultural commodity will be of a certain kind and quality. No institutional embodiment of the author–work relation, however, is more fundamental than copyright, which not only makes possible the manufacture and distribution of books, films, and other commodities but also, by endowing it with legal reality, helps to produce and affirm the very identity of the author as author."[6] In a gloss on Foucault, Simon During puts it this way: "In modernity there has been a shift of author function: the authorial name has become a *property*—in a process we can trace by examining the history of copyright laws."[7]

This narrative is not totally wrong; there is too much evidence in its favor. Take Trollope's autobiography as an example. Vigorously defending authorship as a trade, Trollope declares of copyright: "Take away from English authors their copyrights, and you would soon take also from England her authors." The connection between the name "Trollope" and the commercial value of the commodity is also quite clear. As an established author in the mid-1860s, and suspecting that his work was well-received only because he signed his name to it, he experimented by publishing two stories anonymously in *Blackwood's Magazine*. But Blackwood offered him, as he says, "perhaps half what they would have fetched with my name," and since neither story was successful the experiment was dropped.[8]

What I want to argue, nonetheless, is that the widely accepted narrative put in circulation by Foucault, if not wrong, is not nuanced enough, and thus creates significant distortions and misunderstandings. By the terms of its formulation, even if not meaning to, it throws in the shade or tends to ignore a very large field of actual publication practice. The gaps begin to appear the moment we take perspective from the widespread practice of anonymous and pseudonymous publication.

The history of publication shows unequivocally that there is no cause-and-effect relation between the ownership of literary property, or the lack of it, and the presence or absence of the name of the author. Even when the name is marketed as a commodity, the copyright is not always retained by the writer; even when the copyright is retained, the writer can remain unknown. Authors could (and did) either sell or retain copyright. Authors could (and did) either sign their name to the work or not. While Trollope was signing his name to his books he did not always retain copyright, which caused him difficulties when he wanted to collect and publish his Barchester novels together. Byron gave away the copyright of *Childe Harold's Pilgrimage* as a gift, but signed his name to the book. On the other hand, he sold the copyright of the first five books of *Don Juan* to Murray, and the other eleven to John Hunt, but did not sign the book. Byron's motives are worth noting. Since *Queen Mab*—which challenged both monarchy and Christianity, and which Shelley had signed—had been used against Shelley in court, Byron, who had recently divorced and was engaged in a custody battle, took heed and instructed Murray to keep his name off the book.[9] All of Jane Austen's novels published during her lifetime appeared without her name, yet she tended to retain copyright, paying the cost of printing herself and using the bookseller as a distributor who took a percentage of the profits.[10] Charlotte Smith's husband was legally entitled both to her copyrights and any earnings from them, a situation for women writers that ended only with the Married Women's Property Act of 1870. But Smith signed her books and called attention to her financial plight in her prefaces.

The conclusion is inescapable: naming and copyright protections operate on separate levels of discourse and involve separate sets of decisions on the part of the writer (if indeed the writer is even consulted). When copyright historians discuss the author as owner, that author is an abstract legal identity that does not need to have a specific name for it to function in legal discourse. No copyright law ever required the name of the author to be printed on the title page of a book or pamphlet. In a cogent critique of certain assumptions made by the pioneers who brought copyright history to the attention of literary critics, David Saunders and Ian Hunter have made the point that the legal and artistic identities of the author have been conflated but must be kept apart.[11]

If we consult the laws that regulated printing in England, we discover an interesting fact. At times, various laws and proclamations did indeed require the name of the author to be given on the title page. A Royal Proclamation in 1546 directed that "every book should bear the author's and the printer's name, and exact date of printing."[12] Yet, when the Stationers' Company was incorporated eleven years later in 1557 with the charge of regulating printing and publishing, such language was not in evidence. From the mid-sixteenth century when the regulation of printing was established, there has been only a brief period of roughly twenty years, beginning with the Star Chamber Decree of 1637, when the laws of England required the name of the author to be printed on the title page of a book or pamphlet. After the Star Chamber was abolished in 1641, it was thought expedient during the interregnum not simply to reinstate licensing, which Milton opposed, but also once again to require the name of the author on the title page. Yet, with the Licensing Act of 1662, that requirement was dropped.[13] Following 1695, when pre-publication censorship ended, proposals to require the name (and sometimes the address) of the author on title pages were put forward at various times, but were never adopted into law.[14] At every phase of what Mark Rose calls the "regime of regulation," licensing laws were directed primarily at those who manufactured and distributed the goods. Even when authors were mentioned in the statutes as liable to penalties, including after pre-publication censorship had lapsed, it was the names of the printer or the bookseller that needed to be given in the imprint at the bottom of the page. John Murray could refrain in 1819 from putting his name on the title page of the anonymous poem, *Don Juan*, but following the Seditious Societies Act of 1799 the printer's name, Thomas Davison, was compulsory.[15]

One of the things this means is that authorial anonymity in England was, essentially, an officially tolerated form of sanctuary, for even in cases where the printer was successfully prosecuted, the author could not always be found. Daniel Defoe eventually was captured by the authorities, and stood in the pillory, and went to jail for writing the anonymous pamphlet, "The Shortest Way with the Dissenters" (1702). But Percy Shelley escaped punishment. One copy of his anonymous broadsheet ballad, "The Devil's Walk" (1812), with its attack on the Prince Regent, survives in the Public Record Office where it was discovered in 1871. Shelley's Irish servant, Daniel Healy (the name he gave the judge was "Daniel Hill"), sat in jail for distributing it and the equally illegal *Declaration of Rights* because neither had an imprint indicating the printer. But Shelley was not arrested even though he was the author and mostly likely had a hand in the printing as well.[16] With the exception, then, of a very brief period in the seventeenth century, governments were reluctant to force all authors out into the open.

I have suggested that Foucault's large narrative about the connection between copyright and naming does not correspond to the historical record, at least in England. This brings us back to the question of numbers. Even without the detailed statistics provided by Raven, an educated guess tells us that anonymity, when defined broadly as the absence of reference to the legal name of the writer on the title page, takes in a very large number of books published at least up to the twentieth century. It involves nearly every author. Anonymity during this period, I would argue, was at least as much a norm as signed authorship. Even if a gradual tapering off is eventually documented, there is still clear evidence that anonymous publication continued to be an option for authors well into the nineteenth century. As late as 1835, John Galt observed that "critics universally regard all authors who give their names as actuated by vanity," a climate that in many cases must have worked against signing.[17] As late as 1871, a review of an anonymous novel, *Desperate Remedies*, speculates whether the author is male or female:

> *Desperate Remedies*, though in some respects an unpleasant story, is undoubtedly a very powerful one. We cannot decide, satisfactorily to our own mind, on the sex of the author; for while certain evidence, such as the close acquaintance which he or she appears (and, as far as we can judge, with reason) to possess with the mysteries of the female toilette, would appear to point to its being the work of one of that sex, on the other hand there are certain expressions to be met with in the book so remarkably coarse as to render it almost impossible that it should have come from the pen of an English lady. Yet, again, all the best anonymous novels of the last twenty years— a dozen instances will at once suggest themselves to the novel-reader—have been the work of female writers. In this conflict of evidence, we will confine ourselves to the inexpressive "he" in speaking of our present author, if we chance to need a pronoun.[18]

I cannot, for the moment, linger over this passage and that "inexpressive 'he'." But at least the reviewer, after a display of prejudices, concludes inconclusively. Other readers and reviewers of anonymous books are less delicate—in 1848 a rumor circulated in Mayfair that Thackeray's governess, supposedly the model for Becky Sharp, was the author of

Jane Eyre and that Rochester was her vision of her former employer.[19] But, to continue, our author's second book, *Under the Greenwood Tree* (1872), is signed "By the Author of *Desperate Remedies*," and only with the third novel, *A Pair of Blue Eyes* (1873), would the Victorian reader learn that the author's name is Thomas Hardy.

The review itself, naturally, is anonymous, as were most reviews and magazine articles. In the 1860s, *The Fortnightly* was one of the first to sign all its articles, which started a trend, but reviews in the *Times Literary Supplement* remained anonymous until the early 1970s, and articles in *The Economist* still are. Debates in the *TLS* twenty-five years ago repeated arguments that had been made as early as the *Gentleman's Magazine* two hundred years before.[20] Some thought that signing guaranteed integrity because writers could not escape accountability; others thought signing would allow them to gauge the weight of an opinion by knowing its source. On the other side, the argument went that it was anonymity that guaranteed integrity because it freed writers from social and political pressures. Nonetheless, in 1871, the year of the review of Hardy's first novel, an anonymous writer in the *National Quarterly Review* of New York observed that "the amount of anonymous and pseudonymous writing has been enormous within the last half century." In the periodical press of Europe, the writer continues, "anonymous writing is the rule, pseudonymous common, and (except in France) avowed authorship is rare." Yet, it is curious that even in a time of widespread authorial anonymity the reviewer begins his article by noting that "few are aware of the extent and variety of anonymous literature."[21] Even when ubiquitous, anonymity rarely calls attention to itself.

The motivations for publishing anonymously have varied widely with circumstances, but they have included an aristocratic or a gendered reticence, religious self-effacement, anxiety over public exposure, fear of prosecution, hope of an unprejudiced reception, and the desire to deceive. This list is hardly exhaustive. The wish to keep one's identity in the dark could extend so far as to drive authors to communicate with their publishers through an intermediary or under a pseudonym as in the cases of Swift, Burney, Austen, and George Eliot. Swift sent the manuscript of *Gulliver's Travels* to Benjamin Motte with a cover letter signed "Richard Sympson," the sea-captain's cousin. Fanny Burney disguised her handwriting in the manuscript of *Evelina* because, as amanuensis to her father, her hand was known to London publishers; the manuscript was delivered by her brother, in disguise, at night. Charles Burney read the novel out to the family circle, not knowing that his daughter had written it. Austen's brother communicated with her publishers, but she wrote to a prospective publisher under the name "Mrs. Ashton Dennis," and Lewes handled negotiations for "George Eliot" referring in his letters to the author as "he."

Authors also chose anonymity if they felt that their authorial persona conflicted with their daily one. Scott signed his poetry, but he did not sign *Waverley*, or so he wrote in a letter, because he felt the dignity of an officer of the court in Edinburgh would be compromised if he were publicly known to be an author of popular fiction: "In truth I am not sure it would be considered quite decorous for me as a Clerk of Sessions to write novels. Judges being monks clerks are a sort of lay-brethren from whom some solemnity of walk and conduct may be expected." Jane Millgate adds in a note that Scott had thoughts of becoming a judge himself.[22] Even today, not all writers of thrillers, romances, and detective fiction sign their legal names and for similar reasons. Signing or not signing may depend on genre, but also on specific cultural circumstances. If, in some cases, anonymity protected one's social position, in others it could successfully obscure it. Paul Hammond makes the point that, in the case of the late seventeenth-century poet John Oldham, anonymity conferred authority by hiding his relatively low social status.[23]

It was common for writers to test the waters before revealing their identity in a second edition. The first Gothic novel, Horace Walpole's *The Castle of Otranto* (1765), a work purporting to be a translation by "William Marshall, Gent.," from a sixteenth-century Italian original "printed in Naples, in the black letter," is a well-known example. But it could also work the other way around: a known author could retreat into the shade for whatever reason, perhaps in order to slip out from underneath an authorial identity that had become confining. I have already cited Trollope, who wanted to know if his books sold because they were good, or because his reputation was already established. A twentieth-century version of this is Doris Lessing, who published *The Diaries of Jane Somers* (1983) as Jane Somers because, she states in a later preface to the same work, she did not want reviewers to frame their judgments in terms derived from their reading of "Doris Lessing."[24] Stephen King, who published several novels in the 1970s under the name Richard Bachman, offers a variation of this dilemma in *Misery* (1990), a fable of an author trapped, literally, by his reader into writing the kind of story the reader wants to read.

If it is sometimes true that the professional situation puts a premium on the name of the writer, this is not always so. There are also times when the exigencies of writing for bread enforce disguise—it may be counterproductive to flood the market. This is certainly the case with

Mary Robinson who, together with Southey, provided many of the poems published in the *Morning Post* in 1800. Robinson routinely signed her novels, which undoubtedly capitalized on her notoriety as a famous actress and former mistress of the Prince of Wales; she had also collected her previously anonymous poetry into signed volumes in 1791 and 1793. But to disguise the fact that so many of the newspaper's poems were coming from the same hand, poems of hers were printed under the signatures "Tabitha Bramble," "Tabitha," "T. B.," "Bridget," "Oberon," "Laura Maria," "L. M.," "Sappho," and so on.[25] Some of these, it is true, point to Robinson, such as "Laura Maria," the name under which it was already known she had published her Della Cruscan poems. But Tabitha Bramble is a character in Smollett's *Humphrey Clinker*. Here, the pseudonym functions as a signal to the reader to expect a dramatized, and clearly fictional, point of view; educated guesses would not lead back to the real author.

This last point leads us back to the author-function and the way it can be fruitfully applied to the case of anonymity. For although Foucault identifies the author-function and its historicity with the name of the author, his focus is on how the name circulates in discourse apart from its designation as the proper name of an empirical person. Rather than invoke the flesh-and-blood writer, the name signals the status of a certain kind of writing, works as a principle of classification, and establishes a relation of homogeneity and filiation between texts. But, as is clear from Foucault's example of "Hermes Trismegistus," the relation of filiation between texts obtains even when the author is a fiction. More than that, filiation exists even when the author remains unknown, as in the example of texts that are signed "by the author of." Well-known instances are "by the author of *Waverley*" and "by the author of *Sense and Sensibility*." But a search through a catalog of titles arranged according to year of publication, such as the one at the Huntington Library, shows that, although this designation appears occasionally in the late sixteenth and early seventeenth century, it is used with greater frequency in the late seventeenth century and is common practice in the eighteenth and nineteenth centuries. The author of *The History of Jemmy and Jenny Jessamy* (1753) is given as "By the Author of *The History of Miss Betsy Thoughtless*," a book that was itself published anonymously in 1751. Eliza Haywood's name appears nowhere; her *Female Spectator* is advertised opposite the title page, but without attribution to an author. Charlotte Lennox's *The Female Quixote* was published anonymously in 1752; *Henrietta* appeared in 1758 as "By the Author of *The Female Quixote*." Indeed, as I have already mentioned, the title of Hardy's second novel in the 1870s employs this phrase as well.

The phrase "by the author of," it should be noted, refers us not so much to a situated person as to a previous performance and acts as a kind of advertisement. My favorite example of this latter type is "*Discipline*, By the Author of *Self-Control*" (1815). This title suggests, for example, that if you liked *Self-Control* (1811), you'll love *Discipline*. (It is one of those unaccountable oddities of cultural history that this book was published by "Manners and Miller.") In these cases, a relation is established between two texts according to their authorship and yet the author remains nameless. In fact, a book can have several of the characteristics of the author-function as Foucault defines it—status, copyright, relation to other books by the same author, and so on—and yet not have a named author. This is because the author-function describes precisely a function that may be fulfilled by a name but does not require one. It is first of all an empty function, a structural blank space, which may be signed or unsigned depending on the circumstances. And when signed, of course, the name may just as easily be a pseudonym.

Genette makes this point well in coining the term "onymity" (signing the legal name) to go together with pseudonymity and anonymity: "After all, to sign a work with one's real name is a choice like any other, and nothing authorizes us to regard this choice as insignificant."[26] The author's name is another artifact, at a distance from the empirical writer, a signifier within the semiotics of the text that can be manipulated strategically. Over half of what Shelley published during his lifetime appeared either anonymously or pseudonymously, under such rubrics as "By a Gentleman at Oxford," or "Edited by John Fitzvictor," or "By Philopatria, Jun." Signing one's legal name is not an automatic choice, but part of a strategy for associating only certain pieces with a projected persona.

Such logic is behind my choice of the title for this collection of essays. If the legal name and the fictional name are types of masks, I understand anonymity also not as a lack or absence, but positively, as another mask. There is not, as the standard narrative suggests, an opposition between identity and anonymity (identity emerging out of anonymity with the arrival of modernity), but rather a play of subject positions, because even unnamed texts project a "presence." Without a name to individualize the author, an implied authorial consciousness is still inferred by the reader, and, in that process, the historical, social, and cultural codes that comprise the text come to the fore. This does not mean that all readers will see the same face. As Susan Lanser's essay demonstrates, a single text can give rise to two opposing constructions of the implied author. Moreover, although readers tend to assume that a text is the product of an individual, both anonymous and pseudonymous texts may project a persona that hides their multiple authorship. In other cases, anonymity stands for not a single but a corporate persona, a point made by Paul Hammond in relation to a manuscript collection of erotic poems that project "an ethos, a style of life, a group of attitudes and poses, a shared idiom" (133), and by Dallas Liddle in relation to the corporate persona adopted by anonymous writers in journals and newspapers (54).

This introduction is not meant to present an exhaustive taxonomy. But I hope enough has been said to suggest that, even taking into account the constraints of the structural givens that condition writing and publishing, the historical particularity of authorship in each case must be respected. The essays in this collection illustrate the importance of contingency and context even as they address issues that are posed, thematized, and encoded in a range of anonymous texts.

Working in very different periods, the late seventeenth and the late nineteenth centuries, Kristine Haugen and Leah Price analyze how anonymity reflects the concerns of a particular cultural moment. Haugen's essay takes up a crucial moment in the Battle of the Books. In the late seventeenth century, the authority of authors and critics was attenuated by their awareness of the shadow of the ancients. But once ancient authority was put in question by Bentley's exposure of a supposedly ancient text as a pseudonymous hoax (the letters of "Phalaris"), what were the implications for the authority of contemporary writers? Haugen increases our sensitivity to the self-reflexivity of the issues at stake in this famous quarrel, while simultaneously calling attention to the nature of Bentley's hard-won authority and to the instability at the heart of all textual constructions.

Leah Price shows how the new social phenomenon of the female secretary–typist in the late nineteenth century intersects with ghost-writing. Secretaries were often not just typists but also ghostwriters for their employers. Surveying novels and stories about hack writers who ghostwrite for wealthy patrons, and juxtaposing them with ones about the new type–writer girl, Price argues convincingly that the anxieties these stories address revolve around gender. While some of the works were published under pseudonyms, Price's focus is less on the semiotics of the title page than on ghostwriting as both theme and cultural allegory of the New Woman in the marketplace. If some of these fictions attempt to reinforce traditional gender roles, others destabilize the power relations that were apparently naturalized in the gendering of the boss–secretary relation by exposing and in some cases reversing that relation.

Without denying either the social constraints on women in the early modern period or prejudices against women writers, matters addressed by the women themselves in their works, Margaret Ezell, in surveying the functions of the phrase "By a Lady," questions whether anonymity is simply imposed on women writers of the time. For, in these cases, women employed neither anonymity nor a male pseudonym, but chose instead, while suppressing their name, to foreground gender and social position. The question then becomes: What did the feminine signify and how might it be deployed? By careful analysis, Ezell establishes both the commercial value of female authorship and its potential political force.

Holly Laird, in her account of the Victorian "Michael Field," the pseudonym of coauthors (and lovers) Katherine Bradley and Edith Cooper, argues that collaborative authorship presents a challenge to ingrained thinking about authorship as "solitary genius" (in Jack Stillinger's phrase). But, if the pseudonym appears to deny the fact of collaboration, Laird asks us to understand the union between Bradley and Cooper as the creation of a third entity. Laird focuses on the authors' self-understanding of their writing as a romantic marriage that subsumed their identities, and traces the set of associations that led them to choose the name Michael Field as its signifier.

Susan Lanser addresses one of the central methodological problems posed by an anonymous or pseudonymous text: in the absence of reliable extra-textual information about the writer, how in fact does the reader construct the meaning of the text? The case of the anonymous text foregrounds the circularity of reading and the centrality of the notion of the implied author by highlighting the extent to which, as Lanser neatly puts it, "reading abhors an authorial vacuum." By analyzing a text that has received two diametrically opposed readings from modern critics—a narrative (among other things) of a woman who tours Europe dressed as a man and who eventually puts aside her disguise in order to settle down with another woman—Lanser suggests the problem inheres in the notion of *the* implied author. Once we understand that it may not be possible to identify the sex of an implied author, we understand further that the notion of the implied author itself implies a unified construction of a plural text, whereas "a text's consciousness may be general without being singular."

Marcy North asks a different question about reading. Since many authors are no longer anonymous, how can we recover the original context of their anonymity, specifically, how does a modern reader recover the context of anonymity for an author as famous as Shakespeare? Here, recovering anonymity means recuperating aspects of meaning encoded in the circulation of manuscripts that have become obscured through the conventions of book publishing. North analyzes manuscript anonymity as a material and thematic frame for reading sonnets by Shakespeare copied into seventeenth-century commonplace books and manuscript compilations, and then speculates on the milieu in which the sonnets circulated before they were published by Thomas Thorpe in 1609. A common and expected condition of many texts, North warns that anonymity signifies in more than one way and could "denote both choice and accident, name suppression and negligence."

Is there any relation between the anonymity of the author and the content of a book? Clearly not in every case, otherwise a majority of books published before, let us say, 1900 would dwell on their own anonymity in self-reflexive fashion. Yet, clearly also, in some books the theme of a lack of identity is pursued so consistently within the text that authorial anonymity needs to be seen as more than a convenient convention of disguise. Several contributors open up the self-reflexive dimensions of an anonymous text in which anonymity (or pseudonymity) is simultaneously theme and allegory.

Susan Eilenberg and Brian McHale, especially, place reflexivity in the foreground. While critics of *Frankenstein* have previously drawn a parallel between Mary Shelley's anonymity and her monster's, Eilenberg explores just how various and subtle the meanings of anonymity may be. By showing how deeply Mary Shelley meditated the nature of social anonymity as the threat of an unassimilable Other, Eilenberg aligns herself with critics who have traced the political or psychological allegory of the monster as a figure for oppressed social groups or repressed psychic contents. But she develops these issues in relation to the specific linguistic peculiarity pointed out by Catherine Gallagher, which is that nothing is signified by something: the substantive "nothing." If "nothing" and "nobody" are substantives holding a positive place in the chain of language, the monster embodies the paradox—he is not so much alive as undead. In him, negation is animated. Eilenberg's essay stimulates thought in several directions, one of which must be the implications of the unstable and uncanny nature of human subjectivity, grounded as it is in language.

Brian McHale trains his sights on a contemporary controversy, poems that purport to be translations into English of Yasusada, poet and survivor of Hiroshima. But since Yasusada is a mask adopted most likely by Kent Johnson of Ohio, the ethics and purposes of impersonation take center stage. For Charles Bernstein, Yasusada is a hoax motivated by white-male resentment at the preference given to women and minorities by editors of poetry. McHale disputes this reading by producing a taxonomy of literary hoaxes from Ossian and Rowley to Ern Malley and Alan Sokal, arguing that Yasusada is a mock-hoax in which the whole point of the impersonation is to expose its own inauthenticity, and hence the fictional quality of national identity construction. As a parody of Japanese poems translated into English, Yasusada foregrounds the factitiousness of the construction of Japanese-ness in American culture.

Vincent Carretta presents us with an attribution question by reprinting here for the first time, and thus making more widely available, ten letters that originally appeared in the *Morning Post* in the late 1770s under the name "Gustavus Vassa," an attack on the slave trade in the Glasgow Courier in 1792 signed "Gustavus," and an anti-war piece signed "Othello" that appeared in 1794 in *The Cabinet*. Is this the same Gustavus Vassa whose African name was Olaudah Equiano and who published his autobiography, *The Interesting Narrative of the Life of Olaudah Equiano, or Gustavus Vassa, The African, Written by Himself*, in 1789, and did he subsequently sign "Othello" in a journal operated by known friends? It is crucial to the political force of Equiano's autobiography that he is a named historical person. The oddity pointed out here by Carretta, though, is that Equiano's slave name, Vassa, which is also his legal name, was the name of an early Swedish king who freed his people and thus had become the generic name for a liberator in eighteenth-century journals. This situation raises the possibility that one's legal name can function as a pseudonym in print.

James Raven's overview of anonymous novels in the late eighteenth and early nineteenth century is based on solo and collaborative research over many years. Aside from statistics, he provides a sociology of the book trade during this period. Empirical evidence of this sort has the power to radically adjust our notions of authorship. For instance, how many scholars would have guessed that in the 1810s, while 56 percent of all novels were published anonymously, the great majority of the 44 percent of those that were named, were by female authors? Thus, counter to intuition, during this period the female name is not being suppressed; rather a certain model of feminity is actually being promoted, apparently for commercial reasons. Raven's numbers make us hungry for more. For instance, we know that anonymous publication was still widespread in the late nineteenth century, but how widespread was it really? Would reliable numbers for this period similarly challenge current assumptions about authorship? Only the most complacent will answer in the negative.

In conclusion, taken together, these essays show that anonymity is not simply a residual characteristic of oral or manuscript culture, but continues for several centuries to be a dominant form, perhaps the norm, of print culture as well. Anonymity was not always a form of ethical, or religious, or socially imposed self-effacement, but had commercial uses as well. It intersects with different social and cultural contexts across several centuries. Moreover, neither anonymity nor pseudonymity have disappeared in the present, and are especially in evidence in electronically distributed writing of all kinds. Therefore, some historical understanding of anonymous publication must be integral to our understanding of authorship and writing generally. This volume hopes to stimulate further research in that direction.

Notes

1. See Archer Taylor and Fredric J. Mosher, *The Bibliographic History of Anonyma and Pseudonyma* (Chicago: University of Chicago Press, 1951); Samuel Halkett and John Laing, *A Dictionary of Anonymous and Pseudonymous Publications in the English Language* (Edinburgh: W. Paterson, 1882–88); and William Prideaux Courtney, *The Secrets of Our National Literature: Chapters in the History of Anonymous and Pseudonymous Writings of our Countrymen* (London: Archibald Constable & Co, 1908).

2. For further study see: J. W. Saunders, "The Stigma of Print: A Note on the Social Bases of Tudor Poetry," *Essays in Criticism* 1 (1951), 139–64; Marcy North, "Ignoto in the Age of Print: The Manipulation of Anonymity in Early Modern England," *Studies in Philology* 91 (1994), 390–416; Paul Hammond, "Anonymity in Restoration Poetry," *The Seventeenth Century* 8 (1993), 123–42; Catherine Gallagher, *Nobody's Story: The Vanishing Acts of Women Writers in the Marketplace, 1670–1820* (Berkeley and Los Angeles: University of California Press, 1994); Alexander Welsh, *George Eliot and Blackmail* (Cambridge, MA: Harvard University Press, 1985); Jane Millgate, *Walter Scott: The Making of the Novelist* (Toronto: University of Toronto Press, 1984); Peter Manning, "The Nameless Broken Dandy and the Structure of Authorship," *Reading Romantics: Texts and Contexts* (Oxford: Oxford University Press, 1990), 145–62; Jerome J. McGann, "Byron and the Anonymous Lyric," *The Byron Journal* 20 (1992), 27–45; Jan Fergus, *Jane Austen: A Literary Life* (London: Macmillan, 1991); Sharon Marcus, "The Profession of Author: Abstraction, Advertising, and Jane Eyre," *PMLA* 110 (1995), 206–19; Geraldine Friedman, "Pseudonymity, Passing, and Queer Biography: The Case of Mary Diana Dods," *Romanticism on the Net* 23 (August 2001) <http://users.ox.ac.uk/~scat0385/23friedman.html>; Dallas Liddle, "Salesmen, Sportsmen, Mentors: Anonymity and Mid-Victorian Theories of Journalism," *Victorian Studies* 41 (1991), 31–68; Marc DaRosa, "Henry James, Anonymity, and the Press: Journalistic Modernity and the Decline of the Author," *Modern Fiction Studies* 43 (1997), 826–59; Brenda Silver, " 'Anon' and 'The Reader': Virginia Woolf's Last Essays," *Twentieth Century Literature* 25 (Fall/Winter 1979), 356–441; E. M. Forster, "Anonymity: An Enquiry," *Atlantic Monthly* 135 (1925), 588–95; Henry Seidel Canby, "Anon is Dead," *The American Mercury* 8 (1926), 79–84; James Fergusson, "The Life and Works of Anon," *The London Mercury* 27 (January 1933), 246–49; Robert Wells, "Distinctive Anonymity," in *The Poet's Voice and Craft*, ed. C. B. McCully (Manchester: Carcaret, 1994), 167–81. This list is necessarily selective. A special issue of *New Literary History* [33 (Spring 2002)] devoted to anonymity appeared while this book was in production.

3. For the argument that follows I draw heavily on my article, "Anonymity and Authorship," *New Literary History* 30 (1999), 877–95.

4. Michel Foucault, "What is an Author?" in *Textual Strategies: Perspectives in Post-Structuralist Criticism*, ed. Josue V. Harari (Ithaca: Cornell University Press, 1979), 149.

5. Roger Chartier, *The Order of Books: Readers, Authors, and Libraries in Europe between the Fourteenth and Eighteenth Centuries*, trans. Lydia G. Cochrane (Stanford: Stanford University Press, 1994), 58.

   Papyrus rolls in ancient Greece and Rome were labeled by titles written on tags, called "syllabi," attached to their vellum covering. Collected works of authors were kept together in a separate bucket that would be marked "Plato," "Homer," or "Thucydides." For further information see Fredric G. Kenyon, *Books and Readers in Ancient Greece and Rome* (Oxford: The Clarendon Press, 1932), 60 ff.

   Much earlier, among others whose names we know, a Sumerian poetess of the twenty-third century B.C.E., Enheduanna, "left a considerable body of compositions of a very high order— seventeen centuries before Sappho. Her portrait has survived and her biography can be reconstructed in outline." See William W. Hallo, "Assyriology and the Canon," *The American Scholar* 59.1 (Winter 1990), 108. Hallo states that literature written in cuneiform (which continued in use until the first century B.C.E.) constitutes the oldest non-anonymous poetry in existence.

6. Mark Rose, *Authors and Owners: The Invention of Copyright* (Cambridge, MA: Harvard University Press, 1993), 1–2.

7. Simon During, *Foucault and Literature: Towards a Genealogy of Writing* (London: Routledge, 1992), 124.

8. Anthony Trollope, *An Autobiography*, ed. Michael Sadleir (Oxford: Oxford University Press, 1980), 107, 205.

9. Byron to Murray, 4 December 1819, cited in Luke, 202. Byron first wrote to Moore on 19 September 1818, that he would not sign his poem because it is an experiment that he will discontinue "if it don't take." Later, in order to maintain the poem's formal anonymity, he wrote to Murray on 8 October 1820: "Recollect that if you put my name to 'Juan' in these canting days—any lawyer might oppose my guardian right of my daughter in Chancery ... ." See *Byron's Letters and Journals*, ed. Leslie A. Marchand (Cambridge, MA: Harvard University Press, 1976), vol. 6, 68; vol. 7, 196.

10. Jan Fergus, *Jane Austen: A Literary Life* (London: Macmillan, 1991), 14 ff.

11. David Saunders and Ian Hunter, "Lessons from the 'Literary': How to Historicize Authorship," *Critical Inquiry* 17 (Spring 1991), 479–509.

12. D. F. McKenzie, "Stationers' Company Liber A: An Apologia," in *The Stationers' Company and the Book Trade 1550–1990*, eds. Robin Myers and Michael Harris (New Castle, Delaware: Oak Knoll Press, 1997), 39. I thank Douglas Brooks for bringing this instance to my attention.

13. Susan Stewart, in *Crimes of Writing* (Oxford: Oxford University Press, 1991), 13, states that after 1662 the author's name was required, but this is not so; the 1662 act required only the printer's name, but also that the printer know the name of the author *if asked*.

   A copy of the 1637 decree can be found in *A Transcript of the Registers of the Company of Stationers of London, 1554–1640 A.D.*, ed. Edward Arber, 5 vols. (London: Priv. print., 1877), vol. 4, 529 ff; the relevant text is section 8. The 1642 Parliamentary order was collected in the Thomason Tracts (B.M.E. 207.2; Wing E2639). When Parliament passed an ordinance for the licensing of the press on 14 June 1643 there was no mention of the author's name. Renewals of this ordinance (30 September 1647, 20 September 1649, and 1 January 1652/3), however, specifically require the name of the author to be printed on title pages; see *Acts and Ordinances of the Interregnum, 1642–1660*, eds. C. H. Firth and R. S. Rait, 3 vols. (London: Pub. by H. M. Stationery off., printed by Wyman and Sons Limited, 1911). An order issued in the name of the Lord Protector on 26 August 1655 tried to effect more efficient enforcement of the these ordinances; see Thomason Tracts, B.M.E. 1064.58. For the 1662 Licensing Act, see 14 Car. II, c. 33, in *Statutes of the Realm*, vol. 5 (London: George Eyre and Andrew Strahan, 1822). The relevant text is section 16: "And be it further enacted and declared that every person and persons that shall hereafter print or cause to be printed any Booke Ballad Chart Pourtracture or any thing or things whatsoever shall thereunto and therein print and set his or theire owne Name or Names and also shall declare the Name of the Author thereof if he be thereunto required by the Licenser…" (430). This act was subsequently renewed without change until it was allowed to lapse in 1695.

14. Daniel Defoe, *An Essay on the Regulation of the Press* (1704), ed. John Robert Moore (Oxford: Blackwell for the Luttrell Society, 1948). Bolingbroke made a similar proposal around the time of the Stamp Act in 1712; cited in Irwin Ehrehpreis, *Swift: The Man, His Works, and the Age*, 3 vols. (Cambridge, MA: Harvard University Press, 1962–83), vol. 2, 568. In 1799, while the Seditious Societies Act was going through the House of Commons, it was suggested that "all anonymous works should have the name of the author printed on the title-page"; cited in C. H. Timperley, *A Dictionary of Printers and Printing* (London: H. Johnson [etc., etc.] 1839), 800. In 1835, John Galt argued that all works should be signed because it was unfair for printers to be prosecuted while authors had a means of escape; "Anonymous Publications," *Fraser's Magazine* 11 (May 1835), 549–51.

15. Hugh J. Luke, Jr., "The Publishing of Byron's *Don Juan*," *PMLA* 80 (1965), 200. The Seditious Societies Act of 1799 (39 George III, ca. 79) required that all presses be registered, and the name and address of the printer be given on the front of each single paper published, and "upon the first and last leaves of every paper or book which shall consist of more than one leaf"; cited in C. H. Timperley, *A Dictionary of Printers and Printing* (London: H. Johnson [etc., etc.] 1839), 800.

16. For this fascinating incident, see Richard Holmes, *Shelley; The Pursuit* (London: Weidenfeld and Nicholson, 1974), 158 f.

17. John Galt, "Anonymous Publications," *Fraser's Magazine* 11 (May 1835), 551.

18. *Athenaeum*, 1 April 1871, 398; reprinted in *Thomas Hardy: The Critical Heritage*, ed. R. G. Cox (New York, 1970), 1. The review in *Spectator* considers the book's anonymity to be a wise move: "By all means let him bury the secret in the profoundest depths of his own heart, out of reach, if possible, of his own consciousness. The law is hardly just which prevents Tinsley Brothers from concealing their participation also" (3). Herbert Tucker called my attention to the phrase "inexpressive she" in *As You Like It* III.ii.10, and suggests that, although the meaning of "inexpressive" changed from "inexpressible" to "neutral," the reviewer must have had Shakespeare's line in mind.

19. *The Quarterly Review* 84 (December 1848), 174.

20. For a recent comprehensive survey of the debates on anonymity in Victorian journalism see Dallas Liddle, "Salesmen, Sportsmen, Mentors: Anonymity and Mid-Victorian Theories of Journalism," *Victorian Studies* 41 (1991), 31–68. For the *Times Literary Supplement*, see John Gross's policy statement, "Naming Names," *TLS* 7 (June 1974), 610–11, and letters to the editor on June 21 and June 28. See also Martin Amis's recollection of the transition, "The Coming of the Signature," *TLS* 17 (January 1992), 18. For an earlier version of the argument based on the position of the person writing, see a letter to Sylvanus Urban, *Gentleman's Magazine* (December 1787), 1044, given the title "Utility of the real names of our Correspondents" in the Table of Contents.

21. *National Quarterly Review* 23 (1871), 42–3.

22. Jane Millgate, *Walter Scott: The Making of the Novelist* (Toronto: University of Toronto Press, 1984), 60, 204 n. 3.

23. Paul Hammond, "Anonymity in Restoration Poetry," *The Seventeenth Century* 8 (1993), 130.

24. Doris Lessing, *The Diaries of Jane Somers*, 2nd ed. (New York: Vintage Books, 1984), vii.

25. R. S. Woof, "Wordsworth's Poetry and Stuart's Newspapers: 1797–1803," *Studies in Bibliography* 15 (1962), 152 n. 5.

26. Gerard Genette, *Paratexts: Thresholds of Interpretation*, trans. Jane E. Lewin (Cambridge: Cambridge Univeristy Press, 1987), 39–40.

CHAPTER ONE

Rehearsing the Absent Name: Reading Shakespeare's Sonnets Through Anonymity

Marcy L. North

Modern editions of Tudor and Stuart literary texts consistently relegate early anonymity to a footnote. We read these texts as Spenser's *Shepheardes Calender*, Marlowe's *Tamburlaine*, and Milton's *Maske presented at Ludlow Castle* despite the fact that important early editions appeared anonymously.[1] Even the title of this essay on anonymity conforms to the modern expectation that early authors' names will frame any critical discussions of their works.[2] As missing names have resurfaced over the years, scholars have attached them to texts (or reattached texts to authors' names) with the assumption that attribution belongs to that illusive category of authors' intentions. The anonymity instigated by the author is no exception; scholars simply read the author's choice to remain anonymous as subordinate to the assumed ambition of the author. One could argue that replacing authors' names is necessary for our modern system of information management, but the practice unfortunately obscures several of the ways that texts were received, read, and interpreted in early modern England. For many types of early literature, anonymity worked as a meaningful frame, signaling the genre or publication medium of the work, its legality or illegality, and its institutional sponsorship or patronage. Anonymity pointed to the author's class status or gender, to his or her claims about the worth of the work, or to the particular time in an author's literary career (youth, for instance) with which the work was to be identified. Anonymity also defined certain texts as common wisdom or popular fable; these texts required no author because they belonged to everyone and to no one. Even as late sixteenth-century booksellers discovered that popular names could sell books, anonymity remained incredibly common.[3] Lyric poems, ballads, controversy pamphlets, political satires, and play texts, to name only a few examples, circulated frequently without authors' names. Few writers of the period succeeded in avoiding anonymity; if they did not choose this familiar authorial stance themselves for some particular work or occasion, it might be chosen for them or happen to them at any point in the transmission of their works.

Although Shakespeare's name dominates the title of Thomas Thorpe's 1609 edition of the sonnets, more than one-half of the twenty-four individual Shakespeare sonnets that have been located in early manuscripts appear anonymously—a fact that has attracted little critical attention from scholars studying the sonnet variants.[4] Almost all of the anonymous manuscript copies of the sonnets appear in commonplace books from the second quarter of the seventeenth century, and it is possible that Shakespeare's name was simply lost in the intervening years between the Thorpe edition and the later circulation of these poems. There is reason to believe, however, that at least some of these sonnets appear anonymously because they originally circulated in a manuscript culture where names were highly unstable texts and where alternative, often discrete modes of authorship and text presentation thrived.[5] This essay asks what the anonymity of these post-publication copies of the sonnets can tell us about the sonnets' initial circulation and reception. Do the anonymous sonnets reveal assumptions about authorship and transmission that Shakespeare shared with coterie authors of his period? Do they contain traces not only of textual derivation but also of the material conditions under which Shakespeare worked? Could anonymity reveal something about the very author it threatens to conceal?

My argument builds upon Peter Beal's reluctance to dismiss these late manuscript copies of the sonnets as insignificant textually. "It is at least a possibility," he argues, "that certain of the texts found in miscellanies of the 1620s and 1630s ultimately derive from early MS copies of individual sonnets and have no connection whatsoever with the 1609 edition."[6] If Beal's qualified guess proves true, Shakespeare might have had manuscript circulation and even anonymity in mind as the medium and frame for his sonnets when he composed them. Using the seventeenth-century evidence and the few contemporary references to the early circulation of the sonnets, my essay recreates manuscript anonymity as a material and thematic frame for the sonnets and rereads them through that anonymity. Borrowing the critical technique in Arthur Marotti's essay on

Shakespeare's sonnets as literary property, I look within the sonnets for Shakespeare's awareness of contemporary attribution practices and for his familiarity with the unstable material conditions of poetry circulation.[7] Revisionist textual theorists such as Marotti, Beal, and Margreta de Grazia have made the terms "textual instability," "malleability," and "mediation" much more familiar in recent years, and they have argued convincingly that one cannot always categorize non-authorial mediation as an "error."[8] Yet few of these scholars have discussed anonymity's complex relationship to mediation, that is, anonymity's functionality at almost all levels of text production. Shakespeare, I want to argue, was acutely aware of that relationship.

My discussion highlights Sonnet 71, "No longer mourn for me when I am dead," which imagines its own anonymity and which appears anonymously along with Shakespeare's Sonnet 32 and poems by Drayton, Herbert, Donne, and Suckling in a mid-seventeenth-century commonplace book. Several of the other anonymous Shakespeare sonnets help me to build a credible context for this reading. Sonnet 116, "Let me not to the marriage of true minds," appears in an anonymous expanded version in a seventeenth-century songbook.[9] Sonnet 128, "How oft when thou, my music, music play'st," appears anonymously in a composite collection in the Bodleian Library.[10] Of particular interest are the many anonymous copies of the popular "When forty winters shall besiege thy brow" that vary in important ways from the Thorpe edition. Although information about the transmission of Shakespeare's sonnets before 1609 is scarce, the seventeenth-century evidence captures and preserves certain aspects of the earlier circulation, and it identifies anonymity as a valuable interpretive frame and an important step in the early transmission process. The seventeenth-century manuscript copies of the sonnets show us a poet who faced the realistic possibility that, as he put it in Sonnet 72, "My name be buried where my body is."[11]

Shakespeare and Social Anonymity[12]

Shakespeare is one of the most difficult authors to reread through early anonymity, for not only did his name develop into a market commodity quite early in his career, his name also functions today as a seemingly indisputable icon for the English literary canon and as a sacred standard of quality and genius.[13] Modern students struggle to imagine a Shakespeare text for which the author's name and reputation are not central editorial and literary frames.[14] Scholars, likewise, look to the written or printed name, the "William Shakespeare" or "W.S.," as the starting point for authorship debates, and their studies often serve to protect that name, no matter which side of the argument they take.[15] It is not surprising that Michel Foucault used Shakespeare as one example of the complexity of the author-function and asked us to consider how the function of Shakespeare's name would change if we learned that he had not written the sonnets or that he *had* written Bacon's *Organon*.[16] It is the modern reader rather than Shakespeare, Foucault reminds us, who has invested so much in the cultural import and functional breadth of Shakespeare's name and who is unable to tolerate anonymity except "in the guise of an enigma."[17] The operations of modern authorship that we "force texts to undergo" have little to do with Shakespeare's own view of authorship.[18]

Shakespeare's modern iconic status, de Grazia confirms, has its roots not in the early modern period, but in the Enlightenment, when, in the name of authenticity, editors effectively severed the author from the social origins of his texts.[19] When one looks at those social origins, it is clear that Shakespeare did not necessarily write with a concern or desire for the immediate or clear attribution of his work. *Romeo and Juliet, Titus Andronicus*, and *Henry V* were published anonymously in the late sixteenth century.[20] The quarto title pages, which announce the "circumstances of the performances" but not Shakespeare's name, are, according to de Grazia, evidence of "the subordinate role of authorship to performance" in the early publication of play texts.[21] These early printed plays capture the collaborative ethos of the early modern theater where the author was one player among many.[22] The first editions of *Venus and Adonis* and the *Rape of Lucrece*, which are attributed beneath their dedications but not on the title pages, also suggest Shakespeare's familiarity with less conspicuous modes of self-presentation.[23] Together, these plays and poems argue against the assumption that Shakespeare wanted or expected his name to be a prominent source of authority early in his career.

The contemporary anecdote most often used to argue for Shakespeare's later authorial self-consciousness does not stand up to close scrutiny. In 1599 and in 1612, William Jaggard attributed his miscellany, *The Passionate Pilgrim*, solely to Shakespeare even though it contained works by other authors. Thomas Heywood's angry response to the misattribution of the 1612 edition is famous, because Heywood leads his readers to believe that he and his ally, Shakespeare, are reclaiming their respective works in the interest of protecting their intellectual property.[24] "The Author," Heywood professes of Shakespeare, is "much offended with M. Iaggard (that altogether unknowne to him) presumed to make so bold with his name."[25] Yet when the printer cancels the title page that advertised

Shakespeare as the sole author of the *Passionate Pilgrim*, neither Heywood nor Shakespeare appears to have protested the resulting anonymity. This anecdote actually demonstrates that, in early modern England, authors and book producers perceived anonymity as a legitimate and practical alternative to attribution (or misattribution) rather than as a bibliographical error.[26] Heywood's initial protest was not really typical; there were dozens of authors who said little about the misuse or neglect of their names and who might have expected (if not partially encouraged) the anonymity that claimed their works. One cannot read Heywood's description of Shakespeare's outrage, for instance, without wondering why we have no clear record of Shakespeare protesting the earlier editions of the *Passionate Pilgrim*, which were also attributed to him but were never entirely made up of his works. Perhaps Shakespeare had no control over the publisher at that point in his career. It is just as likely, however, that he had no interest in straightening out the misattributions.

To explore more fully how Shakespeare, his readers, and the collectors and publishers of his day understood anonymity, one must look at a number of overlapping conditions. Many early texts located their authority in a source other than that of an autonomous and individuated author.[27] Ecclesiastical texts often leaned on the authority of institutionalized truth or on the divine author for affiliation, while printed play texts frequently advertised their association with a theater company rather than with the primary author. During Shakespeare's lifetime, the author's name had not yet been established as the deciding marker of intellectual property, and readers, compilers, and printers manipulated attribution, just as they did texts, with impunity.[28] Hilton Kelliher calls attention to the collector of a few extracts from Shakespeare's *Henry IV, Part 1*, who took the liberty late in Elizabeth's reign to manipulate Shakespeare's lines for possible inclusion in a commonplace book.[29] Like many personal compilers of the period, he did not record the author's name with these excerpts. In both print and manuscript, book producers and compilers utilized a wide variety of conventions to present "authors" to their readers. Among the most popular were extensive prefatory materials, initials instead of full names, subscripts after authorial clusters, anagrams, the practice of attributing a miscellany to one prominent author, and, most important, anonymity. These conventions often obscured the intellectual claim of specific authors and called attention to the collaborative production of the text. Just as significant is the fact that the conditions of manuscript transmission and early printing rarely guaranteed that an authorial name would remain permanently fixed to a text; idiosyncrasies, carelessness, and ignorance helped to make

anonymity even more familiar to early modern readers.[30] The society
within which Shakespeare wrote and initially transmitted his sonnets, the
society that allowed Jaggard in 1599 to acquire, print, attribute, and later
make anonymous some of Shakespeare's sonnets, understood that
anonymity could denote both choice and accident, name suppression
and negligence. It read and accepted anonymity as a common and
expected condition of many texts.

The possibility that Shakespeare's sonnets circulated in manuscript
during the late sixteenth century allows one to imagine a context within
which Shakespeare might have tolerated or even cultivated anonymity.
A remark by Francis Meres in 1598 concerning Shakespeare's "sugred
Sonnets among his private friends" has led to a great deal of speculation
about the transmission of the sonnets before their publication by Thorpe
in 1609.[31] Meres's brief account of English literary activity in *Palladis
Tamia* suggests that Shakespeare was known to have written several of his
sonnets by 1598 but that only a few privileged readers had seen them.
Although the extant manuscript versions of the sonnets are all from
the mid-seventeenth century, Marotti and Gary Taylor have guessed
with Beal that these later versions point back to manuscript sources in
circulation before the Thorpe edition.[32] The appearance of the two
Shakespeare sonnets in Jaggard's 1599 *Passionate Pilgrim* lends credence to
these claims. The lack of any extant manuscript copies from the early
period, however, denotes a very limited circulation, especially if one
compares Shakespeare to other poets of the period such as Sidney,
Ralegh, and Donne, who wrote for private audiences and whose works
appear with some frequency in contemporary commonplace books and
personal anthologies. The private circulation of poetry encouraged certain kinds of anonymity. An unsigned poem could serve as a gesture of
intimacy in small social circles where poems passed from hand to hand.
Anonymity also allowed authors to assume an air of nonchalance or
a posture of humility regarding their literary endeavors. If Shakespeare's
sonnets were kept within a restricted circle of readers, his name also
became the property of a few protective acquaintances, for whom,
perhaps, privileged knowledge was a badge of membership. Authorial
discretion is only as good as the knowing reader's discretion, however,
and Jaggard and Meres prove that exclusive transmission circles were, to
some extent, penetrable.

Anonymous Sonnets and the Matter of Authorship

Several of Shakespeare's sonnets acknowledge the media and materials of
manuscript transmission. Sonnets 77 and 122, for instance, mention the

table-books into which a collector or patron copied circulating poems. Whether or not collectors recorded an author's name in such books was largely a matter of individual taste and occasion, and extant personal compilations reveal an incredible variety of attribution practices. British Library Sloane MS 1792, a manuscript of the early 1630s which contains an anonymous version of Shakespeare's Sonnet 2, rarely attributes its works unless an author's name forms part of a poem's title.[33] Other commonplace books reveal different choices; some identify only the items by family and friends, some utilize authors' initials, and a few leave almost all of their included authors anonymous.[34] The attribution decision made by the author or by a poem's first copyist was rarely the last word. Anonymity could become part of a text at many stages in its transmission history, both in the beginning when the text circulated among close acquaintances and much later when the text reached readers and collectors less familiar with the author. Shakespeare's sonnets variously imagine private immediate transmission and a more distant reception. Sonnet 26 addresses a patron with the expectation that a physical copy of the verse will soon be in the patron's hands:

> Lord of my love, to whom in vassalage
> Thy merit hath my duty strongly knit,
> To thee I send this written ambassage
> To witness duty, not to show my wit
> (ll. 1–4)

The poem has us believe that its transmission will immediately follow its composition. On the other hand, many of the much-noted sonnets which describe writing as a lasting memorial to the lover anticipate a future audience beyond the immediate gift or gesture. Sometimes that audience is hostile, as in Sonnet 17, where the author fears that his "papers, yellowed with their age" will be "scorned, like old men of less truth than tongue" (ll. 9–10). The audience in Sonnet 81 is gentler, however, with "eyes not yet created" which "shall o'er-read" the lover's image in the poet's verse (l. 10). Sonnet 25's "painful warrior famoused for fight" who is "from the book of honour razed quite" (l. 11) reveals the danger that a future audience might forget the poet entirely.

The Shakespeare sonnet that was most popular with seventeenth-century manuscript compilers, Sonnet 2, contains no specific images of text transmission, but it demonstrates another internal characteristic that sometimes determined the popularity of a manuscript poem, a vulnerability to appropriation. "To One that would Die a Maid" or "Spes Altera," as the poem is often titled, has a subtle proverbial echo and general applicability that opens its lines up to less individualized readings. When compared to the other sonnets dealing with youth's beauty, aging, and procreation, the images in Sonnet 2 are less focused on characteristics specific to the particular lover, and the direct address to the young man is less immediate and confrontational. Sonnet 2 is built from images pertaining to a hypothetical time of life and to a life decision. When read anonymously, these images renew their value and immediacy for each new reader. I cite Folger Library MS V.a. 170, an Oxford commonplace book from the 1630s:

> When forty winters shall besiege thy brow,
> And trench deepe furrowes in that lovely field:
> Thy youths fayre livery, so accounted now,
> Shall bee like rotten cloaths of no worth held.
> Then being askt where all thy beauty lies
> Where all the lustre of thy youthfull daies:
> To say, within these hollow sunken eyes
> Were an all beaten Truth, & worthlesse prayse.
> O how much better were thy beauties use
> If thou couldst say, this pretty child of mine
> Saves my account, & makes no old excuse
> Making his beauty by succession thine!
> This were to bee new borne, when thou art old
> And see thy blood warme, when thou feelst it could.
>   (163–4)

Since almost any poem can be made to seem proverbial when taken out of its initial context, and since specific occasional poems also had great value for collectors, theories about a poem's popularity must remain speculative. Mary Hobbs argues that the copies of this poem may have been transmitted as a popular song, and Gary Taylor notes that many of the collectors were probably bachelors at the university who found the poem pertinent to their own social situations.[35] Whether or not these are the factors that attracted collectors, the poem appears in twelve different manuscripts, while the next most popular sonnet, number 106, appears in only two.[36] Shakespeare's name does not seem to have been the key to this poem's popularity, since at least eight of the sonnet copies either do not identify the author or downplay the author's identity.[37]

A broader look at Folger V.a. 170 uncovers more than one explanation for the anonymity of Sonnet 2. The sonnet sits among a number of popular seventeenth-century poems, many of which are attributed with initials to William Strode, Richard Corbett, Donne, Jonson, and others. The Shakespeare sonnet is one of the few poems in this cluster without some form of attribution. One would like to think that the compiler acquired the poem without an author's name and appreciated the quality of the poem independent of the poem's authorship, for this explanation would help legitimate Shakespeare's reputation today. Several other possibilities complicate this theory, however. What attracted the compiler to this sonnet may simply have been the poem's currency in the university circles of the seventeenth century. There is also a possibility that Shakespeare's anonymity is not an accident of transmission. The Folger compiler may not have wanted to confuse William Shakespeare with William Strode, a very popular Oxford author of the period. Since Strode's works monopolize this section of the manuscript and are identified with the initials "W.S.," the compiler may be using anonymity to signify that this particular poem is not Strode's. This explanation does not deny the poem's attractiveness to the compiler, but it establishes that Strode's "authorship" was much more important than Shakespeare's. Whether the anonymity was accidental or intentional, the fate of Sonnet 2 in Folger V.a. 170 is hardly unusual. In fact, Shakespeare may have partly anticipated this fate when he first composed and initially circulated his sonnets.

In a commonplace book composed slightly later than Folger V.a. 170, the complex authorial conceits of Sonnet 71, "No longer mourn for me when I am dead," give us an even clearer sense that Shakespeare imagined anonymity as a step in the transmission process of manuscript poetry. Even though this sonnet is not one of those identified by scholars as deriving from early manuscripts, it nevertheless thematizes just such a transmission history. Sonnet 71 appears anonymously on folio 12v of Folger Library MS V.a. 162, which Beal identifies as a mid-seventeenth-century commonplace book compiled within Oxford University circles and owned by a Stephen Welden.[38] Shakespeare's Sonnet 32 appears in this same manuscript almost fourteen folios after Sonnet 71. Although it is unlikely that the two sonnets reached the compiler as an authorial cluster, they share a picture of a reader–lover who peruses their lines after the author's death, a picture which seems oddly appropriate to this mid-century manuscript. Unlike Folger V.a. 170 where authorial initials are prevalent, almost all of the poems in the Folger V.a. 162 are anonymous, indicating that editorial choice lies behind at least some of the anonymity. The two sonnets blend in with a variety of lyric complaints, devotional verses, epitaphs, epigrams, and university satires. Nothing about the material or literary frame marks these poems as Shakespeare's.

From its position below Herbert's anonymous, visually intriguing "Altar" and across from a moralistic verse on the condition of man, Sonnet 71 explicitly links the creation of an authorial self to the poem's transmission and reception in a context like Folger V.a. 162, a manuscript where anonymity is a dynamic probability. "No longer mourn for me when I am dead" speaks to an intimate audience about a time immediately following the author's death. This moment is a crisis point for the memory of the author's name, love, and work; it is a time when the private reception of the poem and the public opinion of the author collide. Unlike sonnets such as 81, which promise the nameless addressee that "your name from hence immortal life shall have" (l. 5), Sonnet 71 makes the *addressee* responsible for the fame, remembrance, or obscurity of the *author*. The poem depicts an initial reader who is familiar with the poet's work and intimate enough to be affected by the world's opinion of the author. That close relationship is partially defined by the poem's quiet assumption that its own lines remain unsigned and that the poet's name rests in the reader's memory. The poet begins with a deceptively simple wish:

> Noe longer morne for me when I am dead
> then you shall heere the sullen surly bell
> giue warning to the wor^l^d that I am fled
> from this vile world wth vilest wormes to dwell
>
> (ll. 1–4)

Mourning has little to do with naming at this moment in the poem, for the bell supplies the voice of the mourner. When the ringing of the bell ends, so should the mourning for the author. The next quatrain develops the poem's essential tension. The physical presence of the poem, its attention to the memory of the author, and perhaps even the handwriting of the manuscript version urge the reader to remember the poet at the same time that the poem's lines instruct the reader to forget:

> nay if you read this line remember not
> the hand that writt it, for I loue you so
> that I in your sweet thoughts would be forgott
> if thinking on me then should make you★ woe
>
> (ll. 5–8)

★ I have emended "me" to "you" using the 1609 edition for reference.

The reminder to forget is inscribed in the written text where it outlasts the subject of its lines, both the hand that writes and the poet's name. If we assume that the poem is unsigned at this point, the reminder to forget creates an absence within the lines where the author perpetually is not. This is an absence, however, that continually acknowledges the possibility of the author's presence and the possibility that the addressee will eventually name the author. If the poem is signed or attributed, however, its dynamics are far less complex. The addressee has ignored the instructions to forget the poet, and the sonnet comments ironically on the impossibility of Shakespeare having been forgotten.

The final six lines of the sonnet imagine the author's name as an oral text that accompanies the poem, not as a written text. The reader's ability to forget the author begins with a refusal to "rehearse" or speak the name:

> o if (I say) you looke vpone this verse
> when I (perhaps) compounded am with clay
> doe not so much as my poore name reherse
> but lett your loue euen with my life decay
> least the wise world should looke into your moone*
> and mocke you with me, after I am gon./
>
> (ll. 9–14)

Once again, the poem claims to outlast the love and the author to which it eternally refers. If the poem maintains the anonymity it assumes, then the words "poore name" will live longer than the name itself. The introduction of the outside world's gaze into the couplet closes the poem around the lovers, dividing the audience into two. Although the phrase, "wise world," in the penultimate line evokes an image of a kind but stern audience that seeks to learn the author's name from the lover, the last line describes a crueler audience. It is not entirely clear at the end of the poem whether the lover's silence can protect the poet from the world's mockery, even though silence promises to protect the lover.

Sonnet 71 juxtaposes reminding and forgetting, attribution and anonymity, whether the poem is experienced by secondary readers as anonymous or not. Almost any reading leaves one wondering if the author truly wants to be forgotten or if the poem is not precisely meant to be the instrument of remembrance. Line 11's request, "doe not so much as my poore name reherse" embraces its antithesis by rehearsing

---

* moone] moan.

itself. Similarly, the handwriting mentioned in line 6 identifies the poet while it instructs the lover to "remember not." The anonymity of this poem adds another complexity that the poem itself anticipates. If the poem is signed or in some way attributed, then the suspense that animates the addressee's choice to rehearse or not to rehearse the name fades. Either the power to forget the poet was never really given over to the initial reader, or the poem records that reader's choice to deny the poet his literal request (though perhaps not his underlying desire) and to fix his name to the poem. When the poem is read anonymously, however, its lines preserve the reader's choice as a dynamic and perpetual tension.

In spite of Shakespeare's many self-referential moments in the sonnets, one might want to resist the initial inclination to read Sonnet 71 through a signature as a thoroughly ironic gesture toward obscurity or as an equally ironic prophesy of its own immediate attribution. It is far more fascinating to consider that, in early manuscript culture, names were indeed transmitted frequently by word of mouth, by "rehearsing" or "mocking," either to be lost as the poem reached less informed readers or to be fixed to the text eventually. Shakespeare's Sonnet 71 confronts this possible fate by making attribution the responsibility (or irresponsibility) of the initial reader. Whether the poet seeks obscurity or fame, the guarantor of these wishes is imagined to be someone other than the author and to exist outside of the text. Shakespeare has complicated his fascination with the lasting nature of text here to reveal that authorial names, as a category of meaningful expression, are not consistently put onto paper and made into material text. An author's name is not always rehearsed and controlled by the author.

The material version of this sonnet in the leaves of Folger V.a. 162, with its anonymity and handwriting, replays many of the complexities of authorial identity described within its lines. The handwriting becomes a kind of signature, one that the copyist may have wanted a knowing reader to identify when he appropriated this poem for his own use. Since each possessor of a text in manuscript culture could create a new frame for the text without too much concern for authorial intention, it is entirely possible that this poem has been collected because it is *no longer* Shakespeare's rather than because it is Shakespeare's. The anonymity of the sonnet in Folger V.a. 162 also plays out the drama of authorship, and it does so in two dimensions. Read as the work of its early author, the anonymous poem speaks to the success of the author's admonition to forget. Read as a poem appropriated by the compiler, the anonymous poem reestablishes the tension between its inside audience and outside audience, between its capacity to protect and to expose the rehearser of its lines. What one also notices in this relatively late copy of Sonnet 71 is that anonymity performs a double function here, first, as a coterie convention that keeps a name in an intimate circle and, second, as a convention that may have encouraged the poem to move out of its circle. The lover and the wise world continue to compete for the "author" of this anonymous sonnet.

It is important to note at this point that the transmission histories of many early modern texts do not exhibit any linear progression toward or away from attribution. Correctly attributed and anonymous versions of texts often circulated simultaneously. The attribution of a poem in a published work did not guarantee its attribution in later manuscripts and publications. Compilers familiar with an author's name sometimes chose to leave it off of a copy that they were manipulating for a specific occasion. Henry Lawes' adaption of Shakespeare's Sonnet 116 as an anonymous song lyric, for instance, might be a case where Lawes' musical goal outweighed issues of authorial identity and textual authenticity.[39] Therefore, we cannot assume that all early modern authors and compilers would have accepted the modern narrative whereby attribution is an improvement on anonymity. Early modern anonymity was more accurately a set of conditions and conventions that framed a text, that marked the accident of text transmission, the courtly nonchalance of the author, or the authorial stance created by author, compiler, or book producer for the presentation of the text. In Folger V.a. 162, the possibility of lost names is no more or less credible than the possibility of discretely hidden names. The fact that the manuscript follows the Thorpe edition historically does not necessarily mean that Sonnet 71's anonymity records the compiler's ignorance.

Sonnet 71 asks us to read its anonymity as the ambiguous and paradoxical product of both discretion and accident, as the record of a process of reception and transmission instigated by the addressee of the poem but never quite finished. The poem illuminates the paradoxically private and public context that anonymity creates. The poet seeks some guarantee that the privacy of the intimate message between himself and his addressee will be preserved. To halt the transmission of authorial identity seems to promise that privacy. Ironically, the same anonymity that guarantees the privacy of the poet and addressee and closes the poem around them also opens the lines of the poem up to public appropriation, to reuse of the poem, to repeatability. In the end, the anonymous poet and his addressee lend their voices to any poet or lover who rehearses the lines again. The reminder to forget continues to remind, and the anonymity that allowed the poem the aura of a unique and particular communication between two individuals finally denies the poem its particularity.

The complexity of Sonnet 71's authorial conceit is hardly matched by the other Shakespeare sonnet in Folger V.a. 162. Nevertheless, Sonnet 32, which appears anonymously on folio 26, demonstrates convincingly that anonymity can provide an interpretive frame even without the thematic resonance. Sonnet 32 never raises the issue of the author's name, though it mirrors 71 in its premise that the lover will read the author's poetry after his death. Sonnet 32 also echoes the material implements of manuscript transmission in Sonnet 71 as it prophesies that its own lines will be artifacts in a future material context. Rather than facing the criticism of the wise world, Sonnet 32 will live to compete with the poets of the next age even though the author will not live to view the outcome:

> If thou surviue my well contented daie
> when that churle death my bones with dust shall couer
> and shalt by fortune once more resuruay
> theis poore rude lines of thy deceased louer
> Compare them with the bettering of the tyme
> and though they be out-stript by every penn
> reserue them for my loue, not for theire rymn
> exceeded by the high of happier men
> oh then vouchsafe me, but this loueing thought,
> had my frends Muse growne wth this growing age
> a dearer loue then this his loue had brought
> to march in ranckes of better equipage:
> but since he died and Poets better proue,
> theirs for there stile, Ile read, his for his loue./.

Fortune, rather than the author's careful intention, has set these lines in the reader's hands again and given the reader the power to resurvey and to reserve the poem. One can imagine the addressee finding or perhaps copying these lines into a manuscript such as Folger V.a. 162, where the sonnets appear among the works of Shakespeare's contemporaries and the poets of the next generation. Sonnet 32 sits across from the anonymous "Goe and catch a falling starre" by Donne and above Drayton's anonymous "Nothing but No and I and I and No." A poem attributed to John Suckling appears a few folios earlier, and seventeenth-century epigrams and witty verses dot the pages around folio 26. The last line of Sonnet 32 brings the new and old together through the imagined interpretation of a loving but critical reader, but the material proximity of the new and the old in Folger V.a. 162 allows this interpretation to be enacted. The anonymity of many of the poems in the manuscript requires an inside reader like the one depicted in Sonnet 32 to distinguish the old from the new and the Shakespeare from the Herbert and Suckling. The manuscript, however, cannot promise any such reader. Although Shakespeare hopes for his reader's affirmation that his work has surpassed the next generation's lyrics, Folger V.a. 162 refuses to grant him that status easily and shows us instead a world where juxtaposition and comparison are a continuous process encouraged by anonymity. Shakespeare's presence in this manuscript might indicate that his work has indeed outlasted the greater number of poets in his own generation, but his work has survived only to be placed within a context where no more attention is paid to his work than to that of any other poet.

If Sonnets 32 and 71 echo the many Shakespeare sonnets that locate the fame of the poet and subject in the future, that echo may also be a cue for the modern reader to re-imagine an early material frame other than the printed text. The manuscript is often a monument without a name, yet it can inscribe and preserve a meaningful mode of authorship and reception as well as print can. Manuscript transmission is often social and collaborative rather than individual, but it could and did carry a poem from one generation to the next. In one sense, Sonnet 32 claims to be a closed and finished poem, a text that at the poet's death can no longer be improved to keep up with the literary trends. Like Sonnet 71, however, the poem also imagines itself as open to manipulation. The words that it asks the reader to think in lines 10–14 convey a hope for preservation yet put the act of preserving into the reader's hands. Shakespeare attempts to control unstable future reception through a polite ventriloquism, but he does so within the very object that must be preserved. This irony is closely related to the irony in Sonnet 71, where the poet uses an object of remembrance to tell the reader to forget. Within the instructions to forget and to preserve, one sees Shakespeare's recognition of the vagaries of transmission, especially the impossibility that an author can control the material aspects of attribution and physical preservation after the poem has left his hands.

The material characteristics of Shakespeare's sonnets in these later manuscripts are not unique when compared to the sonnets of his contemporaries, even those belonging to poets who circulated their poems predominantly in manuscript or who considered themselves manuscript poets. Sonnets by Sidney and Spenser were misattributed in manuscript and also appeared anonymously, even after publication. Drayton's sonnets appear anonymously in Folger V.a. 162 with the two anonymous Shakespeare sonnets. Verses by other sonneteers were often transmitted individually or in small clusters rather than in their large sequences, just as Shakespeare's sonnets were. Spenser's Sonnet VIII, for instance, ends up in the Henry Lawes' songbook along with Shakespeare's Sonnet 116. Donne's and Jonson's poems are almost too numerous in manuscript to catalog, but their poems, too, appeared anonymously in seventeenth-century anthologies. What all of these examples tell us is that manuscript circulation had slightly different patterns of presentation than print did, and attribution in manuscript transmission was even less in the control of the author than the poems themselves. Although Shakespeare and his contemporaries may not have exhibited the concern about attribution that authors and scholars do today, and although some of these names may have been lost in transmission, there is no reason to assume that these authors were oblivious to the patterns of transmission or that they saw print as the normative model for text presentation. Both the press and the pen contributed to the authorial self that speaks from Shakespeare's sonnet, but the images from manuscript offer the most evocative depiction of the instability inherent in the early modern idea of the "author."

The picture of text attribution that Shakespeare paints for us in another source, his plays, leaves no doubt that manuscript transmission contributed to his repertoire of creative images. Characters in the plays regularly manipulate unstable authorial identity for the purpose of executing pranks, treachery, and character identification. In *Twelfth Night*, Maria writes an anonymous letter that she knows Malvolio will mistake for Olivia's (II.iii.159–61). Malvolio subsequently interprets a few cryptic initials in this letter as an anagram for his name (II.iii.38–41). Orlando's love poems to Rosalind in *As You Like It* are hung in the trees and carved into the trunks anonymously, though he is soon discovered as the author. Of more tragic consequence, Edmund in *King Lear* forges his brother Edgar's hand and signature and frames him for treachery against their father (I.ii). Hamlet also rewrites his uncle's commission to England so that Rosencrantz and Guildenstern are executed instead of himself (V.ii). In several plays, the handwriting of an unattributed or misattributed manuscript, rather than the signature, is trusted to identify the author. Malvolio thinks he recognizes Olivia's hand in the letter he has found (II.v.86–8), and Gloucester asks Edmund about Edgar's letter, "You know the character to be your brother's?"(I.ii.62)[40] The sonnets that expose Beatrice's and Benedick's love for each other at the end of *Much Ado About Nothing* are deemed authentic because they are written in the lovers' hands (V.iv.86, 89), and the rediscovery of Perdita in the

Winter's Tale is partly confirmed by recognition of Antigonus' hand in a letter that had been left with the abandoned infant (V.ii.34–5). Shakespeare was acutely aware that the transmission of identity was both material and textual, but that neither the material (handwriting) nor the textual (the name) could guarantee the accurate transmission of authorial identity.

The many anonymous manuscript copies of Shakespeare's sonnets and the patterns of transmission and attribution found in the works of his contemporaries indicate that poets of his period expected attribution to transform and evolve as their poems circulated. This is a very different legacy, but an important one, from our image of Shakespeare as a writer who left the literary equivalent of marble monuments to his name. Scholars have begun to chip away at this image by resurrecting some of the Quarto versions of the plays, analyzing the reception and editorial history that created this image, and focusing on particular material texts rather than on ideal editions, but Shakespeare's understanding of the name as an unstable marker of authorial identity deserves much more attention. The handwriting, the anonymity, and the textual manipulations that characterize early manuscript culture commonly find their way into the images crafted by Shakespeare and his contemporaries, but they have more often been read for their comment on the art of writing than for their interesting perspective on text transmission and authorship. There has been a critical reluctance to explore how early authors dealt with the bibliographic realities of their literary culture, perhaps because we want to imagine authors in control of their literary property, but more probably, in light of the new studies of Shakespeare, because many bibliographic realities still seem incidental to the practice of being an author. This chapter will, I hope, encourage readers to question that reluctance. Reading Shakespeare's sonnets through their early anonymity opens his texts up to several rich interpretations that his early readers would have recognized easily, but which are partly obscured from us today because the name of the author frames even our most probing analyses.

Notes

1. Spenser's *Shepheardes Calender* was first published in 1579. In 1611, it appeared for the first time with Spenser's name attached in *The faerie queen: the shepheards calendar: together with the other works of England's arch-poet, Edm. Spenser.* The authorship of *Tamburlaine the great* (1590) is still speculative. *The Maske at Ludlow Castle* appeared in print in 1634 and was first printed together with Milton's name in the 1645 *Poems*. For details, see Halkett and Laing, *A Dictionary of Anonymous and Psuedonymous Publications in the English Language*, Third (Revised and Enlarged) Edition, 1475–1640, ed. John Horden *et al.* (Harlow and London: Longman, 1980).

2. Margreta de Grazia offers an astute discussion of how the editorial apparatus that modern scholars have inherited from the Enlightenment prescribes our expectations about authorship. See *Shakespeare Verbatim* (Oxford: Clarendon Press, 1991).

3. See my article on anonymity's function within early print culture, "Ignoto in the Age of Print: The Manipulation of Anonymity in Early Modern England" *Studies in Philology* 91 (Fall, 1994), 390–416.

4. Of the Shakespeare sonnets listed in Peter Beal's *Index of English Literary Manuscripts*, 2 vols (London: Mansel, 1980), I have determined that the following items are anonymous: ShW8 (Sonnet 2), BL Add. MS 10309, f. 143; ShW 9 (Sonnet 2), BL Add. MS 21433, f. 114v (W.S. in author's list at end); ShW 10 (Sonnet 2), BL Add. MS 25303, f. 119v; ShW 11 (Sonnet 2), BL Add. MS 30982, f. 18; ShW 12 (Sonnet 2), BL Sloane MS 1792, f. 45; ShW 13 (Sonnet 2), Folger MS V.a. 170, pp. 163–4; ShW 14 (Sonnet 2), Folger MS V.a. 345, p. 145; ShW 19 (Sonnet 2), Yale, Osborn Collection, b 205, f. 54v; ShW 21 (Sonnet 32), Folger MS V.a. 162, f. 26; ShW 24 (Sonnet 71), Folger MS V.a. 162, f. 12v; ShW 25 (Sonnet 106), Pierpont Morgan Library MS 1057, p. 96; ShW 28 (Sonnet 116), New York Public Library, Music Division, Drexel MS 4257, no. 33; ShW 29 (Sonnet 128), Bod. MS Rawl. Poet. 152, f. 34; ShW 30 (Sonnet 138), Folger MS V.a. 339, f. 197v. At least seven manuscript copies are ascribed to W.S. or Shakespeare. I have not been able to determine the status of three of the manuscript copies.

   The scholars who have analyzed the manuscript copies of the sonnets or collated them with the Thorpe edition include John Kerrigan, ed., *The Sonnets and a Lover's Complaint* by William Shakespeare (Middlesex and New York: Viking, 1986), 441–54; Gary Taylor, "Some Manuscripts of Shakespeare's Sonnets," *Bulletin of the John Rylands University Library* 68 (1985–86), 210–46; Peter Beal, *Index* 1, 449–63; Mary Hobbs, "Shakespeare's Sonnet II—'A Sugred Sonnet'?" *Notes and Queries* 224 (April, 1979), 112–13.

5. Early modern manuscript culture and its importance to our understanding of early lyrics, ballads, newsbooks, and other manuscript genres have been described by Arthur Marotti in *Manuscript, Print, and the English Renaissance Lyric* (Ithaca and London: Cornell University Press, 1995), H. R. Woudhuysen, *Sir Philip Sidney and the Circulation of Manuscripts: 1558–1640* (Oxford: Clarendon Press, 1996); and by Harold Love in *Scribal Publication in Seventeenth-Century England* (Oxford: Clarendon Press, 1993). Looking at print culture, Wendy Wall discusses the complexity of early modern authorial presentation in *The Imprint of Gender* (Ithaca and London: Cornell University Press, 1993).

6. Beal, *Index* 1:450.

7. Arthur Marotti, "Shakespeare's Sonnets as Literary Property" in *Soliciting Interpretation: Literary Theory and Seventeenth-Century English Poetry*, ed. Elizabeth D. Harvey and Katharine Eisaman Maus (Chicago and London: University of Chicago Press, 1990), 143–73.

8. Beal, *Index* and *In Praise of Scribes: Manuscripts and Their Makers in Seventeenth-Century England* (Oxford: Clarendon Press, 1998); de Grazia, *Shakespeare Verbatim*; Marotti, *Manuscript, Print*. See also Margaret Ezell, *Social Authorship and the Advent of Print* (Baltimore: Johns Hopkins University Press, 1999). The theories utilized by these scholars were influenced, in part, by the work of Jerome McGann and D. F. McKenzie; McGann, *A Critique of Modern Textual Criticism* (Chicago: University of Chicago Press, 1983); McKenzie, *Bibliography and the Sociology of Texts* (London: British Library, 1986).

9. New York Public Library, Music Division, Drexel MS 4257, No. 33.

10. Bodleian MS Rawl. Poet. 152, f. 34.

11. All sonnet quotations except those from early manuscripts are taken from Stephen Booth, ed., *Shakespeare's Sonnets* (New Haven and London: Yale University Press, 1977).

12. The term "social anonymity" echoes intentionally the term "social authorship," which Ezell defines so well in *Social Authorship and the Advent of Print*.

13. Marotti, "Shakespeare's Sonnets," 154, notes that Shakespeare's name started to appear on published play quartos in 1598 and 1599, and that his name "began to have a commercial value" about the time that William Jaggard attributed the *Passionate Pilgrim* to him in 1599.

See de Grazia, *Shakespeare Verbatim* for a discussion of the development of modern Shakespeare scholarship and the importance of the 1790 Malone edition to Shakespeare's modern iconic status. MacD. P. Jackson also addresses many of the issues surrounding the formation of the Shakespeare canon and the modern assumptions about Shakespeare as author; "The Transmission of Shakespeare's Text" in *The Cambridge Companion to Shakespeare Studies*, ed. Stanley Wells (Cambridge: Cambridge University Press, 1986), 163–85.

14. de Grazia also points out that the presence of an author is a necessary criterion for the modern definition of "literature"; "What is a Work? What is a Document?" in *New Ways of Looking at Old Texts', Papers of the Renaissance English Text Society*, ed. W. Speed Hill (Binghamton, NY: Medieval & Renaissance Texts & Studies, 1993) 199.

15. For a particularly fitting example, see the arguments of the 1980s concerning the authorship of "Shall I die, shall I fly" and the "Funeral Elegy." Gary Taylor, "A New Shakespeare Poem? The Evidence," *TLS* 4316 (Dec. 20, 1985), 1447–8; Donald W. Foster, "Shall I Die' Post Mortem: Defining *Shakespeare*," *Shakespeare Quarterly* 38 (1987), 58–77; Donald W. Foster, *Elegy by W. S.: A Study in Attribution* (Newark: University of Delaware Press, 1989).

16. Michel Foucault, "What is an Author?" in *Textual Strategies: Perspectives in Post-Structuralist Criticism*, ed. Josué V. Harari (Ithaca: Cornell University Press, 1979), 146.

17. *Ibid.*, 150.

18. *Ibid.*

19. de Grazia, *Shakespeare Verbatim*.

20. *RJ* STC 22322, 22323; *TA* STC 22328; *HV* STC 22289.

21. de Grazia, *Shakespeare Verbatim*, 90.

22. For an extended study and theory of early modern collaboration, see Jeffrey Masten, *Textual Intercourse: Collaboration, Authorship, and Sexualities in Renaissance Drama* (Cambridge: Cambridge University Press, 1997).

23. *Venus and Adonis* was published in 1593, and *The Rape of Lucrece* was published in 1594.

24. Hyder Rollins, ed., Introduction, *The Passionate Pilgrim*, 3rd ed. (1612), facsimile reproduction (New York and London: Charles Scribner, 1940), xxvii–xxviii. See also, Marotti, "Shakespeare's Sonnets as Literary Property," 150–54.

25. Rollins, ed. *Passionate Pilgrim*, xxviii. Heywood's protest appeared in a letter at the end of the 1612 *Apologie for Actors*.

26. I offer a somewhat different reading of this incident in "Ignoto in the Age of Print," 410–12.

27. Evelyn Tribble, *Margins and Marginality* (Charlottesville: University Press of Virginia, 1993), deals with this topic at length. For a good example of an author who made anonymity a source of authority, see Joan DeJean's discussion of Madame de Lafayette, "Lafayette's Ellipses: The Privileges of Anonymity," *PMLA* 99 (1984), 884–902.

28. The histories of authorship and copyright are discussed by W. W. Greg, *Some Aspects and Problems of London Publishing Between 1550 and 1650* (Oxford: Clarendon Press, 1956); Joseph F. Loewenstein, "*Idem*: italics and the genetics of authorship," *Journal of Medieval and Renaissance Studies* 20 (1990), 205–24; Jacqueline Miller, *Poetic License: Authority and Authorship in Medieval and Renaissance Contexts* (New York: Oxford University Press, 1986); Ian Parsons, "Copyright and Society" in *Essays in the History of Publishing*, ed. Asa Briggs (London: Longman, 1974); Mark Rose, "The Author as Proprietor: Donaldson vs. Becket and the Genealogy of Modern Authorship," *Representations* 23 (1988), 51–85; Martha Woodmansee, "The Genius and Copyright: Economic and Legal Conditions of the Emergence of the 'Author,'" *Eighteenth-Century Studies* 17 (1983–84), 425–48.

29. Hilton Kelliher, "Contemporary Manuscript Extracts from Shakespeare's *Henry IV, Part 1*," *English Manuscript Studies 1100–1700*, ed. Peter Beal and Jeremy Griffiths (Oxford: Basil Blackwell, 1989), vol. 1, 144–81.

30. Marotti describes many of the characteristics of text transmission to which lyric poems were particularly vulnerable in "The Transmission of Lyric Poetry and the Institutionalizing of Literature in the English Renaissance" in *Contending Kingdoms: Historical, Psychological, and*

Feminist Approaches to the Literature of Sixteenth-Century England and France, ed. Marie-Rose Logan and Peter L. Rudnytsky (Detroit: Wayne State University Press, 1991), 21–41.

31. Francis Meres, *Palladis Tamia; Wits Treasury*, facsimile of the 1598 edition with preface for the Garland Edition by Arthur Freeman (New York and London: Garland, 1973), 281–2.

32. Marotti, "Shakespeare's Sonnets as Literary Property"; Beal, *Index*, 1:450; Gary Taylor, "Some Manuscripts of Shakespeare's Sonnets."

33. This poem and manuscript are described in C.C. Stopes, "An Early Variant of a Shakespeare Sonnet" *The Athenaeum* (26 July 1913), 89.

34. A sample of those commonplace books available in modern editions demonstrates the variety of attribution practices. John Lilliat carefully signed his own poems in his late Elizabethan commonplace book; *Liber Lilliati: Elizabethan Verse and Song (Bodleian MS Rawlinson Poetry 148)*, ed. Edward Doughtie (Newark: University of Delaware Press; London and Toronto: Associated University Presses, 1985). Similarly, the tutor Henry Stanford noted the authorship and circumstances of his pupils' works; *Henry Stanford's Anthology: An Edition of Cambridge University Library Manuscript Dd. 5.75*, ed. Steven May (New York: Garland, 1988). The Dalhousie manuscripts from the early seventeenth century, which may represent the patronage circles of the Essex family, are mostly anonymous; *The First and Second Dalhousie Manuscripts: Poems and Prose by John Donne and Others*, A facsimile edition, ed. Ernest W Sullivan, II (Columbia, MO: University of Missouri Press, 1988). See also, Max W. Thomas, "Reading and Writing the Renaissance Commonplace Book: A Question of Authorship" in *The Construction of Authorship: Textual Appropriation in Law and Literature*, ed. Martha Woodmansee and Peter Jaszi (Durham and London: Duke University Press, 1994).

35. Hobbs, "Shakespeare's Sonnet II," 13; Taylor, "Manuscripts of Shakespeare's Sonnets," 223–4.

36. I have not counted a quatrain of this poem that appears in Folger MS V.a. 148.

37. At least seven manuscript copies are anonymous; see note 4. BL, Add. MS 21433 does not include Shakespeare's name with the poem, though his initials appear in an author's list at the back of the manuscript with no specific cross-reference to the poem; see Taylor, "Manuscripts of Shakespeare's Sonnets," 214, for details. Univ. of Nottingham, Portland MS Pw V 37, according to Beal, 2:453, ascribes the poem to "W.S."

38. Beal, *Index*, 2:454.

39. For a description of this version, see Willa McClung Evans, "Lawes' Version of Shakespeare's Sonnet CXVI," *PMLA* 51 (1936), 120–2.

40. *The Riverside Shakespeare*, 2nd ed. (New York: Houghton Mifflin, 1997).

CHAPTER TWO

Death of an Author: Constructions of Pseudonymity in the Battle of the Books

Kristine Louise Haugen

Literary scholars were eagerly anatomizing the history of pseudonymous writing long before the twentieth century. In the process, they quarreled about which particular texts were pseudonymous or forged, and also, inevitably, about their own theories and methods. Just how did one know that a given text was not by its supposed author? How much proof, and what kind of proof, could demonstrate that a text was fake (or for that matter, authentic)? What, finally, was the payoff for any such argument over textual history? What difference did it make for readers when an apparently robust author was revealed as a vacuous pseudonym? I trace here a vehement and famous controversy from the late seventeenth century in which all of these levels of argument were provocatively brought into play.

To give us a point of access into the texts of the Battle of the Books—which were often as puzzling and technical in their details as they are celebrated in general—I propose to set them in conversation with the now-classic arguments of Roland Barthes, Jacques Derrida, and Michel Foucault about authorship and its discontents. These writers, as we know, aroused both great excitement and deep suspicion in their immediate contemporaries, much as their seventeenth-century counterparts in the Battle had done. If twentieth-century theory can point us toward undiscovered facets of the Battle of the Books, however, we will also find that some aspects of the Battle remain resistant to modern comparisons. The Battle, I will argue, was in large part an exercise of and a meditation on the humanistic habits of reading and writing that enjoyed such a remarkable efflorescence in England following the Restoration. To discover how that alien soil gave rise to questions and anxieties so often resembling those of the recent past is the challenge that awaits us now.

In 1968, Roland Barthes triumphantly announced the death of the author. Pointing to early modern Europe as the scene of the author's portentous birth, Barthes famously called for a return to the authorless paradise still observable in "les sociétés ethnographiques," the domain of the endlessly repeated but ever-changing traditional narration. Like the primitive oral narration, the modern written text according to Barthes is a tissue of citations, which the writer (never the "author") simply assembles, recombines, and varies. It is not the author that speaks in a text, but language itself; accordingly, the "author" does not precede or originate a text but is precisely coeval with it. And since the "critic" is also a historically determined creature who came into existence only to recover putative authors in and through texts, the critic will necessarily share in the author's demise. As the author gives way to the writer, the critic must yield to the reader, who is purely the space on which all citations are written—in effect, a monumental encyclopedia or dictionary, not unlike the lexicon of Greek which Thomas de Quincey compiled to recycle his ancient reading into modern writing.[1]

In 1704, Jonathan Swift published a prose mock epic, *The Battle of the Books*, in which authors try to kill each other.[2] In the eminently martial setting of the Royal Library, ancient and modern books fight ferociously for supremacy, with the ancients making much the better showing. Aristotle slays Descartes, Vergil at the last moment spares the life of Dryden, while Homer dispatches Davenant's hero Gondibert, Sir John Denham, Samuel Wesley, Charles Perrault, and Bernard de Fontenelle. In an episode with especially biting reference to recent events, the Royal Librarian Richard Bentley attempts a stealthy attack on two venerable authors, Aesop and Phalaris, as they sleep unarmed near a tree. But despite his formidable equipment—a flail, and a bucket of manure for slinging—Bentley is suddenly seized by the goddess Affright, and he retreats with only the sleepers' armor for his pains.

Barthes' text and Swift's are both the products of vehement intellectual quarrels that probably seemed likely, at their respective times, to determine the whole future direction of the study and use of received texts. I juxtapose them to point out that the France of the 1960s is not the only setting in which theoretical challenges to authors, individually or as a class, have been successfully mounted. Swift's *Battle* appeared as a late installment in a controversy itself also known as the Battle of the

Books, which had lasted throughout the 1690s in its English incarna-tion.[3] In what came retrospectively to be seen as the quarrel's beginning, Swift's patron Sir William Temple had propounded an argument as attractively paradoxical as Barthes's, with the difference that Temple believed the fallen condition of his contemporaries to be irreversible. According to Temple, the author had died sometime in the second century CE: all subsequent writers of poetry, history, philosophy, and scientific texts, though they might pretend to the status of authors, were in fact ignoble copiers of the true ancient originals.[4] The modern age was thus inferior to antiquity in all significant respects—Temple's notion of culture is centered to a remarkable degree on texts—and the death of authorship is not a triumph but a tragedy.

The quarrel that ensued can be read in several ways. Many interpre-tations have focused on Temple's deeply pessimistic view of the history of human culture, and have accordingly found the seeds of modernity and enlightenment in the writings of Temple's opponents, above all William Wotton, who published a painstaking essay in 1694 in which he delineated modern achievements in fields such as medicine, natural his-tory, historiography, philology, and theology.[5] Wotton's "modern" view, founded on what historians of ideas have called the "idea of progress," has been alternately linked to the efflorescence of natural science in seventeenth-century England or, more recently, to the study and philos-ophy of history in the same period. An account of changing social roles and social approaches to texts has been plausibly added as a further dimension of this interpretation. For the self-consciously genteel Temple, classical texts were objects purely to be admired and (imper-fectly) imitated; for the scholarly Wotton, and even more clearly for Wotton's scholarly partisan Richard Bentley, classical texts were objects to be intensively studied, mastered, and revised or even occasionally rejected on the basis of modern knowledge.[6]

Although I will not take issue here with this interpretation as I have just outlined it, the time seems right to examine the Battle from a some-what different angle. As my account of Temple's essay has suggested, problems about the general status of texts and how to define authorship also figured prominently in the writings of the Battle, above all in the controversy over the pseudonymous letters of Phalaris, the author to whose death this paper's title refers. To focus on authors and texts as the topics of polemic is not only to disclose an unfamiliar aspect of the Battle, but also to see it in the wider climate of epistemological debate, historical interrogation, and readerly anxiety which marked much writ-ing by elites in later seventeenth-century England.[7] I will argue that the

Phalaris controversy reveals both points of contention and points of consensus about the relations that were taken to obtain between the text of Phalaris's letters, their alleged author Phalaris, other texts, and the extratextual world; I will also show some ways in which these initially localized arguments came to be applied, with the broadest implications, to seventeenth-century practices of writing and reading. This is to say that the debate over Phalaris involved not only theoretical or evaluative arguments about the nature of ancient and modern texts, but also pressing problems for the contemporary enterprise of writing about texts, with the controversial texts of the Battle itself serving as primary targets for one another. These arguments and problems can, then, be taken as a kind of anatomy of pseudonymy as it was constructed in one late seventeenth-century episode. They demonstrate the theoretical and technical ways in which contemporaries might attempt to expose a text as pseudonymous, as well as the cultural anxieties that attended this concrete case of pseudonymy. Since, according to Temple, all modern texts were only copies, were all they also pseudonymous insofar as they purported to be by authors? Could the general distinction between antiquity and modernity be upheld if an ancient "author" was also exposed as a pseudonym? Given a debate in which both sides assumed that reading ancient texts was a worthy and necessary activity, could the center hold if it was impossible for a given reader to tell a pseudonym from an author?[8]

In order to survey the initial state of affairs in the controversy, and to introduce the highly mortal figure of the author Phalaris, let me return to Temple's essay and offer a somewhat expanded reading. We recall that according to Temple, the ancient Greeks and Romans had set examples in every learned pursuit that Temple's contemporaries could never match or excel.[9] Temple had a theory as to why this was so. It was not merely that the classical age as a whole or in general was preferable to the present, but the (to Temple) indisputable observation that the first known practitioner of every discipline or cultivated endeavor had been the best (*E* 58). Thus, the finest fables ever written were by Aesop, the first fabulist in prose, and the finest personal letters ever written were those of the Sicilian tyrant Phalaris, who had lived in the sixth century B.C.E and was thus the first letter-writer. In view of the tragic role soon to be assumed by Phalaris, it seems worthwhile to quote Temple at length on his excellence and originality:

> The two most antient, that I know of in Prose, among those we call prophane Authors, are *Æsop*'s Fables, and *Phalaris*'s Epistles, both

living near the same time, which was, that of *Cyrus* and *Pythagoras*. As the first has been agreed by all Ages since, for the greatest Master in his kind, and all others of that sort, have been but imitations of his Original; so I think the Epistles of *Phalaris*, to have more Race, more Spirit, more Force of Wit and Genius than any others I have ever seen, either antient or modern. I know several Learned Men (or that usually pass for such, under the Name of Criticks) have not esteemed them Genuine, and *Politian* with some others have attributed them to *Lucian*: But I think, he must have little skill in Painting, that cannot find out this to be an Original; such diversity of Passions, upon such variety of Actions, and Passages of Life and Government, such Freedom of Thought, such Boldness of Expression, such Bounty to his Friends, such Scorn of his Enemies, such Honor of Learned Men, such Esteem of Good, such Knowledge of Life, such Contempt of Death, with such Fierceness of Nature and Cruelty of Revenge could never be represented, but by him that possessed them; and I esteem *Lucian* to have been no more Capable of Writing, than of Acting what *Phalaris* did. In all one Writ, you find the Scholar or the Sophist, and in all the other, the Tyrant and the Commander.

(*E* 58–9)[10]

This redoubtable passage is fascinated, even obsessed, with the origins of things, in two senses. First, and most obviously, the origin of a given genre is taken to be its finest hour, its whole subsequent history becoming a narrative of decadence and abjection. This logic would seem to imply, in fact, that Temple's contemporaries *could* make contributions to world culture if only they initiated new genres and enterprises at which they would, as founders, be the best; but Temple naturally suppresses this idea in the pursuit of his gleefully despairing argument. In the second place, we notice that Temple's argument metonymically identifies texts with their origins—that is, with their historically situated authors—to a degree that scarcely admits any separation. The letters of Phalaris are valuable precisely because Phalaris is present in them; they transparently embody his royal virtues. Thus, it is not Phalaris himself, but the text of his letters that possesses "more Race, more Spirit, more Force of Wit and Genius than any others I have ever seen." Indeed, Phalaris is not only the author and origin but also the meaning of his letters, and their invariable semantic referent: the letters are the product of Phalaris's faithful mimesis of himself ("such diversity of passions ... could never be represented, but by him that possessed them"). And given Temple's principle that the first author in a genre writes the best text, it appears that the identity of the author is the sole criterion for judging the text he writes. It is impossible at this point not to think of Barthes's critique: "the image of literature to be found in ordinary culture is *tyrannically centered* on the author, his person, his life, his tastes, his passions" (*DA* 142 [emphasis added]; *MA* 491).[11]

Temple was hardly the first to suppose that the personal letter was a peculiarly vivid and unmediated means of expressing a writer's character. Claims for the special authenticity of letters were a commonplace in the later seventeenth century, although such claims coexisted uneasily with the recognition that even authentic personal letters were composed by rhetorical means.[12] To some twentieth-century critics, indeed, real letter collections and fictional letter collections of the period seem virtually indistinguishable to the reader, and it is an irony of the seventeenth-century obsession with epistolary authenticity that so many fictional letter collections were in circulation.[13] It seems noteworthy too that although letters were increasingly considered a feminine genre, Temple presents Phalaris's letters as highly masculinized, perhaps hearkening back to an early modern conception of the letter as a vehicle of male friendship.[14] After Temple's death, his own letters were published by his former client Jonathan Swift, tending to perpetuate not only Temple's notion of the letter as a document of the man of action, but also, somewhat inevitably, an equivalence between Temple and Phalaris.[15]

Bound up with Temple's concern for authenticity was a complementary metaphor that would recur in shifting guises throughout the subsequent debate. If ancient texts (or at least certain ancient texts) were originals, then for Temple all modern texts were copies, bloodless imitations that Temple seems to find not only aesthetically but even ontologically attenuated. This account of modern intellectual life as the realm of the abject copy constitutes what we might call the general or ideal level of Temple's argument. What makes Temple's claims more than purely nostalgic is that they sometimes extend to a more particular and concrete plane as well. For Temple suggests that concrete early modern practices for dealing with ancient texts were also inevitably practices of copying. The causal link between modern copying and the loss of authorship is straightforward in passages such as Temple's claim that "very few" modern writers "can pretend to be Authors, rather than Transcribers or Commentators of the Ancient Learning" (*E* 10). Here the images of transcribing and commenting ask to be read literally, as references to humanistic writing practices known to Temple and to all of his classically educated contemporaries. Transcription of passages from classical texts into topically organized commonplace books had been encouraged by private and university tutors in England since the sixteenth century, and the resulting compendia could be (and were) drawn on in the production of everything from school themes and poems to learned treatises.[16] "Commentators" might conceivably be writers of discursive texts that summarized and elaborated ancient texts—a rather fluid line would separate this kind of writing from transcription—but the production of actual line-by-line commentaries on ancient texts was also a staple enterprise not only of early modern scholars and teachers of poetry, oratory, and the like, but also of physicians, mathematicians, astronomers, and antiquarian historians.[17] If Temple's notion of authorship excludes these practices—and it certainly appears to exclude them—then Temple is hardly an apologist for early modern humanism, but a merciless critic of it.[18] This is the case whether we regard humanism as essentially rhetorical and belletristic, or essentially scholarly and even empirical: both kinds of enterprise must succumb before Temple's indictment of the copy. Nor, incidentally, is writing the only humanist discursive practice that incurs Temple's displeasure: "pedants," whom he accuses of bringing learning into disrepute, can be known by their incessant and malapropos quotations of classical texts in conversation (*E* 69). In the modern era according to Temple, then, virtually all writing is citation, and so is a disturbing proportion of speech itself.

Both the general and the concrete levels of Temple's critique of modernity made their way into the debate over Phalaris of the later 1690s. The chronology of that debate is complex, but it is necessary to outline it briefly here. In the first place, Temple's claims for Phalaris were controversial in themselves, in that not all contemporaries assumed that Phalaris had written the letters attributed to him. Temple himself mentioned the fifteenth-century scholar Angelo Poliziano's suggested attribution to Lucian; Erasmus had also taken the letters' fakeness for granted in his widely read pedagogical texts.[19] One speculates that Temple had been told as a young man that the letters were real—perhaps by his Cambridge tutor Ralph Cudworth, who was never an especially skeptical person.[20] In any event, in 1695 Temple's claims were seemingly seconded by the appearance of a new edition of Phalaris's letters at the Oxford University Press under the name of the Hon. Charles Boyle, a nephew of Robert Boyle who was then an undergraduate at Christ Church.[21] In the preface to this edition, Boyle complained of his ill-treatment by the Royal Librarian, Richard Bentley, who he said had allowed a collaborator of Boyle's to borrow a manuscript of Phalaris from the Royal Library but demanded its return before a collation could be finished.[22] Since Bentley was an associate of William Wotton, who had argued for the modern age against Temple in his 1694 *Reflections upon Ancient and Modern Learning*, Boyle's invectives against Bentley tend further to align Boyle with Temple. They also provoked Bentley to write a fairly short *Dissertation upon the Epistles of Phalaris*, which he published as an appendix to the second edition of Wotton's *Reflections* in 1697; here Bentley gave his own account of the manuscript episode and argued on many grounds against the Phalaris letters' authenticity. In reply, partisans of Boyle published *Dr. Bentley's Dissertations ... Examin'd* in 1698, a book that appeared under the name of Boyle alone. This book more or less conceded that the letters were likely to be inauthentic, but attacked Bentley's individual arguments as well as his allegedly pedantic character. Finally, in 1699, Bentley published a greatly expanded second edition of his *Dissertation*, in which he elaborated and defended his arguments against Phalaris and accused Boyle of ignorance, ineptitude, and impoliteness. Many pamphlets by other parties also appeared.[23]

Bentley's *Dissertation* is the most impressive and perhaps the strangest of all these texts. Bentley was already a classical scholar of international stature in 1697, when he was 35 years old.[24] Thanks to the specifically clerical nature of his classical training, he was versed in historical chronology, Near Eastern languages, and the religions and philosophies of the ancient world, as well as the minutely detailed mode of argument by which English clerical scholars generally treated these subjects. But although some of the kinds of information and mental habits at Bentley's disposal were alien to an educated amateur like Temple, the two opponents' contributions to the Battle of the Books reveal that they shared fundamental evaluative assumptions about authors and authorship. Like Temple, Bentley assumed that authorship is good, that copying is bad, and that copying entails the loss of authorship. We will shortly see how Bentley exploited this common scheme of values in his arguments against Phalaris: for Bentley, the Phalaris letters were not only pseudonymous and authorless, but also copies in more than one sense. At the moment, it is worthwhile to notice that the same scheme of values is also implicit in Bentley's other writings, showing that the dynamic of author and copy was not simply a momentary appropriation from Temple on his part. In Bentley's practice as a classical editor, an absolute antithesis between authorship and copying was perhaps the central methodological assumption: Bentley took his task to be the restoration of the text an author had written, yet the surviving manuscripts of any classical text were inevitably copies of copies, sometimes at many removes. Perhaps more acutely than any of his scholarly contemporaries, Bentley distrusted these copies, meaning in practical terms that he regarded no one manuscript as authoritative on all occasions, and that he often felt licensed to ignore the manuscripts altogether in favor of what he believed the author had really written. Bentley had many techniques for going directly to the author without passing by way of manuscripts: he might appeal to possibly parallel passages within the text under examination, possibly parallel passages in other writers' texts, the laws of poetic meter, or merely what Bentley called "reason, the light of the meaning, and necessity itself" as he understood these.[25] On the one disastrous occasion when Bentley applied himself to a non-ancient text, Bentley began his work by theoretically reducing that text to a faulty copy as well, so as to justify his own bold interventions: according to Bentley, the original manuscript of Milton's *Paradise Lost* had been corrupted before publication by a devious printing-house worker who had clumsily revised and interpolated the text. The first printing of *Paradise Lost* was thus already a debased copy, and only Bentley could reveal what Milton had really written.

Coexisting with Bentley's disdain for textual copies was a further conviction shared with Temple, namely that when an original text was finally arrived at, its author was vitally present in that text, perhaps even identical with that text. Now a certain degree of conflation between author and text was virtually necessary for all contemporaries, not only in ordinary phrases such as "Temple reads Phalaris" or "Bentley edits Horace," but also in the technical language of textual criticism: a passage in a text might be either "healthy" *(sanus)* or "corrupt" *(corruptus)*, and a manuscript was either "sound" *(integer, incolumis)* or "mutilated" *(mutilus, laceratus)*. The metaphor of the text as the author's body could be indefinitely and quite graphically elaborated, as when Bentley wrote to a friend about his project to edit Horace, "when I was young, I believe I successfully healed a number of that author's ulcerous passages."[26] But in Bentley's case, this metaphor also tended to turn into a text-critical method, perhaps most spectacularly in his edition of Horace. Unlike Temple, Bentley in his Horace edition spends relatively little time listing the aesthetic qualities of his author and his text, although he does occasionally remark that one or the other is "elegant" *(elegans)* or "poetical" *(venustus)*. Bentley does strongly resemble Temple in his insistence that he, Bentley, can infallibly recognize what is and is not "Horace" in an immediate and total way. Fairly typical is the peroration to a long note in which Bentley proposes the conjecture *rectis oculis* in place of the manuscripts' unanimous reading *siccis oculis*: "I think I have now sufficiently and abundantly proved that either Horace wrote *rectis oculis*, or by all means he should have done. If you deny either one of these, you have no idea what Horace is; if you deny both, I am afraid we know very well what you are."[27] Elsewhere, Bentley is even more peremptory in issuing commands to his reader, as when he directs us to accept another conjecture: "Do not doubt that Horace wrote thus."[28] That Bentley himself thus assumed something close to authorial status was an implication he never denied. Contemporaries often pointed this out in scandalized tones, and complained further that Bentley's editorial behavior came close to setting up a tyranny in the putatively free republic of letters.[29]

When Bentley attacked Temple's claims about Phalaris, then, he did so from essentially parallel working assumptions about what the normal or ideal relationship between a text and an author was—a relation of identity. The Phalaris letters were aberrant, for Bentley, because the relationship between the letters and their putative author was also aberrant: Phalaris was a name attached to "his" letters in a purely conventional way in their material circulation, not an undying essence permeating the text and animating it from within. Bentley made great rhetorical capital of his and Temple's shared abhorrence for all things copied when, at the opening of his *Dissertation*, he compared Phalaris's letters to a proverbial ancient painting of grapes which appeared so realistic that birds gathered in droves to peck at it (*D1* 10–11).[30] Temple was, of course, the seventeenth-century version of these deluded birds, whose deception was all the more humiliating because of Temple's own insistence on the poverty of the copy and the enduring value of the original.

In technical terms, Bentley conducted his assault on Phalaris in two ways. In the first place, he called attention to particular passages of the letters that, he claimed, could not have been written by the historical Phalaris. Phalaris had referred to a vessel called the "Thericlean cup," but Bentley claimed that the Thericles after whom this cup was named had not lived until more than a century after Phalaris's death (*D1* 110–11). Phalaris had addressed admiring letters to the philosopher Pythagoras inviting him to the palace for a visit, but Bentley thought it quite possible that the lifetimes of these two figures had not overlapped at all (*D1* 27–8). Phalaris had threatened his enemies using what was later a proverbial Greek expression, saying "I will cut you down like a pine tree," but in fact this proverb had a literary source which, again, Phalaris could never have read (*D1* 169–71). Bentley also pointed out that no other Greek writer had referred to any letters of Phalaris until a thousand years after they were supposed to have been composed, not even writers on the history of Sicily who should have mentioned the letters had they really existed (*D*1 506–8). Thus, Bentley combined arguments from historical chronology and literary history to drive a wedge between the surviving text and the author whose life and thoughts they were supposed to reflect.

At the same time, although less extensively, Bentley argued on the aesthetic and ethical grounds that Temple had made his own. Bentley claimed that to anyone with as thorough a knowledge of Greek as his own, the letters' style made it patently obvious that they came from a later period. Bentley did not, however, offer any stylistic analyses beyond the individual phrases he had already singled out as inauthentic—he explained, perhaps rightly, that no one was likely to see the light on the basis of a stylistic analysis if their own knowledge of Greek had not already told them the letters were late. Bentley also denied that the letters possessed the intuitive feeling of humanity, authenticity, and presence that Temple had ascribed to them. Claiming powers of ethical intuition of his own, Bentley argued that when the real letters of ancient or modern statesmen were compared with the Phalaris letters, "… you feel by the emptiness and deadness of them [the Phalaris letters], that you converse with some dreaming Pedant with his elbow on his desk; not with an active, ambitious Tyrant, with his Hand on his Sword, commanding a Million of Subjects" (*D*1 487).

In fact, Bentley continued, the Phalaris letters were "a fardle of Common Places" (*D*1 487), a string of the clichés developed by Greek rhetoricians precisely in order to capitalize on their hearers' stereotyped ideas about virtue, tyranny, and the like.[31] If Temple thought the letters were the perfect mirror of monarchy, then, the image in that mirror was nothing other than Temple's own commonplace preconceptions as they had been cannily anticipated by an ancient sophist. Like the unfortunate birds, Temple had mistaken what was plastery, flat, and fake for what was juicy, round, and real.[32]

Yet, according to Bentley, the Phalaris letters were not without an origin of sorts once their putative author was removed from the picture. In Bentley's account, the letters derived from a mass of other texts, from ancient dictionaries and from geographical and historical works. Their nameless forger had simply assembled and recombined these texts, seeking above all to efface the traces of his own involvement from the finished product. Accordingly, the Phalaris letters were not only a copy in the general sense of being unreal, like the ancient grapes, but they had been literally constituted by the copying of other texts. Like virtually all modern texts in Temple's account, this putatively ancient and original text was a mass of citations.

Bentley's clearest arguments for this citational aspect of the Phalaris letters fall in the long central portion of the *Dissertation* concerning what Bentley calls the "language" of the Phalaris letters. In this part of his argument, Bentley repeatedly shows that the letters contain parallels with texts that were only written long after the life of the historical Phalaris (*D* 169–427 [sections 5–13], esp. 169–309 [sections 5–11]). His often unspoken further claim is, of course, that these parallels constitute citations of intertexts on the part of the Phalaris forger, rather than citations of Phalaris by the writers of the intertexts. For example, Bentley picks out a passage in which Phalaris delivers "a Sentence of Moral" to the effect that "wise men take Words for the shadow of Things"—an idea with reverberations for the problematic relationship between Phalaris's letters and the world of Phalaris which they purportedly reflect—and points out that the same saying was attributed to the philosopher Democritus by Diogenes Laertius and Plutarch (*D1* 189–90). But since Democritus had composed his aphorism more than a century after Phalaris' death, and moreover possessed "the character of a man of Probity and Wit; who had neither inclination nor need to filch the Sayings of others," Bentley concluded that the forger had taken the saying from Democritus and inserted it into the letters of Phalaris: "He should have minded his hits better, when he was minded to act the Tyrant." Again, Phalaris's "Moral Sentence" that "Mortal Men ought not to entertain Immortal Anger" was really drawn from Euripides (*D1* 195–6), and his reference to the "other daemon" who brought misfortune was really drawn from Pindar (*D1* 216–17). In this respect, Phalaris's letters truly were "a fardle of Common Places," an artful arrangement of quotable quotes from all departments of ancient literature.

On the one hand, these arguments served Bentley's general strategy of separating the historical Phalaris from the letters, thus rendering them authorless: since the historical Phalaris could not have quoted Democritus, Euripides, or Pindar, the letters were not by him. On the other hand, these arguments also emphasized the forger's strategy of textual copying in a very concrete way. Bentley suggested, for example, that when the writer of the Phalaris letters quoted a phrase from Herodotus word for word without variation, "he had *Herodotus's* passage in his Eye" (*D2* 177), by which Bentley apparently means not only that the forger was thinking of the Herodotus passage, but that he actually had Herodotus's text (or a phrasebook containing the passage) open in front of him. In fact, Bentley seems to have assumed that citation and compilation were central techniques of forgery in general and not limited to the case of the Phalaris letters. When Bentley argues, in the *Dissertation*, against the authenticity of the laws of Zaleucus—these laws, which are preserved only as quotations in other writers, are generally considered to be authentic today—he makes the corpus's parallels with other attestations of Zaleucus's laws into evidence of forgery, rather than of authenticity: "The Impostor had taken care to insert those Laws of *Zaleucus*, which he had met with in Ancient Writers, into his counterfeit System" (*D2* 343). Again, in his arguments against the authenticity of the fables of Aesop, one of Bentley's central proofs is that the fables sometimes quote or paraphrase a poetic version of the Aesopian fables that had been written by one Babrius in the postclassical period.[33]

In fact, it is not only Bentley's account of Phalaris's language that relies on citation as a primary tool of exposing imposture. The complex chronological arguments with which Bentley begins the *Dissertation* (sections 1–4) can be understood in much the same way. Since Bentley believed, for example, that the real Phalaris had never written to the real Pythagoras, the "Pythagoras" who is addressed in the letters is little more than a name taken by the forger from philosophical and historical texts. This Pythagoras, like Phalaris's "Moral Sentences" and the author "Phalaris" himself, is essentially a citation: the Phalaris letters might appear to refer to a real world outside themselves, but in fact they only derive from and refer to other texts. As a result, the only sensible way to read the letters was to avoid assuming, as Temple had, that they gave access to anything in the concrete world at all, whether it were Phalaris, his correspondents, or his drinking implementa. One must instead read the letters exclusively for their parallels with and divergences from other texts. And this is the procedure Bentley followed throughout the *Dissertation*, as individual passages from "Phalaris" led him again and again through labyrinths of other writing.

Copying and citation thus rose to the level of a proof, although not the only possible proof that a text was not by its alleged author. At the same time, Bentley acknowledged that the whole of postclassical Greek literary writing partook of citation in a broader sense, in that this writing was done in a classicizing linguistic idiom that had progressively less in common with ordinary spoken language. Against Boyle's remark that the Greek language had remained essentially unchanged for many centuries, Bentley countered that "it was Imitation only, that makes the Greek Books of different Ages so alike" (*D2* 406).[34] The citations in the Phalaris letters suddenly begin to seem less like an aberration and more like a convention, even a cultural necessity, at the time when the letters were compiled. This is only the first of many ways in which Bentley's account of the aberrant Phalaris letters was eventually to slip the boundaries of the case of Phalaris and attach itself to apparently normal ancient (and seventeenth-century) texts.

It has sometimes been suggested that Bentley's *Dissertation* is primarily valuable because Bentley recognized the importance of historical context to the meaning and nature of texts. In this account, Bentley's historicism would distinguish him sharply from Sir William Temple, for whom privileged ancient texts were eternal in their own right and eternally accessible to readers, like him, who possessed a minimum of contextual understanding.[35] It is certainly true that Bentley was more knowledgeable about the ancient world than Temple. But given the extent of Bentley's knowledge, what seems surprising is Bentley's utter indifference to the question of what the real historical context of the letters was. Bentley tells us a good deal about the context to which the letters do not belong, that is, the archaic Sicilian world of Phalaris; yet he says virtually nothing about the motivations and the cultural environment of their forger, which would certainly seem to be the path through which a contextual or historicist account of the letters must lie.[36] Bentley does indeed begin his treatise with the observation that textual forgery was widespread in the Hellenistic period, as book consumers were prepared to give good prices for books to which famous names were affixed. But by the time of the Roman empire, when Bentley believed the Phalaris letters were written, Bentley asserts that even financial gain was no longer an important motive (*D*1 10). Nor does Bentley ever suggest reasons why the personal letter as a genre or the figure of Phalaris in particular might have seemed interesting either to a forger or to his Greek-speaking audience. Pure deceit had become forgers' sole *raison d'être*. The successful imposition of their forgeries "no doubt, was great Content and Joy to them [the sophists]," although for obvious reasons, successful forgeries could never make their writers famous in their own right (*D*1 10–11). Deceit was likewise the sole motive of the Phalaris forger, an accusation Bentley periodically repeats via metaphors of theatrical performance and the use of masks: Bentley boasts, for example, that he will "unmask the recent Sophist under the person of the old Tyrant" (*D*1 395; cf. 17, 195). Greek forgeries, including the letters of Phalaris, apparently have a single meaning—if it can be called a meaning—namely, their falseness. Like the "writer" in the most gothic twentieth-century version of the death of the author, the Phalaris forger according to Bentley is a man without qualities, a disembodied hand through which citations mysteriously flow.

Was Bentley's assault on Phalaris a simple and localized tyrannicide, or do Bentley's arguments figure as a symptom of anything larger about Bentley and the enterprise of late seventeenth-century scholarly writing? By rights we might expect that they would not. Bentley did not argue, after all, that all language is citation, that no text has an author, or the like. Only in the case of the Phalaris letters, as well as the sharply delimited group of other texts that Bentley defined as forgeries, did these fascinating and deviant conditions obtain.[37] Yet, if the category of forgery served as a kind of conceptual firewall for Bentley, allowing him to dirty his hands with the Phalaridean type of textuality without compromising the normal world of originary authors and mimetic texts, the ensuing controversy showed that this firewall was by no means impermeable. We have already seen that the citational practices of the Phalaris forger, according to Bentley, bore a close resemblance to the humanist techniques of using texts that Temple had derided and Bentley had so intensively employed. Bentley acknowledged this on the many occasions when he called the Phalaris forger a "pedant," which had been one of Temple's most loaded terms of censure for the modern age. But the equivalence between the Phalaris letters and modern scholarly texts became spectacularly explicit when Bentley and his opponent Boyle began to accuse one another of ignorant copying, bogus citations, and, in the end, full-blown pseudonymy. If Bentley had argued that Phalaris was like the derivative modern texts described by Temple, both sides now argued that their respective opponents' modern texts were like Phalaris. The charges are worth examining not only because of the way in which they equate modern texts with a problematic ancient one, but also because the charges posed a significant dilemma for contemporaries: assuming that scholarly writing did consist largely in citation, how could any standards be fixed that would indicate which citations were acceptable and scholarly and which citations were infelicitous, irresponsible, or simply wrong?

Bentley was the first to recognize that his account of Phalaris had legs, so to speak. In the first edition of his *Dissertation* in 1697, Bentley strongly insinuated that the undergraduate Boyle was not primarily responsible for his edition of Phalaris: it had been largely prepared by Boyle's Oxford tutor after much of the research had been done by an anonymous and humble assistant. In effect, "Charles Boyle" was a pseudonym. These charges were not directly denied in Boyle's 1698 pamphlet *Dr. Bentley's Dissertations ... Examin'd*, but they were reinflected and redirected against Bentley himself. Bentley was accused at length of being a "pedant" precisely like the supposed forger of the Phalaris letters.[38] He was also accused of copying everything he wrote: Boyle suggested that Bentley's apparently exhaustive learning derived only from dictionaries and the printed indexes of books (*DBD* 164–5), and he claimed that Bentley had stolen two parallels to a passage in Phalaris from Boyle's own edition (*DBD* 143). Finally, in an expertly handled comic appendix, it was calmly argued that Bentley was not the author of the *Dissertation* circulating under his name: the *Dissertation*'s rustic use of English, its bad manners, and its pedantic learning could not be fathered on a famous scholar and library keeper without insult. The case was reinforced with long quotations from the *Dissertation* itself in which the name "*Dr. Bentley*" was substituted for "*Phalaris*." Bentley replied in a similar vein in the 1699 second edition of his *Dissertation*. Boyle was not the author of his 1698 pamphlet either, Bentley now claimed (*D2* 168, 174, 329), and if he had written any of the text he expressed himself, as the Phalaris forger had done, with "common-place Eloquence" (*D2* 171). Not Bentley but Boyle (or rather Boyle's "under-jobbing assistant") was the one who relied on indexes, other people's commentaries, and predigested quotations in reference books (*D2* 215, 219, 230–1, 381, etc.). Meanwhile, Bentley defended himself against Boyle's parallel charges, managing to convert even his own previous errors into virtues: had the first edition of the *Dissertation* been correct in every detail, Bentley really would have been proven to be "a Turner of *Index*'s and *Lexicons*" (*D2* 422).

Bentley also found time to suggest that not merely Boyle, but the whole of seventeenth-century scholarly writing, was implicated in practices of citation. Take, for example, a telling statement in the *Dissertation* about the nature of neo-Latin, the language in which Bentley had published his pre-*Dissertation* philological works and Boyle had published his edition of Phalaris. Apropos the largely imitative or citational nature of postclassical Greek literary language, Bentley commented that modern Latin offered an even more perfect case of the same phenomenon: modern Latin derived exclusively from previous Latin writing, without any influence from changes in spoken language. Neo-Latin was thus "no longer liable to those Changes, to which living Languages are naturally obnoxious; but by being Dead, it's become Immortal" (*D2* 406).[39] And if all language actually was citation in the international scholarly community of the late seventeenth century, so, too, was a great deal of scholarly argumentation, as we have already seen in the case of Bentley's *Dissertation*. If the forger had put Phalaris together out of texts, Bentley could only take Phalaris apart by resolving him into his elements of quotation and misquotation, in short, by citing.

Bentley's own argumentative reliance on quotation is clearly the point at which his accusations against Boyle seem in danger of collapsing under their own rhetorical weight. If Boyle's habits of citing made Boyle something less than the author of his text—and this is certainly the direction of Bentley's argument—just what kind of citing did Bentley suppose he was practicing so as to remain responsible for his own *Dissertation*? What kind of citing could any seventeenth-century student of texts perform and remain something other than a "transcriber," "commentator," and "pedant"? Is Bentley involved in a fundamental misrecognition of the nature of his own practices, driven by the binary rhetoric of original and copy he shared with William Temple?

It seems to me that Bentley did attempt to address this difficulty and to differentiate his own methods of citing from Boyle's, a project that necessarily implied moving beyond a simple division between authorship and citation. Bentley did suggest a criterion that would distinguish acceptable scholarly citation from unacceptable, irresponsible citation, and he located that criterion in the nature of the text from which a citation is drawn. Bentley claimed that his own citations derived from his readings of entire ancient texts, but he often accused Boyle of being ignorant of the complete contents of the texts he quoted or referred to. This was because Boyle had relied on predigested quotations in two forms: standard ones he drew from dictionaries and encyclopedic scholarly treatises, and custom-made ones gathered for Boyle by his nameless assistant. Boyle's citations thus led not even to ancient texts but only to previous citations of them, as Bentley gleefully demonstrated more than once.

We immediately notice that Bentley's account of good and bad citation still relies, at one remove, on a metaphysical and indeed Temple-like notion of authorship, now transferred to the level of the text. According to Bentley, for example, he himself cites Plutarch's *Theseus* (or, to incorporate fully the incipient slippage from text to author, Bentley cites Plutarch) while Boyle pretends to be citing that text but has really taken his information directly from early modern treatises by Julius Caesar Scaliger and G. J. Vossius (*D2* 280–1). It seems quite possible, however, to restate Bentley's account in a way that focuses not on the authorial or nonauthorial nature of the text that is cited, but instead on the kind of reading and citing that is done in the present. Citation can, after all, be a very definite form of linguistic agency.[40] Bentley could have claimed, in this case, that he himself actively made excerpts from texts, defining and producing his quotations as quotations. The obvious fact that Bentley did not literally copy out the entire texts he cited would itself indicate that his citations were cases of strategic practice, not a form of mechanized repetition without agency. Boyle, on the other hand, merely repeated the text of prefabricated quotations in their entirety, without doing the work of marking them out as quotations himself. This procedure would in fact approximate to the parrot-like, subjectless repetition that figures in the gothic version of the death of the author—we recall that the reader, for Barthes, is precisely the sum total of all the texts he or she has ever read with nothing left out. Where Bentley's own rhetoric claimed that his citation was legitimate because it engaged with whole, authorial texts, I am suggesting instead that citational agency lies in the act of producing parts, in the act of interventionist, productive reading.

Whether we think in Bentley's terms or in terms of citational agency, it is clear that Bentley's differentiation of his own writing procedures from Boyle's was also a riposte to Temple on the subject of modernity. Bentley had already shown that Temple's arguments about the originary status of antiquity were mistaken in their details; he now suggested that Temple's understanding of the modern age as a uniformly abject realm of the copy was too simplistic to account for the divergence of modern writing practices. It seems likely, in fact, that the controversy with Temple and Boyle stands behind many of Bentley's most florid subsequent statements about the quasi-authorial status of his own philological work. Consider, for example, Bentley's assertion in the preface to his Horace edition that he possesses not merely the great stock of historical and linguistic knowledge which any ordinary commentator must master, but also "an inordinately keen faculty of judgment ... cleverness and cunning ... [and] what the ancients ascribed to Aristarchus, a certain aptitude for divination and prophecy. These can never be acquired through hard work or longevity; they are the gift of nature alone to those who are born lucky."[41] As he explicitly contrasts himself as *philologus uates* with the moderns whom Temple had condemned as "transcribers" and "commentators," Bentley also seems to suggest that it is philological work like his own, not Temple-like veneration of antiquity, that offers the best avenue for communing with authors and reproducing authorship in the present.

Without, of course, subscribing to Bentley's extravagant notion of authorship, I think there is great importance in his project of recuperating some sort of status for writing practices that appear marginal to some because they are non-originary or citational. I would like to conclude by looking briefly at two further cases—one relatively modern and one ancient—in which we might do this. First, consider a work of criticism by an eighteenth-century emulator of Bentley, John Jortin's *Remarks on Spenser's Poems* of 1734. Jortin's treatise is a characteristic moment in what has often been treated as a hopelessly dark age in the criticism of English literary texts, the early- to middle-eighteenth century period in which essentially "verbal" commentaries and treatises were the norm.

While some students have sought to locate the birth of English historical criticism in the commentaries of this time, the most glaringly obvious aspect of these texts is their almost single-minded devotion to intertextual citation. The exclusive task Jortin set himself in this treatise was the identification and reproduction of parallel passages, which he often discussed to the effect that Spenser had made a "true" or "false" use of them. Not only Jortin was thereby involved in the practice of citation, but by implication so was the poetic text being discussed: Jortin's treatise gives the distinct impression that *The Faerie Queene* mostly interested Jortin insofar as it was itself constituted by citation. Yet, to cite a parallel passage, as Jortin did again and again, was not just to repeat it, but, as Bentley's differentiation between forms of citation suggests, actually to construct and name it as both a passage and a parallel. The reading that yielded parallels was not merely a case of "collection"—the usual contemporary term for it—but a case of production. So, in turn, was the writing of heavily citational poetry: if Jortin's intertextual Spenser is hard to understand as an author, he is without question an active and productive reader.

Finally, let us turn to the unfortunate and, until now, almost completely blank figure of the Phalaris forger. For Bentley, we recall, the forger was little more than a citer of texts determined to efface his own identity, motivated by nothing more than the desire to deceive. Yet, without speculating about the forger's subjective intentions we can still accord him a certain, perhaps unstable, measure of personal and cultural agency—an agency actualized through the very citations that make up his text.[42] For the forger, reiteration of bits and pieces from texts of the classical period (and, most likely, from compendia or lexica into which those texts had already been digested) was a form of engagement with the textual past that also constituted a re-creation or re-presentation of that past.[43] The forger added a new text to the literary tradition which he cited and rearticulated, and thereby marked the tradition in his own right. Of course, it is a paradox inherent to forgery that this marking could not be done in the writer's own name, but only under cover of a name— Phalaris—that itself constituted another citation and rearticulation of transmitted material. Yet it is possible to go even farther and ask, as Serena Bianchetti has done, whether the Phalaris letters could ever have been meant to deceive anyone at all. In Bianchetti's view, the literary Attic dialect in which the letters are written would have signaled immediately to ancient readers that the letters were an imaginative reconstruction, not an authentic personal document of the historical Phalaris.[44] In that case, the letters' citational and non-originary character was never an unspeakable scandal hidden behind a tyrant's mask, but rather the most obvious and central fact confronting the letters' first audience. In that case too, the Phalaris letters come to seem more and more like the characteristic texts of early modern humanism, in which citation was not a secret but an avowed and indispensable technique of writing and of reading. When Temple celebrated Phalaris and decried modern humanist writing, then, it seems that he was engaged above all in an educated form of forgetting.[45]

Notes

1. Roland Barthes, "La mort de l'auteur" (hereafter, *MA*) in *Œuvres complètes*, ed. Éric Marty, vol. 2 (Paris: Seuil, 1994), 491–5 (first published *Manteia*, 1968); Eng. trans., "The Death of the Author" (hereafter, *DA*) in Barthes's *Image Music Text*, ed. and trans. Stephen Heath (London: Flamingo-Fontana, 1984), 142–8.

2. Jonathan Swift, *A Full and True Account of the Battel Fought last Friday, Between the Antient and the Modern Books in St. James's Library*, published with *A Tale of a Tub* (London: John Nutt, 1704).

3. On the English Battle, see, above all, Joseph M. Levine, *The Battle of the Books: History and Literature in the Augustan Age* (Ithaca: Cornell University Press, 1991). On the French *querelle des anciens et des modernes*, see Joan DeJean, *Ancients against Moderns: Culture Wars and the Making of a Fin de Siècle* (Chicago: University of Chicago Press, 1997) and Hans Kortum, *Charles Perrault und Nicolas Boileau. Der Antike-Streit im Zeitalter der klassischen französischen Literatur* (Berlin: Rütten & Loening, 1966).

4. Temple, "Essay of Ancient and Modern Learning" (hereafter, *E*) in his *Miscellanea. The Second Part* (London, 1690), 10: "[S]ince that time [the reign of Antoninus Pius, 138–61 C.E.], I know very few that can pretend to be Authors, rather than Transcribers or Commentators of the Ancient Learning ... ." See also 28: the moderns "have hardly ever pretended more, than to learn what the others taught, to remember what they invented, and not able to compass that it self, they have set up for Authors, upon some parcels of those great Stocks, or else have contented themselves only to comment upon those Texts, and make the best Copies they could, after those Originals."

5. William Wotton, *Reflections upon Ancient and Modern Learning* (London, 1694). See Levine, *Battle*, and R. F. Jones, *Ancients and Moderns: A Study of the Rise of the Scientific Movement in Seventeenth-Century England* (Berkeley: California, 1961).

6. In addition to Levine, see Simon Jarvis, *Scholars and Gentlemen: Shakespearian Textual Criticism and Representations of Scholarly Labour, 1725–1765* (Oxford: Oxford University Press, 1995).

7. A broad range of recent work is relevant: see, for example, Michael McKeon, *The Origins of the English Novel, 1600–1740* (Baltimore: Johns Hopkins, 1987), Steven Shapin, *A Social History of Truth: Civility and Science in Seventeenth-Century England* (Chicago: University of Chicago Press, 1994); Adrian Johns, *The Nature of the Book: Print and Knowledge in the Making* (Chicago: University of Chicago Press, 1998); Joseph M. Levine, *Dr. Woodward's Shield: History, Science, and Satire in Augustan England* (Berkeley: California, 1977).

8. Michel Foucault famously discussed cases of pseudonymy and historical criteria for determining pseudonymy as a way of elucidating historical constructions of the author: "What is an Author?," in Foucault's *Language, Counter-Memory, Practice*, ed. Donald F. Bouchard and trans. Bouchard and Sherry Simon (Ithaca: Cornell University Press, 1977), 113–38, esp. 121–31.

9. The picture is actually somewhat more complicated, because Temple initially described Greek and Roman culture as derivative also—it came by various channels from a syncretically conceived Orient that included the Near East, Ethiopia, India, and China. But since Temple knew of no exemplary texts from these places (and doubtless for other reasons), the texts and authors that he actually discussed as exemplars were Greek and Roman.

10. The fables of Aesop were as pseudonymous as Phalaris's letters, something pointed out in Richard Bentley's *Dissertation upon the Epistles of Phalaris* (1697)—this is the reason why Bentley's ill-fated assault in Swift's *Battle of the Books* is on both Phalaris and Aesop. See D. K. Money, *The English Horace: Anthony Alsop and the Tradition of British Latin Verse* (London: British Academy, 1998).

11. Precisely because of the relatively traditional categories employed in Barthes's thought, he makes a good sounding-board for the questions canvassed in the Battle; of course, this is not to suggest that his is the final word on the subject of the author. See, above all, Jacques Derrida, *Of Grammatology*, trans. Gayatri Chakravorty Spivak, corrected edn. (Baltimore: Johns Hopkins, 1997) and "Signature Event Context," in *Limited INC*, ed. Gerald Graff (Evanston: Northwestern, 1988), 1–23. Derrida's account of presence and absence seems particularly relevant to Temple's text. Apropos Phalaris, is it a coincidence that the author in Derrida's critique is also royal ("the sovereign author")?

12. On claims for authenticity, John W. Howland, *The Letter Form and the French Enlightenment: The Epistolary Paradox* (New York: Peter Lang, 1991), 24–6 and Robert Adams Day, *Told in Letters: Epistolary Fiction Before Richardson* (Ann Arbor: University of Michigan Press, 1966), 90–1; on rhetoricity, Howland, 45 and Claudio Guillén, "Notes toward the Study of the Renaissance Letter," in *Renaissance Genres: Essays on Theory, History, and Interpretation*, ed. Barbara Kiefer Lewalski (Cambridge: Harvard University Press, 1986), 70–101, esp. 85–98.

13. Peter V. Conroy, Jr., "Real Fiction: Authenticity in the French Epistolary Novel," *Romanic Review* 72 (1981), 409–24; Day, *Told in Letters*, passim.

14. Feminine letters: Elizabeth Heckendorn Cook, *Epistolary Bodies: Gender and Genre in the Eighteenth-Century Republic of Letters* (Stanford: Stanford University Press, 1996), Katharine A. Jensen, "Male Models of Feminine Epistolarity: Or, How to Write Like a Woman in Seventeenth-Century France," 25–45 and Elizabeth C. Goldsmith, "Authority, Authenticity, and the Publication of Letters by Women," 46–59 in Goldsmith, ed., *Writing the Female Voice: Essays on Epistolary Literature* (Boston: Northeastern University Press, 1989); masculine letters: Guillén, "Notes," 78–9.

15. *Letters Written by Sir W. Temple, Bart. and other Ministers of State*, 2 vols. (London, 1700), completed by *Letters to the King, the Prince of Orange, the Chief Ministers of State, and Other Persons. By Sir W. Temple Bart* (London, 1703).

16. On commonplace books, François Goyet, *Le sublime du "lieu commun"* (Paris: Champion, 1996); Ann Blair, *The Theater of Nature: Jean Bodin and Renaissance Science* (Princeton: Princeton University Press, 1997); Ann Moss, *Printed Commonplace Books and the Structuring of Renaissance Thought* (Oxford: Clarendon, 1996); and Terence Cave, *The Cornucopian Text: Problems of Writing in the French Renaissance* (Oxford: Clarendon, 1979). For an indication that the commonplace book was still taken seriously in the late seventeenth century, Peter Beal, "Notions in Garrison: The Seventeenth-Century Commonplace Book," in *New Ways of Looking at Old Texts: Papers of the Renaissance English Text Society, 1985–1991*, ed. W. Speed Hill (Binghamton: Renaissance English Text Society, 1993), 131–47.

17. For line-by-line commentaries, especially in the sixteenth century, see, for example, Anthony Grafton, "Renaissance Readers and Ancient Texts: Comments on Some Commentaries," *Renaissance Quarterly*, 38 (1985), 615–49; Ann Blair, "Ovidius Methodizatus: The *Metamorphoses* of Ovid in a Sixteenth-Century Paris College," *History of Universities* 9 (1990), 73–118; Kees Meerhoff and Jean-Claude Moisan, "Précepte et usage: Un Commentaire Ramiste de la 4e *Philippique*," in *Autour de Ramus: Texte, théorie, commentaire*, ed. Meerhoff and Moisan (Montreal: Nuit Blanche, 1997); Kristine Louise Haugen, "A French Jesuit's Lectures on Vergil, 1582–83: Jacques Sirmond between Literature, History, and Myth," *Sixteenth Century Journal* (forthcoming, 2000), Nancy Siraisi, *The Clock and the Mirror: Girolamo Cardano and Renaissance Medicine* (Princeton: Princeton University Press, 1997); Anthony Grafton, "Barrow as a Scholar," in *Before Newton: The Life and Times of Isaac Barrow*, ed. Mordechai Feingold (Cambridge: Cambridge University Press, 1990), 291–302; William McCuaig, *Carlo Sigonio* (Princeton: Princeton

University Press, 1989). Biblical commentaries are also relevant, although Temple's text nowhere engages with theology or Christian subjects; for representative commentaries from late seventeenth-century England, see Marcus Walsh, *Shakespeare, Milton, and Eighteenth-century Literary Editing* (Cambridge: Cambridge University Press, 1997).

18. Cf. John F. Tinkler, "The Splitting of Humanism: Bentley, Swift, and the English Battle of the Books," *Journal of the History of Ideas* 50 (1988), 453–72.

19. For Erasmus, see "De ratione studii," ed. J.-C. Margolin, in *Opera omnia* ser. I, vol. 2 (Amsterdam: North-Holland, 1971), 111–46 at 135–6; "De conscribendis epistolis," ed. Margolin, *Opera omnia* ser I., vol. 2, 205–579 at 224; and "Institutio principis christiani," ed. O. Herding, *Opera omnia* ser. IV, vol. 1 (1974), 136–219 at 180.

20. On Temple and Cudworth, *Dictionary of National Biography* s.v. Temple; for Cudworth, see D. P. Walker, *The Ancient Theology: Studies in Christian Platonism from the Fifteenth to the Eighteenth Centuries* (Ithaca: Cornell, 1972) and Anthony Grafton, *Defenders of the Text: The Traditions of Scholarship in an Age of Science* (Cambridge: Harvard University Press, 1991), 17–18.

21. For the annual series of editions, known as New Year's Books, to which the Phalaris edition belonged, E. G. W. Bill, *Education at Christ Church Oxford 1660–1800* (Oxford: Clarendon, 1988).

22. British Library, MS Royal 16.D.II; Bentley later collated it on the margins of his copy of Boyle's Phalaris edition, now British Library shelfmark 682.b.7.

23. For the other controversial texts and details of the controversy, Levine, *The Battle of the Books*; J. H. Monk, *The Life of Richard Bentley*, 2nd edn., 2 vols. (London: Rivington, 1833), 1:58–133, and A. T. Bartholomew and J. W. Clark, *Richard Bentley D.D.: A Bibliography of his Works and of all the Literature called forth by his Acts or his Writings* (Cambridge: Bowes and Bowes, 1908). The 1698 text refers to "Dissertations" by Bentley, but in 1697 Bentley had published a single *Dissertation* subdivided into sections that treated different pseudonymous texts. In references to the *Dissertation* (hereafter, *D*), I cite from the 1699 edition and indicate whether the passage at hand first appeared in the first edition (*D1*) or in the second edition (*D2*).

24. For his career in general, the most valuable accounts remain R. C. Jebb, *Bentley* (London: Macmillan, 1882); and Monk, *The Life of Richard Bentley*; for particular aspects, see further John Gascoigne, *Cambridge in the Age of the Enlightenment* (Cambridge: Cambridge University Press, 1989); William Kolbrener, *Milton's Warring Angels: A Study of Critical Engagements* (Cambridge: Cambridge University Press, 1997); Walsh, *Shakespeare, Milton*; Adam Fox, *John Mill and Richard Bentley: A Study of the Textual Criticism of the New Testament 1675–1729* (Oxford: Blackwell, 1954); and C. O. Brink, *English Classical Scholarship: Historical Reflections on Bentley, Porson, and Housman* (Cambridge: James Clarke, 1986).

25. This notorious passage is from the preface to *Q. Horatius Flaccus*, ed. Bentley (Cambridge, 1711), c1 v°: "in conjecturis vero contra omnium Librorum fidem proponendis & timor pudorque aurem vellunt, & sola ratio ac sententiarum lux necessitasque ipsa dominantur" ("but when we propose conjectures against the testimony of all books, fear and modesty are tugging on our ears; they can be overcome by reason alone, and the light of the text's meaning, and necessity itself"). I discuss Bentley's methods in more detail in *Richard Bentley: Scholarship and Criticism in Eighteenth-Century England*, PhD. dissertation (Princeton, 2001).

26. "In his [a series of editions Bentley contemplated] primus prodibit Horatius, cujus olim, cum juvenis essem, ulcerosa aliquot loca feliciter sanasse videor": Bentley to J. G. Graevius, Cambridge, 20 August 1702, in *The Correspondence of Richard Bentley, D.D.*, ed. C. Wordsworth and J. Wordsworth, 2 vols. (London, 1842), 1:193–7 at 194.

27. "[S]atis iam, opinor, & abunde pervicimus, aut scripsisse RECTIS OCULIS Flaccum, aut saltem ita debuisse: quorum alterum modo si negas; qui Horatius sit, omnino nescis: sin utrumque; vereor ne, qui tu sis, optime sciamus": *Q. Horatius Flaccus*, notes p. 8, ad C 1.3.18.

28. "Noli dubitare, quin sic Horatius scripserit": *Q. Horatius Flaccus*, notes p. 304, ad S 2.3.212.

29. For overt claims about the authorial status of the competent critic, Wotton, *Reflections* (1694), 316–21. This passage in Wotton bears a remarkable resemblance to parts of the preface to

Bentley's Horace edition (1711). For Bentley as tyrant, Pieter Burmann, ed., *Quintus Horatius Flaccus Ad fidem codicum manuscriptorum emendatus* (Utrecht, 1713), "Lectori," ★6 r°.

30. The story comes originally from Pliny, *Natural History*, 35.65–66 and had appeared more recently in Charles Perrault's *Parallele des anciens et des modernes* (Paris, 1688), 199–200 and Wotton's *Reflections* (1694), 72.

31. For the ancient and early modern theory and practice of the discursive commonplace, see Goyet, *Le sublime du "lieu commun"* (Paris: Champion, 1966).

32. Helpful modern accounts of the letters include D. A. Russell, "The Ass in the Lion's Skin: Thoughts on the *Letters of Phalaris*," *Journal of Hellenic Studies* 108 (1988), 94–106, setting the letters in the context of rhetorical practice, and Niklaz Holzberg's discussion in the context of fictitious epistolary texts, in *The Novel in the Ancient World*, ed. Gareth Schmeling (Leiden: Brill, 1996), 649.

33. *Dissertation* (1697), 142–3 (the section on Aesop was omitted from the 2nd edn.).

34. Bentley used the term κοινὴ διάλεκτος to mean literary Attic (*D2* 406), whereas in modern usage it refers to the ordinary spoken Greek attested in documentary texts and the New Testament.

35. The most erudite argument on these lines is presented by Levine, *Battle of the Books*; see also A. H. De Quehen, "Richard Bentley's Spider-Web," *International Journal of the Classical Tradition* 1 (1994), 92–104 and Tinkler, "The Splitting of Humanism."

36. See Glenn Most, "Classical Scholarship and Literary Criticism," in *Cambridge History of Literary Criticism*, vol. IV: *The Eighteenth Century*, ed. H. B. Nisbet and Claude Rawson (Cambridge: Cambridge University Press, 1997), 742–57 at 754–5.

37. Other recognized forgeries that Bentley mentions in the *Dissertation* include the Sibylline oracles, the Letter of Aristeas, the *Antiquitates* of Annius of Viterbo, the Etruscan history of Curzio Inghirami, and humanist forgeries of works by Cicero and Petronius: *D1* 11–12.

38. "Charles Boyle," *Dr. Bentley's Dissertations on the Epistles of Phalaris and the Fables of Æsop Examin'd* (London, 1698), 91–9 (text cited hereafter as *DBD*).

39. Cf. Wotton, *Reflections* (1694), 29.

40. See, for example, Judith Butler, *Excitable Speech: A Politics of the Performative* (New York: Routledge, 1997).

41. *Q. Horatius Flaccus*, "Praefatio ad Lectorem," c1 r°-v°: "Formam vero & institutum operis sic mihi definivi terminisque his circumscripsi; ut ea sola attingerem, quae ad sanitatem sinceritatemque Lectionis pertinerent: cetera illa pluraque, quae ad Historiam & Mores antiquos grandem illam Commentariorum silvam & instrumentum spectarent, prorsus praeterirem .... [D]iffusa illa lectio & eruditio, veterisque totius Latii & Graeciae notitia, quae in illa studiorum materie totum constituit, in hac Nostra partis duntaxat infimae & initiorum apparatusque locum obtinet. Omnia quippe tibi ista in numerato esse prius oportet, quam de quovis Scriptore sine dementissimae temeritatis nota censuram agere audeas: est & peracri insuper judicio opus; est sagacitate & ἀγχινοία; est, ut de Aristarcho olim praedicabant, divinandi quadam peritia´ μαντικῇ quae nulla laborandi pertinacia vitaeve longinquitate acquiri possunt, sed naturae solius munere nascendique felicitate contingunt." "The form and purpose of the present work I defined and restricted as follows: I would discuss [in my annotations] only questions pertaining to the soundness and correctness of the text; I would completely pass over the many other questions that had to do with ancient history and culture, that enormous storehouse and stockpile for commentaries .... To study such topics requires nothing but that vast reading and erudition, that knowledge of all ancient Rome and Greece, which in my work holds the very lowest place, as a mere preliminary and preparation. To be sure, all that is cash you must have on hand before venturing to pass censure on any author, unless you want to give proofs of the most insane temerity. Yet you also need an inordinately keen faculty of judgment; you need cleverness and cunning; you need what the ancients ascribed to Aristarchus, a certain aptitude for divination and prophecy. These can never be acquired through hard work or longevity; they are the gift of nature alone to those who are born lucky."

42. Serena Bianchetti's source-criticism powerfully demonstrates the citational character of the letters, although her hypothesis of a fourth-century B.C.E. origin for the corpus would be difficult to prove definitively: *Falaride e Pseudofalaride: storia e leggenda* (Rome: L'Erma di Bretschneider, 1987).

43. Simon Swain, *Hellenism and Empire: Language, Classicism, and Power in the Greek World, AD 50–250* (Oxford: Clarendon, 1996) emphasizes the degree to which the Second Sophistic's engagement with the past was centered on language.

44. Bianchetti, *Falaride e Pseudofalaride*, 149.

45. I am extremely grateful for comments and advice about Phalaris, Bentley, and other matters from Anthony Grafton, Jonathan Lamb, Robert Griffin, and Richard Serjeantson.

CHAPTER THREE

" 'By a Lady': The Mask of the Feminine in Restoration, Early Eighteenth-Century Print Culture"

Margaret J. M. Ezell

It is a commonplace among literary critics that early modern women writers as a group shared a need for anonymity and developed authorial strategies to protect their reputations as socially acceptable females. Virginia Woolf's observation in *A Room of One's Own* that "Anon, who wrote so many poems without signing them, was often a woman," is frequently taken as being not only a description of an authorial practice, but also as a critique of the patriarchal culture which demanded that women artists—if they indeed could exist—hide their gender as a price for their artistic expression. We expect early modern women writers to give up their individual names, not because they wished to do so, but because of the cultural constraints placed upon them.

In such interpretations, anonymity is imposed, not selected. The relationship between early modern women writers and the practice of anonymous or pseudonymous authorship is seen as a direct response to gender conflicts within a culture, an authorial device which acts as a disguise for the protection of the writer, a masking device which indeed creates the physical space on the title page for her to be a poet or an essayist within the pages of a published text.

As satisfying as such interpretations have been, there remain some other questions which arise when one looks at the particulars of the texts where women gained anonymity through employing either a pseudonym or, in particular, the mask of "a lady." The first, and most obvious, is, that if cultural sanction against women being on public display in print was so encompassing and if the function of selecting anonymity of a pseudonym was to disguise the gender of the author to permit her speak, what are we to make of the selection of "By a Lady" as being one of the period's more popular solutions, a label which confronts the reader with the writer's gender, often as part of the very title of the work? Why was the choice of women writing during this period not simply "Anon" or the strategy adopted by nineteenth-century women writers, the adoption of male names?

From this point, further questions arise about "By a Lady" as acting primarily as a disguise assumed by women writers for social protection. How well did such sobriquets function as a shield for the female author, hiding or disguising her identity and protecting her from acquiring a "reputation"? Could they serve more as a costume rather than as a disguise, a means to signify to the reader that a certain type of role was being performed, a type of personality was being staged, rather than being simply a way to hide the true identity of the individual?

I. The Pseudonym as the Shield of the Anonymous Female

The theory that the use of a sobriquet or pseudonym functions as a protective cloak of anonymity for the gender and individual identity of the female writer has a mass of evidence to support it. There is the explanation, which in early modern England, to voice one's views in public was unfeminine. A woman who wrote down her views and published them was in direct violation of her culture's very definition of femininity.[1] Charlotte Otten begins a recent collection of early modern women's writings with the observation that, "the climate for women writers in sixteenth- and seventeenth-century England was not congenial. Commanded for centuries to be "chaste, obedient, and silent," women who violated the prohibition of silence risked disapproval, even castigation, by a society dominated by males. Moreover, a woman going into print was a challenge to the theological and medical grounds that supported the inferiority of women—an inferiority that demanded silence."[2] Otten's collection of texts by women obviously demonstrates that there were women who were not silenced, but Otten points out that "the implications for female writing are obvious. First, women hesitated to write at all; second, they felt the need to apologize for everything they wrote," (3) and the practices of anonymous publication would seem to be a continuation of this defensive strategy to shield and excuse the woman writer.[3]

What were the constraints involved in enforcing such a code that women hide their identities? The modern novelist Christina Wolf observed about nineteenth-century women writers who declined to publish under their own names that the practice "... can be understood in terms of the atmosphere of the time. I think there are certain things we refrain from doing nowadays, some of them consciously, that won't be understood later... because a lot of taboos must actually be understood not in terms of what is stipulated, but the whole ambience and mood of the time, and the limits in one's self."[4] Wolf's point is made in the context of the larger argument about citizens of the present passing judgment on the acts—or the lack of activity—by individuals in the past, but there are several features of her observation that are suggestive when looking at the authorial strategies of early modern women writers too.

This modern sense of the "mood of the time" and its ability to dictate "limits in one's self," would appear to be graphically outlined in Anne Finch's late seventeenth-century assessment of her situation as a woman author in her poem, "The Introduction." This text is frequently cited as a representative view from inside the cultural cage surrounding early women writers.[5]

> Did I my lines intend for public view,
> How many censures would their faults pursue!
>
> ★ ★ ★ ★ ★ ★ ★
>
> True judges might condemn their want of wit;
> And all might say, they're by a woman writ.
> Alas! a woman that attempts the pen,
> Such an intruder on the rights of men,
> Such a presumptuous creature is esteemed,
> The fault can by no virtue be redeemed.
> They tell us we mistake our sex and way ...
>
> ★ ★ ★ ★ ★ ★ ★
>
> ... if some one would soar above the rest,
> With warmer fancy and ambition pressed,
> So strong the opposing faction still appears,
> The hopes to thrive can ne'er outweigh the fears.
> —Anne Finch, Countess of Winchilsea, "The
>   Introduction"

Implicit in Finch's observations is the feeling that in addition to the universal situation of poets of having to face intimidating dissection of one's literary abilities from hostile critics, a woman poet is vulnerable to criticism of more than her versification, upon her publication of her writings. Another facet of the cultural prohibition against women being in print would be, in addition to being labeled a bad poet, the risk of being labeled as a "masculine" or an "unwomanly" woman who intrudes the space of men.

Why would a woman's *name* in print make her "masculine"? For a woman to sign her name was the equivalent of declaring her proprietorship of the ideas expressed, her possession of mastery over the artistic techniques employed, but under early modern law, of course, a woman not a widow had no automatic, guaranteed right to own property.[6] Legally, proprietorship could be assigned a male name, not a female one. A text with a woman's name could be read symbolically as a public declaration of her possession of intellectual and artistic property, a situation that did not exist under English law at that time even for a married woman's possession of material property.

Thus, while one might say that there was no "law" forbidding a woman writer from putting her name on her printed text, there was a clear cultural concern over whether such a declaration of ownership was legitimate—or even possible—thus, it would seem, generating a need to hide the author's identity and gender to permit print publication. Modern commentators interpret the authorial strategies used by women writing in the late seventeenth and early eighteenth centuries as cramped contortions of the author-function, where the writer, apparently driven by some irresistible need to see her words in print, ventured to do so behind the supposed cover of anonymity or by the use of a pseudonym to disguise her presence in print as a female author.

McGovern cites Katharine Rogers' assessment of Finch as "a woman imprisoned in man-made conventions," and Gilbert and Gubar's view of Finch as the woman poet trying "to escape the male design in which she feels herself enmeshed" (3). Given such a masculine culture, anonymity or pseudonymity is interpreted as functioning primarily as a protective device for the female author, a necessary strategy to permit expression. But the protective cloak of anonymity for a woman writer is also viewed in such interpretations as a constricting choice, smothering the individual identity of the writer as well as protecting it, denying her a chance at true, direct self-representation as an artist.

In addition to such sympathetic interpretations of anonymous or pseudonymous publication practices by early women, there is also, however, a darker reading of the practice shadowing other contemporary interpretations: women who chose to hide behind certain masks were complicit with the cultural forces that constrained them. The author (anonymous) of the entry on "pseudonyms" in *The Feminist Companion to English Literature*, for example, characterizes one of the most popular pseudonym selections, by "A Lady" as being a "discreet, conciliating" choice.[7] The implication here is that the woman writer, recognizing the social forces arrayed against her, simultaneously acknowledged their power by adopting one of their code words for appropriate feminine utterance, "lady."

Dorothy Mermin likewise believes that Finch and Philips manipulated the model of "male amateurism" to create a personae that permitted them to be the speaking voice in the poem, rather than the object described. "Philips, Behn, and Finch follow the old convention of assuming literary names to transform themselves into women fit for verse," Mermin asserts, but her opening premise is that such use of these conventions "is unavoidably duplicitous, with overtones of sexual coquetry, teasing withdrawal and self-display."[8] Interestingly, in both interpretations of early modern women's use of anonymous and pseudonymous publication, the language of the critic is charged with sexual innuendo itself—while early modern male critics might call a woman writing under her own name "loose" and "exposed," we call those writing under the mask of a pseudonym a "coquette," "complicit" with the masculine literary economy, or, as Mermin calls it, "being on their best behavior" (337), and thus, it is implied, reifying the constrictive regime.

II. Pseudonyms as Disguise

As I have written elsewhere, the selection of pseudonyms that are actual names rather than labels such as "a lady," which characterize English literary productions during the latter part of the seventeenth century and the start of the eighteenth are noteworthy in that they are typically gender specific. The late seventeenth, early eighteenth-century reader would encounter a host of pseudonyms for which the gender was clear— Orinda, Ardelia, Galesia, Corinna (Katherine Philips, Anne Finch, Jane Barker, Elizabeth Thomas) and Poliarchus, Palaemon, Strephon, Daphnis (Sir Charles Cotterell, Francis Finch, John Locke and the Earl of Rochester [among many], and Thomas Creech).[9] Such selections do not hide the author's gender, but instead highlight it. This generation of women writers clearly made a different choice of authorial self-representation than that made by George Eliot and Currer, Ellis, and Acton Bell in the nineteenth century.

And, pragmatically, what are we to make of how well such pen names, whether Orinda or "by a lady," disguised the individual identity of the author? How "anonymous" were the identities of the authors of texts "by a lady"? In this context, the title of one of Elizabeth Thomas's poems proves interesting: "To the Lady Chudleigh, the Anonymous Author of the *Lady's Defence*."[10] It appears that there is some question about how effective the use of a pseudonym would be not only to disguise the sex of the author, but even her very name. Alexander Pope's early quarrel with Edmund Curll over the pirated publication of a collection of satires entitled "Court Poems," (1716) concerned in part the damage it might do to the reputation of one of its authors, Lady Mary Wortley Montagu; Curll in his preface had suggested that the author was either "a LADY of QUALITY" or John Gay, but the mask of "a Lady" apparently would not have sufficiently hidden Lady Mary.[11] Likewise, the use of the pseudonym "Corinna" in no way served to protect the identity or reputation of Elizabeth Thomas; in one critic's interpretation, her adoption of this particular name actually damaged Thomas's personal reputation because of its historical associations.[12]

Thus, it seems odd that "a lady" was the "conciliatory" choice for many writers in the latter part of the seventeenth century, if indeed the goal was to avoid social censure for encroaching on masculine proprietary sensibilities. One could argue that by assuming it, the women were also invoking the shield of their social class. However, as we shall see, the materials most often associated with title pages attributed to "a lady" do not always support the political or social aims of an elite social class.

Let us look at some individual examples and see the ways in which "a lady" functioned on the title page of different types of printed texts during the Restoration and the early eighteenth century. Was its primary function, as we have assumed, to disguise the identity of the author and to shield feminine modesty?

One of the first features to note about anonymous print texts or those that announce authorship "by a lady" or "by a young lady" on the title page is that the accompanying introductory materials frequently reveal information about the authors' identities. Often, prefatory materials such as the epistle to the reader or the prefaces are indeed signed with the woman writer's name, initials, or other indications of her identity. In William Hicks's *London Drollery* (1672), the poem "On Captain Hicks his Curiosities of Nature" is listed under its title as being "By a Young Lady." It is signed at the end, however, by "E. C."[13]

Likewise, the table of contents of Aphra Behn's 1685 collection, *Miscellany, Being a Collection of Poems by several Hands*, offers a survey of possible ways to identify oneself as an author, male or female. It is a confusing mixture of poems with clear author attributions ("A Song by the Earl of Rochester"), poems with the author's initials where it is clear to all who the writer is ("A Pindaric to Mr. P. who sings finely. By Mrs. A. B."), poems attributed to persons since lost to us ("To Mertill, who desired her to speak to Clorinda of his Love. By Mrs. Taylor"), and poems employing descriptive labels rather than names ("Ovid to Julia. A Letter, By an unknown Hand" and "The Female Wits. A Song, By a Lady of Quality"). It is obvious that Behn is not attempting to hide her identity or gender by signing herself "Mrs. A. B."; to what extent did "Mr. J. W." or "Mr. T. B." expect their readers to likewise decode their identities?

One should also note that print texts that appeared initially as "by a lady" sometimes reappear in later editions with the author's name. Anne Finch's *Miscellany Poems* was printed originally in 1713 with "Written by a LADY" on its title page; shortly afterwards in 1714, it is reissued with a title page reading by "Lady Winchilsea." If appearing in print was a violation of cultural constraints defining feminine modesty, was being reprinted somehow less so? Ann Messenger interpreted the switch from "by a LADY" to the name and rank as an indication that a "countess had less to fear from a largely hostile public than a plain Mrs.," an interpretation seconded by Charles Hinnant.[14] Finch, however, had been a countess since 1712 and was recognized as such by her contemporaries; Jonathan Swift observed in a letter written in 1712, "my old acquaintance, Mrs. Finch, is now Countess of Winchilsea, the title being fallen to her husband but without much estate."[15] Therefore, her initial venture into print would have had the same measure of protection from her aristocratic status as the reprint did. If, as Finch's poem "The Introduction" suggests, texts by women are more severely and unfairly criticized than those by men and their authors held up to personal attack, why choose to announce oneself as a "LADY" on the first cover, and by one's name on the second?[16]

McGovern interprets the change to financial motives, "perhaps in hopes that sales of the book might be increased" (100). Given the enthusiasm for aristocratic connections displayed on the title pages of miscellanies and songbooks of the period, this certainly would seem to be a valid argument—at least from the bookseller's point of view. For Anne Finch, who would not have received any financial profit from the increased sales, it seems less compelling. Indeed, we have no knowledge at this point who decided what would appear on this particular title page—the author or the bookseller—but following modern practice, we have assumed it was the author's decision. Given the complete control booksellers had over the printed text during this period before the establishment of copyright, the selection of anonymity, pseudonymity, or the author's name on this title page might well have been the decision not of the individual writer, but of the manager of the commercial printed product.

There are certainly clear instances of women's texts being manipulated without their knowledge or consent by booksellers and printers. Mary Chudleigh published *The Ladies Defence* without her name on the title page in 1701; the poem is a sprightly retort to John Sprint's lugubrious representation of wifely submission in his sermon *The Bridewoman's Counsellor* (1699). In her preface to *Essays upon Several Subjects* (1710), Chudleigh reveals that she had denied the request of her publisher, Bernard Lintot, to include that early piece when he reprinted her collection, *Poems on Several Occasions* (1703); Lintot, however, purchased the text from the bookseller and printed it without Chudleigh's consent, which angered her considerably.

She was angry in part because the version he used corrupted the original text and left out the epistle to the reader and the preface, "by which means, he has left the *Reader* wholly in the Dark and expos'd me to Censure."[17] She notes that the first printing, too, mangled her preface, "that I hardly knew it to be my own: but it being then publish'd without a Name, I was the less concern'd" (248). She concludes that "but notwithstanding the great Care I took to conceal it, 'tis know to be mine, I think my self obliged, in my own Defence, to take some notice of it."

How does the 1701 text demonstrate the "great Care" she originally took to conceal her identity as the author? Obviously, her name does not appear on the title page. In her prefaces, she clearly identifies herself as a woman, writing to other women—her gender is not disguised but made the central feature of her appeal to her readership. Also, she signs the dedication to "all Ingenious Ladies," "M—y C—." Furthermore, she opens the subsequent "preface to the Reader" with the information that "the Book, which has been the occasion of the ensuing Poem, was presented to me by its Author," who had been clearly identified in his book as John Sprint residing in Sherbourn, Dorset.

Thus, while on the one hand the 1701 appearance of *The Ladies Defence* satisfies our model of the woman writer seeking to escape social censure by not putting her name on the title page, it does not in fact serve to either conceal or disguise her individual identity. The combination of the initials and the implied social connection between the authors would certainly provide an easy means for not only determining that the author was, indeed, a female, but also her name (certainly

Sprint and Chudleigh's immediate social circle would have known who "M—y C—" was). It is, furthermore, a good example to remind us that early modern authors did not always have the same direct control over the physical presentation of their materials in print as later generations of writers did.

The seeming contradiction between Chudleigh's assertion that she took great care to conceal her identity as the author (although she does say that the piece that was circulated and commented upon in manuscript was "known" to be hers) and the presence of her initials and autobiographical information in the prefaces is not unique to Chudleigh. Barbara McGovern notes that in 1709, Anne Finch had two poems printed in Delariviere Manley's *The New Atlantis*; McGovern observes that "though these poems were published biographical information about the poet's previous attachment to the court and her subsequent move to the country so that Finch's identity was probably generally known."[18]

Charles Hinnant in his study of Finch's subsequent literary reputation also points to her practice of publishing anonymously in "ephemeral" miscellany collections. Hinnant observes about the content of her volume that, "Finch conforms to a popular convention of seventeenth-century women's poetry: she adopts a pastoral sobriquet ('Ardelia') that is intended to preserve her privacy and yet present a construction of the self. These poems were not to be thought of as anonymous or authorless, yet the true identity of their author was intended to be recognized only by members of her circle."[19] Hinnant's last statement is interesting in the context of considering how manuscript texts from this period move into print. As with Chudleigh's poem in reply to Sprint, the audience for Finch's poems, too, had originally been a social group for whom a signature or statement of the author's individual identity was simply unnecessary. This practice is not "anonymous" in the sense that the author is hidden or unknown—she is so well known to the readers of her manuscript texts that her name is irrelevant.

III. Pseudonyms and Print Conventions

What were the print conventions governing the author's appearance on a late seventeenth-, early eighteenth-century title page? A look at the texts produced after 1660 suggests that the conventions for what information was included as part of the title on the title page situate the author's name differently than those of a nineteenth-century title page. Unlike later title pages, where the convention is to delineate clearly by

means of font and spacing between the title of the text and the name of
the author, in early modern printed texts from the latter part of the seventeenth and early eighteenth centuries, the title itself of a work often
contains much more information than merely announcing the subject
matter.

As seen in the following selection of examples, the title informs the
reader not only of the topic, but also the context, and the authority of
the text's origins. All of the following examples feature women authors,
although they are of different genres: *Triumphs of female wit, in some
pindarick odes, or The emulation together with an answer to an objector against
female ingenuity, and capacity of learning: also a preface to the masculine sex by
a young lady* (1683), *Maria to Henric, and Henric to Maria: or, The Queen to
the King in Holland, and His Majesty's answer; two heroical epistles in imitation of the stile and manner of Ovid. Written by a young lady* (1691), *Six familiar essays upon marriage, crosses in love, sickness, death, loyalty, and friendship,
written by a lady* (1696), *Alcander and Philocrates: or, The pleasures and dis-
quietudes of marriage A novel. Written by a young lady* (1696), *The Unnatural
mother, the scene in the kingdom of Siam: as it is now acted at the new theatre
in Lincolns-Inn-Fields, by His Majesty's servants written by a young lady*
(1698). No stark and striking headline-style titles here; clearly the
emphasis was not on producing the catchy, memorable, "sound bite"
titles that currently grace contemporary best-seller lists. The title page in
these seventeenth-century examples serves instead as a promotional
advertisement for the volume.

Assuming that the intent of the design of the title page was to attract
the browser to purchase and read the text, it then is noteworthy that the
announcement of female authorship could be considered an inducement
to buy. If it were a cultural transgression for a woman to publish her
thoughts, what type of text would advertise the sex of the author as part
of its commercial appeal?

As seen in the case of the first example, *Triumphs of Female Wit*, the
title and the announcement of the author's gender is essential for height-
ening the appeal of a text which is openly a "battle of the sexes."
Purchasers of this text, one presumes, wanted to read about conflict with
the social status quo. While, as Virginia Woolf noted in *A Room of One's
Own*, there are scores of books available written by men explaining
women ("have you any notion how many books are written about
women in the course of one year? Have you any notion how many
are written by men? ... women do not write books about them—a fact
that I could not help welcoming with relief"[20]), it is clear that there was
a perception by the publisher of *The Triumphs of Female Wit* that it was

important and desirable to represent this text as speaking in a female voice.

One should note, however, that there were still other commercially driven factors at play leading to an announcement that a text was by a female other than this seemingly sensationalist one. When one scans the electronic version of the ESTC for publications "by a lady" of its variations between 1660 and 1720, it is ironic to discover how many of the entries retrieved are now attributed to Richard Allestree.[21]

The title of one work "by a Lady" attributed to Allestree in Wing and the ESTC is worth pondering in its full, glorious early modern length. *The Whole duty of a woman: or a guide to the female sex. From the age of sixteen to sixty, &c. Being directions, how women of all qualities and conditions, ought to behave themselves in the various circumstances of this life, for their obtaining not only present, but future happiness. I. Directions how to obtain the divine and moral virtues of piety, meekness, modesty, chastity, humility, compassion, temperance and affability, with their advantages, and how to avoyd the opposite vices. II. The duty of virgins, directing them what they ought to do, and what to avoyd, for gaining all the accomplishments required in that state. With the whole art of love &c. 3. The whole duty of a wife, 4. The whole duty of a widow, &c. Also choice receipts in physick and chirurgery. With the whole art of cookery, preserving, candying, beautifying, &c. Written by a lady* (1696). The attribution of this text is still under question, with several theories ranging from Allestree, a single anonymous woman, to a collection of women's texts.[22]

Regardless of the identity of the author, one naturally presumes the intended readership for this volume was women. This, too, becomes problematic on the examination of specific volumes: the 1696 edition at the Bodleian Library, for example, reveals that it was owned by at least three men, Henry Ramsbottom, Lindsey Wolsey, and James Stork (the latter signature dated 1763), who signed their names and also used its empty spaces to take down notes.[23] It was such a successful title that it was reprinted six times before 1720 and clearly made its way from library to library through generations of readers.

The representation of this text as being in a feminine voice is reinforced in the prefatory materials. The Preface is addressed to "Ladys, Gentlewomen, and others, of all Degrees" and the speaker carefully identifies herself as having had "a Liberal Education and many Opportunities to Improve what my Younger years were Seasoned with." The speaker continues that having reached an advanced age it is time for a "Seasonable Publication" of the useful knowledge she has collected since "it is but necessary I should do all the good I can, before I go out of this World, that I may find the Comfort of it in another."

If this text is indeed by Allestree, why would a male author deliberately choose to hide himself behind a female pseudonym? As we see in
today's publishing practices, certain genres such as "bodice-ripper"
romances apparently demand a female name on the title page. If the
intended readership is designated as being primarily female, clearly the
desire for a female author on the title page is to promote the volume as
a female text, by a woman, for women. But the example of *The Whole
Duty of a Woman* goes beyond a simple appeal to a perception of female
shared interests. The writer—whether male or female—creates for
the reader a sense of a particular type voice to convey instruction, a wise,
educated, older woman with a moral mission, a type of "universal" wise
woman.

In short, as it was used by Allestree (or not) and his publishers, the
sobriquet "a lady" did serve to cloak the writer's gender, but not with
the design of protecting his reputation or shielding him from criticism.
Instead, the projection of a female presence, a female voice from behind
the feminine mask on the title page and in the prefatory materials was a
means of engaging the desired consumers of the texts, in effect of
appealing to a female community as having shared interests—an authoritative woman speaking to women. The fact that it might well have been
used by a man in order to attempt to shape the mentality of women, to
reinforce socially (society as defined by him in this text) acceptable roles
as virgin, wife, and widow does not eliminate the way in which the use
of a feminine mask acts as an amplification device as well as a cloaking
one, an attractive advertisement rather than a humble excuse.

IV. Pseudonyms and Cultural Costuming

If Allestree were *not* the author, what would be the advantages for
a female author, or a bookseller who had collected several texts by
women, of using this speaker rather than a woman's actual name? What
is the effect on the reader's perception of the author if it is presented as
being "By a Lady" rather than a specific female name?

Once again, Virginia Woolf suggests a productive way of altering our
perception of the function of anonymity, by looking at the effect on the
reader rather than the author of the text. In her last essays, "Anon" and
"The Reader," Woolf was engaged in a speculative literary history of
Britain from the troubadours to the present, what she described as "an
amusing book on English literature."[24] The opening chapter of this
book, she apparently envisioned as being entitled, "Anon."

She begins with an evocative description of primitive England and an early English lyric being sung in a pastoral landscape. "The voice that broke the silence of the forest was the voice of Anon. Some one heard the song and remembered it for it was later written down, beautifully, on parchment. Thus the singer had his audience, but the audience was so little interested in his name that he never thought to give it. The audience was itself the singer, ... filling in the pauses, helping out with a chorus. Every body shared in the emotion of Anon's song, and supplied the story.... Anon is sometimes man; sometimes woman. He is the common voice singing out of doors" (382). This representation of the author as "the common voice," where author and audience are equal participants in the process is later contrasted with later authors. "It was the printing press that finally was to kill Anon," she observes, "Caxtons [sic] printing press foretold the end of that anonymous world" (384, 385). Woolf's point is that with print came the attribution of a text—a fixed object—to a single individual, with no space to acknowledge any participation of a reader: "the first blow has been aimed at Anon when the authors [sic] name is attached to the book. The individual emerges. His name is Holinshed; his name is also Harrison" (385).

Scholars of medieval literary history may not be convinced by Woolf's representation of medieval texts, script or printed. But the concept of "Anon" as functioning as a means of creating a "common voice" in which the reader/audience participates is an intriguing one to contemplate in the context of later "by a Lady" texts. Woolf's vision of the difference between "Anon" and later writers, whether historically correct or not, provides us with another way to look at the choice to sign a work "by a Lady" rather than with one's name.

By adopting the cultural label for appropriate female behavior and deportment, writers selecting the sobriquet "a Lady" create a sense of not an individual author but a composite one—a "generic" lady, such as we have seen in *The Whole Duty of a Woman*. Chudleigh, in her expositions by "a Lady" to "The Ladies," is, in effect, creating a shared community of writers and readers, not distinguished by individual features, but a shared femininity and shared concerns. But is this femininity conformable to the cultural definitions of it? What scenarios are the masked ladies performing in these texts?

Let us consider, for a final example, Anne Finch's publication of "An Elegy on the Death of King James" (1701). Critics have routinely explained her choice of printing it as being "By a Lady" as being her means of protecting herself, both because of gender and political reasons. Hinnant points to Finch's "Jacobite" identity as a central factor in shaping her decisions to publish or not and Barash sees her loyalties to the Stuart monarchy as at "the heart of Finch's construction of herself as a public poet."[25]

What if, however, one applies Woolf's notion of "Anon" being a "common voice" to this text? The mask of "a Lady" may permit Finch a different relationship with her audience. Instead of being a conciliatory, protective strategy, "a device used by Finch simultaneously to assert class privilege and to gain both sexual and political protection," as Barash sees it (337), one could see the adoption of this particular mask as being subversive rather than abashed.

What does it say about the universality of social constraints that a poet, speaking as a "lady" in general, a representative of a gender and class rather than speaking as an individual in particular, holds the politically provocative view that the death of James was a national tragedy? The event is deemed worthy of comment by a poet who identifies herself as female and as a "free disinterested Muse;" she does not so much excuse her writing as satirize male public poets, since they, the "Abler writers," shun the task of eulogizing James as not being likely to provide sufficient remuneration (Barash, 331). Furthermore, the Lady also appeals to the shared feelings of a specific group of readers, feelings she, too, holds, in opposition to the dominant political power's wishes:

> O you who in his frequent Dangers stood,
> And Fought to Fence them at the Expense of Blood,
>   Now let your Tears a heavier Tribute pay,
>   Give the Becoming Sorrow Way:
>   Nor bring bad parallels upon the Times,
>   By seeking, thro' mistaken Fears,
> To Curb your Sighs, or to Conceal your Tears;
> 'Twas but in *Nero's* Days, that Sighs and Tears were Crimes
>   (Barash, 334)

If this is what the "ladies" of England were thinking about current conditions, one could certainly be concerned what the Jacobite rabble might be saying and doing. The choice of signing "By a Lady" does not hide the sex of the author and the views expressed are not "ladylike" in the scheme of society at large. Instead, this Lady appears to be speaking to and for a group of sympathetic readers, but speaking against the appropriate norms.

The potential for subversion through the mimicry or ironic performance of the cultural expectations of the dominant group in power is central to recent psychoanalytic and postcolonial theories of the survival strategies of members of muted, or colonized groups.[26] The woman "re-enacts" male expectations of femininity, usually in a heightened form, "being on one's best behavior" so to speak, and thus fulfils the requirements of the viewer, all the while maintaining an ironic self-determination and control from behind the mask.

A consideration of the multiple functions of the pseudonym "by a Lady,"—shield, disguise, costume—permit us to consider the possibility that sometimes the lady might be less a victim of restrictive cultural definitions of feminine modesty than an authorial strategist seeking the right audience. Works "by a Lady" in their very existence as print texts subvert the assumption that women writers must not speak as women. Likewise, when one considers the subject matter of many of these titles, the works are frequently less conciliatory than contrary in their relationship to the status quo, from Chudleigh's response to Sprint's definition of a bride's submission to Finch's lament for the virtues of the deposed monarch.

Notes

1. See, for example, Angeline Goreau's early formulation of this theory, encapsulated in the statement that in addition to the sense of intellectual inferiority early modern women felt on account of their education, "a much more subtle and complex inhibition [existed] that women repeatedly mentioned as a reason they hesitated to publish their work: feminine modesty." Angeline Goreau, *The Whole Duty of a Woman: Female Writers in Seventeenth-Century England* (New York: The Dial Press, 1985), 9. A later and more extensive exploration of how early modern women wrote and published under the prescription to be silent and chaste is Elaine Hobby's *Virtue of Necessity: English Women's Writing 1649–88* (Ann Arbor, MI: University of Michigan Press, 1989):

   "Women belonged in the increasingly private sphere of the home: they were not supposed to be so bold—or so immodest—as to venture into the public world of print. The charge of 'immodesty' was a serious one. Whatever the initial grounds of the attack on a woman's reputation, an association with sexual misbehavior, with a lack of concern for her family's 'honour', was always in danger of following" (9). While Hobby emphasizes the dynamic nature of the cultural constraints and women's constant shifts to challenge a patriarchal framework of femininity, other texts such as the introduction to the "Early Seventeenth Century" section of *The Norton Anthology of English Literature* present the cultural constraints as being crippling: "a woman of great wealth and social prestige, like the duchess of Newcastle, was less inhibited from writing and publishing; but Lady Mary Wroth, after one rash act of publication, was silenced for the rest of her life ... the women struggled (and with only partial success) to find voices of their own ..." (1079). *The Norton Anthology of English Literature*, ed. M. H. Abrams *et al.*, 6th ed., vol. 1 (New York: W. W. Norton, 1993).

2. Charlotte F. Otten, "General Introduction," *English Women's Voices, 1540–1700* (Miami: Florida International University Press, 1992), 1.

3. In this context, it is interesting to compare James Raven's findings that in the latter part of the 1780s, the tag of "By a Lady" or "By a Young Lady," appeared on as many as a third of the novels marketed (Raven, x). Interestingly, Raven points to the benefits accrued rather than

the liabilities of presenting oneself as a female author in that periodical press avowed a critical leniency toward women's novels, which Raven suggests, might induce a male writer to adopt this guise; however, as Raven also points out, the declaration of partiality for female authors did not in fact result in much positive praise for them, so one wonders whether this was much of an inducement for eighteenth-century men in search of a pseudonym.

4. Christina Wolf, "Culture is What you Experience—An Interview with Christina Wolf," *New German Critique* 27 (Fall 1982), 94.

5. Finch's recent biographer, Barbara McGovern, sees the literary life of Anne Finch as representative of the ways in which early modern women had to work to construct an identity as a poet. Speaking of women writers in general, "those few [women] who, like Finch, overcame these obstacles [of education and leisure] faced one more insidious impediment. Having nurtured their talent as authors, they frequently found themselves denied opportunities for publication and serious public recognition, or had their writings denigrated and trivialized by a patriarchal literary world." *Anne Finch and Her Poetry: A Critical Biography* (Athens, GA: The University of Georgia Press, 1992), 2.

6. On early modern women, law, and property, see Antonia Fraser's early study, *The Weaker Vessel* (New York: Vintage books, 1985); Lawrence Stone, *Uncertain Unions: Marriage in England 1660–1753* (New York: Oxford University Press, 1992); and Susan Staves, *Married Women's Separate Property in England, 1660–1833* (Cambridge, MA: Harvard University Press, 1990).

7. "Pseudonyms," in *The Feminist Companion to English Literature*, ed. by Virginia Blain, Isobel Grundy, and Patricia Clements (New Haven: Yale University Press, 1990), 874. Here, too, I am disagreeing with Carol Barash's assertion that "virtually no one but Finch" was using the title-page appellation "By a Lady" in 1701, finding in fact from a survey of the ESTC that the signature "By a Lady" was tied in popularity with "by a young lady" during the 1670 to 1720 period, a count that does not include its frequent use with individual pieces in miscellanies. Carol Barash, "The Political Origins of Anne Finch's Poetry," *Huntington Library Quarterly* 54 (1991), 330.

8. Dorothy Mermin, "Women Becoming Poets: Katherine Philips, Aphra Behn, Anne Finch," *ELH* 57 (1990), 338, 347.

9. Margaret J. M. Ezell, "Reading Pseudonyms in Seventeenth-Century Coterie Literature," *Essays in Literature* 21 (1994), 14–25. Thanks here to Elizabeth Hageman for her extensive knowledge of sobriquets employed by Katherine Philips and her literary associates.

10. Elizabeth Thomas, *Miscellany Poems* (London, 1722).

11. See Isobel Grundy, "The Politics of Female Authorship: Lady Mary Wortley Montagu's reaction to the printing of her poems," *The Book Collector* 31 (1982), 19–37.

12. Indeed, in her article "Elizabeth Thomas and the Two Corinnas: Giving the woman writer a bad name," Anne McWhir argues that John Dryden's supposedly complimentary suggestion that Thomas assumes "Corinna" as her poetic name links her both to a famous courtesan and a female poet referred to by Pindar as the "Boeotian [Theban] sow." *ELH* 62 (1995), 105–19.

13. William Hicks, *London Drollery* (London, 1672), 56–60.

14. Ann Messenger, "Publishing Without Perishing: Lady Winchilsea's *Miscellany Poems* of 1713," *Restoration* 5 (1981), 27–37 (28); Charles H. Hinnant, *The Poetry of Anne Finch: An Essay in Interpretation* (Newark: University of Delaware Press, 1994). Hinnant is less direct in stating his interpretation than Messenger, but the implication is the same: "Finch's first volume was published anonymously in 1713. The late 1714 issue—after Finch had become a countess—was the first issue to deliver the author's name on its cover" (18).

15. Quoted in McGovern, *Anne Finch*, 98.

16. It is also interesting in this context that the earliest known manuscript text of her collected poems, with a title page entitled "Poems on Several Subjects" states that it is "Written by Ardelia," not "by a lady" or Finch's name, but it was a name by which she was known to her circle of friends and script readers. See Barash, "The Political Origins of Anne Finch's Poetry," for a reproduction of this title page (348).

17. Mary, Lady Chudleigh, "To the Reader," *Essays upon Several Subjects* in *The Poems and Prose of Mary, Lady Chudleigh*, ed. Margaret J. M. Ezell (New York: Oxford University Press, 1993), 248.
18. McGovern, *Anne Finch*, 93.
19. Hinnant, *The Poetry of Anne Finch*, 19.
20. Virginia Woolf, *A Room of One's Own* (New York: Harcourt Brace Jovanich, 1929), 26–7.
21. Allestree was a productive author of numerous didactic treatises. See his entry in *The Dictionary of National Biography*. See George Ballard's account of the controversy over the attribution of *The Whole Duty of Man* to Lady Pakington and Allestree's involvement. *Memoirs of Several Ladies of Great Britain* (1752), ed. Ruth Perry (Detroit: Wayne State University Press, 1985), 290–303.
22. Angeline Goreau attributes *The Ladies Calling* (1673) to Allestree, but not *The Whole Duty of a Woman*, which she believes was by "an anonymous female author" (10). Still others believe that the text is a composite volume of the writings of several women. The attribution of it to Allestree would seem to be linked to the attribution to him of *The Whole Duty of Man* (1658), which is still thought by some to be by Lady Pakington.
23. *The Whole Duty of a Woman* ... (London, 1696), Bodleian Library shelfmark Vet.A3f.177.
24. Quoted in Brenda R. Silver's introduction to Virginia Woolf, " 'Anon' and 'The Reader': Virginia Woolf's Last Essays," ed. Brenda R. Silver, *Twentieth Century Literature* 25 (1979), 356–418 (357). I am indebted to David McWhirter for drawing my attention to these pieces.
25. See Charles H. Hannant, "Anne Finch and Jacobitism: Approaching the Wellesley College Manuscript," *Journal of Family History* 21 (1996), 496–502 and Barash, "Political Origins," 329. Barash helpfully reprints this interesting long poem, with its elaborate apparatus of historical notes; there is a third copy of the poem (Bodleian Library shelfmark Vet.A4e.2853) in addition to ones she cites at the British Library and the New York Public Library.
26. Luce Irigaray's use of mimicry or performance in order to subvert systems of thought through "re-presenting" it, is most clearly seen at work in the collection of essays *Ce Sexe qui n'est pas un* (1977; *This Sex which Is Not One*, trans. Catherine Porter [Ithaca: Cornell University Press, 1985]); she describes it as a deliberate act to "disturb the staging of representation" (155). This concept is also expanded by the postcolonial critic Homi K. Bhabha in discussing the ways in which colonized populations perform back to the dominant social force their expected and anticipated roles as a means of preserving autonomy. "The Other Question: Difference, Discrimination and the Discourse of Colonialism" in *"Race," Writing and Difference*, ed. Henry Louis Gates, Jr. (Chicago: University of Chicago Press, 1985) and *Nation and Narration* (New York: Routledge, 1990).

CHAPTER FOUR

The Author's Queer Clothes: Anonymity, Sex(uality), and The Travels and Adventures of Mademoiselle de Richelieu

Susan S. Lanser

And now Reader, let me tell you, that by what you have read hitherto, you may ghess what you are like to have for the future, this that I have written already, is an Essay of what I intend for you, by this piece of Stuff you may judge what Garment you shall have.

Francis Kirkman, *The Unlucky Citizen*[1]

In his famous *Practical Criticism: A Study of Literary Judgment* (1929), the critic I. A. Richards rebuked hundreds of smart Cambridge students, "products of the most expensive kind of education," for their "feeble capacity to understand poetry." The students' "widespread inability to construe meaning," their generalized "bewilderment," and their "fatal facility" for the stock response (symptoms more prominent among male students on account of the "greater familiarity with poetry that is certainly possessed by the average girl")[2] had been exposed by anonymity: Richards had given out thirteen poems without offering any clues to their origins. While pleased that the anonymous readings exposed the canonical process whereby "approval and admiration is being accorded not to the poetry but to an idol," so that poems by Donne and Lawrence were serious losers against the work of Philip James Bailey, Richards lamented that reputation had become a shortcut for reading authors in place of texts, revealing "what a comparatively relaxed and inattentive activity our ordinary reading of established poetry is. Even those who have won a deserved eminence through their critical ability, who have worthily occupied Chairs of Poetry and taken their part in handing on the torch of tradition retrimmed, would probably admit in their secret souls that they had not read many poems with the care and attention that these anonymous items, under these conditions, invite."[3]

What Richards deplored as critical laxity I want to propose as critical axiom: authorship conventionally underwrites readers' engagements with literary texts.[4] Even in the climate of "close reading" that Richards helped to foster as an antidote, readers commonly strive, with an insistence not unlike the desire to know the sex of a newborn (or of an ambiguous person sitting next to one), to establish "true" authorship and to construct the text in its light. Although, as Robert Griffin rightly reminds us, the vast majority of writing both present and past is anonymous,[5] institutions of literary scholarship are still heavily organized around authorship despite the impact of "new historicisms" that have taught us to look at texts as documents rather than monuments (to reverse René Wellek's terms[6]). In organs such as *The Age of Johnson*, the Jane Austen Society, and the *Wordsworth Circle*, in bitter contests over the authorship of Shakespeare's plays, in publishers' claims that there is no market for reprints of anonymous novels, the author-function that Foucault so importantly recognized still thrives as literature's "mode of existence," circulation, and functioning despite efforts to dismantle and displace it.[7] It is not accidental that a vast amount of material published anonymously in the eighteenth century is now attributed, if only provisionally and sometimes on slight evidence, to a Proper Name.

This adherence to authorship, I would suggest, encourages a tautological construction of authors and texts in which the projects of authorial identification and textual interpretation that Richards sought to separate become circular. Although *Roxana* was originally an anonymous work called *The Fortunate Mistress*, I approach it today as a metonym of Daniel Defoe, who is already known to me as a set of texts (mostly named for their eponymous characters) and a historical personage named Foe (1660–1731), both of which have been filtered through historical responses and critical scholarship. At the same time that I create *Roxana* through Defoe, I (re)create Defoe through *Roxana*. When I then encounter a possible new "Defoe"—say, a piece of unattributed journalism—my decision to accept or reject this work as Defoe's is likely, barring external evidence, to be predicated on my existing construction of the author; if the text fits, it gets added to the canon that, in turn, (re)constitutes Defoe. If I determine that Defoe could not have written the piece because he was a Whig or a Dissenter, the work is cast back to the oblivion of anonymity—and deprived of considerable cultural capital.

This mutual construction of authors and texts also underlies the concept of "implied authorship" despite contrary intentions. First articulated by Wayne Booth and pondered since by numerous narrative theorists, the "implied author" designates the *idea* of the author, or the sense of authorial norms and values, that emerges from the text, or what Shlomith Rimmon-Kenan described as the "governing consciousness of the work as a whole."[8] A vexed concept that returns in spite of repeated efforts to evict it, the "implied author" is not a textual "speaker which can be pointed to," but is rather what Ansgar Nünning sees as a "structural whole,"[9] nowhere and everywhere, the source yet paradoxically also the effect of the text whose consciousness it signifies. Not all critics agree that this "whole" is appropriately represented through the anthropomorphic language of implied authorship, and there is no *formal* basis for positing such an authorial entity. Rather, implied authorship is *functional*, a *reading effect* that can serve as a (putatively stable) ground against which the reliability of various textual voices and messages is measured and through which the text's aesthetic, intellectual, moral, and ideological authority is produced.[10]

In theory, "implied authorship" applies equally to anonymous and attributed texts. But I do not think it mere chance that *The Rhetoric of Fiction* focuses on the most canonized novels of the last three centuries and that Booth's references to implied authors retain the rhetoric of the proper name ("Lawrence," "Austen," "Flaubert"). Booth conceives the implied author as a writer's "second self," "usually a highly refined and selected version, wiser, more sensitive, more perceptive than any real man [sic] could be."[11] In this way, "implied authorship" preserves the author-function by relocating it "inside" the text, and the historical author reenters the configuration as the anchor for the implied author thought to reside in the text.

Booth's recourse to actual authors is not surprising, for however useful the notion of a purely textual author, figuring out how the sense of an author inheres in a text turns out to be daunting both ontologically and practically. Authorship is, I suspect, inferred continuously and mostly subliminally as a reader processes a text (even for you who are now reading my essay). We read rather as the Francis Kirkman of my epigraph, suggests: by what we have read hitherto, we guess at what is to come; we imagine the "Garment" by sampling the "Stuff." But this sampling does not begin with a *tabula rasa* of the given text, nor is the text ever a *tabula rasa*. In *The Narrative Act*, I identified what I called "extrafictional" structures (structures that I would now, *d'après* Genette, call paradiegetic or paratextual): elements conveyed through the physical book and through the process of textual transmission, such as the information on a title page, a dedication or preface, indicators of genre, accompanying blurbs—all of which inaugurate and delimit the project of inferring authorship even before we encounter the text "proper."[12] Even when these paratextual features are absent in a specific instance, well-trained readers will provide conventional substitutes. I think readers bring at least two distinct but related types of prior inferential knowledge to their construction of an implied author: the assumptions about reliability, credibility, and wisdom that a given culture confers on authorship, and some rudimentary sense of a particular authorial biography, even if "biography" is as limited as a suggestion of the author's sex or nationality. Handed a Regency romance with its covers torn off, for example, I am likely to infer an American or British female author addressing a middlebrow readership.

Readers become most conscious of this process of inference, I suggest, when the author produced in the course of this heavily conditioned reading is either troubled by textual dissonance or challenged by external facts. I think, for example, of two widely publicized and politically charged cases in which an author's real identity differed dramatically from that implied by a pseudonym. *Famous All Over Town*, a 1983 "autobiography" by Danny Santiago, was hailed as the first "authentic" account of a Chicano adolescent's life in the Los Angeles *barrio* until it was revealed, to a storm of outrage, to be the work of an elderly social worker named Daniel James. Even more distressing was the revelation that the award-winning *Education of Little Tree*, by a man thought to be a native American, turned out to be the work of a former and repentant member of the Ku Klux Klan. If such deceptions underscore the exceptional ability of humans to inhabit subject positions far different from our own—and hence to mark the potential gap between real and implied authorship—the outrage underscores readers' attachment to a particular authorial body in relation to a particular text, whose "garments" are supposed to confirm the image of the author that the text puts forth.

On the other hand, the sense of an author can emerge quite unproblematically even from an anonymous text when that text is highly conventional in ideology or genre. A few years ago, I came upon a twelve-page *Satyr Upon Old Maids* published anonymously in 1713. Its title already identifies the work as a satire directed at never-married women, whose denigration is also already evident in the choice of the term "old maids." The virulent attack on single women—as "odious" and "impure," "nasty, rank, rammy, filthy Sluts" destined for "Pestilence" on earth and the "Devil's Dish" thereafter—is so monoglossic that there is little difficulty grasping the "general consciousness of the work as a whole" without the knowledge of the work's authorship.[13] Whether this text turns out to have been written by one Marshall Smith, as the English Short Title Catalogue records as a possibility, or whether it might even be discovered to be the work of an unmarried woman, the text's "governing consciousness," its "norms and values" would be difficult to interpret in more complicated ways.

But how do readers infer the "general consciousness" of a text that is radically uncertain at once in authorship, genre, and ideology? I want to ask this question through an unusual work probably first published in 1743 and tantalizingly titled *The Travels and Adventures of Mademoiselle de Richelieu. Cousin to the present Duke of that Name. Who made the Tour of Europe, dressed in Men's Cloaths, attended by her Maid Lucy as her Valet de Chambre.*[14] A lengthy production narrated by a woman who has passed as a man, written in English but purporting to be drawn from a French original, a complicated mix of travelogue, adventure, satire, and sexual intrigue intermingled with essays on subjects from writing to religion to politics and culminating in a love plot that transgresses gender norms, *The Travels and Adventures of Mademoiselle de Richelieu* is in multiple ways one of the queerer texts of its time. For that very reason, I suggest, it offers us the opportunity to interrogate the problem of textual authorship in ways that *The Rhetoric of Fiction*'s corpus of famous authors and well-read texts cannot provide.

The Travels and Adventures of Mademoiselle de Richelieu is not anonymous in a simple way. Rather than saying nothing at all about authorship, the title page announces that the work was "Now done into English from the Lady's own Manuscript. By the Translator of the Memoirs and Adventures of the Marques of Bretagne and Duke of Harcourt." If we take this intelligence at face value, we have both an author (Mademoiselle de Richelieu) and a translator (the person who rendered into English a particular volume of Prévost's *Mémoires d'un homme de qualité*). Further investigation provides the translator's putative last name: in 1741 the Dublin publisher Oliver Nelson released a *Memoirs and Adventures of the Marques of Bretagne and Duke of Harcourt. Written originally in French; and now done into English by Mr. Erskine.* That Nelson also published the Dublin edition of *The Travels and Adventures of Mademoiselle de Richelieu* supports the possibility that the works have a common English source.

But with what kind of authoring shall we credit "Mr. Erskine" if we are to credit him at all? Has he "done" *The Travels and Adventures of Mademoiselle de Richelieu* as he "did" Prévost's novel? If so, what is his relationship to Mademoiselle de Richelieu, and how did he come by her manuscript? For *The Memoirs and Adventures of the Marquis de Bretagne and Duc d'Harcourt* is patently an English rendering of a known French novel, and the role of "Mr. Erskine" is limited more or less to his function as a translator of someone else's narrative, a narrative available to the bilingual reader for comparison. It is far from certain that *The Travels and Adventures of Mademoiselle de Richelieu* has any French source at all, and there is no suggestion of a printed source. If there is a French manuscript, who is "Mademoiselle de Richelieu," and is her manuscript really a memoir, or is it a fiction exploiting the conventions of historicity so popular in the period? If there is no French source—and none has yet been unearthed—might the text be a memoir of the travels and adventures of an Englishwoman masquerading as a French aristocrat? Is the work simply a fiction originating in English and masquerading, as English novels sometimes did, as a memoir from the French? If there is a French source, does the English version render it faithfully? Are we to take at face value the title's claim that the eponymous Mademoiselle is related to the real Duc de Richelieu? Are the dates in 1728 and 1729, mentioned by the text, a key to historicity or merely a lure to strengthen the formal realism of the text? Is this a "French" text, bearing French "norms and values," perhaps mocking the straight-laced English? An "English" text mocking the lascivious French? A hybrid representing a cosmopolitan Anglo-French alliance?

The status of the "Mr. Erskine" associated metonymically through the Prévost translation is equally unclear. Is s/he a person actually born to that name, or is this name a pseudonym, a front for someone else's narrative? If "Mr. Erskine" is a real person, might s/he be one of the dozens of Erskines who wrote religious works, political pamphlets, translations, and local histories in the eighteenth century—for example, the Sir Henry Erskine who published a *Story of the Tragedy of Agis* in 1758 with one of the publishers who produced an edition of *The Travels and Adventures of Mademoiselle de Richelieu*? Shall we trust the source that attached the name "[William?]" to the Erskine who translated the *Marques of Bretagne* even though no William Erskine matching the dates of this author appears in the *DNB* or any other standard reference work? Might "he" actually be the Lady Frances Erskine who also published in the period, or one of the other female Erskines mentioned in the British Library Catalogue? Or is the allusion to the translator of Prévost simply a ploy by author or publisher to encourage a belief that this text also has a French original, in which case the Mr. Erskine who translated Prévost might have nothing whatever to do with *The Travels and Adventures of Mademoiselle de Richelieu*?

This lack of reliable information about the text's authorship is intensified by the almost total absence of a reception history. No one has yet located any contemporary reviews of the work or references in letters or diaries. At this point, therefore, we cannot know how eighteenth-century readers may have speculated about the work's authorship or how the book's unusual content was received and perceived. While anonymity cannot entirely explain this silence since anonymous texts were reviewed in the period, the absence of comment is odd given the number of editions of the work. I would wager that if *The Travels and Adventures of Mademoiselle de Richelieu* were discovered tomorrow to have been written by a known author, it would be read avidly and returned to print and scholars might more diligently hunt down allusions to it; in this sense, the fate of *The Travels and Adventures of Mademoiselle de Richelieu* signifies the author-centeredness of critical practice itself.

The mystery of authorship—in this instance less a complete absence than a confusing half-presence—is intensified by the narrative project of the work. If questions of authorial identity are never idle ones, they are particularly tantalizing in relation to a text that flaunts the ease of concealing and changing one's name, one's sex, and one's social identity. As its title predicts, *The Travels and Adventures of Mademoiselle de Richelieu* presents a cross-dressing woman touring Europe as a (very convincing and most attractive) man, but writing her story as a woman well aware of the conventional construction of the author as male but also passing off sections of her work as taken from other authors. Such a scenario in which the autodiegetic narrator/character is sexed female but crosses divides of gender, surely intensifies curiosity about the historical author, all the more as the title page already signals some collusion between "a lady" and the man who has "done" her (manuscript) "into English."[15]

To make guesses about the author even more tempting, *The Travels and Adventures of Mademoiselle de Richelieu* takes the trouble to insist that authorship should govern reading. In a passage that recalls the tautological project I described above, the narrator lays out an elaborate procedure by which we may "judge of a Book" by evaluating its author and its paratext; we are to "observe the Title, the Author's or Editor's Name, the Number of the Edition, the Place where, and the Year when it was printed, and the Printer's Name, especially if he be a celebrated one: Proceed thence to the Preface, and look for the Author's Design, and the Occasion of his writing: Consider also his Country, (each Nation having its peculiar Genius) and the Person by whose Order he wrote." We are even asked to consider the author's profession, rank, and associations with "learned Men," which may sometimes be learned from the

Dedication: "If his Life be annexed, run it over, and note his Profession, what Rank he was of, and any thing remarkable that attended his Education, Studies, Conversation, or Correspondences with learned Men; not forgetting the Elogies which have been given the Author, which often occur at the Beginning, or even any Critique or Censure, especially if made by a Man of Judgment. If the Preface do not give an Account of the Method of the Work, run briefly over the Order and Disposition of it, and note what Points the Author has handled; observe whether the Things and Sentiments he produces be trite and vulgar, or solid, and fetched from greater Depths. Note, whether he go in the common Road, or make any Innovation, and introduce any new Principle" (II, 143–4). We are further to ask whether "the Author be known to excel in that Talent more immediately necessary for [the book's] Subject, or have already published any Thing on the same that is esteemed," to consider the writer's age and whether s/he was "an Eye-Witness of what he relates" or "has Access to the public Records" or was "hired by any great Man," and of course to attend to "the Time or Age wherein the Author lived" (II, 143–50). Yet, *The Travels and Adventures of Mademoiselle de Richelieu* denies us almost every one of these supposed interpretive indices. And indeed the narrator undermines this entire discourse by imagining resistant readers: "What does this Girl mean, will some of my Readers I dare say cry, to teize us with a long Story about Books, as if she could persuade us that she knew any thing of the Matter, and which is worse, said nothing after all upon the Subject, but what we have read a Hundred times." (II, 150). Is the text implying that if we have a "Girl" author, all bets are off?

This is not impossible, since *The Travels and Adventures of Mademoiselle de Richelieu* is a queer text in form and content as well as in authorship. The opening pages promise both a primary narrative—in which the Alithea de Richelieu rejects "the shameful Drudgery" of propagation for cross-dressed adventures—and a tissue of "Digressions," which will be "regularly inserted" as essential to "Work[s] of this Kind" (I, 7). Yet the digressions turn out to be far from "regular"; each volume displays a different pattern as tales about characters present and past, essays on topics from kingly succession to national character, and descriptions of various European sites are threaded unevenly with the narrator's own adventures as she tours Europe disguised as the Chevalier de Radpont. Readers of the first volume might be prepared for Swiftian satire when the narrator announces that "This is a Tale of a Tub with a Witness"—though the "Tub" has already been redefined as a figure for the reproductive womb. But these readers would be treated first to a long discussion of hereditary monarchy, after which nearly half the volume would be occupied with two inserted tales of male–female love, with little attention to the "travels and adventures" of the eponymous heroine. Readers of the middle volume might focus on travelogue and picaresque as the "Chevalier de Radpont" recounts her journey across France and the flirtations with women from which she must extricate herself. But late in this second volume the tide would turn again, yielding the unexpected beginnings of a love affair in which the narrator, to gain the heart of her beloved Arabella, reveals her true sex. Readers of the final volume might focus on the descriptions of European cities including London, or upon a plot that becomes increasingly singular as the narrator and Arabella, both in masculine disguise, complete the tour, after which they resume female clothing and settle down together in a relationship the more erotic if one recalls that "whim" was eighteenth-century slang for female genitals: "the longer we are together, the more we love one another, and are happier in our Friendship and Freedom, than we could possibly propose to be in any other Condition of Life. *Arabella's* Temper is sweet with a little Mixture of Reserve; mine is gay with a little of the Ingredient called *Whim*; my Gaiety rouses her now and then out of a Fit of Thoughtfulness, and her Reserve bridles my Vivacity, so that we play to one another's Hands; and if there be such a Thing as Happiness in Life, we are the Persons who enjoy it" (III, 358). How are we to read this queer plot that I have somewhat artificially extricated from the uneven complexities of *The Travels and Adventures of Mademoiselle de Richelieu*, a plot that is barely suggested in the first volume but that vies with travelogue as the dominant presence of the third? Is this book a celebration of homoerotic connections, or is it making a mockery of its narrator's desires? How might readers produce an author for this text? In raising these questions, I have already singled out one aspect of a text whose implied author would have to be produced by the entire range of the work's commitments on matters as diverse as monarchical succession, Jesuits, and national character.

I want to explore this question of authorship by looking at the very different "implied authors" already inferred for *The Travels and Adventures of Mademoiselle de Richelieu* by what I believe are the only two published essays about the text. The first, which brought the book to scholarly attention, is Carolyn Woodward's " 'My Heart So Wrapt': Lesbian Disruptions in Eighteenth-Century British Fiction," which appeared in the feminist journal *Signs* in 1993. The second, which places itself in dialogue with the first, is Susan Lamb's " 'Be Such a Man as I': Mademoiselle Makes the Tour of Europe in Men's Clothes," published in the 1998 volume of *Studies in Eighteenth-Century Culture*. In ways already suggested by their titles, these essays make quite different assumptions about the text's authorship, and both invoke eighteenth-century literary and social conventions to enable larger claims about gender, genre, and ideology. I present these essays not to judge between their readings (although my own views will sometimes emerge), but to look at the grounds on which two sophisticated, informed, self-aware and refreshingly honest scholars can reach different conclusions when contextual knowledge is limited.

Carolyn Woodward, writing in 1993, saw *The Travels and Adventures of Mademoiselle de Richelieu* as a feminist celebration of lesbian love, subversive for its time and for that reason generically complex. Woodward's judgment of the work, she readily tells us, was already conditioned by the reference source in which she discovered it: Angela Smallwood's 1989 study, *Fielding and the Woman Question*, which describes Mademoiselle de Richelieu as "an apologist for women's rights."[16] For Woodward, *Mademoiselle de Richelieu*—as she tends to title the work in a practice that underscores the role of a central female figure—asserts the "right to parody gender expectations, the right to desire and love women, and the right to write about desire," all of this "represented in a playful and tender story that ended with two women settling down together in sweet contentment for the rest of their lives"[17]. Responding to the perplexing question of why this work seems to have escaped notice for so long, Woodward points to the conventions of the eighteenth-century novel, which she sees structured by male quest and female subordination. Woodward's *Mademoiselle de Richelieu* is thus a transgressive lesbian narrative camouflaged within a multi-generic work. The narrator's masquerade is repeated by the narrative structure: just as the text hides beneath an unknown author, and the female narrator hides beneath men's clothes, a nonlinear and many-genred text with little apparent structure conceals a transgressive and linear lesbian novel in which girl meets girl, girl falls in love with girl and girl more or less marries girl.

Woodward understands that *Mademoiselle de Richelieu* is generically fuzzy, with "no hierarchy ... by which we might settle into reading the text as primarily either 'essay' or 'novel' " or even autobiography (849). She is the first to acknowledge that she "may have missed something important" in a book where "travelogue outdoes love story by something like six to one" (849); as evidence of a very different interpretive possibility she cites Percy Adams's *Travel Literature and the Evolution of the Novel*, which reads over the homoerotic story entirely. But once Woodward "caught on to its story of girl-meets-girl," she says, "I read

quickly through details of the succession of the kings of France, pictur-
esque descriptions of the Alps, and listings of the principle manufactures
of Milan to get to the juicy bits" (849).

Ultimately, then, Woodward finds a novel in this text, and one that
thwarts heterosexual expectations: "As I read, I was prepared for the
moment when the right young men would come along. Two weddings,
I thought. But as I kept turning the pages, and getting nearer and nearer
to the back cover of the final volume, that moment did not come" (853).
She is then able to place *Mademoiselle de Richelieu* in relation to several
other novels by women (Sarah Scott, Sarah Fielding, Charlotte Lennox)
that also represent female friendship or community, establishing for the
text both a genre and a lineage. This move, in turn, allows her to read
the "other" material in the book as "experimental devices such as gaps
in narrative, genre mixing, and avoidance of closure" designed as a kind
of cover story for the book's transgressive plot. In what Woodward
describes as a "period of increasingly intense anxieties about sex and
gender distinctions" and "increasingly rigid sex-role expectations"
(842–4) in which "the gender ambiguities of cross-dressing" (848) were
a site of contest, *Mademoiselle de Richelieu* is set against such antisapphist
works as Henry Fielding's *The Female Husband* (1746) as a subversive,
feminist text that "cracks open patriarchal narrative" (854).

As she constructs the text as a lesbian novel—if a lesbian novel buried
as but "one of various entwined narratives" and "formally not the most
prominent" (855)—Woodward has already inferred an implied author
who affirms lesbian affiliation against perceived patriarchal hostility and
who has intentionally created a confusing, generically messy text for
subversive purposes. This production of an implied author sets the stage
for inferring a real one: fully acknowledging the speculative nature of
her guesswork, Woodward imagines a female, possibly sapphic author,
rejects the possibilities of either a French original or a real Mr. Erskine,
and speculates that this author might even have been the "witty and
adventurous English writer Lady Mary Wortley Montagu" (859), who
spent time in France, wrote travel narratives, had strong bonds with
women, and in January 1744 attended a masquerade ball in honor of the
Duke of Richelieu, governor of Languedoc, whose cousin is allegedly
the narrator of the text. For Woodward, then, it is not only the narrator
but also the author who is cross-dressed: "Mr. Erskine" is a Lady in drag.

As a self-aware and careful critic, Woodward of course recognizes, and
indeed discusses, the ways in which her own desire helps to fashion
both the text and its author. Her constructions of the two are of a piece,
and hence consistent with what I have posited as normative scholarly

reading practices. This procedure also illustrates a widespread interpretive practice by feminist critics, myself very much included, in which the privileging of female authorship, of the novel as a genre, of female transgression as a topos, and of narrative subversion as a textual strategy all coalesce to uncover in this generically mixed and anonymous work a feminist find.

For Susan Lamb, this feminist practice, one that she acknowledges guided her own first reading of the work, has resulted in a serious misreading of the text; it has "wrongly" turned *The Travels and Adventures of Mademoiselle de Richelieu* into "an apology for women's rights" and "a transgressive celebration of lesbian desire."[18] By taking the narrator at face value, says Lamb, readers have mistaken the text's authorship, genre, and ideological purposes. Lamb reads *The Travels and Adventures of Mademoiselle de Richelieu* as a conventional satire at once on "women, early feminism, and same-sex eroticism and sexual love" in which gender categories are transgressed not to dismantle but to confirm them (76). For Lamb, *Travels*—her shortened version of the title, which redirects our attention away from the "lesbian" protagonist—is not only no "apologist for women's rights" but a complete misogynist. Lamb sets up this reading by opening her essay with the satiric poem "Petit Maitre," an anonymous attack upon cross-dressing and its attendant confusion of sexual boundaries that appears at the end of a much wider critique of British sexual practices, the 1749 *Satan's Harvest Home*. For Lamb, the *Travels* is not a subversive text but a work like the "Petit Matire" that mocks the practices it inscribes.

Lamb's argument, like Woodward's, rests on three mutually constituted aspects of the text: its genre, its sexual politics, and its implied authorship. She too acknowledges that the work is "highly heterogeneous" (76). But where Woodward sees a novel, Lamb discovers satire, and where Woodward saw the text as mocking conventions of gender and sexuality through its narrator, for Lamb it is the narrator herself who is being mocked. Where Woodward sees a lesbian in love with another lesbian, Lamb sees "a male impersonator who is in an erotic relationship with another male impersonator" (96). Where Woodward located *Mademoiselle de Richelieu* in the company of novels by women like Scott, Sarah Fielding, and Lennox, Lamb places *Travels* in the sphere of Menippean and Varonian satire by way of Dryden and Manley. Where Woodward sees the text as burying a discourse of women's love for women, Lamb sets it into a culture in which "female same-sex sexuality was fully and visibly imaginable" even though it was "legally actionable and publicly condemned." While Woodward's narrator is a reliable if sly recorder of her adventures, Lamb's is an untrustworthy and "facetious" figure with a "satirical voice"—"by conventional contemporary mores, monstrous"—whose monstrosity exposes the machinations of same-sex adventuring (76–8).

In constructing the narrator of the *Travels* as unreliable, Lamb also infers an author who is no champion of female friendship or lesbian desire, no "apologist for women's rights," but a conventional, conservative, anti-feminist satirist working within traditions created primarily by men. Like Woodward, Lamb moves readily, if tentatively, from implied to real authorship. "*Travels* was probably written by a man," she argues, or—in a nice evocation of the dynamics of the narrative itself—"perhaps by a woman careful to pass as a man" (79). Like Woodward, Lamb recognizes that either a woman *or* a man could in theory have written the *Travels*, but ultimately she assigns the author a masculine identity because of what she sees as the text's conservative and anti-feminist stance. She explains the probably-male author's use of a female *narrator* by this same stance: in a Richardsonian climate dedicated to female self-improvement, she argues, "the ideas [in the text] are so misogynist that they would be unacceptable coming from a male speaker" (91) and have therefore been placed strategically in a female voice.

Against Woodward's tentative proposal of Lady Mary Wortley Montagu, therefore, Lamb tentatively proposes a specific man. Removing the quotation marks Woodward had placed around "Erskine," she names the author Erskine, refers to Erskine as "he," and suggests in a footnote a particular William Erskine, a Jacobite who lived on the Continent, as a possible author of the work.[19] If Woodward removes the female author's male clothes, Lamb removes the male author's female clothes, describing a complicated dance in which "a male author (or a female author passing as one) pretends to be the translator of a female author who has the skills, education, land holdings, economic privilege, and independence of a man and who actually pretends to be a man" (81). For both critics, it is worth noting, the author is not a French memoirist but an English fictionist who has lived on the Continent and who has donned the literary clothing of a French aristocrat.

Both Woodward's and Lamb's interpretations of *The Travels and Adventures of Mademoiselle de Richelieu* rely on a "close reading" of the text, yet their readings diverge dramatically. A reference to female-female sexuality as "impossibility" is for Woodward an ironic inside joke, while for Lamb it underwrites the belief that "at least one male body is necessary for sex" (83).[20] While Woodward stresses the love plot featuring Arabella and Alithea over other textual material, Lamb emphasizes the travel narrative and the episodes of flirtation that do not result in liaison. Woodward does not take up the moments of "misogyny" to which Lamb points; Lamb does not take up the happy ending of the love plot or the two women's resumption of female clothes. And where Woodward's implied author vaunts women's intellectual capabilities, Lamb's author mocks these pretensions as "obviously flawed" (94). Lamb also turns the tables one more time, for she recognizes that "Erskine's choice of a cross-dressed woman as the one who will encounter, collect, and describe the evidence to support ideas of women's sexual rapaciousness and god-determined moral and intellectual bankruptcy undermines itself in the very performance of its mission" inadvertently opening readings that "would probably be unimaginable to Erskine and his contemporaries" (95). We are led back in this way to the transgressive text Woodward describes, but this time the transgression is an accident, a function of modern reading practices and inconsistent with the norms of the period.

Both scholars acknowledge a personal investment in their particular reading of the text: Woodward foregrounds her desire for "lesbian literary community" and states forthrightly that on "that summer's day in the British Library" when she discovered *Mademoiselle de Richelieu*, she "desired to connect with the story of Alithea and Arabella" and with the author whom "by now I imagine as a literarily cross-dressing woman" (859). Lamb offers an intellectual motive when, after acknowledging that she was "prepossessed" on her first reading "with the notion that the narrative has as its agenda debunking misogynist myth" (94), she says she now thinks that "to identify *Travels* in the way it has been considerably diminishes the work's sophistication and its implications" (76). For Lamb, the satiric *Travels* is a more rewarding read. Perhaps because of her own first, Woodward-like reading, she is then led to admit that the text may evade its authorial purposes: "The validity of Erskine's culture's misogyny, gender, and sexual categories, is necessarily undermined by" a narrator "whose narration is so joyous and playful in tone" that the text is "tempting and likely to be read against the grain" (96). In a sense, then, Lamb imagines a real author who is not wholly successful in controlling the implied author of his text.

It is hardly unusual for scholars to create divergent readings of texts, especially of texts that are generically complex or that enter so charged and contested a field as gender and sexuality. In this case, however, I think the divergences would be much more difficult to sustain, or might not even have arisen, if this text were not anonymous. My own reading of the text stands less at the points of difference between

Woodward and Lamb than at the intersection that occurs in Lamb's final paragraph, when she acknowledges the "disarming playfulness of the narration" and its ultimate permission to the reader, despite any contrary authorial intentions, to believe that "two women can do it too" (96). Certainly Woodward's reading conditioned mine until Lamb's inquiry challenged me to confront the generically more complicated and satiric possibilities I had previously overlooked. Even now that Lamb's suggestion that the text gets away from its author allows me to see the text as satiric, I see no evidence that the text ever undermines or mocks the relationship between Arabella and Alithea: the two women are indeed successful in touring Europe in men's clothes, and they do end up together, publicly, for life.

In pondering these essays with their divergent readings and in facing my own frustration with this text, I am struck by the extent to which reading abhors an authorial vacuum and seek to displace anonymity with identity. I myself have spent dozens of hours trying to identify "Mr. Erskine" and to track down a possible French original for *The Travels and Adventures of Mademoiselle de Richelieu.* I suspect that if the text were reprinted, scholars would be advancing still other alternatives according, for instance, to their belief in the existence of a French source text or to their interest in the text's attitudes toward Jacobite politics. It is not my purpose here, however, to propose a third authorial contender, although I confess I will be ecstatic if a real author for this text turns up. What I want to do instead is to ask what kinds of questions might help us think further about this text's—and any text's—implied authorship. I will restrict myself to the questions already raised by Woodward and Lamb, or more accurately by the tension between them: questions about the implied author's sexual identity and ideology.

I delimit my attention here because as I suggested at the beginning, fully reconstructing an implied author would be a monumental feat. Just as it could take volumes to describe the rules deployed by those who engage in conversation without giving those rules a thought, so the continuous process of inferring authorship would have to be described sentence by sentence, if not word by word. Reproducing this textual author would not simply mean distinguishing voices and structures after the fashion, say, of Genette's *Figures III*, but would entail minute and laborious processes like those Roland Barthes identifies in *S/Z*. Were I to chart out the authorial consciousness of *The Travels and Adventures of Mademoiselle de Richelieu*, in other words, I would have to describe the entire system of norms, conditions, and associations through which this text signifies its consciousness. Each time I processed a bit of text,

I would need to ask what potential range of "general consciousness" could produce the work thus far, and how this might be amalgamated to my range of reference for actual authors. Through accretion and revision, I would delineate with greater or lesser assurance the values and concerns of the text, relating them as well to (my sense of) the culture text. I would, in short, attempt to identify the grounds for what is ultimately, after all, an impression, an inference. And I would need to ask at every turn to what extent any knowledge of the historical author or the context of authorship might be operating in tandem or tension with my reading of the text. I would be operating as the narrator of *The Unlucky Citizen* asks in the passage that serves as my epigraph: I would be "ghessing," from whatever "Stuff" I can assemble, piece by piece, what "Garments" that text will wear.

To take on a more modest challenge, then: is it possible to designate a probable sex or sexuality for the implied author of *The Travels and Adventures of Mademoiselle de Richelieu* by apprehending the book's attitudes toward gender and sexuality? Both Woodward and Lamb appeal to the sexual ideology of the 1740s to ground their reading, yet they characterize that ideology differently and use it for different ends. This difference is possible, I think, because if there is ever a stable sexual ideology, England in the 1740s is not the place to find it. A rather broad range of discourses circulated in that decade about women, their rights, their sexuality, and their relationships—a range that would become less plausible a decade or two later, in part precisely because of the texts that circulated in the 1740s. I have elsewhere defined this period as a watershed decade in England, when a certain kind of play within practices and constructions of sex and gender is being rejected in favor of more rigid articulations; a number of texts of the 1710s through 1740s which I call "sapphic picaresque," among them *The Travels and Adventures of Mademoiselle de Richelieu*, inscribes homoerotic adventuring in celebratory or at least not condemnatory ways, but that fluidity begins to shut down in works like Fielding's *Female Husband* (1746), Cleland's *Fanny Hill* (1749), and Richardson's *Sir Charles Grandison* (1753). Both Woodward's story of subversion and Lamb's scenario of satire are plausible in the England of the 1740s, and it is not impossible that the text is at once celebrating *and* fretting about women's intimate relationships; as Catherine Belsey reminds us, "at times of crisis in the social formation" we are able "to glimpse a division within the subject" that yields ruptures and dissonances within a text.[21]

Even if we could identify a single ideological position for this work, would that identification lead us to the author's sex? Feminist critics have for several decades associated particular ideological and formal con-figurations of texts with a particular sex of authorship. From critiques of women's representations in men's works to studies that separate out women writers and read them *as* women, feminist scholarship (my own *Fictions of Authority* decidedly included) has been deeply invested in authorial sex. But notwithstanding Virginia Woolf's proclamation that "Anon ... was often a woman,"[22] the disarming condition of anonymous authorship reminds us that there is finally no way to guarantee the sex of a real author on the basis of the text alone. Attempts to deduce that sex have usually meant applying the most stereotypical assumptions about gender, and such attempts to ascribe authorship to anonymous or pseudonymous works have been frequently and often famously wrong.

But the impossibility of determining a *real* author's sex on the basis of textual content does not make it impossible to deduce the sex of an *implied* author, since the implied author is always only a reading effect.[23] Indeed, it is a matter such as sex that leads me to argue, against the posi-tions of both Booth and Genette, that a text's implied author is neither a real author's "second" and "better" self nor a tautological equivalent to the real author, but an authorial *position* that the text wittingly or unwit-tingly assumes. I would argue, for example, that the implied author of the *Satyr Upon Old Maids* constructs and inhabits a man's subject position whether or not a man actually wrote the work.

Determining the sex of the implied author of *The Travels and Adventures of Mademoiselle de Richelieu*, is more complex, and not only because of the work's gender-bending proclivities or ideological instabilities. To this sea of troubles I would add the indeterminacy that stems from its narrative form: with a pervasively present first-person narrator–protagonist, the text offers no access, beyond the words on its title page, to a framework or overvoice through which the narrator can be perceived. When all we have is a single, and fictional, consciousness, how do we measure that consciousness or infer an authorial one that presumably takes precedence?

It has been a critical axiom, of course, that no narrator, and especially not an autodiegetic narrator, should be confused with an implied author. I'm going to stick my neck out and claim that as a default, even sophis-ticated readers are likely to equate the narrator with the text's "general consciousness" in cases when the autodiegetic narrator is nowhere superseded or displaced by another voice of equal or greater diegetic status, when the norms of the narrator strike the reader as reliable (a tricky and subjective issue in itself[24]), when the narrator's image is both internally consistent and also consistent with whatever notion of "author" in general or *this* author in particular the reader is already carrying, and when the resolution of the plot permits the reader to sustain this connection between narrative and authorial consciousness. I would acknowledge immediately that the *grounds* for sustaining or rupturing this connection may very from reader to reader and moment to moment as much as they clearly will vary from text to text. I would also acknowledge the ontological *groundlessness* for the connection of implied author with autodiegetic narrator that I am guessing readers nonetheless make.[25]

If this default connection between the autodiegetic narrator and the implied author is indeed a conventional link by which readers infer textual consciousness, then one could argue that readers will most readily create a female implied author for *The Travels and Adventures of Mademoiselle de Richelieu*. Certainly, the narrator declares herself to *be* an author at the start, and grounds in her sex the very oddness of her text: "Were I a common Writer, I should follow common Form, that is to say, deduce my Origin from a long Race of illustrious Ancestors, and conclude the pompous Introduction with a Word or two to the Male Sex, who think it is a monstrous Presumption in a Woman to pretend to write" (I, 1–2). Later she reminds us that "Women began early to be Authors; and let any of the audacious Male Sex, who cannot bear that Women should be Sisters of the Quill, remember this, and read my Book with Reverence" (II, 136). But if, at any point in reading such passages, I perceive or experience a dissonance between the text and my own assumptions, all bets are off. If, for example, I read passages like these as mockery, I may well, as Susan Lamb does, reconstruct the implied author as male. There is certainly ground for constructing an implied author who, like the narrator, is complex and dissonant in gender and sexuality. Both Lamb and Woodward construct such a queer author, if differently: for Woodward, the authorial consciousness is female and lesbian; for Lamb it is male and homosocial if not homosexual.

And perhaps the author's queerness extends beyond sexuality. Even as I have tried to pin down an implied author for *The Travels and Adventures of Mademoiselle de Richelieu*, I have been pointing to the ways in which this work resists categories and gives mixed messages. If a truly careful and open-minded reader were to attempt constructing the implied author of *The Travels and Adventures of Mademoiselle de Richelieu*, might s/he not decide that the implied author is irreducibly queer in a range of ways? Might s/he recognize that to create an implied author in the Boothean sense s/he would have to purge out textual elements and interpretive features and fictionalize authorial—and textual—coherence? What if there *is* no way to make sense of these differences because the implied author is not singular at all? What if we have a "division within the subject" who is the "author" of this text?

To raise this question is to problematize not only the implied authorship of *The Travels and Adventures of Mademoiselle de Richelieu* but also the entire project by which authorship is understood in Western modernity. For whenever we speak of *the* implied author we are already reducing a text's possible pluralities to a singularity. Foucault says as much when he claims that the author as "functional principle" "impedes the free circulation, the free manipulation, the free composition, decomposition, and recomposition" of the text."[26] When Booth frames the implied author as a superior, godlike, refined, better and wiser—hence not only incidentally male—version of a "real" self, he is very obviously relying on what is more or less the nineteenth-century "classic realist" figuration of the author that Catherine Belsey describes. Such an author confers coherent and non-contradictory meaning, "apparently not in the words on the page," wherein somehow author and reader participate in an ideological compact that erases its own contingency.[27] In short, the prevailing notion of implied authorship, like the author-function it reflects, creates the "readerly" text that controls and contains the queerness of plurality—the kind of plurality Barthes sought to open up when he performed in *S/Z* his slow "*step-by-step*" "decomposition" of "Sarrazine." Barthes reminds us that "if we want to remain attentive to the plural of a text" we must "renounce structuring this text in large masses";[28] surely to speak of *the* implied author, as I have done here, is to structure authorship as a mass. If, however, we set aside this classic sense of implied authorship in favor of a queerer sort, we may even have an implied author who could have written both Lamb's and Woodward's *Travels and Adventures of Mademoiselle de Richelieu*.

In this sense, the anonymous text is liberating because it reminds us that the creative mind can project facets of itself that might not be visible through the lens of biography, that a text's consciousness may be general without being singular. As a text that is *about* queerness—queerness of voice, identity, desire, ideology, behavior—as a text that shows us how easily a "woman" can be a "man" and "Mr. Erskine" speak for a French "Lady," *The Travels and Adventures of Mademoiselle de Richelieu* stands as a sign of the ultimate incoherence of the very project of authorship to which literary scholarship has so insistently subscribed. Instead of trying to figure out whether the implied author of *The Travels and Adventures of Mademoiselle de Richelieu* is a man or a woman, heterosexual or homosexual, even feminist or misogynist, we might have to recognize that s/he is all of these at different moments, and that the meaning of this text lies precisely in these dissonances that are also a sign of their times.

Perhaps, then, it is useful to figure the implied author not simply as a person but as a person dressed—or cross-dressed: a person whose garments can be altered, discarded, tried on, and changed before—or behind—our eyes. It may be no accident that a number of eighteenth-century writings deploy the image of garments to describe the behaviors of texts—Swift's *Tale of a Tub* comes immediately to mind, as does Defoe's *Roxana*, in whose preface the author speaks of "dressing up the Story" in "Cloaths" that suit it for "the World." Its own claims notwithstanding, the text that furnishes my epigraph tells us very little about the "Garments" that will follow from the "Stuff" already there; *The Unlucky Citizen* is a complicated work that takes many unexpected turns, giving us its "stuff" piecemeal. Perhaps, then, *The Travels and Adventures of Mademoiselle de Richelieu* should remind us that all authors may wear queer clothes, and that it is the reader's pleasure to guess not only what Garments s/he is wearing but what garments we shall have.

Notes

1. Francis Kirkman, *The Unlucky Citizen Experimentally Described in the Various Misfortunes of an Unlucky Londoner* (London: Anne Johnson, 1673), 105. This passage appears as an epigraph in Wayne Booth's *The Rhetoric of Fiction* (Chicago: University of Chicago Press, 1961), 210.
2. I. A. Richards, *Practical Criticism: A Study of Literary Judgment* (New York: Harcourt Brace, 1929), 292–9 passim.
3. Ibid., 297. Thus Donne's seventh Holy Sonnet becomes the "rotten" work of a "simple man" with "bad" technique and "temperamental" metrics, Lawrence's "Piano" a work of "gross sentimentality," and a Longfellow poem "a bastard of spurious rectitude and false simplicity."
4. The word "literary" is important here, for some kinds of texts rarely evoke the question of authorship at all. In my essay in progress "The 'I' of the Beholder," I argue for the intimate relationship between a text's genre and our reliance on knowledge of a text's authorship. In this framework, advertisements, hymns, and road signs lie within a group of "detached" genres for which authorship is conventionally not a determinant of textual significance. At the opposite pole lie "contingent" or "attached" genres such as the letter to the editor, the memoir, and the scholarly essay, all of which rely on assumptions that connect a particular author to the text. Literary genres, I argue, operate in an equivocal mode: they can usually be understood without recourse to a sense of the author, but that sense of the author usually fashions our understanding of the text.
5. Robert Griffin, "Anonymity and Authorship," *New Literary History* 30.4 (Autumn 1999): 891 and passim.
6. See René Wellek, "The Name and Nature of Comparative Literature," in *Comparatists at Work*, ed. Stephen G. Nichols, Jr. and Richard B. Vowles (Waltham, MA: Blaisdell, 1968), 13. I have engaged this question of literature as monument in "Compared to What: Global Feminism, Comparatism, and the Master's Tools," in *Borderwork: Feminist Engagements with Comparative Literature*, ed. Margaret Higonnet (Ithaca: Cornell University Press, 1994), 280–300.

7. Michel Foucault, "What Is an Author?" in *Language, Counter-memory, Practice: Selected Essays and Interviews* (Ithaca: Cornell University Press, 1977), 123 and passim.

8. Shlomith Rimmon-Kenan, *Narrative Fiction: Contemporary Poetics* (London: Methuen, 1983), 86. In a more recent essay, Rimmon-Kenan strives for a more plural sense of authorship; see Ruth Ginsburg and Shlomith Rimmon-Kenan, "Is There Life after Death? Theorizing Authors and Reading *Jazz*," in *Narratologies: New Perspectives on Narrative Analysis*, ed. David Herman (Columbus: Ohio State University Press, 1999), 66–87.

9. Ansgar Nünning, "Deconstructing and Reconceptualizing the Implied Author," *Anglistik* 8 (1997), 110 ff.

10. I have argued elsewhere that the "implied author" can take many forms and that the concept itself is a matter of belief. In other words, not only the nature of implied authorship but the very "existence" of an implied author "in" a text is a function of some readers' ways of reading some texts. See my "(Im)plying the Author," *Narrative*, 9:2 (May 2001), 153–60.

11. See Wayne Booth, *The Rhetoric of Fiction* (Chicago: University of Chicago Press, 1961), 71–86, and Booth, "Distance and Point of View: An Essay in Classification," *Essays in Criticism* (1961): 67. It goes without saying that Booth's language of the 1960s constructs the author, his inclusion of Austen notwithstanding, as a "man." This masculinity, as I will suggest later, is not a mere accident of language practices but adheres to his larger sense of authorship as a position of cultural authority.

12. See Lanser, *The Narrative Act: Point of View in Prose Fiction* (Princeton: Princeton University Press, 1981), 122 ff., and Gérard Genette, *Paratexts: Thresholds of Interpretation* (Cambridge: Cambridge University Press, 1997). For a useful critique of "extrafictional," see Werner Wolf, "Framing Fiction. Reflections on a Narratological Concept and an Example: Bradbury, *Mensonge*," in *Grenzüberschreitungen: Narratologie im Kontext/Transcending Boundaries: Narratology in Context*, ed. Walter Grünzweig and Andreas Solbach (Tübingen: Gunter Narr, 1998), 110–11.

13. *A Satyr Upon Old Maids* (London, W. Denham, 1713), passim.

14. Further references to *The Travels and Adventures of Mademoiselle de Richelieu* will be from the three-volume London edition (M. Cooper, 1744) and will appear in the body of the text. The English Short Title Catalogue also identifies a Dublin printing by O. Nelson in 1743 and an undated London printing by S. Ballard. In his *Check List of Prose Published in England 1740–1749* (Charlottesville: University Press of Virginia, 1972), Jerry C. Beasley names a second Dublin version by Greenough in 1744 and points to a piracy entitled *The Entertaining Travels and Surprising Adventures of Mademoiselle de Leurich. Who travelled over Europe, dressed in Man's Apparel, attended by her Maid-Servant as her Valet de Chambre. Now done into English from the Lady's own Manuscript. By a Masterly Hand.* I have seen a Dublin 1758 edition (by Alex. McCulloh) of this abridgment, but Beasley believes there is a 1748 edition as well.

15. In this essay, I am using the term "sex" to denote a biological condition and "gender" to designate the qualities of appearance, behavior, character, and temperament culturally associated with one or the other sex. I have no doubt that sex is in truth a spectrum rather than a dichotomy, indeed that sex is arguably, like gender, a cultural construct as Judith Butler has argued in *Bodies That Matter*. For the purposes of this essay, however, I am adopting the simpler and more commonplace binary of male/female that operates in the grammatical designation of authors as "he" or "she."

16. See Angela J. Smallwood, *Fielding and the Woman Question: The Novels of Henry Fielding and Feminist Debate, 1700–1750* (Hempstead/New York: Harvester/St. Martin's Press, 1989), 191. Smallwood's mention occurs in a valuable appendix of "Documents debating Issues relating to Women, 1680–1760." Percy Adams, her apparent source here, actually calls Richelieu a "lively, curious apologist for women's rights"; see Adams, *Travel Literature and the Evolution of the Novel* (Lexington: University Press of Kentucky, 1983), 190 (emphasis mine).

17. Carolyn Woodward, "'My Heart so Wrapt': Lesbian Disruptions in Eighteenth-Century British Fiction," *Signs* 18:4 (1993), 838–9. Further references will appear in the body of the text. I owe to Woodward my own introduction to *The Travels and Adventures of Mademoiselle de*

Richelieu, and we have had numerous conversations about the book and its range of possible authors and readings. This discussion represents only the "Carolyn Woodward" of the *Signs* essay.

18. Susan Lamb, " 'Be Such a Man as I': Mademoiselle Makes the Tour of Europe in Men's Clothes." *Studies in Eighteenth-Century Culture* 27 (1998), 76. Further references to this essay will appear in the body of the text.

19. Lamb considers the text to have "openly Jacobite politics" and on this basis rejects Montagu's possible authorship in favor of William Erskine, brother to the Earl of Pittodrie, who lived on the continent. I myself read the discussion of "Kingly Government" in Volume I (9–28) as a critique of succession that would seem to undermine a Jacobite politics.

20. Lamb argues that the narrative is ultimately a displacement of *male–male* desire and "a disguised account of a sexual liaison between men" (84), and that Erskine "uses the voice of a woman, as the men in the Molly houses did." She makes this claim because, she says, "all of the expressions of love between them are made between two people who look and act as men, are economically and socially independent, own large estates, have somehow received an identifiably male classical education, and who fake sexual interest in women to comply with social expectations" (84). Certainly the novel evokes male homoeroticism even as it is evoking desire between women. However, not all expressions of the women's love are made when they are cross-dressed, and the relationship between Alithia and Arabella is made possible precisely by the narrator's *removal* of male dress to reveal her female body: she literally bares her breasts to Arabella, upon which Arabella embraces her and the two vow to love one another for life. At the novel's end, moreover, they resume female clothing to live together.

21. Catherine Belsey, *Critical Practice* (London/New York: Methuen, 1980), 86.

22. Virginia Woolf, *A Room of One's Own* (London: Harcourt Brace, 1957), 51.

23. In one sense it is of course a complete fiction to attribute sex—a biological condition—to a "reader effect," but insofar as that reader effect generates an anthropomorphism, I would argue that sexing the implied author is not much more absurd than sexing a narrator or a character.

24. Nünning perceptively argues that the reliability of a narrator is measured not against the norms of the implied author, finally, but against the reader's "preexisting conceptual knowledge of the world." See "Unreliable, compared to what? Towards a Cognitive Theory of *Unreliable Narration*: Prolegomena and Hypotheses" in *Grenzüberschreitungen: Narratologie im Kontext*, 70.

25. I take up this issue of autodiegetic narration and implied authorship in "(Im)plying the Author."

26. Foucault, "What is an Author?"

27. Belsey, *Critical Practice*, 72.

28. Roland Barthes, *S/Z*, trans. Richard Miller (New York: Farrar Straus Giroux, 1974), 12–13.

CHAPTER FIVE

Possible Gustavus Vassa / Olaudah Equiano Attributions

Vincent Carretta

Since the publication in 1995 of Olaudah Equiano's *The Interesting Narrative and Other Writings*, several published works have been discovered that either may have been written by, or were attributed to, Gustavus Vassa/Olaudah Equiano. Ten letters signed "Gustavus Vassa" appeared between 24 July 1777 and 10 July 1778 in the pro-government London newspaper the *Morning Post, and Daily Advertiser*.[1] An attack on the slave trade and slavery, signed "Gustavus," appeared in the *Glasgow Courier* on 15 March 1792. And an anti-war statement signed "Othello" was published in late 1794 in *The Cabinet*, a periodical produced by several of Vassa/Equiano's known Norwich associates.

All of these writings must be treated as pseudonymous. If the *Morning Post* letters were not written by the Vassa/Equiano who authored *The Interesting Narrative*, they were definitely published under a false name. The name Gustavus Vassa had been given the author of *The Interesting Narrative* by his slave owner Michael Henry Pascal in 1754 and remained his legal name used at his baptism in 1759 and in his will in 1796. With the addition of the epithet, the African, Vassa announced that that slave name was an imposed pseudonym masking his true name, Olaudah Equiano. He did not publicly reveal his Equiano identity until he sought subscribers in November 1788 for his *The Interesting Narrative of the Life of Olaudah Equiano, or Gustavus Vassa, the African. Written by Himself* (London, 1789). But recently discovered documentary evidence has raised the possibility that the name Olaudah Equiano itself may also have been a pseudonym used by an author whose true identity has not yet been, and perhaps never will be, determined.[2]

The newspaper essays in the *Morning Post* may have been by Vassa/Equiano, who published letters and advertisements in at least 18 other British newspapers during the 1780s and 1790s. Because these later publications identify the author either by Vassa/Equiano's short-lived government role as commissary for the projected Sierra Leone settlement, or by his known association with fellow African co-signers, or by internal evidence, they can be assigned with certainty to the author of *The Interesting Narrative*. But during the 1770s, someone other than Vassa/Equiano may have assumed the name of Gustavus I, or Gustavus Vassa (1496–1560), the noble Swede who led his people to freedom from Danish rule in 1521–23 and went on to become a very successful king of liberated Sweden. In British political discourse, the figure of Gustavus Vassa had been associated with the opposition since the publication in 1739 of Henry Brooke's anti-ministerial play, *Gustavus Vasa, The Deliverer of His Country*, which the government had kept from being staged in 1738. The continued political currency of the figure was maintained by re-publication of the play in 1761, 1778, 1796, and 1797, all years in which Britain was at war. The last paragraph of the first of the series of letters in the *Morning Post* closes with the author's hope that his comments will be so well received that he may "think [him]self entitled to the name of GUSTAVUS VASA." Such a hope would be appropriate to anyone, including Vassa/Equiano, sending public advice to the ministry. But for Vassa/Equiano to hope to deserve his slave name would be ironic in a way unavailable to others. The absence in the 1770s of the epithets "the African" or "the Ethiopian," which Vassa/Equiano added to "Gustavus Vassa" in Equiano's published letters in 1788 and 1789, does not in itself rule Vassa/Equiano out as the Vassa of the *Morning Post* series because he signed all his known pre-1788 letters as simply Gustavus Vassa, without the epithets. I know of no one else who was publishing under the pseudonym Vassa during the last quarter of the eighteenth century.

The *Morning Post* letters appeared during a period when we know that Vassa/Equiano was in London, and they would fill a gap between his arrival there in 1777 and his employment in early 1779 by Matthias Macnamara, who had been dismissed in August 1778 as governor of Senegambia in Africa. Vassa/Equiano tells us that having spent "some little time at Plymouth and Exeter" (219) after he had arrived at Plymouth on 7 January 1777, he went to London. A letter Vassa/Equiano includes in his *Narrative* proves that he was in Macnamara's employ by 11 March 1779 and that he was then living on Hedge Lane, Charing Cross, in

Westminster. The *Morning Post* letters are sent from various locations, moving from east to west—Anderton's Coffee House, Fleet Street, Peel's Coffee House, Fleet Street, and Hungerford Coffee House, Strand (near St. Martin-in-the-Fields church and Charing Cross). These sites are consistent with the westward movement from the City of London to Westminster that the *Narrative* indicates Vassa/Equiano made between 1777 and 1779.

The *Morning Post* letters would also fill the gap of the American Revolution, a subject almost completely untouched in Vassa/Equiano's *Interesting Narrative*. (One might note that this subject is untreated as well in Benjamin Franklin's contemporaneously written though much later published *Autobiography*.) Vassa's first letter argues that, had the British capitalized on their victories under the leadership of William Pitt, the elder, during the Seven Years' War (1756–63) by retaining their conquests in the West Indies, Britain "would for all ages to come have remained the *metropole* of the commercial world, and *mart* of general trade for all Europe, Asia, Africa, and America; as well as the most formidable naval power on earth." He implies that "the inadequateness of the peace" established by the Treaty of Paris in 1763 laid the groundwork for the present war with the American colonies and the threat of military intervention by France and Spain on behalf of the rebels.

Vassa is a royalist who supports the cause against the American rebels, like the African-born former servant Ignatius Sancho. Sancho published similar newly discovered letters under the pseudonym "Africanus" and his own name, respectively, in the *Morning Post* on 28 August 1778 and 29 December 1779. In his 1 January 1778 letter addressed to Lord North, the prime minister, Vassa, however, is much harsher than Sancho ever is in his criticism of North's conduct of the war.[3] But even Sancho, who through his former employer, the duke of Montagu, had connections to North and his family, acknowledged that North "is a good husband! father, friend, and master—a real *good man*—but I fear a bad m[iniste]r" (*Letters*, 191). Vassa's harsh comments were prompted by the defeat at the battle of Saratoga, New York, on 17 October 1777, of the British forces under general John Burgoyne by the American general Horatio Gates. Having marched from Canada and taken the American fort at Ticonderoga on the route to Saratoga, the overextended Burgoyne was defeated when Sir Henry Clinton failed to reach him with British troops brought up the Hudson River from New York City. Vassa, and many others, faulted Clinton and fellow British general Sir William Howe for failure to prosecute the war vigorously. The defeat at Saratoga was the military turning point of the war, convincing France and Spain to join forces with the Americans early in 1778, and led to increased political pressure for a negotiated end to the rebellion.

Vassa and Sancho both opposed Lord North's Reconciliation Bill for offering what they thought overly generous peace terms to the American rebels. Vassa's letters of 4 and 10 March 1778 express his growing anger as the original Bill became increasingly conciliatory. On 4 March he welcomes the Bill, but on 10 March he withdraws his previous support for the rapidly changing proposal. Sancho's letter of 28 August 1778, on the other hand, expresses his relief at the Americans' apparent rejection of the ultimate offer: "I am very glad to see by the newspapers the American rebels have thought fit to reject the much too favourable terms, that, it is said, have been offered to them ... ."[4] Vassa's stance in the newspaper letters is consistent with the patriotic pro-British position maintained by Vassa/Equiano in the *Narrative* and by Sancho in his *Letters*.

The Vassa letters reveal a familiarity with French and Latin and Classical history not found elsewhere in Vassa/Equiano's work. But the quite limited level of familiarity displayed is less impressive than that found in the posthumously published letters of the self-educated Sancho. It could easily have been achieved by an autodidact like Vassa/Equiano through reading translations. Some of Vassa's learning is clearly a bit uncertain. His 10 March 1778 letter opens with an invocation of Galgacus (Calgacus), who rallied Britons to stop the advance of Julius Agricola, the Roman governor of Britain, into the Scottish Highlands (Caledonia) in A.D. 83. Vassa probably expected his readers to remember that Galgacus motivated his followers by exhorting them to resist enslavement by the Romans. Tacitus, Agricola's son-in-law, records in *Agricola* that although Agricola won the battle at Mons Graupius because of superior weapons and tactics, the courage and ferocity of the Caledonians led by Galgacus ultimately compelled the Romans to withdraw. Vassa's Galgacus seems to speak directly to Caesar, but in Tacitus's *Annals* Caratacus (Caractacus), not Galgacus, is the defeated Briton who addresses Claudius Caesar in Rome in A.D. 51. The speech Tacitus gives Caratacus does not include the sentiments cited by Vassa, though those sentiments are similar to some voiced by Galgacus in *Agricola*. Neither Galgacus nor Caratacus would have spoken the eighteenth-century Irish used by Vassa as an epigraph. And the inaccuracy of that anachronistic Irish indicates that Vassa was neither a fluent nor native speaker.[5] In several of the other *Morning Post* letters Vassa is more obviously engaged in fiction writing. For example, the 23 June 1778 letter is historical fiction, and that of 2 July 1778 is an oriental tale.

Missing in the newspaper essays are the subject of religion and the use of biblical quotations so frequently found elsewhere in Vassa/Equiano's writings, but the same may be said of Sancho's *Morning Post* letters as compared to his other writings. And the *Narrative* itself leaves out references to events we would expect to appear in his autobiography. The most noticeable example is that of the *Zong* atrocity of 1781, which Vassa/Equiano brought to the attention of the abolitionist Granville Sharp in 1783 when the case was heard in court against the captain of a slave ship who had ordered 132 enslaved Africans thrown overboard in an attempt to collect the insurance on his lost cargo. The absence of references to slavery in Vassa's *Morning Post* letters should not be surprising: they are not found in Sancho's newspaper letters either. Slavery was much more frequently discussed in print in England after the mid-1780s than before.

If Vassa/Equiano is the Vassa who wrote these letters, he clearly fictionalizes his identity—in effect, using a pseudonym for a pseudonym—though little autobiographical information is offered, and virtually no attempt is made to create a Swedish persona. The emphasis on military affairs and the references to the martial experience of the speaker in Vassa's letters do not appear to me to be too alien to the experiences of the Seven Years' War Vassa/Equiano recounts in his *Interesting Narrative*. Rhetorical inflation enhances Vassa's *ethos* and hence credibility as a military advisor: "To tell you, that I have been a *Soldier*, would be of no consequence, unless I told you, that I have been a commander of men. Battles and sieges I have frequently been in; and sometimes I have been eminently successful, Mr. Editor. I never quitted the field unsuccessfully but once—that fatal day ended all my hopes of glory!" (23 June 1778).

As Vassa/Equiano does in his *Narrative*, and Sancho in his posthumously published correspondence, Vassa rhetorically positions himself in his *Morning Post* letters as the stranger in a strange land. As an outsider, he observes the events around him: "The discourse turned upon the antiquity, and origin of the inhabitants of their different countries [England, Scotland, Wales, and Ireland]. Woes me! quoth I, who am not a native of either of the happier isles, but a continental spawn of accident; I can only be an humble hearer in this grand dispute" (11 June 1778). Vassa, like Vassa/Equiano, presents himself as a citizen of the world, a man without a country, and at one point tells of a man who appears to have much in common with the Vassa/Equiano of *The Interesting Narrative*:

An illustrious person, whose early misfortunes, from the mistaken zeal, and principle of his predecessors, obliged him to become a man of the world, and to endeavour the acquirement of such treasure, as no mortal power could deprive him of, while life remained, travelled Europe, Asia, Africa, and America, as a merchant, and philosopher; both honourable characters, and both of infinite advantage to society!

In his youth he was bred to arms, and bore a distinguished rank before he was twenty years old. A series of misfortunes changed his turn of mind, and he felt a secret pleasure in pursuing, unknown, a scheme of life becoming a private gentleman.

(2 July 1778)[6]

Furthermore, Vassa/Equiano, Sancho, and the Vassa of the *Morning Post* share a belief in the civilizing and pacifying powers of international commerce, an interest in people at the social and geographical margins of English society and the British empire, a fascination with the unusual, a recognition that a person may have more than one identity, and the possession of a sardonic sense of humor.

The 9 November 1777 essay on the notorious Chevalier d'Eon, with its sociopolitical comments on hermaphroditism and cross-dressing and its anti-Gallicism, demonstrates a satiric side only occasionally and briefly displayed in *The Interesting Narrative*. Like his knowledge of events in America, Vassa's information about d'Eon could easily have been gleaned from the daily press, including the *Morning Post*, which extensively covered the dispute over the Chevalier's sexual identity, especially when a jury in July 1777 ruled that a bet on d'Eon's gender was legal and in so doing recognized the Chevalier as a woman. (That d'Eon's gender was male was not proven until after his death in 1810.)

Definite attribution to Vassa/Equiano of the Gustavus Vassa letters in the *Morning Post* will probably never be possible; the question of who lies behind the pseudonym remains open to dispute.

Vassa/Equiano was not a public figure during the 1770s; so assuming his identity by writing under his pseudonym then did not offer an author any obvious rhetorical or financial benefit. By 15 March 1792, however, when "Gustavus" published his attack on the slave trade in the *Glasgow Courier*, Vassa/Equiano had achieved the status of a celebrity in the abolitionist cause. In addition to the four editions of his *Interesting Narrative* published by then, he had also published at least twenty-five times in various English and Irish newspapers. His voice had authority. And between 27 April and 20 August 1792, Vassa/Equiano would advertise his autobiography at least four times in Glasgow, Edinburgh, and Aberdeen newspapers during his tour of Scotland on behalf of himself and the struggle against the slave trade.[7] But for several reasons "Gustavus" is very probably not Vassa/Equiano, even though his persona is African, referring to Africans as "my fellow countrymen," and the sentiments of "Gustavus" were certainly shared by Vassa/Equiano. As far as we know, Gustavus Vassa never identified himself as simply "Gustavus," and in March 1792 Vassa/Equiano was still in England, preparing for his 7 April marriage in Cambridge to Susanna Cullen. The pseudonymous "Gustavus" may have known and taken advantage of Vassa/Equiano's impending trip to Scotland to assume his identity in his response to the pro-slavery argument of the equally pseudonymous "Columbus" in the 6 March issue of the *Glasgow Courier*.[8]

Of all the letters included below, the one most likely to have been written by Vassa/Equiano is "Mischievous Effects of War" by the pseudonymous "Othello" that first appeared, probably in early March 1795, in the biweekly periodical *The Cabinet. By a Society of Gentlemen*. It was published in Norwich for about a year, starting in October 1794, and collected in three volumes late in 1795. The known contributors to the reformist *Cabinet*, all writing under pseudonyms, included several of the younger men and women who had subscribed in March 1794 to the eighth edition of Vassa/Equiano's *Interesting Narrative*, published in Norwich: Amelia Alderson (later Opie), William Dalrymple, William Enfield, H. Gardiner, John Pitchford, Anna Plumptree, John Taylor, John Stuart Taylor, P. Meadows Taylor, William Taylor, and William Youngman. Mary Wollstonecraft, who had reviewed the first edition of Vassa/Equiano's *Interesting Narrative* in 1789, was a possible contributor to *The Cabinet*.[9] And John March, publisher of *The Cabinet*, had subscribed for two copies of Vassa/Equiano's Norwich edition. The contributors to the periodical were opposed to the slave trade and the war with Revolutionary France. Vassa/Equiano had been in Norwich in February and March 1794, advertising for subscribers, and attending meetings of the Tusculan School, a local debating club that included several of his future subscribers. The name "Othello" obviously suggests a Black writer, but the antiwar essay never comments on the author's ethnic identity. Consequently, unlike "Gustavus" in the *Glasgow Courier*, the author of "Mischievous Effects of War" has no apparent rhetorical reason for assuming a Black identity. Why would a contributor to *The Cabinet* arbitrarily choose the name "Othello?" Vassa/Equiano was the only person of African descent known to have associated with contributors to the periodical. And, perhaps inevitably, one of the earliest reviewers of Vassa/Equiano's autobiography had likened him to Othello in July 1789, a link Vassa/Equiano recalled in every subsequent edition of his *Interesting Narrative*.

Whatever the true identities of Vassa/Equiano, Gustavus Vassa, Gustavus, and Othello may have been, they all chose to write in pseudonymous disguise.

....

1. *The Morning Post, and Daily Advertiser*, 24 July 1777

For the MORNING POST

Mr. EDITOR,

Had Great Britain turned her political views to the extention of colonies, in the West Indies, instead of enlarging her territorial dominions upon the continent of America, to secure the great avenues of trade, and commerce to her in-land colonies, or the continent from falling into the hands of France, and Holland, our only rivals in commerce, this nation would for ages to come have remained the *metropole* of the commercial world, and *mart* of general trade for all Europe, Asia, Africa, and America; as well as the most formidable naval power upon earth. A limited commercial monarchy should always have had in view the colonization of countries, where her marine power could not only command the respect, and obedience of the inhabitants, but also where the current of trade, and produce of her colonies, centered in the mother country. Such is the nature of our West India establishments; first because they are islands; and secondly, because they never can, from their situation, become either manufacturers, mechanics, or artists, that could anyway affect the consumption of merchandize from Britain; and, thirdly, because all their produce, and labour, must come to this mart for sale.

It would have required but very little sagacity to have penetrated the views of a growing people, extending their settlements over a waste fertile continent; nor is the design of this essay, to enter into reasoning upon the ingratitude of a people, which owe their existence to the parent state—I shall only observe, that even in domestic life, when children grow to maturity, they shake off gradually their dependency upon their parents, however they may otherwise respect them; what happens in private life, arises comparatively, and bears an allusion to the actions of men in an aggregate situation. America has now declared her independency of the mother; it is the duty of every honest man, who has the real good of his country at heart, to wish a reconciliation, that will prove of equal advantage to Britain, and her colonies;—those who wish otherwise, if any there should be, are enemies of the state, and traitors to their King and country.

The great misfortune that attended this nation at the end of the last war, which was carried on so successfully, and ended so gloriously to the honour of the British arms, was the inadequateness of the peace, which was concluded between Great-Britain, France, and Spain; the arrangements of territorial cession, and division, therein established, are too conspicuous for a total ignorance of geographical knowledge in the British Ministry, and their negotiations, to require a comment.

The ratification of the treaty of Paris, was a more desperate wound to the commercial glory of this country, than any that had ever before been given; and it was from that moment that America began to think seriously of independancy, and that France beheld the sun-shine of commercial splendor, breaking in upon her empire.

It was then that the French administration displayed to all Europe their penetration and superior wisdom, in establishing a treaty of peace, after an unsuccessful war, that would not only repay the nation the many millions they had lost, but they also saw an ample field opening to their view, that would soon gratify their revenge upon this country without drawing a sword against her:—they now exult, and glory, that their hopes are come to pass.

It is neither the virtue, nor piety of the Prince, nor his Ministers, that can secure wisdom to his Councils; and this is not the age of inspiration,—without a competent share of acquired, and experimental knowledge.—Natural abilities eminently improved, produce great men in their different walks of life:—but a minister of state, who takes upon him the arduous task of guiding the helm of public affairs, should weigh well in his own mind, the stupendous work he undertakes for the public;—for upon his conduct may depend the utter ruin, or the glory of his country.

If I can point at some outlines for the future conduct of Ministers, to regain the immense loss we have sustained by the late treaty of peace with France, and offer a few leading, and permanent observations, respecting a reconciliation, which timely attended to, may yet take place, I shall deem my time exceedingly well spent, as well as think myself entitled to the name of

GUSTAVUS VASA

Anderton's Coffee-house, July 19

....

2. *The Morning Post, and Daily Advertiser*, 18 August 1777

For the MORNING POST

AMERICA

Mr. EDITOR,

There never was a period in the annals of this country, that required more wisdom, resolution, and spirit, in the administration, than our present situation with America, France, and Spain; notwithstanding the universal complaint of indifference, inactivity, and inappositeness, there appear in all the measures adopted by our present race of statesmen for ascertaining the natural rights and maintaining the dignity of the empire.

To illustrate this truth, we need only take a back view of their measures, which gendered the soul of rebellion in America, by the stipulations agreed to, and ratified by the last treaty of peace with France, and Spain; the same perseverance in a chain of false politics, with an equal degree of supineness, and self-sufficiency which characterized our peace makers, seem hereditary in their successors.

The plan adopted for sending legions of foreign troops to the American continent, is so pregnant of a profound ignorance of the real interest of Britain in those regions, that even the most superficial speculator who looks but a little forward, can at once discover the injurious tendency of sending foreign mercenaries to aid us in the reduction of our colonies.

The numberless proofs, which may be adduced from antient as well as modern history, of the evils brought upon empires, kingdoms, and states, who made use of mercenary strangers to assist them in the conquest of distant countries, are so many and striking, that it would be needless to quote them in this place.

German auxiliaries in Flanders, Mr. Editor, where it is the interest of the different sovereigns to take care, that at the end of a peace, each division of foreigners shall return to their own country, differ widely from Germans, or Russians transported from slavery, penury, and an ungrateful soil, into a land of *Canaan* flowing with milk, and honey. Where they are not only far removed from their tyrant masters, but invited by the very people they are sent to conquer, not only to join, and share with them those rights, and privileges they set up for, but also offering them a most liberal share of the property of a rich extensive fertile country; where they behold with astonishment in every province they pass, a luxuriance of nature they never beheld before;—where they daily meet with townships, and settlements of numbers of their own countrymen, who either quitted their land for want of bread, or were traffick'd for, and sent thither as bond servants, but now having regained their freedom, they find thousands of them settled in properties, estates, and farms of their own, living in comfort, ease, and even luxury in comparison with their former miserable and indigent state.

These, with numberless other reasons improper to be exposed in the speculations of a public paper, ought to have had some weight with administration before they had agreed to send armies of foreigners into our continental colonies.

Indeed had the spirit of true wisdom, and good policy guided their resolutions, and councils in disposing of a number of foreign troops, to aid in the conquest of *islands*, and such situations as sagacity, and true policy could have suggested, and have often but in vain been pointed out to our demagogues in power; instead of pouring in an addition of strength to the cause of rebellion, and furnishing new vigour by virtue of veteran adventurers to the spirit of independancy,—we might by this time have not only negotiated an honourable reconciliation with the refractory colonies,—and even had the flower of their army, and navy, to have joined Great Britain in such conquests as would have repaid us the expences of the war, but restored harmony to the continent, and re-united our former friendship with these people upon a lasting, solid, and mutual foundation of commercial, alliance, and dependancy on each other.

But what can be expected in a country where every natural good is sacrificed to partial views, and schemes of interest merely calculated to prolong the calamities of an unprofitable, and unnatural war, by which a few are enriched, and the nation perhaps effectually ruined?

Twenty or thirty thousand foreign troops might be happily, and advantageously employed, with the power of the British navy, to superintend round *islands*, where they might answer the end of garrisons from the *Cape Devarde* islands, to the *Havannah*, there, Sir, is a field for employing both the wisdom, and genius of a capacitated, spirited, and liberal minded administration?—The dominion of the seas, and the possession of islands, which are the grand, and leading avenues to the *East Indies*, *South Seas*, and *West Indies*, is the only empire Britain should contend for;—troops drafted into islands, where from the nature of the climate, and establishment of the inhabitants, they cannot mingle with the people, nor in any shape quit, or refuse their duty,—may answer a great, and good end, as auxiliaries; but once set upon a continent, and initiated, as well as invited to all the advantages of wide extended dominions, where they can settle *ad libitum*, are considerations worthy of much more attention than has yet distinguished our present ministers.—If these observations can point out to their conviction some errors, which have crept into their most recent measures with respect to the mode of carrying on the continental war in America;—there may yet be pointed out a line of turning the current of war into an advantageous channel to Britain, before the opening of another campaign.

The number of adventuring foreigners, which have emigrated from Europe, to join the American cause is astonishing, Mr. Editor, and they continue to flock thither, particular[ly] from Germany, France, and Holland, as well as from Great Britain, and Ireland, the views of France, and Spain are deep, and interested in this scheme, because if they can lengthen out the war until a third power genders, and takes root on the continent, it answers every end to them they wish, which is division;— they are ready, or nearly so, in their West India colonies, to take the first advantage they see will answer the purpose of distressing Britain in those regions. Their present mode of encouraging piracy and depredations by their own people, fitted out under American colours, and the distresses our trade and plantations suffer in those seas, are too alarming not to merit more attention, and some spirited measures. One thousand eight hundred foreign emigrants, within these three years have joined the American cause. This is a fact I have, Mr. Editor, in my power, if necessary, to ascertain. It is therefore high time for this country to act with resolution and vigour, to defeat the views and purposes of her hereditary natural foes, and to come to speedy measures to re-unite, if possible, the mother country with her natural offspring by means adequate and honourable to both,—is the ardent wish and prayer of

GUSTAVUS VASA

Anderton's Coffee-house, August 4

....

3. *The Morning Post, and Daily Advertiser*, 7 November 1777

For the MORNING POST

Mr. EDITOR,

Last Tuesday, between two and three o'clock in the afternoon, going from St. Paul's to Charing-cross, in Fleet-street I perceived the passengers on each side the street looking earnestly, with a mixture of surprize that bespoke amazement, indignation, contempt, and such other sensations as different minds are agitated with on beholding an object that calls up immediate astonishment from its appearance. This *phenomenon*, which called forth the attention of every creature that beheld it, and seeing every eye directed to the street behind me, I, of course, turned round,—and was in a moment planet-struck at the object which thus attracted every eye.—The windows and doors were as full of gazers as if it had been Lord Mayor's day, or any new solemn procession.—The subject of their astonishment was indeed new,—and to me appeared to be an *exotic* of the neuter gender; for no one, to behold it, could possibly determine in their own mind whether it was *male* or *female*, and yet it had something of the resemblance of a production, wherein some of the human species had a share in its formation.—A good looking old *English Gentleman*, who stood by me, said, It was a young *British Nobleman*, who had lately returned from his travels. On which an honest *Hibernian* who stood near us, exclaimed, 'By *Jasus*, Sir, I beg your pardon for contradicting you (quoth Paddy); for by my shoul [soul] I take it to be one of the new animals brought home by some of your curious voyagers; who, as is said, have *crossed* round the world, and have brought home some of the strange creatures found in their way when they came through the northwest passage, by the *Archipellago of St. Lazarus*.—The creature must be the production of a southern climate, for sure I am such a beast never was vegitated in a northern soil!' 'Troth (said a studious looking *Scot*, who overheard the Irish Gentleman) I am entirely of your opinion, Sir; for I will be crucified if there is a single atom of the human composition of either of our country folk in sick a strange monster as that thing is; for although it has at first sight a something of the human species in its figure, on a close view of its features you will find yourself disappointed, and on contemplating a little more, you will perceive that from its stupid, indolent look, mixed with the appearance of a self consequence in its mode of gazing upon the spectators, as it is carried along; that it has nothing of the *vive risible* features of any of the monkey, or mangumbo kind.' At which my Hibernian friend cried, 'Stop, stop! I did not tell you it was a monster! and see, my jewels, the owner drives it in that *phaeton* round the streets, as Astley does his great little horse, before he advertises it for a public shew.' Thus ended our conversation.—The being, Mr. Editor, whatever it was, sat upon the left hand of an old man, whose features denoted that of a worn out *Compagnion de Voyage*, and lover of *virtu*. The creature had a man's hat on its head, which was covered, in appearance, with human hair, dressed in the *degagee* courtezan taste, plaited up behind, and its locks carelessly flowing on each side;— over its carcase was thrown a long mantle, seemingly of white freeze cloth, a large cape round its shoulders, with a broad gold lace, and down its breast, or foreside, the lace was continued to its *hoofs* or *toes*. Its face, as already mentioned, had something of a human cast, but of a mixture of features entirely new; its nose was longer than *common*, its complexion seemed made up with *fucus's*, or cosmetics of different kinds; but there broke thro' their colourings a species of sallowness that bespoke its natural *hue*, between the copper and brass-looking skins of old people, who had been long used to paint, notwithstanding the creature cannot be old; its eyes looked something like those of a dead cod,—its mouth rather large, and it grinned not to laugh, but to shew its teeth, which appeared tolerable white. Behind the phaeton stood two well dressed footmen, in green liveries; on the carriage was a coat armour of distinction, and a crest on a *chapeau*. It seemed to chatter to the person who drove it slowly along, as if to give time to the spectators to examine it. The only thing it moved was its lips and head, which it turned from side to side, and seemed to stare at the people with an unmeaning, cold, contemptuous look, as if they were creatures below its notice. This makes me think it is an animal of pitiful pride, full of its own consequence, and deeply in love with itself; for it appears fretful and surly.—These hints may lead some of your learned readers, and lovers of natural history, to inquire into this animal's species and generation, as well as into its place of nativity; whether it be an *amphibi*, or a terrestrial; whether quadruped, or aduped; or whether it may really be a young person of fashion of these times, or what it really is.—I am not, upon my honour, Mr. Editor, any way concerned in the property of this creature, and therefore I hope you will think I do not send you this, in order to get money, by raising the public curiosity, before it be advertised for exhibition,—if it is brought hither for that purpose from beyond seas. I remain,

Sir, your most humble servant,

GUSTAVUS VASSA

Peel's Coffee-house,
Fleet-street, October 30th

4. *The Morning Post, and Daily Advertiser*, 1 January 1778

For the MORNING POST

To Lord NORTH

LETTER I

My Lord,

The turn American affairs have taken, notwithstanding the variety of advice, and information your Lordship has received from the

New England pensioners, to which so much ear has been given, and in whom so much confidence has been trusted, proves that error, or something worse, has operated amongst those who followed, and abetted the system adopted for bringing back to their duty the rebellious Americans.

It is a matter of little consequence to the aggregate body of the British empire, whether your Lordship, or Lord George Germaine, or any other is officially *ostensible* for measures immediately issuing from their departments in administration since his Majesty consigns the superintendency of the whole administration to a Premier, your Lordship is that chief of the King's Ministers.

It is therefore that no scheme, no plan, nor no measure can meet with approbation, or success or be in any way adopted, without your knowledge and concurrence.

A time draws near, when a justification of the fatal measures pursued during the course of this unlucky war will be demanded (I speak not, my Lord, as a modern *patriot*, for I despise the tribe) of Administration; and I am well aware, *Sir*, will be had.

A people who, by excess of freedom, are daily approaching to the verge of slavery, are, my Lord, more formidable than, I fear, your wisdom and sagacity have penetrated.

And however well cloathed Administration may be, by the united sovereign power and concurrence of Parliament, it is nothing new, in this country, to see Ministers deserted, and reduced to pitiful plight:—The present mode of parliamentary representation sufficiently authorizes this suggestion.—I blame not your Lordship for having any hand in changing to corruption and venality, either the spirit of the *electors*, or those they make a choice of to represent them. These premises drawn, we need not wonder at the clamours of the present demagogues of opposition; their political refinement on our constitution, with other like great changes, we owe to the glorious, immortal revolution, which opposition so much idolize.

As the Premier of the day, my Lord, it is a matter of surprize, and wonder, you should not be better informed respecting the original, and true state of America; as a man of business,—of calculator,—and an adept in financing, it is strange you do not yet understand the great commercial *line of interest* between *America*, and *Great Britain*.—To have been led into such chimerical schemes, and plans, as have been adopted in your *reign*, discovers at least a want of superior abilities. This, my Lord, is not the season of mediocrity; I shall not conceive an idea of your having any other view, than that of being a faithful servant of the Crown, and a good Briton.

Look for a moment to the rise of this war, behold that dreadful supineness, which conducted its first campaigns in America; the war began in New England, in New England it should have immediately *ended.*—No reason can be given for breeding, fostering, and abetting *rebellion.*

General Gage either sacrificed, or had it not in his command to exert his strength, and power, or rebellion never would have been what it is;— why was not *Boston* afterwards supplied with sufficient troops to keep that important *station.*

The retreat to *New York*, and the plans afterwards adopted to send such an expedition as went through Canada, is full of ignorance, full of absurdity, and I wish they may not turn out designs inimical to the sovereign dignity of this country in its contrivance; when New York was in our possession, a few troops from Canada were sufficient to possess them of *Ticonderoga*; that post gained, they need attempt no further.—The British arms could with ease have reached Albany, and its environs; but great Ministers, my Lord, do not think it worth their while to become *geographers.*—Why did not Gen. Sir William Howe attack Mr. General Washington, with nearly equal numbers? You will perhaps say, Sir William Howe is of the *Fabian* line; if so Mr. Washington is no bastard;—but it was necessary to wear out the war, to sacrifice to avarice, not only this country, but many thousands of excellent subjects;—and those who gain by *legal spoil*, if they survive, will laugh at poor old England, as do, my Lord, your modern chiefs of patriotism for whom you care not a button,—because they only gull the credulous, ignorant, and unwary, with the tale of a *tub*; who labour to sell those whom they have bought for seven years,—and indeed that is the only plausible excuse which can be made for them: I speak only of those chiefs, who bring in auxiliary adventurers to assist them in their parliamentary opposition.—A few enthusiasts, who have native interest, are to be pitied for their folly, and imbecility.

Had an expedition from New York taken place, in concert with the taking of *Ticonderoga*, Mr. General Gates's army would, if they would have stood, have been in the same humiliating state, which Gen. Burgoyne's army is in now.—The principal expedition necessary to forward the King's interest, and the service of this country, should have been carried on from New York to *Albany*, and *further*, for a tenth part of the expence it has cost from *Quebec*, to where the British *army* were made prisoners; but that would not have answered the end of those, who contrived this diabolical plan.

I address this to your Lordship as *Premier* only; when I have done with you, my Lord, I will of course address your colleagues.

December 27, 1777

GUSTAVUS VASSA

....

5. *The Morning Post, and Daily Advertiser*, 4 March 1778

For the MORNING POST

Mr. EDITOR,

FACTION, opposition, and mock patriotism are at last drove into confusion, by Lord North's Reconciliation Bill.—Whatever serious effect Administration may hope to derive from it, I know not: but I trust the wisdom of the Ministry foresaw, that before it is published in America, those Colonies in rebellion will be convinced thoroughly, it is their interest to reunite themselves, upon liberal terms, to the mother country.—It is high time not only to shew the world, that wisdom only guides the helm of the state, but that resolution, and a speedy exertion of power, shall convince our natural enemies of the national indignation for their perfidy and infidelity to *Britain*, for the part they have so long acted with impunity, to aid, supply, and support the Rebels in America.—By cutting off all communication between the rebellious *Americans*, and *France* and *Spain*, or any further intercourse, either in *Europe*, or the *West Indies*, these deluded people will soon return to their duty, and they may yet make *Britain* amends for the losses sustained during this disagreeable war.—No man, but an enemy to the *British monarchy*, can wish *America* to be independant, merely because our Ministers may not have been so fortunate, and successful as those who directed the last war.—I own I have felt very sensibly for the loss of many opportunities I have seen slip, since the commencement of the *American* troubles, by which they might have been ended; but I have the charity to believe, that our Ministers have done as much as their line of abilities could lead them to do.—It is not every age that produces a *Sully*, or a *Marlborough*, nor so fortunate a Minister as *Pitt*. The current of fortune drove furiously for a time in the last Minister's favour; but, *alas!* he has lived to see that his former system of politics, altho,' in war—successful, became, when reduced into *a peace*, the means of blasting all the laurels he had acquired for his country.—May the present set of Ministers profit by his example! May they be able to conquer from the common, and hereditary foes of *Britain*, with equal rapidity, all those valuable islands, which were sacrificed, at the end of the last war, for Mr. *Pitt's* favourite *Canada*. *Britain* is formed by nature to be the Empress of the Main, and the Sovereign of Islands; but it is contrary to every idea, that even common sense can form, to imagine a commercial, limited monarchy, should grasp at the unlimited empire of a continent like *America*.—If the Commissioners, who are to carry the Reconciliation Bill to *America*, can announce, that *Britain* is determined to revenge herself immediately on her perfidious enemies, where she can at once crush their marine power, I should not be surprized to hear of Gen. *Washington*, and his whole army having joined the Royal Standard at *Philadelphia*, or *New York*, by the middle of *May* next; otherwise the Commissioners, and their Missionaries may, if they please, use all the Acts of Parliament they carry to *America*—for a certain purpose!

GUSTAVUS VASSA

....

6. *The Morning Post, and Daily Advertiser*, 10 March 1778

For the MORNING POST

To Lord NORTH

*Is e Mian Naduir gu Graidhamid ar Duthick

LETTER II

My Lord,

We are taught by nature the love of our country! Such was the reply of *Galgacus* to *Caesar*, when he accused the *British Prince* of temerity, and boldness, for driving the Romans out of *Caledonia*; but, *alas*, my Lord, what shall we say of you, at a time when the soul of loyalty, native valour, and love of their country, animated every gallant spirit that breathes the air of free born Britons, from utmost *Thule* to Dover *Cliffs*, when the Sovereign had it in his power to command the lives and fortunes of every real lover of constitutional liberty, to support, and sustain the dignity of the British Empire, and to reduce audacious disobedience, and rebellion to a state of lawful, and natural obedience?

---

* Old British manuscript, from which Tacitus took the famous speech of Galgacus.

At a moment when the torrent of good fortune was breaking in upon the efforts of your Sovereign, to bring back to their duty a race of unnatural, and ungrateful bastards, in order that they might be in due time legitimised;—at such a crisis to offer, in the face of a British Parliament, *terms of humiliating reconciliation*, beggars, my Lord, in my mind, all description *of pusilanimity*, if not depravity in the management of the public cause.

The bill you have brought into parliament, as a measure of reconciliation between Britain, and her revolted Colonies, lays down a precedent for any, or all the nations of Europe, to consider them as an independent people, confessing by your own tacit acknowledgement, that they are invincible.—It was all they wanted, my Lord; and they will speedily shew you, that they have the wisdom, and gratitude to despise your measures, notwithstanding they are sanctified by the consent of parliament.

I have long seen, and lamented, my Lord, that you little know the people you have to deal with, and that you will not be advised by men who are really willing, and able to give you a true idea of American virtue.—If the terms you offer are accepted by the Congress, you may live to see the most populous streets in London overgrown with grass. The Americans only wanted an opportunity to depopulate Britain and Ireland. Your reconciliation bill, my Lord, effectually opens a new avenue to the grateful Americans,—to draw from this country every subject worthy of their acceptance. It were a thousand degrees better for Britain, that America was separated from us for ever, than for them only to be nominal subjects.

Take courage, my Lord! carry on the war with spirit, only change its present channel.—The Americans will sue for *mercy, peace*, and *protection*.—Revive again the fire of true patriotism, which you have nearly extinguished. Let the British lion once more be fairly roused; give the command of the army, and navy to men of spirit, courage, and abilities;—let the fury of our revenge fall where it ought to do, on the perfidious House of Bourbon:—then, my Lord, you will truly merit the name of a great, and good Minister!

March 5

GUSTAVUS VASSA

....

7. *The Morning Post, and Daily Advertiser*, 11 June 1778

For the MORNING POST

Mr. EDITOR,

DURING this vacancy of politics, the following essay may afford many of your enlightened readers some amusement.—The other day I was agreeably entertained by the conversation of some ingenious gentlemen, of the *British*, and *Irish* nations.

The discourse turned upon the antiquity, and origin of the inhabitants of their different countries. Woes me! quoth I, who am not a native of either of the happier isles, but a continental spawn of accident; I can only be an humble hearer in this grand dispute.—The Englishman, as a matter of right, began; said he, I am firmly of opinion, whatever innovations have crept in amongst us, by the propensity of our mothers to novelty, the original inhabitants of Britain were all of them *True-born Englishmen*; and as to the people called by *Tacitus* and other Historians *Aborigines*, I am, with that illustrious author, of opinion, their origin is very difficult to trace.

A *Scotch gentleman*, with great humour, agreed with the English gentleman, that *Tacitus* was very just in his remarks upon the difficulty of tracing, with any degree of certainty, the origin of *True-born Englishmen*; for, said he, altho' no nation on earth produced more originals than Old England, she might challenge all that ever wrote of antiquity, or that ever may write, to give any thing like a true account, who were the *Aborigines* of that part of South Britain called *England*.—A gentleman of Ireland, happy to find an apt occasion to speak of his *Milesian* descent, "By my shoul, said he, you have hit him home: I will soon shew you, gentlemen, how your whole nation of Britain was originally peopled by the descendants of *Milesius*;—first of all, we peopled Scotland out of Ireland with *Milesians*, and then we sent a few tribes over to England, in order to people that country too: You may therefore rest satisfied, that all of you are originally of Irish Aborigine, for there is no doubt but the Irish nation was the first, and only nation in those seas whose first people was taught to walk upright, or as I may say, go upon their *hind legs*."

An ancient *Briton*, who was rather impatient to hear the Irish Gentleman's mode of peopleing Great Britain, said, "Sir, I allow that no nation on earth satifies their appetite with false, and unfounded notions of their antiquity more than those Irish, who call themselves *Milesians*; for the truth is, you have no documents of any date that can be said to savour of antiquity: all your accounts of yourselves are merely tales of a *tub*. *Look you*, my friend—for we have undeniable records, and stubborn facts, to prove, that Wales did people all South-Britain, as the original *Albions* did that of *North-Britain*; for to be plain, and pleasant with you, we never had any great notion of your *Milesians*, as you call them; and as to you, Mr. True-born Englishman, it is nothing new from your motley tribe, to speak with ingratitude of your founders, since ye know not one in ten thousand of ye who were your *mothers*, much less who were your *fathers*.

"Moreover it is clear, that neither *Scotland* nor *Wales*, could possibly have been peopled from southern climes. Who the devil would quit a land of *milk* and *honey*, to live upon *clifted rocks*, and mountains of *ice* and *snow*? Besides there is nothing but the dialect, that affords the least affinity between the fat, brawny, fleshy *Milesian*, and the iron-faced hardy *Scot*, or the short, stout, athletic raw-boned *Welshman*. The true spirit of the north is perseverance, and conquest. The northern nations have often re-peopled all Europe; and as ungrateful as their colonies and children have ever been to them, after they planted them in rich soils, and forgetting their origin by being sunk in luxury and vice, they always find fresh supplies of natural veterans to guard them in times of danger, and secure their legal freedom. Another proof that no people of the north could ever originate from the south, is, that even the Roman empire with all her legions, never could entirely subdue *Wales*, nor did they ever get above a third of Scotland; when they were so tired of their futile attempt during near 400 years, that at last they evacuated Britain, as an unconquerable nation. In what period of history can the Milesian valour speak to such a subject, I would be glad to know look you," said the ancient Briton?

"We have no instance since the Romans of any nation of spirit coming from the south to the north, to conquer barren mountains and leave fertile fields. It is much more likely, that the Scots bordering upon Ireland, made at various times descents into that rich country, and finding it a happier climate and soil than their own, remained amongst the natives; and hence the old Irish acquired their barbarous language; for the *Erse* affords not any thing to discover its affinity with any southern ancient languages, but continues to be spoken in all the remote parts of the northen nations, particularly among the Delicarlians of *Sweden*, and thence to the northern *Tartars*."

GUSTAVUS VASSA

Hungerford Coffee-house,
June 9, 1778

....

8. *The Morning Post, and Daily Advertiser,* 23 June 1778

For the MORNING POST

A MILITARY PARALLEL

Mr. EDITOR,

YOU have lately indulged me with a place in your paper; I could not therefore resist my propensity for sending you the following short *Gallic* piece of history, as it does honour to the chief who commanded the *Gauls* at that time.

But it brought into my mind a groupe of things, which a short essay can but poorly explain. To tell you, that I have been a *Soldier,* would be of no consequence, unless I told you, that I have been a commander of men. Battles and sieges I have frequently been in; and sometimes I have been eminently successful, Mr. Editor. I never quitted the field unsuccessfully but once—that fatal day ended all my hopes of glory! and I soon beheld myself in a different point of view to what I had looked at myself before. Indeed it may have been for me a happier change, otherwise unavailing pride, loaded with vanity, and embroidered with self-conceit, might in time have made a very ridiculous fellow of me.

You may remember I long ago reprobated the idea of an expedition from *Canada* across the Lakes. There were but two principles upon which I could possibly see it founded: the one was speculation, without a shadow of real knowledge of the undertaking; the other was a superficial knowledge of some flattering parts, supported by an amazing fund of self-applause, in imagining the possession of superlative ability merely because of being by the stroke of the hand of Providence, the child of Good Fortune. I would not have dared to have solicited my Sovereign for such command, much less, Mr. Editor, professed the imbecility of planning so moonshine-like an expedition. You will perhaps say no, because you profess yourself an old soldier: I say that is not the fault of those who set the Canadian expedition on foot as it was carried into execution.—But to the story of Belgius the Gaul.

Belgius with his clans having left their native country in search of a more favourable clime, (for they had little or nothing to eat at home) undertook, without any heavy *artillery,* to traverse the alps; a region which nought but *Hercules* ever had attempted, and for which *Hercules* was deemed a god. The glory of the *Gallic Chief* was only to be thought amongst the first of men. Pardon the reflection, Mr. Editor; those Gauls were called Barbarians; alas! how they differed from our modern heroes. Our great moderns write long letters, and tell you a story that fills two or three sheets of paper about taking a few old iron guns, and killing some forties or fifties of men. Oratory, and senatorial eloquence, are necessary to make a Christian General of our day. But a General of Gaul could neither read, nor write, else why call them Barbarians? yet they could manage such expeditions, and make such conquests, that no nation before them, nor since their time, have equalled. Had *Belgius* been at Saratoga, I should not have had occasion to have quoted this part of his history. *Ptolomy*, King of *Macedonia*, was the only monarch who "treated the irruptions of the Gauls into *Italy* and *Greece* with contempt. The Gauls having sacked *Rome*, and laid the *capitol* in *ashes*, turned their face to Greece, having heard of *Alexander's* fame; they were told *Macedonia* was rich with the spoils of the world!—Quoth *Belgius*, 'my brothers, friends, and fellow soldiers, let us find out those *Macedonians*, and share at least the plunder of the universe with them.—I wish to meet a brave people in arms, it is no mark of a true soldier to look with indignation and contempt on an enemy with whom he is not at war!' 'None,' said he to *Mulucha Minichan*, his companion, 'are invincible but the Gods! We are, my fellow soldier, but men! and it is beneath a chief of *Gauls*, my brother, to be proud, and full of mean arrogance, because the Gods may have occasionally crowned him with fortune, and fame. A man of pride is but a shadow, which perishes as he rises into fortune's lap; but wisdom, modesty, and perseverance will crown the possessor with endless glory!'—The Gauls were now on the borders of *Macedon*, and *Belgius*, their leader, sent ambassadors to *Ptolomy*, who treated them with disrespect and arrogance, because their mission was to offer peace, provided the Macedonian King would give a moderate price for it! *Ptolomy's* vanity was raised to such a pitch at the demand of peace, that he told his people, the *Gauls* after their long march and great fatigues, were afraid to come to a battle. 'Besides,' said he, 'they dread the very name of a *Macedonian* soldier': and to the ambassadors, he answered, 'ye shall have no peace unless your principal officers are left as hostages, that your people shall lay down their arms!' The ambassadors returned to *Belgius*, and told him what had passed; that *Ptolomy* in a rage, cried out, 'What, shall *Macedon*, who gave laws to the wide and extended world, treat for a peace with a few tribes of undisciplined bare ar[se]d Gauls? no! away, away!'—The Gauls could not forbear a general laugh throughout the army at this reply!

   " '*Ah!*' said *Belgius*, 'is it so *Ptolomy* replies to us?—The Gallic legions will teach the mistaken proud *Ptolomy* manners and humility, to his superiors;' and turning to his army, says, 'Gauls, will ye fight, or will ye become the captives of *Macedon*? What say ye, my children of the North!

will ye follow me, and make your way through the mighty phalanx of Macedonia, or will ye afford them a triumph, and become their slaves?'—The *Gauls*, shouting with one voice, cried, 'Conquest, or death!—*Belgius* lead on!'"—The Gauls were not more than 30,000, the Macedonians 200,000: the Gauls were far from home, ill cloathed, ill fed; with no arms but the short black spear and a lance: The Macedonians were armed with all the new-invented arms of Alexander the Great, and every other invention of defence used in those days; well cloathed, and well fed.—For all this the Gauls gained a compleat victory, and *Belgius* immortal honour!

GUSTAVUS VASSA

....

9. *The Morning Post, and Daily Advertiser*, 2 July 1778

For the MORNING POST

REVERSE OF FORTUNE

Mr. EDITOR,

AN illustrious person, whose early misfortunes, from the mistaken zeal, and principle of his predecessors, obliged him to become a man of the world, and to endeavour the enquirement of such treasure, as no mortal power could deprive him of, while life remained, travelled Europe, Asia, Africa, and America, as a merchant, and philosopher; both honourable characters, and both of infinite advantage to society!

In his youth he was bred to arms, and bore a distinguished rank before he was twenty years old. A series of misfortunes changed his turn of mind, and he felt a secret pleasure in pursuing, unknown, a scheme of life becoming a private gentleman.

At Cairo, in Egypt, he fell in with the following adventure, amongst many others which he met with; and, as it brought him to the possession of a friend, whose misfortunes in youth arose from the same cause with his own, their meeting may afford many feeling hearts a sympathy unknown but to virtuous minds, and a contemplation, which none but the wise can reach.

Our traveller had an interpreter, Mordecai, an Armenian Jew, who was likewise a child of sorrow, having once been a merchant of great worth, and reputed a man of honour, tho' a *Jew*. He lost his fortune by the hand of Providence, in a storm, and now for bread became an interpreter.

As they were passing in the streets of Cairo, a great multitude stood round an old, venerable, tall man, whose hair, as white as the milk-white lamb, hung careless round his shoulders: he sung, with a melodious voice, a melancholy tune, in a tongue which none round him could understand; but so powerful and fascinating was his harmony, and so commanding of respect was his countenance, and manner, that the rude rabble of Cairo stood with an awful muteness round him, which at once bespoke a mixture of pleasure and venerable admiration!

"Mordecai," (said the traveller,) "who is that fine old prophet, whom the ruffian mob of Cairo stand so silent to hear?" "Ah! my Lord," (said Mordecai), "he is like me, a child of dire fortune!—That venerable wanderer, Sir, was once in a most exalted line of life, tho' now he earns his *quotidien*, by singing his mournful, pleasing, harmonious ditties to the ruffian tribes of Cairo. When I was in India, in the days of my prosperity, that noble Christian was prime Minister, and General to one of the first Sovereigns in the East. His wisdom, and valour, rendered him the admiration of all good men, Mahometans, Gentoos, Jews, or Christians, as he was the dread, and envy, of all villains, of either sect or religion. Tho' generally victorious, he never appeared lifted with pride; nor at reverses, some of which he met with, was he ever dejected. I have seen him at the head of 50,000 victorious troops. Once I saw a letter he wrote after a battle to his Sovereign,—'*I have vanquished the enemy, by the valour of your soldiers!*'—After a series of long services, his Prince permitted him to retire, with a vast treasure, acquired by honourable means, and the liberality of his sovereign. He loaded a very large ship with his treasures, which he designed for Egypt, from thence to remit them to France, where he intended to go, altho' he is a native of some northern nation.—But, alas! how uncertain is human grandeur!—he fell in with a nest of pirates, who attacked his ship, who after a desperate engagement took her, with all his wealth, stripped him naked, and put him on shore, covered only with wounds!—The very barbarians of our Egyptian shore took pity on him! and you behold him now, fallen from what he was, to what he is!"—The traveller let fall the sweet tear of sympathetic compassion! Mordecai, with uplifted eyes, and hands, exclaimed, "O God of Abraham, what a poor creature is man!"

The traveller drew near the subject of their observation. In his countenance, tho' furrowed with age, and sorrow, he could trace the lines of a face at once familiar to his *ken*. It was the companion of his youth, the illustrious son of—.

This meeting would be too tender a tale for me to relate; but, after an absence of thirty years, two sincere friends met, and now enjoy, with each other, the satisfaction of retirement, and that happiness, which virtue only can afford.

The song he sung to the tawney mobility of Cairo, was the following, to the Tune of "*Lochaber no more!*"*

> LET mortals take warning whom splendor adorn,
> Nor virtue, nor valour, secures them from *scorn*;
> When *Fate* has decreed them to pay an auld score,
> Like me, they may wander on some foreign shore!
>   If virtue's allied to a life without blame,
> And laurels obtain'd, without thirst of fame;
> Tho' Fortune's turn'd cruel, I had them *galore*;
> E'er plunder'd and ruin'd, on Egypt's fam'd shore.
>   Wherever I pilgrim, whate'er comes of me,
> Fair *Albion*! may blessings show'r ever on thee,
> May thy sons fam'd for valour, as always of *Yore*,
> Maintain their great fame,—and from conquest their *shore*!
>   And, oh! may that *Scotia*, from whence I'm exil'd,
> Still flourish in virtue, tho' barren and wild;
> Her sons rich in honour, far distant explore,
> More worth than the di'monds on India's bright shore.
>   Ye daughters of ALBION, whose beauties disclose
> More sweets than the lillies, or soft blushing rose;
> Whose honour preserves you, from tainture or guile,
> Preserve that bold race, who will guard the *old isle*!

GUSTAVUS VASA

Hungerford Coffee-house,
June 27, 1778

....

---

* Mordecai had given the unfortunate chief as much ivory as made him tubes to a set of *bagpipes*, after the manner of the martial Highland *pipes*. On that instrument he often played to the wild Arabs, who seemed highly pleased with its rude noise. The traveller says, that the bagpipe was a Scythian instrument of martial music, which in preference to all others in those countries, finely figured, and distinguished in their statues, and bas reliefs.

10. *The Morning Post, and Daily Advertiser,* 10 July 1778

For the MORNING POST

Mr. EDITOR,

The arrival of General Howe has awakened the public anxiety, with an expectation of his reasons being made public for so long, and passive a conduct to the rebels in America. Mr. Howe, as a military man, will no doubt, for his own honour, give his reasons for not having given a decisive blow to rebellion during so many campaigns, and so many unavailing movements of his army.

All the military men of experience, and judgment throughout Europe, are puzzled to account for those delays, and procrastinations to a decisive action with Gen. Washington, which have marked the British General's operations through the different campaigns of his command. The intent of this essay is not to enter into the *minutiae* of Mr. Howe's generalship; but it is hoped he will step forth, and satisfy those, whose judgment, experience, and profession, entitle them to be satisfied of some doubts, that naturally hang round them at so unprecedented a mode of conducting a war.

I may venture to affirm, that no period of ancient, or modern history will furnish the most ingenious speculator with any thing that can be brought forward, as a parallel to the campaigns of which General Howe has had the command, for inactivity, and decision!

This war having been carried on upon entire new principles, military men of course are anxious to know its political, and military ratios: the British army has, on all hands, been acknowledged to have been every way qualified for attack, or defence; they were likewise the flower of our veterans,—soldiers, who had already traversed America, although not with the same Commander in Chief at their head. The rebel army, in opposition to them, admitting for a moment they were thrice the number of the British, were not in fact any way equal to them, either in experience, discipline, appointment, arms, ammunition, artillery, or implements of war, for attack, and defence. Let their bravery be deemed as high as possible, there is a want of steadiness in irregular troops, which nothing but a long military command, and the habit of war will diffuse through an army, so as to make them equal to stand a long and obstinate engagement. The British soldiers were equal to that; and with no disrespect to the Americans, I may say they had not yet acquired the necessary time by war to make them such veterans.

It is true, the mode in which they have been treated by the British army, has given them every encouragement which such an army could wish, to set a high value upon their own valour, and superiority; at a time, when in a manner destitute of arms, ammunition, cloathing, money, or permanent alliance, they were let lie a whole winter in camp within a few miles of the royal army unmolested, is sufficient reason for them to judge highly of their consequence in the eyes of the enemy.

What would the Roman Senate, or that of Carthage, have said to *Flaminius,* or *Hannibal,* and the one returned from *Asia,* or the other from *Italy,* after such campaigns as Mr. Howe has gone through?—I leave mankind to judge.—In what manner would *Augustus,* or *Julius* have treated a General, whose account must in effect have been no more than this?—"Sire, I embarked your army at New-York, and providentially your royal navy, under my brother's command, landed safe at Chesapeak Bay, when, with equal ease, they might have been landed from the Delaware; but that is not my business. I brought them, except a small skirmish, the which I could not avoid, safe to *Philadelphia,* their destination, where I cantonned them warmly, and snugly in winter quarters; there I made it my business to countenance, and encourage your Majesty's most inveterate enemies; to your friends, there was no need of encouragement—all rivitted to your cause by duty, and loyalty!—The enemy lay buried under snow in their huts, a few miles from us, ill cloathed, ill paid, and every way so despicably, and miserably appointed as an army, either fit for attack or defence, that it would have disgraced your Majesty's arms, and even shocked humanity to have routed the poor devils from their burrows, and cabins, until stores came to their aid, and some foreign reinforcements, to make them worth the notice of your troops to attack."

"Spring brought them into their camp in troops, and summer produced such legions, that I thought it adviseable to leave them the whole country to themselves, and re-embark your troops to New York and Long Island, as more healthful and excellent summer quarters, where diversions without molestation may be enjoyed. Having in all these things done my duty as a general, I am come home to breathe my native air, and to receive such applause and congratulations from my sovereign and country, as my eminent services for the state *deserve!*"

Poor Mr. Burgoyne has been denied the presence of his sovereign, for having saved his army from slaughter and death; but Mr. Howe has been received by his sovereign for his humanity, in not disturbing the poor American army in their winter cantonments, and restoring to the congress their original imperial seat of council, Philadelphia. Had the Duke of Cumberland in April, 1746, so treated the poor starved Highlanders, who for four days before the battle of Culloden, had not one man's proper provisions amongst six of them, the which his Highness well knew, instead of forcing them to a battle, and thereby breaking the neck of the rebellion,—what do you think King George the second would have said to his favourite son, Mr. Editor? You will say that was a different kind of rebellion perhaps; I own it. The clans were headed by men of honour and gentlemen, although unfortunately addicted to mistaken political principles. The Americans are a set of abandoned ingrates, without the shadow of either virtue or principle, to give colour to their rebellion; and unless it be some renegado from either of these three kingdoms, not a gentleman is there to be found in all their armies, that can tell where his grandfather was born; besides they are the sworn enemies of monarchy and Kingly government; no doubt in some measure pleasing in their principles to those who have treated them with such compassion and humanity.

It is time for administration to change their mode of choosing their Commanders in Chief, either for land or sea, and out of minority men! else woe will be the fate of poor Old England!

GUSTAVUS VASA

Hungerford Coffee-house,
July 8, 1778

....

11. To the Editor of the *Glasgow Courier*, 15 March 1792

SIR,

The adherents of the AFRICAN SLAVE TRADE appear now to be sensible, that they must reason upon the subject, and that mere exclamations and complaints against vain philosophy, and the enthusiasm of humanity, will no longer be regarded by the public. Among a few other attempts of this nature, I lately met, in your Paper, with a letter, under the signature of COLUMBUS, in which the writer boldly defends the practice of Slavery, and maintains that its abolition by Government would be contrary to justice. I shall beg leave to offer a few remarks upon that extraordinary performance; and if it should be found, that I belong to that unhappy race of men, who have been the object of this barbarous traffic, I hope the public will give the more indulgence to any errors or mistakes which I may fall into, or to any impropriety of expression which may escape me.

COLUMBUS begins with complaining, that his adversaries, instead of printing the *whole* evidence taken by the Committee of the Commons, have "garbled and selected such parts of it as suited their own views and purposes." It is submitted to the public, whether this be a candid insinuation. The abstract of the evidence, which has been published and circulated, is avowed to contain an abridgement of the evidence only that was brought by the Petitioners; but that it is an unfair or partial abridgement, no person, it is believed, will venture to allege. It exhibits a simple statement of the cruelties with which we have been treated, and the various enormities arising from the Slave Trade, in all its branches. The evidence brought on the other side, by adducing witnesses who, from their situation and rank, had not seen these enormities, can be of little importance. It is merely of a *negative kind*, which can have no weight in opposition to such a large and solid body of *positive testimony*. But if the supporters of the Slave Trade think otherwise, why have they not produced this negative evidence? Why do they complain of what they themselves might so easily rectify? Or rather, how can it be believed, that if this publication could have been of any service to their cause, it would not have appeared long ago? Would they have taken so much pains in retailing the misrepresentations in the Speech made by the white people of St. Domingo, and in spreading groundless reports of the insurrections and disorders committed by the Negroes in the other Islands, if they had been capable of producing any real facts to palliate their conduct, if they could have produced a single rag to cover them from the shame to which they stand exposed in the eyes of the whole world?

After this preface, Columbus opens his defence of Slavery, by observing, that Providence, for wise purposes, has formed mankind of different abilities and ranks, and linked them together in a chain of mutual dependence; from which he appears to conclude, that, in this chain, the Negroes were intended to be Slaves.

I am no stranger to this claim of *natural superiority* over my countrymen, which the white people are so ready to advance. But are not the many disadvantages we lie under, with regard to the cultivation of our minds, sufficient, in a great measure, to account for the inferiority of our endowments?

The superior education enjoyed by the free people of the West Indies, may, on the other hand, go some length in accounting for that superiority of talents, and for that refinement of manners, for which they are so much distinguished.

In how many parts of the world, are even white people plunged in utter darkness and barbarism? In what a miserable state were the Britons, when they admitted the practice of selling their own children? If the Negroes appear to the Europeans in a meaner light than other rude nations, it may be attributed to that very slavery into which they have been reduced, and by which their minds are peculiarly debased. May I not, at the same time, be permitted the vanity of observing, that Egypt, the nursery of science in Europe, was originally inhabited by people of similar colour and features to those unfortunate Africans, who are, at this day, treated with so much contempt?

But admitting that the Negroes are inferior in abilities to every other people upon earth, will it thence be inferred, that it is lawful to injure and oppress them, and to deprive them of those rights which belong to all other men? Is it by such a system of morality, that white men propose to demonstrate their superiority over the Negroes? Is it by a doctrine so absurd, that Columbus means to assert that rank of understanding, by which he supposes himself to be placed at the upper end of what he calls the chain of human dependence? Is wisdom given us by providence, that we may impose upon folly? Are we endowed with strength, that we may be enabled to prey upon the weak. Are we not all children of the same father, possessed of an immortal soul, equally accountable for the deeds done in this life? But it is observed by a great author, that Europeans have been in the right, not to allow us to be men; lest, if we were, a suspicion might arise that they are *no longer Christians.*

To prop a little the foregoing argument, from the natural inequality of ranks, your correspondent is pleased to mention, in justification of slavery, that it arose from the operations of war and conquest; "whereby[,"] he says, "captives became the property of the conquerors." Concerning this *right of conquest*, it is not my intention to employ many words. It seems now to be admitted by every person of a liberal mind, that superior force can never bestow upon a conqueror any right which he did not previously possess. To suppose the contrary, is to suppose that mere power is the foundation of right, and that every man is entitled to do whatever he has the opportunity of executing. According to this hypothesis, which, to the scandal of jurisprudence, was formerly too much countenanced, the people detained in slavery, whenever they acquire the power, have a right to cut their masters' throats; and, if on that occasion, instead of putting them to death, they should only oblige their masters to perpetual service, under the discipline of the *Jumper* [whip] it would be an act of lenity and mercy.

But Columbus has only touched upon these particulars, as he hastens to his main object, which is to prove, that if the Legislature shall abolish the African Slave Trade, it is bound, in justice, to indemnify the West India Traders for the loss which they may sustain upon that account.

The British government, he contends, has introduced and promoted this very slavery, and bestowed upon it the sanction of different acts of parliament. The planters and traders were, in that business, the mere tools of the Legislature, and purchased their estates, or employed their capitals, upon the faith of government; which, therefore, will be forfeited if, without their consent, that slavery, *how immoral soever and unjust in itself*, should be withdrawn and prohibited.

It may in the first place, be remarked, that this writer is guilty of a little misrepresentation, when he insinuates that government took the lead in the introduction of the African Slave Trade. It is well known, that when domestic slavery had been abolished in Europe, it was revived in America by the obstinacy of the European settlers, and in opposition to the remonstrances and prohibitions of the mother country. The settlers urged the necessity of slavery for procuring labourers; and my unfortunate countrymen, without any colour of justice, were dragged from a distant land, and substituted to the weaker and more effeminate natives of America.

The Spanish government first, and the other European governments afterwards, were obliged to comply with their refractory subjects, and to connive at an evil which they were unable to prevent.

But the times are now altered. The meridian beams of knowledge have now brought to light those enormous abuses, which were hid from the public eye; and the feelings of an enlightened age are shocked by a treatment of our fellow creatures so repugnant to the plain rules of justice. The interested clamours of avarice will no longer be endured; and men conscious of the iniquity of their former conduct, must be willing to atone for it, by hastening to abolish those practices, which they blush to have ever permitted.

With all my heart, says Columbus; let this trade be as wicked and unjust as you please. Let it be abolished whenever you think fit. But, the bond! The bond! Justice requires that we be indemnified.

In answer to this demand, I will beg leave to state a parallel case. In all the European Kingdoms, a few centuries ago, every feudal baron enjoyed the privilege of making private war, that is, of robbing and plundering all his neighbours. This privilege was universally admitted, and sanctioned by public authority. But in more civilized ages, a practice, so inconsistent with justice and good order, came to be entirely prohibited. Might not any one of those plunderers, with equal reason to your correspondent Columbus, have demanded an indemnification for the pecuniary loss which he sustained.

"I laid out my capital in this manner, I became a feudal baron, upon the faith of the law as it stood. I was but the tool of government, which encouraged and assisted me in settling in this part of the country. During a good michaelmas moon, I could have seized many hundred head of cattle; but of this, and all *similar* gains, I am now totally deprived. If my neighbours had offended me, I might have murdered or carried off their wives and their children. But I must now tamely put up with every affront. By these new-fangled and unjust regulations, there will be an entire stagnation of all the business of society."

What answer would a sovereign be entitled to make to any of his subjects who had the effrontery to talk to him in this manner? "You are mistaken in thinking that you have a right to rob, or steal, or murder. Though the public was obliged to temporize, and to connive at your practices, they could give you no right to commit crimes. But though the law was bad enough of itself, you have rendered it a thousand times worse by your abuse of it. Instead of indemnification you deserve punishment; and were you to meet with a proper retribution for your offences, the least you could expect is, in the language of the old Scottish historian, *that you should be justified.*"

Such is the answer which, I think, might with propriety be given to Columbus, were it proposed instantly to abolish the institution of slavery in the West Indies. But he knows very well that no such thing is intended; and he has taken a poetical license in stating the facts, that he might obtain the shadow of an argument from his own erroneous statement. The known intention of the proposed application to parliament is, not to abolish, but to regulate the servitude of the West India Negroes. When the further importation of Negroes is prohibited, the planters will be under the necessity of rearing from the slaves which they already possess, and of treating them with some degree of humanity. It is the universal belief that all other attempts for protecting this unfortunate class of men, in the European colonies, will be fruitless, and that all proposals of regulation, by the inhabitants themselves, are mere pretences which will have no effect after the present investigation shall be laid aside.

Now I would ask, whether the British government has a right from views of justice and utility to regulate the trade and manufactures of the kingdom? or whether every regulation of the national commerce must be accompanied with an indemnification to all those who pretend to be suffered by the alteration? When a tax is laid on claret, must the wine merchants be paid for the diminution of their trade in that article? When there is a prohibition of whisky, on account of its being prejudiced to the health or the morals of the people, must there be a pecuniary compensation to the distillers of that spirit, or to the growers of barley?

After all, it is time to inquire what reason Columbus has to apprehend any loss whatever from the proposed regulation. It is clearly proved that, with proper management, the stock of slaves already in the Islands will be sufficient to maintain itself. By allowing them some gratuity, as a reward for extraordinary labour, it is evident that their industry, their skill, and their dexterity, may be wonderfully increased. Thus, by a gradual alteration without any hazard of disorder, the condition of the Negroes may be improved; and even the prospect will arise, that their future emancipation, at a distant period perhaps, may be found of general advantage. At the end of the eighteenth century, when the British House of Commons are every day quoting the celebrated author of "the Wealth of Nations"; and when the eyes of the mercantile world are so much opened to perceive the mischievous tendency of monopoly and restraint in every branch of commerce, is it not a curious spectacle, to observe, that in every part of his Majesty's dominions, there still is a class of restrainers upon trade, so destitute of information, and so overrun with prejudice, as to imagine that the emancipation of the labourers, proceeding from the gradual operation of their masters, would not be beneficial change? I agree with Columbus in thinking that, in point of abilities, mankind are composed of different ranks. At the same time when Sir Isaac Newton discovered the true system of the universe, there were persons, of some education, who still believed in judicial astrology, and the influence of the stars. If the inferiority of un[der]standing in my countrymen lays a foundation for supposing them an *inferior race* to the whites, one would almost be tempted to believe, that there is no small variety of *races* even among the white people themselves.

GUSTAVUS

12.

OTHELLO

The Cabinet. By a Society of Gentlemen, 3 vols. (Norwich: Printed and Sold by J. March. Sold also by J.S. Jordan, Fleet-Street, London, 1795)

> Epigraph: "…The country claims our active aid; / That let us roam, and where we find a spark / Of public virtue, blow it into flame." Thomson

Preface addressed "To the Readers of the Cabinet," dated "Norwich, 17th Jan. 1795," opens, "No work in the English language, perhaps, ever appeared to the world, under circumstances more inauspicious and depressing than the CABINET." "But if tyrants did not read at Milan, do they not read in this country? Not indeed to improve their minds, or to learn the ends and purposes of the authority they are abusing, [1] but to mark for persecution and penalty a careless or unguarded stricture, a warm or intemperate remonstrance" [1–2]. [Charles Marsh (1774?–1835?)].

Mischievous Effects of War

War is a game, which, were their subjects wise,
Kings would not play at.   Bishop of London

Of all the the evils to which weeping humanity is liable, there is no one so much to be dreaded as war, whether we consider it in its most immediate effects, or in its remoter consequences. The truth of this proposition is too palpable to be disputed; nor is there an individual in Europe, whose mind is perfectly free, that does not at this instant deprecate the impending issue which this alarming calamity will produce. But without looking forward to what greater ills may happen, or anticipating sorrows that will too soon arrive—it is sufficient just to dwell for a few moments on the scene already before us, and contemplate the objects it presents.

To a sympathizing mind, what a picture is here! What horrors! What desolation continually opens to view! ... Where are those laughing fields that yesterday waved their golden heads, and bade the husbandman rejoice in an assurance of plenty? Alas! They are destroyed—trodden to the ground, and a de [174]sert remains in their place!—What is become of that noble city, which but a few days ago rose so majestically before us? Where its cloud-capped spires, which appeared to hail the traveller afar off, and its lofty turrets that bade him welcome on his near approach? What is become of those ramparts and fortifications which seemed to defy the destroying-hand of time? Where the sumptuous palaces and costly buildings which existed, the admiration and wonder of every beholder, on which the embellishments of art and the refinements of science had been so lavishly bestowed?—Where is the stately dome—the triumphal arch, through which the hero has oft been conducted, crowned with all the honors of victory? Where the magazines of stores and provisions that supplied a numerous people with the comforts of life? Where the habitations of the artist and mechanic—those schools of industry established for the promotion of universal happiness—for the benefit of all mankind? Ah! Where are they? Behold their ruins! Desolating war has almost levelled them with the ground! No habitation remains—no place where a human being can take up his abode! But, where shall we look for the living multitude that every day appeared in its streets, whose hands were continuously employed in the execution of those schemes which their minds had conceived for the diffusion of happiness among themselves and their fellow-creatures? Surely they are safe—they have been preserved from the general wreck—Alas! no—in defence of their rights and liberties, they were forced to take up [175] arms—but were unsuccessful! Behold, on yonder plains, how their mangled bodies strew the ground—there raged the dreadful conflict—incensed at the bold defence they made against numbers far greater than themselves, their unfeeling conquerors pursued their exterminating plan "til slaughter had no more to do!"

Brave unfortunates! let a stranger shed a tear over your hallowed remains. Your valour shall be remembered with respectful admiration, as long as virtue and liberty shall be esteemed among mankind.

This is not a fanciful picture, an imaginary thing—the scene is real—for a long time it has been exhibited, and is now exhibiting, to the view of all the world. Numbers of our fellow beings from every town and village in Europe have been victims in this fatal tragedy.—Our kindred and acquaintance still form a part in the dramatis personae, and wait the common chance of war.... In the name of heaven, why and for what are they reduced to this alarming situation? Is it necessary for the happiness of one part of the creation that the other part should be made miserable, or totally annihilated? Can such horrid devastation produce so much good to mankind, that instead of endeavouring to stop its progress, every nerve should be strained to make it more extensive? In the sacred name of humanity, which part of a community is it that benefits from such carnage? Is it the labouring poor? Certainly not—they can only expect fatigues and danger, and death, from it—they must bear every hardship and brave every difficulty,—there is no alter [176] native for them—"tis their's to bleed and die in quarrels not their own." Nor is it the honest industrious tradesman that is benefitted. What advantage does he obtain from the most successful war? None—the consequence to him is—decay of trade—decrease of fortune and accumulation of taxes.... If these two classes then, that form the great bulk of a nation, reap no advantage from wars, but on the contrary suffer considerably by them—which part of the community is it that are the gainers, that find an interest in fomenting broils between nations?—'Tis the pampered minion—the sycophantic courtier—the unprincipled placeman—the worthless pensioner, and an undeserving croud [sic], that riot in the distress and ruin of their *country*. It is these, and only these, that find a benefit in war—that feel a pecuniary interest in fomenting national quarrels.—These are the men that can take pleasure in such scenes of blood—that can exultingly laugh at "Victories for which the conquerors mourn, so many fall."

OTHELLO

Vol. 2, 174–7

Notes

1. Throughout this essay I refer to the author of *The Interesting Narrative*, Vassa/Equiano, to distinguish that persona from "Gustavus Vasa," "Gustavus," and "Othello."
2. For questions about the true identity of the author of *The Interesting Narrative*, see my "Olaudah Equiano or Gustavus Vassa?: New Light on an Eighteenth-Century Question of Identity," *Slavery and Abolition* 20 (1999), 96–105.
3. Sancho's letters to *The Morning Post* are reproduced in my "Three West Indian Writers of the 1780s Revisited and Revised," *Research in African Literatures* 29 (1998), 73–86. See also, *Letters of the Late Ignatius Sancho, An African*, ed. Vincent Carretta (New York: Penguin Putnam, 1998).
4. Carretta, "Three West Indian Writers," 77.
5. I thank Linda Coleman, Joan Radner, and Steven Rutledge for advice on Vassa's use of the Irish language and Classical references.
6. For an argument that one of the purposes Vassa/Equiano had in writing *The Interesting Narrative* was to claim the status of gentleman, see my "Defining a Gentleman: The Status of Olaudah Equiano or Gustavus Vassa," *Language Sciences* 22 (2000), 385–99.
7. All the known published and unpublished writings of Vassa/Equiano are reproduced in the revised and expanded edition of *The Interesting Narrative and Other Writings* (USA: Penguin, forthcoming 2003).
8. The March 20 response of "Columbus" to "Gustavus" went unanswered by the latter but elicited a March 27 reply from the pseudonymous "Cassius." I am very grateful to Iain Whyte for bringing this series of letters to my attention.
9. Contributors to *The Cabinet* are identified in Penelope J. Corfield and Chris Evans, eds. *Youth and Revolution in the 1790s* (London: Alan Sutton, 1996).

CHAPTER SIX

The Anonymous Novel in Britain and Ireland, 1750–1830

James Raven

This essay profiles anonymity in novel writing in eighteenth- and early nineteenth-century England. The great majority of these novels are, in literary terms, essentially worthless: their interest is entirely historical, as the colorful and ramshackle foot-soldiers in the advance of the novel during the Romantic period. Investigation of the writing, production, publication, circulation, and reception of these books offers a new understanding of many aspects of the cultural history of these years. For many, the writing of a novel was an apprentice piece—and one from which they did not always recover. Much of this fiction slavishly followed model forms, predictable and with restrained ambition. Several novels even seem to have been put together above the print-room—a few chapters from a hack writer, other parts culled from an old romance, something more translated from a foreign potboiler.[1] The reason for writing was sometimes spelled out in a preface or (not necessarily more succinctly) in a title page. The diversity of writers and circumstances matched the range of success and failure. A few novels were quickly reprinted; others were revived after a few seasons or achieved a limited success in the writer's own circle or locality. The bulk of these novels were soon left to gather dust, summarily disposed of, or returned, after brief reading, to the fashionable circulating libraries for which so many of them were chiefly written.

The following survey is based on a new bibliography of English prose fiction first published between 1770 and 1830.[2] An obvious difficulty with this sort of bibliographical spadework—however exacting its research procedures—concerns our definition of literary genre. The 'novel' has no rigid boundary—it can be pseudo-memoir, mock biography, short romance, children's tale, or fused with several other types of fiction (some, not in prose, but partly or wholly in verse or written in dramatic parts). This confusion of form, indeed, was particularly manifest in the eighteenth century, where the 'memoir' or 'history' embodied in the novel title was used deliberately to persuade of the realism and authenticity commended by readers and critics alike. What 'novels' were depends on subtle interpretation, then and now. Many elaborate or original productions required careful scrutiny before they could be categorized—if at all. At the same time, however, the 'novel' was increasingly secured in contemporary opinion as an acknowledged category of fiction. For periodical editors and reviewers the 'novel' also came to denote specific ideas of composition and purpose.

Use of the *Monthly* and *Critical* reviews and the notices from the later *Edinburgh* and *Quarterly* as basic arbiters to define the novel also tends to broaden the guidelines adopted by many fiction bibliographies, and it is with a slightly different ambit, therefore, that the completed bibliography for 1770–1829 complements previous volumes covering the period from 1700 to 1769.[3] Based on the eighteenth- and nineteenth-century review notices, booksellers' and printers' records, advertisements, and term catalogs, the bibliography has been further constructed from extensive searches of *ESTC*, *OCLC*, and hands-on stack work in hundreds of libraries worldwide. It includes many titles previously unknown, excludes many ghosts, and also lists, after consultation of reviews and printing records, many novels certainly published but no longer surviving in extant copy. Appendix 1 offers basic production totals of new novels, based on the imprint year given on the title page. Many volumes, of course, were predated to maintain the impression of freshness and so each "year" actually ranges over a period of eighteen months or more, overlapping with the earlier and later "year". To repeat, however, even at the time it was often impossible to improve on a general classification for many of these variegated publications. Many, indeed, were rehashed versions of older fictions. "Is it new? Is it old?" the *Critical* asked of *Melwin Dale* in 1786, "We confess we do not know".[4] The broad result of this work is to reexamine the categorization of prose fiction and to ask fresh questions about the authorship, production, and means of circulation of the new novels. We might look again at responsibility for this fashionable and, for many, this shocking thing called a novel. Who exactly were the novelists who fed the demands of ambitious booksellers and circulating librarians and created the rage for the novel in the age of Burney, Austen, and Scott?

One feature stands out immediately. On the basis of the new research, it is clear that the overwhelming majority of the English novels of the eighteenth and early nineteenth centuries were published without attribution of authorship either on the title page or within the preface or elsewhere in the text. As figures 6.1 and 6.2 show, over 80 percent of all new novel titles published between 1750 and 1790 were published anonymously. Only during the 1790s did admitted authorship increase, but even then the majority of writers (some 62 percent over the entire decade) hid behind an anodyne title-page mask, with many of the anonymous novels bearing a very general and unverifiable ascription. Thereafter, as charted by Figures 6.1 and 6.2 (and even more by the profiles of Figure 6.3), the trend continued so that during the first decade of the nineteenth century the sustained total of anonymously issued novels fell for the first time to under half of all new novels published. After about 1810, however, the proportion of anonymous novels increased again, returning by the late 1820s to about 80 percent of all annual new novel titles. An obvious challenge, then, posed by the new profiles of new novel production over these

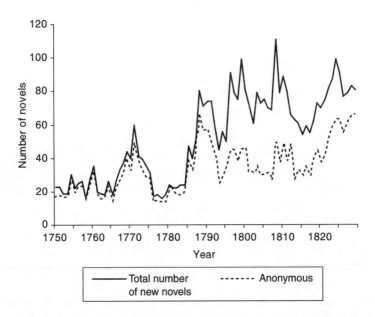

Figure 6.1   Total of new novel titles published compared to the number published anonymously, 1750 to 1829

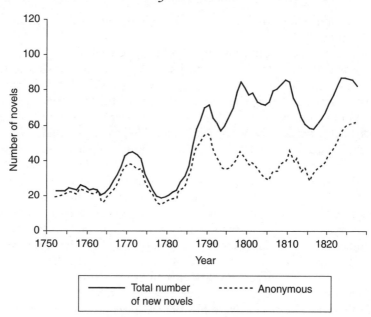

Figure 6.2 Total of new novel titles published compared to the number published anonymously, 1750 to 1829, five year moving averages

80 years is to explain first, why such a very high proportion of novels were first published anonymously, and second, why anonymity was reduced and then revived in the second half of this period.

Both questions turn in part on the degree of anonymity offered in novel publication. Despite the apparent clear-cut title-page distinctions suggested by Figures 6.1–6.3, we must caution against accepting absolute levels of anonymity. The absence of a name on a title page is not quite the same as saying that a reader was kept in the dark about the identity of a novel's author. Our new research base offers a profile of varying levels of anonymous publication, also revealing for the first time certain connections between hidden authors. Many novels carried references to earlier work by the same writer, declaring themselves to be "By the author of ..." This, in fact, has been a critical aid in unravelling relationships between works, even if some of these novels remain unattributable to a specific individual.[5] In other cases, the original anonymity of this "By the author of ..." device was unlikely to have been a secret to enthusiastic novel readers. Frances Burney's "faux-anonymous" *Camilla ... By the Author of Evelina and Cecilia* (1796) was hardly an unattributable

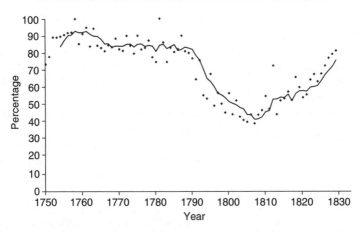

Figure 6.3   Anonymous novels expressed as a percentage of new novel titles, with five year moving average trend line, 1750 to 1829

publication for anyone with current literary interests. The repetition of the "By the Author of" tag on the title page of her 1814 *The Wanderer* was even less likely to limit appreciation of the novel's authorship.

In addition to issuing anonymous novels whose authors were an open secret or very easily discoverable, booksellers and writers adopted other devices of part-disguise and modest allusion. Amongst the three-quarters of all new novels of this period that were published without attribution, the vague and often highly dubious tag of "By a Lady" or "By a Young Lady" gained special popularity. Authors and their publishers resorted to this style with particular enthusiasm in the late 1780s, when the overall publication of fiction advanced markedly. In 1785, nearly a third and in 1787 nearly a quarter of all novel titles were said to be "by a Lady." These and other general gender descriptors cannot, however, be taken at simple face value. Several male writers assumed "young lady" title-page identity, and a few young women pretended to be male. In 1789, William Henry Hall published his tedious *Death of Cain*, an imitation of Gesner's *Death of Abel*, as "By a Lady," and was forced to repeat this (with the addition of "young") three years later for his *Pathetic History of Egbert and Leonora*. Arthur Gifford's 1785 *Omen* was puffed by its publisher, Lowndes, in the newspapers as "by a Lady," and in 1790 Henry Whitfield similarly accredited his *Villeroy; or, The Fatal Moment.*

Amidst this recourse to literary transvestism, a great many novels were boldly entitled "The First Literary Attempt of a Young Lady," especially where an introduction acknowledged the inspiration of a particular model like Burney or Richardson.[6] Prefaces frequently confessed to youth and inexperience. Novels published without any indication of authorship on the title page or in the preface or other preliminary matter, might also be announced in the bookseller's newspaper advertisement as by a juvenile or female hand. Perhaps because of the availability of these general identifiers, pseudonyms were not as prevalent as might be expected, even though it is possible that a small number still escape detection. In a few instances the authenticity of the name appearing on the title page cannot yet be confirmed—was there really a Harriett Squirrel (author of *Original Novels*, 1790)? Did Matilda Fitz-John (author of *Joan!!!*, 1796) ever exist?

The puzzles and absences on the title pages were obviously most apparent with *new* writing, older and reprinted fiction having a much greater chance of acquiring by design or accident author designations (whether or not they were actually the correct ones). But new writing, and hence a tendency to the non-declaration of authorship, was also the stock-in-trade of novel booksellers and circulating librarians. Given the market necessity of producing editions of about 500 or 750 copies only, the demand for new writing often seemed irresistible. Limitations of technology and the determination to avoid excessive risk encouraged booksellers to issue multiple editions of a popular work rather than an abnormally large single edition. The increase in new writing in the later years of this period inevitably brought more writers (although several popular and hack novelists also appear to have been more prolific than their predecessors). This, in turn, affected the proportion of novel titles published anonymously in as much as first-time and write-to-order authors were far more likely to withhold their name from the title page than were more proven writers.

Although difficult to explain further changes in the pattern of anonymity over these eighty years, investigation of the changing sociology of those authors that we can now identify (if only in terms of sex and general age) is suggestive. This is the more so given the gender-influenced disposition of the periodical reviewers. According to the published notices, women novelists might be led to expect leniency (and hence the attraction of a "By a Young Lady" tag), even though it sometimes resulted in shocked recoil from the critics. As Samuel Badcock wrote in the *Monthly* of the 1783 *Burton-Wood ... By a Lady* (actually by Anna Maria Mackenzie): "As this is a *first* attempt, and especially the first attempt of a *female* author, candour should repress the vigour of criticism, even though impartiality could not compliment with the warmth of applause."[7] Both periodical reviewers of the anonymous 1791 *History of Georgina Neville; or, The Disinterested Orphan* made open declaration of their leniency towards women writers before striking down the offering before them. "With all our partiality for female authors," began the *Critical*, "and our anxiety to raise a drooping or a promising genius, we cannot commend this novel." William Enfield in the *Monthly* decided that "this 'first literary attempt' of a young Lady is unquestionably intitled to some degree of indulgence, especially when it is made, as in the present case, under the protection of a long list of noble patrons. If the performance pleases Lords A. B. and C. and Ladies W. X. and Y. though it should not happen exactly to suit the notions of a few old-fashioned critics, who know little of the great world, it must please the ordinary class of readers; who, in judging of works of taste, certainly can wish for no better guides than people of the first fashion."[8] The further association of female authorship with work deemed to be corrupting must have convinced many novelists not to disclose their identity. Take, for example, the verdict of the *English Review* on *Illicit Love* of 1791: "Trash, vile trash!—and sorry are we to say that it is not harmless. The plan is immoral and pernicious—and the chief character is an *unprincipled scoundrel*. We must lament that such a production, which can only serve to corrupt and vitiate the female mind, should proceed from the pen of a *woman*."[9]

Much then, might hang on our retrieval of actual authorship in terms, most notably, of gender, but also of age and background. The profile of those prepared to admit to authorship suggests a motley society, but this is a mix widened even more by the total number of novels from this period with authors now identified (2,809 of 4,185). Taking the 80 years as a whole, novels were written by men and women in roughly equal numbers. Most novelists, not unexpectedly, were from the propertied classes. Beyond this, numerous identifications can be suggested. Writers included leisured gentlewomen, high-profile aristocrats, obscure vicars and curates, sea captains, destitute merchants' wives, reformed and very unreformed prostitutes, over-achieving adolescents, and pious autodidacts. Notably upfront in bearing authors' full names on title pages and prefaces were the several novels by juvenile writers. Minors included Anna Maria Porter, thirteen when *Artless Tales* was written and published in 1793, and Miss Nugent and Miss Taylor of Twickenham, authors of the 1779 *Indiscreet Marriage*, and whose combined ages were said not to exceed thirty.[10] Elizabeth Todd was eighteen when her *History of Lady Caroline Rivers* was published in 1788. Some youthful claimants, however, offered somewhat fanciful claims, and ones hiding behind non-attribution. The non-surviving *Revolution* of 1781 apparently opened with a preface declaring it to have been written by a deceased teenage laborer of no formal education.[11]

Regional loyalties were also occasionally stressed, presumably to encourage the local market, but also to give provincial authenticity to the novel and its author. For her ninth novel, *The Neapolitan*, in 1796, Anna Maria Mackenzie disguised herself as "Ellen of Exeter;" amongst various other examples, Anne Julia Kemble published all her 13 novels issued between 1810 and 1828 anonymously, and all but two as "Ann of Swansea" (four of which, forming no obvious sequence, adopted a final "e" on Ann).[12]

The other obvious feature of novel writers in the early decades of this period was the financial security of most households—something that changed markedly in the later years, with many more novelists attempting to eke out a living by writing (and directly affecting the proportion of writers anxious to remain anonymous). Over a fifth of the writers with novels published between 1750 and 1770 were born into families able to live off private incomes rather than enter trade, the Church, or the law. Only 16 of these 116 writers were the children of fathers who were not gentlemen or from the professional classes, although the fathers of 36 writers, or nearly a third of the total, have not been traced. Many of these may have been of humble background. Amongst the more humble professions, certain trades also contributed further to the support of women writers. At least one female author was married to a bookseller, and two to actor-managers. Only one of the women novelists (Mrs. Haywood) had a father who was not from the landed or professional classes, further suggesting that early access to education was of greater importance to women writers than to men. Establishing the exact educational background of the writers is much the most difficult research task. The schooling received by over half the 116 writers has not been traced. From what can be determined, many attended elite establishments or received expensive tuition. At least 26 of the writers attended university, and several of them were serious scholars. Nine went to Cambridge, six to Trinity College, Dublin, five to Oxford, three to Edinburgh, two to Aberdeen, and one to Glasgow. One other writer completed his education at an Inn of Court. Of those who completed their formal education at school, three went to one of the great public schools, three to small private academies, and at least six to grammar or local schools. At least six authors had no formal education. The income of writers at their death can also be given only impressionistically. The variety in the financial and social station of most novelists of the period has already been suggested. Many gentlemen-writers like

Thomas Amory, the author of *John Buncle* (1756 and continuation, 1766), did not need to push the quill for a living. Two-thirds of all the writers were also able to live by other means. For those who were dependent on their pens, most presumably believed that more than subsistence earnings were possible.

It is this sociology that changed so dramatically between about 1780 and 1820, most notably by the greater prominence of women as authors of the total number of novels published. As detailed by the tables of appendix 2, the balance between male and female novelists changed significantly over this period, both amongst the total of writers openly named in the novels and amongst the total of writers subsequently identified. It must be stressed at the outset that no one should over-interpret figures derived from problematic materials, but the appended tables do give the best available indication of the gender of published novelists of the period. Among the 83 percent of all novels (new and reprints) originally published anonymously between 1750 and 1769 there were many works whose title pages proclaimed that they were "by a Lady." Several, however, were actually penned by male scribblers looking for better sales and review notices. Even here, though, novels entitled "By a Lady" or "By a Young Lady" were outnumbered in most seasons by works bearing other descriptions. There does remain the 36 percent of all novels published during this period whose authors cannot be traced, but even if *all* these novels are assumed to be by women and added to the titles known to be by women, no dominant cohort of women authors emerges. In eleven years, only between 1750 and 1769 were more novels written by women *and* unknown authors than by men. It was also the case that in years such as 1763–64 when the popularity of women writers did increase, this was almost entirely owing to reprints of a few popular authors.

In the final third of the eighteenth century marked changes were apparent. From the total number of novels first published in the 1770s nearly 10 percent provided title page or preface attribution to named men, compared to nearly 6 percent to named women. In only one year of the decade (1775) were more novel title pages issued declaring female rather than male authorship. During the 1780s, however, this relationship was reversed, with 5 percent of all new novel titles announcing a named male author, but some 10 percent of the total naming a female author. The female title-page lead continued, if not so strongly, during the less reticent 1790s, when many more title pages or prefaces boasted names. A total of 17 percent of novels in the 1790s were published with named male writers, but more than a fifth (21 percent) gave named female writers. In particular years a striking number of women authors were acknowledged. Between 1788 and 1790, 33 novel title pages (or prefaces) named women authors. Why this change came about is unclear, but the comparison to eight novel title pages with named male writers in the same years, might suggest that female authorship was being deliberately promoted, and it was exactly at this time, as already noted, that an unprecedented number of otherwise anonymous title pages also bore the attribution to "a Lady." It certainly seems to have been some sort of turning point, although 1791 provided a striking if brief riposte to the trend, with 15 acknowledged male novelists outnumbering the women by nearly two to one.

Far more significant are gender comparisons amongst the total of known writers. Research for this bibliography has uncovered the actual authorship of many anonymous (or mistakenly ascribed) novels, and the summaries in appendix 2 reveal the surprisingly poor showing of known women writers in the earlier decades. Only 14 percent of all new novel titles published between 1750 and 1769 can be identified as by women writers. Moreover, even if all the titles that remain anonymous are assumed to be by women (hardly likely), and this total is added to the known number of titles by female writers, the combined total (58 percent) far from overwhelms the remaining number of novels (42 percent) known for certain to be by male writers.[13] The results of the new research for 1770–79 suggest affinity to the preceding decade, with the number of novel titles with identified female authors remaining at 14 percent of the total (compared to the near third of all titles that can now be given an identifiable male author). Thereafter, the balance shifts, with slightly more novels by women than by men identified for the 1780s and 1790s. During this shift, the tallies of novels remaining anonymous are important, particularly in the 1770s where the authorship of over half of all novels is still unidentified, but also in the 1780s where more than 40 percent of all titles are without a known author. By comparison, well under a third (29 percent) of all novel titles published in the 1790s remain anonymous, boosting the significance of the continuing closeness of the male–female contest (31 percent compared to 37 percent). From the late 1780s, then, the march of the woman novelist is clearly visible, but through the 1790s and to the end of the century it is not at all certain that women greatly outnumbered the male writers of novels.

After 1800, the surge in admitted female authorship of novels continued. During the 1810s the 13 percent of all novels with admitted male authorship compared to 31 percent admitted by women. By now, then, nearly a third of all new novel titles published bore women's names on the title pages or in prefaces, although more than half (56 percent) of all novels were still published anonymously. This makes the change in the 1820s very striking where the already high but declining levels of anonymity sharply revived, and where the admission of authorship by women (17 percent of all new titles) did not greatly exceed that by men (14 percent of all titles). Research to determine, where possible, the actual authorship of all these novels reveals an astonishing resurgence in male novel writing in the 1820s. Whereas about 45 percent of all novel titles published in the first decade of the new century were by women (compared to 34 percent of all new novel titles by men, and the rest remaining with authorship unidentified), and almost exactly half of all new titles published in the 1810s were by women (compared to a quarter by men), in the 1820s almost half (49 percent) of all new novel titles were now written by men (compared to 31 percent by women, with some 20 percent remaining unidentified). In the first two decades of the nineteenth century, therefore, the increase in women novelists seems to have fed through to the admission of female authorship in the books themselves, but the extraordinary turnaround in the 1820s resulted first, in a greater reluctance by women to confess publicly to authorship, but second, in an even greater reticence by the many more male writers now publishing novels. After all, admitted female authorship for these volumes still outranked admitted male authorship in the final decade of this study.

In some of these cases, what amounted to the *avoidance* of anonymity was further forced by the need to declare a purpose in becoming a novelist. Authors sometimes spelled out their reasons for writing in a preface or, at sometimes inordinate length, on a title page. Many different commitments or causes were paraded, but a notable invocation was to charity or destitution. Although often concealed or at least very difficult to determine from the wording of the imprint, many publications were in fact vanity productions in which the author underwrote all or the greater part of the costs. Of various of the more straightforward examples, the imprint of *Burton-Wood* declared it to be "Printed for the Author, by H. D. Steel, No. 51, Lothbury, near Coleman Street: and sold by W. Flexney, Bookseller, Holborn, 1783." Its author, Anna Maria Mackenzie, was not publicly announced. Dozens more examples of authors paying for their own edition of some 500 or 750 copies, almost all hoping to make some return on them by their sale through one or more booksellers, can now only be determined by consultation of surviving printing or bookselling records, including those of the printing ledgers of William Strachan and the Longmans. In a few cases, such as the receipts of payment preserved in the archives of the bookseller

George Robinson (where authors did at least receive a very modest sum of money for complete outright sale of the manuscript), the real identity of the author is further obscured by an agent or a spouse or some other relative apparently collecting copyright payments.[14] Such evidence casts doubt on the authorship of the *Sylph* by Georgiana, Duchess of Devonshire (the novel writer, Sophie Briscoe, was paid 12 guineas for delivery of the manuscript), and also complicates the accepted attribution of *Fatal Follies* (1788) to Anna Thomson, when Robinsons, the booksellers, paid the 50 guinea copy purchase price to her husband, William, also a novelist.[15] Other later examples, where early nineteenth-century receipts and records now suggest that we have to revise attributions to anonymous and pseudonymous novels include volumes by Mrs. Ross and Elizabeth B. Lester (the output of the two is often confused), Henrietta Maria Young, and Elizabeth Thomas, who wrote both as Martha Homely and as Bridget Bluemantle.[16]

As a career, novel writing was almost never self-supporting, despite its apparent attraction to impoverished and desperate gentry. Some of the poorest broadcast their names in order to attract subscribers or to alert readers to their plight. Those prefacing a work with an approved dedication to a local patron or, as in the case of about 60 novels over the entire period, to members of the royal family, almost always gave their names. Ann Skinn certainly published under her own name when attempting to write in 1771 to support herself after leaving her brutish husband. Anna Maria Mackenzie and Eliza Parsons took up their pens as penurious widows with four and eight small children respectively. Mrs. Parsons put her own name to all thirteen of her novels published in the 1790s. Mrs. Mackenzie, more confusingly, published at least six novels anonymously, three under her real name, and a further one under the pseudonym "Ellen of Exeter" between 1783 and 1798. Ann Gomersall (her first 1789 novel, anonymously, the next two under her own name), Elizabeth Hervey (all four novels known to be by her, 1788–97, published anonymously), and Charlotte Lennox (at first in 1790 under her own name and then anonymously in 1791), all wrote to re-establish family fortunes. When published by subscription, many novels boasted quality names in the ranks of subscribers listed at the beginning of the first (and sometimes later) volumes. The great majority, quite obviously, were published with the name of the deserving author emblazoned on the title page and preface, but sometimes a subscription was set up for an undisclosed author. Notable amongst these were *Emma; or, the Unfortunate Attachment* of 1773, listing 116 names, and *Traditions* of 1795 which paraded 640 subscribers' names. *Traditions* can now firmly be attributed to Mary Martha Sherwood; the subscription model must however cast doubt on *Emma* having been written by the Duchess of Devonshire, as is still supposed by some authorities, based on the claim of a later Irish edition.

Many other indigent or allegedly indigent authors published anonymously as hack writers, almost certainly encouraged by booksellers not to disclose their identity so that they could be employed again as writers-on-demand or unacknowledged translators. Eliza Kirkham Mathews wrote tirelessly, apparently in order buy health cures while her actor husband toured the provinces. She published at least five novels between 1785 and 1792, all anonymously. Others soliciting indulgence from the public and the critics included the allegedly widowed author of *Disinterested Love* (1788), although the reviewers were unmerciful. For almost all these writers, an assured income from novel writing was an unrealizable dream, and many, including Skinn, the Lee sisters, Charlotte Palmer, Mary Pilkington, Jane Timbury, and the far more distinguished Lennox, took to teaching to bring home more pennies. In such cases, advertisement of novel writing in the form of their full name on the title page was not always compatible with promotion of a respectable profession like teaching. Not that additional careers always assisted. Gomersall, Mathews, and many other novelists of the period died as parish paupers.

Of particular importance here in the unravelling of authorship are the letters sent to and from the Royal Literary Fund, established in 1790 by a group of philanthropic gentlemen to dispense modest grants to indigent authors. Amongst recipients of relief were Alexander Bicknell, Ralph Fell, Ann Gomersall, Elizabeth Helme, Martha Hugill, Charlotte Lennox, Charlotte Palmer, Eliza Parsons, Mary Pilkington, Samuel Jackson Pratt, and Jane Timbury. Many of those who petitioned had published anonymously. The archives of the Fund prove many unique clues to authorship and also tantalize with letters from poor writers offering grandiose claims to anonymous titles—and claims which they probably knew to be incontestable. In several cases, however, booksellers and other authorities were called upon to verify newly announced claims of authorship to old novels. In one such case, Phebe Gibbes wrote to the Fund in 1804 to claim authorship of *Elfrida; or Paternal Ambition* published by Joseph Johnson in three volumes in 1786, and enclosing a recent authenticating note from Johnson himself.[17] A complication to this (if a rare one) is the subsequent claim of an author to have written a work attributable to another author by some other source. Phebe Gibbes further claimed to have written *Zoriada*, published in 1786 and usually attributed to Anne Hughes, as well as professing authorship of

Heaven's Best Gift, published in 1798, which, Gibbes asserted, she "wrote for the credit and emolument of another hand dec[ease]d" [one Mrs. Lucius Phillips]. In the same letter, Gibbes maintained that she had written in total "twenty-two sets" of novels.[18] If her assertion was true and not simply the hallucinations of an ailing hack, then several other novels ascribed at the time to Anne Hughes and other shadowy figures might have been by Gibbes. Gibbes herself declared that "being a domestic woman, and of withdrawing turn of Temper I never would be prevailed upon to put my name to any of my Productions."[19] We can only guess at the full output of such writers. Elizabeth Helme, for example, insisted that in addition to being the acknowledged author of ten novels and three translations, she had also "translated sixteen volumes for different booksellers without my name".[20]

The Helme petition touches upon one other key encouragement to anonymity in the publication of novels of this period—the borrowing, either explicitly or furtively, from foreign originals. More than a tenth of all novel titles first published in Britain in this period were translations from Continental novels. Some of the source fiction was elderly and obscure; almost all from the1750s until the mid 1790s was from the French, and foreign dependency was especially marked in the early years. At least 95 (or 18 percent) of the 531 novels first published in Britain, 1750–69, were translations. Of these, 84 were from the French, two from the Spanish and only nine from other languages including German. In the 1770s and 1780s a few more novels were translated from the German, but it was a popular source only during the final decade of the century. From 1795, translations from German exceeded those from other languages for the first time. By the beginning of the next century, however, French translations resumed ascendancy, accounting for at least 71 of the total of 770 new novels published in English between 1800 and 1809, and 21 of the 662 new titles published in the 1810s.[21] It has not always been possible to find the date of the French or German original, and some translations were made indirectly (a German novel via a French translation for example) with conflicting evidence about the text used for the translation (whatever the title page or puffing advertisement said). If many translations hid attempts by authors to disguise plagiarism (and lack of imagination), their attraction to bookseller-publishers was also evident. Second-rate novels could be translated by ill-paid hacks with relative ease and cheapness.[22] As noted, already, most novel writers were paid a pittance for their original manuscript (after which they had no rights to any further profit) but even this expense was avoided if the text was borrowed from abroad. Much translation was the resort of indigent writers and scholars huddled in Grub Street garrets or moon-lighting from poorly paid clerical positions. Many still remain transla-tions "By a Lady" without any clue as to their translator, like *The Unfortunate Attachment* of 1795, taken directly from the 1745/46 *Les époux malheureux* of Baculard D'Arnaud. Such refuge in anonymity was often prudent. An advertisement opposite to the opening page of the very advisedly anonymous *Interesting Story of Edwin and Julia* of 1788 warned that "the sentences which the Author has been obliged to bor-row from other Productions are printed without a Mark of Quotation."

Contemporary critics were not unaware of these ploys and approached the question of authorship with great caution. This was par-ticularly the case with the branded claims of female authorship. "We are not without suspicion," wrote the *Critical*, "that in anonymous publica-tions, the words written by a lady are sometimes made use of to preclude the severity of criticism; but as Reviewers are generally churls and grey-beards, this piece of finesse very seldom answers."[23] The dedication in the *History of Eliza Warwick* (1778), "To the Reviewers," was signed by "a female, and a very young one," but the *Critical* reserved judgment, observing that in this matter "there is no such thing as distinguishing men from women" and surmising that this particular author might be of "the masculine gender."[24] The *Monthly* scold observed that *The Ring* (1784) was "said to be the production of a very young Lady. She appears, however, to be so well acquainted with the tricks of the profession, that one would be led to imagine that she had been an old practitioner."[25]

These reviews and notices were themselves anonymous. All critical notices, long and short, appeared without attribution, and the reviewers' anonymity was earnestly guarded by the periodical editors. Almost all contributions to the *Critical* in this period remain unattributable, but the names of *Monthly* reviewers are now identifiable from a surviving run of the periodical annotated with contributors' initials by its editor, Ralph Griffiths.[26] The lifting of the reviewers' veils even reveals novel criticism from several novelists, including John Hawkesworth, John Langhorne, and Thomas Holcroft (the last reviewing 11 novels for the *Monthly* in the 1790s). During the closing decades of the eighteenth century authors can be identified for some 202 of the 315 *Monthly* novel reviews of the 1770s, for 315 of the 404 novel reviews of the 1780s, and, less adequately, for 292 of the 701 novel reviews of the 1790s. All the critics might, of course, have reviewed many more novels.

What is now so striking is that the verdicts on new fiction were deliv-ered from the pens of no more than half a dozen favored hacks. Three *Monthly* reviewers in fact dominated in the final three decades of the eighteenth century. Samuel Badcock, who was the *Monthly's* objector to *The Ring* in 1784, became that periodical's leading novel reviewer. A dissenting minister and associate of Joseph Priestley, Badcock returned to his native Devon in 1778. From then until 1786 he wrote *Monthly* reviews for at least 110 new novels, or, in other words, almost exactly half of all such titles now known to be published in these years. William Enfield was another workhorse for Griffiths. Like Badcock, a dissenting minister and working far from London, Enfield is known to have reviewed 203 novels from 1774 until his death in 1797. London based Andrew Becket reviewed at least 132 novels (or more than half of the 242 new novels published) in an intense four-year period between 1786 and 1789 (including 36 of the 39 author-identified *Monthly* reviews of the 51 novels with 1787 imprints). Amongst other *Monthly* contributors, Gilbert Stuart, historian and critic, was renown as a rapid reviewer, completing notices for 48 of the 180 novels known to have been published between 1770 and 1773. Well known as the author of the *New History of London*, John Noorthouck also worked for the *Monthly*, anonymously like all his fellow critics. He reviewed sixty new novels between 1770 and 1792, although his surviving correspondence is peppered with complaints about impossible deadlines.

An obvious consequence of such a small band of critics anonymously reviewing the novels (also largely anonymous), is the similarity between the published verdicts. The *Critical*, in particular, often borrowed wording from the *Monthly* review when published in advance (as did many other reviews and magazines inserting short critical notices), and in many cases, of course, the report was perfunctory. Reviewing novels was a necessary task if the *Monthly* and the *Critical* were to keep their promise to acknowledge every book published, but dismissive brevity offered a perfectly allowable expedient. The many repeated phrases suggest that the critics spent little time with many of their charges. Reviews often reveal a sense of malicious fun in constructing flippant and ostentatiously horrified opinions. In addition to the amusing quips advising young women to return to churning out butter rather than novels (amongst many such taunts), serious interventions warn of exposure to moral danger by reading fiction. All of this must have confirmed the wisdom of anonymous publishing for both practising and intending authors. Booksellers, apart from those who were silent partners in a publishing syndicate, could not hide so easily when imprints advertised bookseller–publisher, printer, or seller (although exact functions were often unclear), but many booksellers, especially those like Lowndes and the Nobles who operated circulating libraries, must surely have supported authors in their decision to remain anonymous. This was also convenient when, like the Nobles, older novels might be reissued in rehashed form in the pretence of a new publication.

This did not prevent reviewers indulging in guesswork about authorship or offering their readers informed conjecture about possible identities. James Bannister, for example, reviewing *Adeline De Courcy* (1797) for the *Monthly*, wrote that "the story of this novel is romantic .... These volumes appear to be the production of a female pen."[27] The *Critical* called *Maple Vale* (1791) a "chit-chat novel" and added that "we have said that souls have no sexes, yet we think that there is sufficient *internal* evidence to conclude that the author is a female. Are we, in this, inconsistent? We trust not: novels of this kind are constructed mechanically; the mind has no share in the business."[28] Other speculation seems to have been based on some knowledge of who the author was—even of personal contact. William Enfield writing in the *Monthly* of the three-volume *Maiden Aunt: Written by a Lady* (1776), declared that "we should have thought ourselves under the necessity of censuring this female Writer for the incorrect manner in which her work appears before the Public, had we not received *information* [from the author] ... that since the copy passed out of the Author's hands, the beginning of every letter in the first volume was altered, many of them in the most absurd and vulgar manner;—that the carelessness of the publisher has suffered the grossest blunders in sense, grammar, and spelling to pass into print, for which the copy was not answerable, and that he has added fifteen letters just before the conclusion, beginning with the forty-second, and ending with the fifty-sixth, which the Author entirely disclaims, and considers as a compound of inconsistency, added merely to spin out the work."[29]

The public evaluation and dismissal of almost all new novels by the periodical reviewers became, then, a leading cause of title-page disguise and a widespread refuge in anonymity. As the *Critical* reviewer said of the 1774 *School for Husbands*, the artifice of "by a lady" (or, even better, "by a young lady") was used to ward off criticism. The *Monthly* thought this novel to be "hammered out of the brainless head of a Grubstreet hireling".[30] For a few—and it was a minority—timidity did keep the critics at bay. The novelist who signed herself "Sabina" (author of *Laurentia*, 1790) seems to have won her appeal to "the Gentlemen Reviewers" to "in pity spare a simple maid." William Hall later recalled falsifying his identity: "it afforded me some consolation that my name was not announced; but it came to the public eye, as the production of "A Lady".[31] In typical style, the bookseller, James Lackington, made much of the anonymity of his new novel, *Louisa Mathews* (1793), reporting that the author was a "very respectable Lady" but, most regrettably, too shy for her name to appear on the title page.[32] Timidity was understandable given the hostility of the reviewers and responses typically included the prefatory advertisement to *The Maiden Aunt. Written By a Lady*, published in 1776, which declares: "With a heart anxiously trembling for the success it may meet with, does the authoress venture this, her first performance."

One result of so much critical attention and lamentation, indeed, was a certain bravery associated with male authors who declared themselves novelists. Most notable, perhaps, were the clerics who publicly announced themselves, including James Penn, Vicar of Clavering Cum Langley, Essex, and author of *Surry Cottage* (1779), Revd William Cole, author of *Contradiction* (1796), Revd James Douglas of Chiddingford, author of *The History of Julia d'Haumont* (1797). Revd Charles Lucas allowed a coy "C. L." to appear at the foot of his introduction to his 1798 *Castle of St Donats*. Such declarations carried high risk. Of Revd Henry Evans Holder's *The Secluded Man* (1798), the *Critical* reviewer remarked that he was "sorry to see the name of a clergyman, and, we believe, a philologist, in the title-page of so dull a novel."[33] In the preface to *The Irish Guardian* of 1809, Anna Maria Mackenzie wrote that "The Author perceives she cannot conclude without paying a feeble tribute of praise to those male writers, who have thought it no degradation of their dignity … to … improve and amuse in the form of a novel."[34]

As critical scorn escalated by the end of the eighteenth century, and even more clearly during the first decades of the nineteenth century, many writers desisted from putting their names to novels (or were so persuaded by their booksellers) in order to limit the appearance of over-production. Pseudonyms and complete anonymity became the common resort for many novelists in the age of Walter Scott, as was clearly the case in the early years with Mary Meeke, third most prolific novelist between 1800 and 1829. Scott himself published *Tales of My Landlord* in the name of the overtly pseudonymous Jedidiah Cleishbotham, and his other novels were first issued as "by the author of Waverley" (sometimes mentioning other titles also). As Peter Garside has noted, when Amelia Opie allowed her name to stand in full on the title page and in the prefatory dedication to *The Father and Daughter* of 1801, she confessed her trepidation in "To the Reader" "as an avowed Author at the bar of public opinion," insisting that her offering was "not a Novel," but a "a simple, moral tale."[35] In putting her name to *Sherwood Forest*, Elizabeth Sarah Villa-Real Gooch declared that "an acknowledged Novel-writer is, perhaps, one of the most difficult names to support with credit and reputation."[36]

In such a climate, the most obvious force against authors' fears of exposure were the same bookseller–publishers who in other circumstances had been happy to protect the identity of a fledging or hapless writer. As noted already, many booksellers strove to link novels as "by the same author of …," and while maintaining anonymity, this ploy clearly drew on the notions of the good bet from the good stable rather than upon criticisms of over-production. Barbara Hofland, whose 21 novels published between 1800 and 1829 made her the second most prolific novelist of the period after Scott, opened her account with a novel published anonymously, but all but one of her next seven were "by the author of" (the exception being a pseudonym), until she finally claimed public authorship in 1814. Thereafter, we have an increasing number of examples of publishers' interventions aimed at persuading authors that in their own best interests they should either publicly reveal authorship of a novel or highlight a celebrated predecessor work. In 1818, Archibald Constable convinced Charles Maturin that his *Women; Or Pour et Contre* should appear as "by the author of *Bertram*." In 1822, Longmans notified a reluctant James Hogg of his *Three Perils of Man* "that we would wish to have your name in the Title."[37] As Garside also shows, moreover, different preferences of publishers were increasingly distinct during the 1820s at exactly the same time as the tide of anonymity rose again. Of the 43 novels known to be by women and published by Longmans in the 1820s, 30 named the author on the title page, whereas of the 17 novels published by Henry Colburn in the same decade, only three named the author, and each was the result of very particular circumstances. The Longmans' firm was keen on promoting female authorship, but Colburn, "himself by now far more committed to male writers, was more interested in creating a kind of mystique by not naming his authors."[38] What was happening, therefore, was that while some publishers tapped into novel writers' fear of exposure and assisted, for their own devices, in cultivating anonymity, other publishers, adopting very different marketing strategies, were forced to take on the cult of anonymity encouraged even by successful authors like Scott. During the 1820s, even many novelists of repute inclined to retreat behind an anodyne mask or adopted complete anonymity. The final irony here was that reviewers had now begun to participate in the "outing" of novelists, contributing to the pressures, particularly for those writers with professional careers or Society profiles, to conceal their identity from the novel-reading public. Amongst its several revelations, in 1800, the *Monthly* had identified the well-known (and well-established novel writer) Dr John Moore as author of *Mordaunt*, and in 1802 it proclaimed Miss [Margaret] Cullen to be "the fair writer" of *Home*.[39]

It is of course, important not to over-rate either the artistic or the material importance of these novels: most were lamentably written and most were published in very modestly sized editions (as their authors well knew, and indeed, in some cases, financed). Stylistic poverty and transience characterizes the majority. Many were produced in editions of no more than 500 copies (and even some of the most successful in single editions of between 750 and 1,000). Moreover, the majority of titles were never reprinted. All the evidence points to a very large proportion of the novels being produced to service circulating libraries—many owned and managed by the publishers of the new fiction itself. The novels remain true ephemera. A surprising proportion of the works published in the first decades of this period (about 7 percent of all pre-1800 titles listed in the new bibliography) seem not to survive today in any extant copy, even though, in each case, we are certain of their original publication and distribution. Titles issued in the early nineteenth century do seem to have enjoyed a more robust shelf-life, although the contribution of one or two ardent collectors has been instrumental in the survival of many unique copies.

The short life of these "literary gad-flies" as one reviewer called them, ensured that the question of authorship was not easily pursued and very often confused, deliberately or otherwise. The history of the "anonymous popular novel" in this critical period in the development of English prose fiction for a wider and ever more demanding audience, is one of largely impoverished writers caught between their fear of mounting critical disapproval and the varying marketing strategies of their bookseller–publishers. The background and gender of the writers clearly did make a difference to the likelihood of a name appearing on the title page of the novel, but even these trends—of male parity and, in some years, dominance, in the second half of the eighteenth century, and of increasing female authorship of new novels during the early nineteenth century—were mediated by the tensions between critics and booksellers in which the financial bargaining power of the authors of novels was almost always nonexistent. Certainly, by themselves, past success and public confidence were rarely sufficient to persuade authors to countermand the advice of booksellers (even if given the choice), and to run, fully named, the gamut of the periodical reviewers.

Appendix 1

Publication of new novels in Britain and Ireland, 1750–1829

Year	Total	Year	Total	Year	Total	Year	Total
1750	23	1760	35	1770	40	1780	24
1751	23	1761	20	1771	60	1781	22
1752	19	1762	19	1772	41	1782	22
1753	19	1763	18	1773	39	1783	24
1754	30	1764	26	1774	35	1784	24
1755	22	1765	18	1775	31	1785	47
1756	25	1766	27	1776	17	1786	40
1757	26	1767	33	1777	18	1787	51
1758	16	1768	37	1778	16	1788	80
1759	28	1769	44	1779	18	1789	71
Total	231		277		315		405

Year	Total	Year	Total	Year	Total	Year	Total
1790	74	1800	81	1810	89	1820	70
1791	74	1801	72	1811	80	1821	75
1792	58	1802	61	1812	66	1822	82
1793	45	1803	79	1813	63	1823	87
1794	56	1804	73	1814	61	1824	99
1795	50	1805	75	1815	54	1825	91
1796	91	1806	70	1816	59	1826	77
1797	79	1807	69	1817	55	1827	79
1798	75	1808	111	1818	62	1828	83
1799	99	1809	79	1819	73	1829	81
	701		770		662	824	
Grand Total							4,185

James Raven

Appendix 2

Authorship of Novels 1750–1829

Publ. date	Total no. new novels	Proper names from title-pages and prefaces only				Total title-pages with identified proper names		Remaining Anon.
		Male	Female	Anon.	Other[40]	Male	Female	
1750–59								
1750	23	5		17	1	7	2	13
1751	23	5		18		12	1	10
1752	19	2		17		5	3	11
1753	19	1	1	17		6	5	8
1754	30	3		27		10	4	16
1755	22	1	1	20		7	3	12
1756	25	2		23		8	4	13
1757	26	2		24		5	2	19
1758	16			16		3	2	11
1759	28	4		24		8	5	15
	231	25	2	203	1	71	31	128
%		(10.8)	(0.8)	(87.9)		(30.7)	(13.4)	(55.4)
1760–69								
1760	35	2	1	32		6	5	24
1761	20	1		19		7	3	10
1762	19	1	2	16		8	5	6
1763	18		1	17		3	3	12
1764	26	1	3	22		6	7	13
1765	18	2	1	15		8	2	8
1766	27	1	4	22		6	5	16
1767	33	3	2	28		9	5	19
1768	37	5	1	31		10	1	26
1769	44	4	1	39		13	5	26
	277	20	16	241		76	41	160
%		(0.7)	(0.6)	(87)		(27.4)	(14.8)	(57.8)
1750–69								
	508	45	18	444		147	72	288
%		(8.9)	(0.4)	(87.4)		(28.9)	(14.2)	(56.7)
1770–79								
1770	40	5	1	33	1	15*	3	21
1771	60	7	4	49		18	7	35
1772	41	3	1	37		7	6	28
1773	39	4	2	33		12	4	23
1774	35	4	2	28	1	9	2	23

Appendix 2 (*Contd.*)

Publ. date	Total no. new novels	Proper names from title-pages and prefaces only				Total title-pages with identified proper names		Remaining Anon.
		Male	Female	Anon.	Other[40]	Male	Female	
1775	31	—	3	28		10	5	16
1776	17	2	1	14		7	4	6
1777	18	2	1	15		5	5	8
1778	16	1	1	14		2	5	9
1779	18	2	2	14		9	4	5
	315	30	18	265	2	94	45	174
%		(9.5)	(5.7)	(84.1)		(29.8)	(14.3)	(55.2)
1780–89								
1780	24	1	5	18	2	4	7★	11
1781	22			22		5	2	15
1782	22	3	—	19		8	3	11
1783	24	4	2	18		9	9	6
1784	24	2	2	20		10	5	9
1785	47	3	5	38	1	8	17	21
1786	40	2	4	33	1	12	15	12
1787	51	1	4	46		11	14	26
1788	80	3	9	65	2	18	20	40
1789	71	2	10	57	2	14	26	29
	405	21	41	336	8	99	118	180
%		(5.2)	(10.1)	(83)	(2)	(24.4)	(29)	(44.4)
1790–99								
1790	74	3	13	57	1	13	25	35
1791	74	15	8	48	3	24	20	27
1792	58	7	7	44		16	14	28
1793	45	6	10	25	4	12	15	14
1794	56	11	13	30	2	15	24	15
1795	50	8	7	34	1	21	18	10
1796	91	16	25	45	5	31	36	19
1797	79	14	18	45	2	23	31	23
1798	75	16	18	38	3	22	36	14
1799	99	25	27	45	2	37	40	20
	701	121	146	412	23	215	260	205
%		(17.2)	(20.9)	(59)	(3.3)	(30.7)	(36.9)	(29.6)
1770–99								
	1,421	172	205	1,013	33	408	423	560
%		(12.1)	(14.4)	(71.3)	(2.3)	(28.7)	(29.8)	(39.4)

Appendix 2 (*Contd.*)

Publ. date	Total no. new novels	Proper names from title-pages and prefaces only				Total title-pages with identified proper names		Remaining Anon.
		Male	*Female*	*Anon.*	*Other*[40]	*Male*	*Female*	
1800–1809								
1800	81	18	17	46	4	28	35	18
1801	72	13	27	32	3	17	41	14
1802	61	12	17	32	3	18	27	16
1803	79	27	18	34	1	35	32	12
1804	73	21	22	30	5	32	28	13
1805	75	23	22	30	3	29	31	15
1806	70	15	24	31	4	19	35	16
1807	69	18	24	27	6	25	31	13
1808	111	28	34	49	8	34	49	28
1809	79	20	22	37	7	26	35	18
	770	195	227	348	44	263	344	163
%		(25.3)	(29.5)	(45.2)	(5.7)	(34.2)	(44.7)	(21.2)
1810–19								
1810	89	13	27	49	9	19	43	27
1811	80	21	21	38	5	30	34	16
1812	66	6	12	48	5	11	33	22
1813	63	10	25	28	4	16	37	10
1814	61	7	22	32	4	13	39	9
1815	54	7	18	29	4	13	24	17
1816	59	5	20	34	1	14	31	14
1817	55	4	22	29	3	13	30	12
1818	62	5	16	41	7	15	27	20
1819	73	7	22	44	3	18	30	25
	662	85	205	372	45	162	328	172
%		(12.8)	(31.0)	(56.2)	(6.8)	(24.5)	(49.6)	(25.9)
1820–29								
1820	70	16	16	38	4	33	22	15
1821	75	16	17	42	4	30	25	20
1822	82	12	17	53	4	37	26	19
1823	87	11	17	59	2	40	27	20
1824	99	13	23	63	4	45	38	16
1825	91	19	10	62	2	52	23	16
1826	77	8	13	56	1	43	26	8
1827	79	7	11	61	4	38	25	16
1828	83	7	10	66	4	39	25	19
1829	81	9	6	66	1	47	21	13
	824	118	140	566	30	404	258	162
%		(14.3)	(17.0)	(68.7)	(3.6)	(49.0)	(31.3)	(19.7)

Appendix 2 (*Contd.*)

Publ. date	Total no. new novels	Proper names from title-pages and prefaces only				Total title-pages with identified proper names		Remaining Anon.
		Male	Female	Anon.	Other[40]	Male	Female	
1800–29								
	2,256	398	572	1,286	119	829	930	497
		(17.6)	(25.3)	(57.0)	(5.3)	(36.7)	(41.2)	(22.0)
1750–1829								
	4,185	615	795	2,743	154	1,384	1,425	1,345
		(14.7)	(19)	(65.5)	(3.7)	(33.1)	(34.1)	(32.1)

* Includes, in each case, one novel with multiple authors—the gender of the first given author is recorded.

Notes

1. As suggested in many reviews, most notably including *Monthly Review* 46 (1772), p. 78 on the anonymous 1771 *Oxonian*, *Critical Review* n.s. 10 (1794), 349 on George Walker's 1793 *Romance of the Cavern*, and *CR* n.s. 17 (1796), 238–9 on the anonymous 1796 *Magnanimous Amazon*. The author is particularly grateful for the assistance of Prof. Antonia Forster in the very enjoyable and collaborative research that formed the basis for this study; and also to Dr Nigel Hall for his help in preparing the tables and figures.
2. Peter Garside, James Raven and Rainer Schöwerling, eds., *The English Novel 1770–1829: A Bibliographical Survey of Prose Fiction Published in the British Isles* 2 vols. (Oxford: Oxford University Press, 2000), vol. 1 *1770–1799*, ed. James Raven and Antonia Forster; vol. 2 *1800–29*, ed. Peter Garside and Rainer Schöwerling.
3. W. H. McBurney, *A Check List of English Prose Fiction, 1700–39* (Cambridge, Mass., 1960); J. C. Beasley, *The Novels of the 1740s* (Athens, Ga, 1982); James Raven, *British Fiction 1750–1770: A Chronological Check-List of Prose Fiction Printed in Britain and Ireland* (London and Cranbury, NJ, 1987). Coverage errs on the side of generosity. The criteria by which the novel is defined is discussed in Raven and Forster, eds., *English Novel 1770–1799*, 1–5, 21–39.
4. *CR* 61 (1786), 235.
5. Including, for example, *Woodbury* of 1773 and *Suspicious Lovers* of 1777; and *Edmund* of 1790 and *Sidney Castle* of 1792, the last pair not known to be surviving in any extant copy, although they were certainly published and reviewed. In another case, *The Young Philosopher* of 1782, the source of much bibliographical confusion, can now at least be associated with the mysterious author of two other novels of the previous season (*Colonel Ormsby* and *Les Delices du Sentiment; Or the Passionate Lovers*).
6. Including, amongst many, Elizabeth Mathews's *Constance* (1785), and the still anonymous *Lumley-House* (1787), *The History of Georgina Neville* (1791), and *Fanny; or, The Deserted Daughter* (1792), were also entitled "The First Literary Attempt of a Young Lady." In 1786 Martha Hugill more confidently entitled *St Bernard's Priory* as the "First Literary Production of a Young Lady."
7. *MR* 68 (1783), 457.
8. *CR* n.s. 2 (1791), 477; *MR* n.s. 7 (1792), 230.
9. *EngR* 19 (1792), 231.
10. *CR* 49 (1780), 76.
11. *CR* 52 (1781), 76.

12. Despite her prolific output, Kemble is one of the several women writers of (usually abysmal) popular fiction not included in the otherwise indispensable Virginia Blain *et al.*, *The Feminist Companion to Literature in English; Women Writers from the Middle Ages to the Present* (London: B.T. Batsford Ltd., 1990).

13. See Raven, *British Fiction*, esp. p. 18 (this combined total for 1750–59 and 1760–69 (57.7 percent) corrects the error in the calculation for the 1750s given in footnote 46); and Catherine Gallagher, *Nobody's Story: The Vanishing Acts of Women Writers in the Marketplace, 1670–1820* (Berkeley and Los Angeles: University of California Press, 1994), 153–5.

14. These sources and what they reveal about the financing of novels by authors and booksellers are discussed in James Raven, "The Novel Comes of Age," in Raven and Forster, eds., *English Novel 1770–1799*, 51–5.

15. BL Add MSS 38,728 fol. 35; Robinson Archive, Collection of Literary Assignments, Manchester Central Library, MS F 091.A2.

16. Garside and Schöwerling, eds., *English Novel 1800–1829*, 70–2.

17. BL MSS, Royal Literary Fund 2: 74, letter of 15 Oct. 1804.

18. BL MSS, Royal Literary Fund 2: 74, letter of 18 Oct. 1804.

19. BL MSS, Royal Literary Fund 2: 74, letter of 17 Oct. 1804.

20. BL MSS, Royal Literary Fund 3: 97, letter of 20 Oct. 1803.

21. For full details of known translations, see Raven, *British Fiction 1750–1770*, 21, table 5; Raven and Forster, eds., *English Novel 1770–1799*, 58, table 8; and Garside and Schöwerling, eds., *English Novel 1800–1829*, 41, table 1.

22. See Josephine Grieder, *Translations of French Sentimental Prose Fiction in Late Eighteenth-Century England: The History of a Vogue* (Durham, NC: University of North Carolina Press, 1975).

23. *CR* 37 (1774), 317.

24. *CR* 44 (1777), 477–8.

25. *MR* 71 (1784), 150.

26. A cast of critics first assessed by Benjamin Christie Nangle, *The Monthly Review, First Series, 1749–1789: Indexes of Contributors and Articles* (Oxford: Clarendon Press, 1934), and *The Monthly Review, Second Series, 1790–1815: Indexes of Contributors and Articles* (Oxford: Clarendon Press, 1955); and refined by Antonia Forster, *Index to Book Reviews in England 1749–1774* (Carbondale and Edwardsville: Southern Illinois University Press, 1990) and *Index to Book Reviews in England 1775–1800* (London: British Library, 1996).

27. *MR* n.s. 26 (1798), 107.

28. *CR* n.s. 1 (1791), 349.

29. *MR* 54 (1776), 161–2.

30. *CR* 37 (1774), 317–8.

31. William Hall, *Death of Cain*, 4th ed. (London: Crosby and Letterman, 1800), vii.

32. *SJC* 2–5 Feb. 1793.

33. *CR* n.s. 25 (1799), 473.

34. Cited in Peter Garside, "The English Novel in the Romantic Era: Consolidation and Dispersal," in *English Novel 1800–1829*, ed. Garside and Schöwerling, 67.

35. [Amelia] Opie, *The Father and Daughter* (London: Longmaan and Rees, 1801), pp. [vi]–vii. See Garside, "The English Novel in the Romantic Era," in *English Novel 1800–1829*, ed. Garside and Schöwerling, 15–103.

36. [Elizabeth Sarah] Villa-Real Gooch, *Sherwood Forest* 3 vols. (London: Highley, 1804), 1: [ix].

37. Garside and Schöwerling, eds., *English Novel 1800–1829*, 66; Longman Letter Books, I: 101 no. 174C, Longman to Hogg, 18 Oct. 1821.

38. Garside, "The English Novel in the Romantic Era," in *English Novel 1800–1829*, ed. Garside and Schöwerling, 67.

39. Ibid., 68–9.

40. Includes title-page pseudonyms, initials, and names where gender is unclear. Also includes instances where a translator is declared but the original author is not; translators are not counted as authors in this table.

CHAPTER SEVEN

Nothing's Namelessness:
Mary Shelley's Frankenstein

Susan Eilenberg

"I have written a book in <favor> defence of Polypheme—
have I not?"

Mary Shelley to Leigh Hunt[1]

"Nobody's killing me now by fraud and not by force!"

Polyphemus in *The Odyssey* IX: 453[2]

"—And I am nothing."

Mary Shelley to Maria Gisborne[3]

Frankenstein, that anonymous novel, had its origin in a game, a mental blank, and a failure of recognition. Pressed to come up with a ghost story for a storytelling contest, which friends of hers were conducting among themselves for amusement during the wet, dull summer of 1816, Mary Wollstonecraft Godwin—she would not be Mary Shelley until Harriet Shelley's suicide, fast approaching, vacated the surname for her—could not think of anything to tell. She could think of nothing. She could think of *Nothing*. Describing her plight, years later, in the Introduction to the third edition to the novel, she would write:

I thought and pondered—vainly. I felt that blank incapability of invention which is the greatest misery of authorship, when dull Nothing replies to our anxious invocations. *Have you thought of a story?* I was asked each morning, and each morning I was forced to reply with a mortifying negative.[4]

Mary Shelley herself is at first incapable of recognizing in Nothing's reply the tale she seeks. Her incapability is unsurprising. The reply she initially takes for silence is the tale of how a "mortifying negative" comes to possess a face that cannot be faced and a tale that cannot be countenanced.

The Nothing that replies to her, occupying the position of storyteller that she is about to assume, wielding the power to cross identities, redistribute agency, and destabilize certainty, is kin to Nihil, out of which the world may or may not have been created, and to Nemo. The anonym's pseudonym, a radical prosopopeia, an embodied paradox, and a trick of grammar, Nothing (or Nobody) both is and is not. No simple emptiness ("Invention ... does not consist in creating out of void, but out of chaos; the materials must, in the first place, be afforded: it can give form to dark, shapeless substances, but cannot bring into being the substance itself" [*Frankenstein*, 226]), Nothing is full.

As Catherine Gallagher reminds us, Nobody is "a substantive that overtly proclaims the nonexistence of its referent but nevertheless has all

Figure 7.1   A portrait of Nobody. The earliest pictorial representation of Nobody figures in a printed *Sermo de S. Nemine* of about 1500 in the shape of an empty rectangle, "since nobody is depicted therein."[5]

the grammatical functions of any proper noun. One can make Nobody the subject of a sentence, as if one were talking about anyone else, but to posit anything of Nobody is to deny that quality to everybody."[6] A wordly clotting or verbal opacity, Nobody is born of the disingenuous substitution of a sign for its referent. He is the existential analogue to the perceptually ambiguous duck/rabbit, a creature of referential rather than optical instability flickering not between animal forms but between reality and unreality, word and thing, innocence and guilt, first person and third. In his figure agencies and culpabilities multiply and cross. Monstrosity and outrage are his constant attendants.

Though an outcast, Nobody exists only in relation to others, for, as the universal negation, he is the limit (but also the foundation) of everybody's being. Upon his poverty, ugliness (for he has a portraiture), and disgrace depend the prosperity, beauty, and honor of everybody; his misery protects the innocent happiness of all the rest. "The main characteristic of Nobody," Gerta Calmann observes, "was that he was falsely blamed for what everybody did. All through his history he is innocent of the crimes of those who took cover behind his name."[7] He is a scapegoat, a framed man, his adventures told in accusations ("Who broke that window?"/"Nobody!") that deny the deeds for which they blame him.

An early Nobody was Homer's Οὖτίς, sometime pseudonym of Odysseus, storyteller, enemy of Polyphemus the cyclops, and willfully anonymous object of the repeated question, "Who are you?" His story comes to us in a doubly specular frame tale. Odysseus has arrived unrecognized at Alcinous's court, where, listening to a harper unwittingly sing of his famous adventures at Troy, he weeps to remember the past. His tears attract the curiosity of his host. Who is he? asks the king. In answering him, Odysseus tells a tale that, inverting the conditions of the present telling and mocking the relations between this canny guest and his curious host, grotesquely parodies its own frame. He tells him the story of how he responded when Polyphemus asked him, a detected thief, the same question. Who was he? Odysseus tells Alcinous the cyclops had asked, the monster promising him a gift if he would tell his name. Οὖτίς, Odysseus tells Alcinous he answered Polyphemus—Nobody. And so Polyphemus presented his cruel gift, the postponement of death, a reprieve that threatened what it pretended to delay: the cyclops would eat him only after he had eaten his men. Odysseus then attacked the monster, blinding him. The monster cried out. But his monstrous cry undid itself; the words of the accusation cancelled their own sense: "Οὖτίς με κτείνει δόλῳ οὐδὲ βίηφιν";[8] "Nobody's killing me now by fraud and not by force!" Thus a "Who are you" elicits a story of an earlier "Who are you" that ends in the blinded questioner's inability to say what has happened to him.

"I have written a book in <favor> defence of Polypheme—have I not?" Mary Shelley writes. Whom does she think she has defended? One presumes she has in mind Frankenstein's monster, the hideous creature that lives, like the cyclops, apart from society and its laws, promising death by promising its deferral, defying the gods and destroying men. But if he is a Polyphemus, her monster, with his covert parasitism, anonymity, and love of secrecy and of self-replicating, self-undoing tales, suggests nonetheless an identification with the cyclops's enemy as well,[9] the sightlessness of the one doubling the namelessness of the other. Mary Shelley's monster maps both onto Homer's defaced monster and onto the pseudonymically anonymous attacker and narrator whom he cannot intelligibly accuse. Adhering, like Homer's tale, to the paradoxical logic of Nobody, Shelley's tale doubles and crosses and undoes itself, cancelling its sense as it confirms it.

★ ★ ★ ★ ★

A first glance at the causes and the effects of anonymity reveals nothing so clearly as the danger of making something out of nothing. In Mary Shelley's case, this risk of embarrassment is particularly acute. In the circumstances of her life and her writing, there are too many versions of anonymity for critical comfort, too many irregularities in naming and too many explanations for all of them. As instances begin to pile up, one may begin to think it is not anonymity that needs remark, but ordinary proper naming.

Mary Shelley's set played with names incessantly. Nicknames abounded. Aliases proved irresistible to those who wanted to hide, to escape the past, to climb a social ladder, or to remake a self. Claire Clairmont's name changes may be the most familiar; certainly they were the most varied and protracted; but Mary Clairmont, Mary Wollstonecraft, Mrs. Mason, Jane Williams, Edward John Trelawny, and Lord Byron all, at one point or another, went under false or at least not strictly true names. (Some of them, indeed, would now be unrecognizable to us under their real ones.) Percy Shelley himself, not strictly distinguishing between playful literary pseudonymy and seedier fakery, had the infatuated Claire Clairmont direct to "Joe James," at the Pisa post office, the letters that neither of them wanted Mary Shelley to know Claire was writing him.[10]

Mary Shelley too varied her name, though less strenuously than many of those around her. She had at least half a dozen silly nicknames. Signing letters, she was "M.," "Mary W.G." (before her marriage), "Mary W. Shelley," "M.W.S.," "Mary W.<G.>S.," "Mary Wollstonecraft Shelley,"

"Marina W.S.," and "Mary S." Writing to Sir Walter Scott to claim the authorship of *Frankenstein*, she was "Mary Wollst^ft Shelley." Writing to officials or to Lord Byron, she was "Mary Shelley"—a name that during her marriage she reserved for those she needed to impress. After the loss of her husband, she clung to the name he had given her and subordinated the others. To Trelawny she wrote:

> do you think I shall marry?—Never—neither you nor any body else—Mary Shelley shall be written on my tomb—and why? I cannot tell—except it is so pretty a name that tho' I were to preach to myself for years. I never should have the heart to get rid of it.
>
> (*MWS Letters* II, 139)[11]

Although one may be tempted to assume that Mary Shelley's withholding of her name from the title page of *Frankenstein* signified feminine bashfulness, a reasonable response to a culture in which female authorship was frowned upon,[12] there was nothing peculiarly feminine about anonymity, nor anything very uncommon about it, either.[13] In publication, the rules for naming or not naming oneself were flexible. The risk that in keeping one's name from the title page of a work one might be contaminated with that blank and dismissed as a nobody, a nonentity, a "Non-ens,"[14] was no real deterrent to the practice. Eminent anonymous entities abounded. Sir Walter Scott was the Great Unknown, and lesser unknowns were everywhere, many of them in Mary Shelley's own family. Percy Bysshe Shelley published much of his mature poetry—*Alastor, The Cenci, Prometheus Unbound*, "Adonais"—under his own name. But much of his earlier work, and some of his later work too, was either anonymous or pseudonymous. (For Percy Shelley, the two forms functioned equivalently.) Title pages alluded to P.B.S., Victor, John Fitzvictor, "a Gentleman of the University of Oxford," Pleyel, the Hermit of Marlow, Philopatria, Elfin Knight, E.K., and Miching Mallecho, Esq. Sometimes, as in the case of *Queen Mab*, telltale title pages were torn away.[15] At other times they remained affixed to tell no tales at all—they flaunted their silence. Everyone knows about the twenty minutes that *The Necessity of Atheism* sat in the shop window of Messrs. Munday and Slatter before it drew the outraged notice Percy Shelley had aimed at; but had those prominently displayed copies failed to attract attention, the copies the author had sent to luminaries across universities and bishops across the country, together with the advertisements he asked a friend to run "in 8 famous papers"[16] would surely have succeeded. *St. Irvyne, A Vindication of Natural Diet*, and *A Refutation of*

Deism were more quietly anonymous, as was "Julian and Maddalo"; so too was "Epipsychidion," which, as he told his publisher, he "desire[d] should not be considered as my own; indeed, in a certain sense, it is a production of a part of me already dead ... ."[17]

Mary Wollstonecraft had signed her name to most of her major works, including *An Historical and Moral View of the Origin and Progress of the French Revolution, Thoughts on the Education of Daughters, Original Stories from Real Life, A Vindication of the Rights of Men* (the second edition, appearing three weeks after the first), *A Vindication of the Rights of Woman,* and *Letters Written During a Short Residence in Sweden, Norway, and Denmark.* But her *Mary, a Fiction* was published anonymously, as were her translations and works of abridgment.[18]

Godwin himself put his name[19] to his tragedy, *Antonio,* his *Life of Geoffrey Chaucer,* his famous *Enquiry Concerning Political Justice,* the *Memoirs of the Author of A Vindication of the Rights of Woman* that made Mary Wollstonecraft so notorious, and most of his major novels (*Deloraine, Mandeville, Fleetwood, St. Leon,* and *Things as They Are; or, the Adventures of Caleb Williams*). *Cloudesley* was presented "By the author of 'Caleb Williams,'" an attribution easy enough to unravel. Most of the books published for his Juvenile Library under the imprint first of Thomas Hodgkins, a thief willing to lend his name to the enterprise, and then later of M.J. Godwin, Mary Shelley's stepmother, appeared either under the pseudonym Edwin Baldwin, Esq., or else the rather more improbable Theophilus Marcliffe.[20] He published letters and reviews under the name Mucius. Other works, including *History of the Life of William Pitt; Italian Letters, or The History of Count de St. Julian; Damon and Delia, A Tale; Imogen, a Pastoral Romance;* and *Instructions to a Statesman,* appeared anonymously.

Against such a background, the anonymous 1818 publication of *Frankenstein,* following the anonymous publication of the juvenile *Mounseer Nongtongpaw* and that of the collaborative *History of a Six Weeks' Tour,* seems unremarkable—an instance of family tradition. After its issue in 1818, *Frankenstein* appeared twice under Mary Shelley's name[21] before it reverted to official quasi-anonymity. The 1831 revised edition, published as part of Henry Colburn and Richard Bentley's Standard Novels series, upon which most subsequent editions have been based, included an Introduction signed "M.W.S." and a title page that attributed the novel's authorship to "the author of 'The Last Man,' 'Perkin Warbeck' & c & c." From the title pages of *The Last Man, Perkin Warbeck,* & c & c., however, it would be impossible to discover who the author of this particular *Frankenstein* was, as these and the other novels

Mary Shelley would publish during her lifetime all appeared with the legend, "by the Author of 'Frankenstein,' "[22] or sometimes, to vary the formula, "by the Author of 'Frankenstein,' 'The Last Man,' etc." Only pirated editions of the novels and *Mathilda*, which remained unpublished during Mary Shelley's lifetime, escaped the vicious circle. Mary Shelley's short pieces were sometimes signed "M.W.S." Poems and essays signed "Mary S——," "M.S.," and "ΣΖ" may or may not have come from her; certainly most of her short stories, essays, and poems were unsigned.

Mary Shelley felt all her life a strong intermittent disgust at the idea of publicity. "I have an invincible objection to the seeing my name in print," she wrote in 1824 (*MWS Letters* I, 455); "I fear publicity ... it would destroy me to be brought forward in print," in 1829 (*MWS Letters* II, 94); "for my own private satisfaction all I ask is obscurity," in 1837 (*MWS Letters* II, 281). Mary Poovey has suggested we read Mary Shelley's apparent attraction to literary self-effacement[23] in terms of an ambivalence towards what she would have regarded as the unfeminine but nevertheless profoundly desirable self-assertion inherent in authorship;[24] James Carson, on the other hand, finds in this same self-effacement evidence of "an incipient critique of the individualist notion of originary creativity" and an allegiance to an ideal of "non-originary and non-assertive" authorship.[25] Mary Shelley does seem at times to value the signs and perquisites of the authorship of others as little as she does her own. The fact that *Frankenstein*'s narrators quote from poems by Coleridge, Wordsworth, Hunt, and even Mary Shelley's own husband, poems which, if Anne Mellor's dating of the poem's events is right,[26] would not yet have been written at the time of their fictional quotation, suggests, as Peter McInerney notes, an authorial willingness to detach the words of the poems from the facts of their authorship even as she notes them. Figures she describes as authors (or as narrators) exert but little control over their material, their "better-than-Boswellian stenography"[27] and essentially indistinguishable styles effectively subordinating authorship (even realism of character)[28] to the function of narrative transmission. Whether such effects are programmatic or merely inept one would hesitate to say. Certainly, Mary Shelley does not always deprecate authorship. Critics have noted not only the deep investment she would make in her husband's reputation but also the elements of competitiveness and even parasitism in that investment.[29]

However feminist or merely feminine her intentions, soon after her literary life had begun the obscurity of her production ceased to be a matter of choice. Obscurity was required of her by Sir Timothy Shelley, her dead husband's father, who, holding her responsible for his son's ruin, threatened to withhold all financial support if she brought the Shelley name before the public. She withdrew her edition of Percy Shelley's *Posthumous Poems* from circulation and held back from writing a biography of her husband. She managed to win Sir Timothy's permission to publish her 1839 edition of *The Poetical Works of P. B. Shelley* only because literary pirates had by that time so publicized the Shelley name that Mary Shelley's edition could, in his eyes, do it little further damage.

Sir Timothy's horror at the idea of Mary Shelley's use of the Shelley name was more than a dread of public opinion. The name was intolerable to him even in the privacy of the family. He could so little bear mention of his son's name that when his little grandson Charles was buried with the rest of the Shelley family, Sir Timothy ordered the tombstone to omit all reference to his parentage (White, *Shelley* I, 13). The name had a similar, although less durable, effect upon William Godwin, who, after his daughter's elopement, wrote to the poet angrily refusing a check from him and demanding that it be rewritten and (Godwin being Godwin) resubmitted:

> I return your cheque because no consideration can induce me to utter a cheque drawn by you and containing my name.... I hope you will send a duplicate of it by the post which will reach me on Saturday morning. You may make it payable to Joseph Hume or James Martin or any other name in the whole directory. I should prefer it being payable to Mr. Hume.
>
> (Grylls, *Godwin*, 205)

Though unwilling to forfeit Percy Shelley's money for the sake of principled objection to his behavior, Godwin balked at the presence of his name on any check the poet might write. It was as though he believed Percy Shelley's name carried a magical threat of contamination from which he could protect himself only by taking a pseudonym himself.

For, along with the frivolity and negligence in the Shelley circle's attitude towards naming, there was an element of something like superstition, a sense that names were not indifferent labels but things akin to what they named, to be valued or dreaded as their referents (themselves perhaps no more than textual effects) might be valued or dreaded. Godwin for all his rationalism felt this, as his reluctance to allow Percy Shelley to write his name on a check suggests; so did the unimaginative Sir Timothy. Though one might shed a name and take another in order to hide from the consequences of being identified with a particular history—though, that is, the shedding of a name might be an act of powerful (or wishful) self-making—the loss of a name could also signify powerlessness. To be unnamed could signify helplessness to resist exclusion from the community and the memory of the living.

Mary Shelley knew this. Her first child, whom she may have meant to name "Mary Wollstonecraft Godwin III" after her mother and herself, died before she could be named and was buried anonymously (Sunstein, *Mary Shelley*, 97). It was the death Mary Shelley grieved for, not the anonymity, but the event would have been enough to suggest a connection between the two conditions in her mind. Nor was the connection anomalous; in Claire's loss of her daughter Allegra, buried by a combination of malevolence and carelessness in an unmarked grave,[30] Mary Shelley would have recognized a more horrific version of the same association.

Those at least were unintended losses. There were others, even more disturbing. During the time of the writing of *Frankenstein*, in October of 1816, on her way to visit some Wollstonecraft relations, Mary Shelley's half-sister Fanny, daughter of Mary Wollstonecraft and Gilbert Imlay, who had been raised in Godwin's household after Wollstonecraft's death, killed herself. The Swansea *Cambrian* reported her death—that of an unnamed woman who had left a suicide note that read:

> I have long determined that the best thing I could do was to put an end to the existence of a being whose birth was unfortunate, and whose life has only been a series of pain to those persons who have hurt their health in endeavoring to promote her welfare. Perhaps to hear of my death will give you pain, but you will soon have the blessing of forgetting that such a creature existed as

There was no signature, someone—presumably she herself—having destroyed it, thereby creating an anonymity in which Godwin might take refuge from scandal (*Clairmont Correspondence*, 86). Fanny was buried in a pauper's unmarked grave, and none of the family attended the funeral. Godwin put the story about that she had died of a cold, grudging even of this lie; her stepbrother Charles Clairmont was unaware of her death for nearly a year after. She had been allowed to erase herself almost completely: stripped years earlier of her belief that she was a Godwin, she was now, for the sake of the name she could not share, more thoroughly disowned, rendered unreal even in her nonexistence. Two months later—the second loss—Harriet Shelley also committed suicide, she too forfeiting her name in the process. Her body was identified as that of "Harriet Smith," either because that was the name she had given the landlady who later identified her or because the family arranged the fraud to protect themselves from disgrace (White, *Shelley* I, 482). Thus the deaths both of Fanny and of Harriet were simultaneously confirmed and denied in the erasure of their names.

Mary Shelley seems ordinarily not to have believed very much in words apart from their serviceability. But sometimes she behaved, like her father, as though she believed in a magical correlation between naming and being—the possibility of ending one by ending the other or, conversely, prolonging the one through the other. In the aftermath of Percy Shelley's drowning, she expressed what looks very much like superstitious guilt. In a journal entry made three months after his loss, she wrote, "On the 8th of July I finished my journal. This is a curious coincidence. The date still remains—the fatal 8th—a monument to show that all ended then."[31] She cannot really have believed that she could have kept her husband alive past "the fatal 8th" by writing without intermission or conclusion, but some part of her fears that, in coming to the last page of the volume in which she recorded their life together, she has ended his story. If coming to the last page could kill someone, perhaps emptying out a fearsome word could empty it of its terror. Thinking, the following year, about the passage from *The Tempest* that Trelawny had inscribed on her husband's tombstone ("Nothing of him that doth fade,/But doth suffer a sea-change/Into something rich & strange"), she wrote, "This quotation by its double meaning alludes both to the manner of his d____h and his genius" (*MWS Letters* I, 334). So she emptied out the word "death" in order to empty it of its reality; but then, as if to mask what she was about, she went on in the letter to empty Trelawny's name as well, turning him into "T____y." Or is this negligence once again?—or half-belief, a wish to believe in word magic such as her husband had from his incantation-obsessed childhood indulged in? If the latter, it is tempting to read in the vacating of Mary Shelley's name from the title page of *Frankenstein* the same way, an anxious countermagic meant to block whatever power her words might otherwise carry, an uneasy emptying, an equivocation, a gesture expressing her wish for exemption from the claims of words both written and unwritten.

★ ★ ★ ★ ★

Many of the associations anonymity held for Mary Shelley and her circle—with helplessness, with displacement of blame, with magic, with death—appear again in the circumstances of the anonymous publication of *Frankenstein* and in the situation of the novel's anonymous protagonist. Mary Shelley's own explanation of what she meant by publishing *Frankenstein* anonymously came in a letter she wrote to Sir Walter Scott soon after his review of the novel appeared in *Blackwood's Edinburgh*

Magazine, March 1818. She wrote to correct his supposition that the novel's author was her husband:

> I am anxious to prevent your continuing in the mistake of supposing Mr Shelley guilty of a juvenile attempt of mine; to which—from its being written at an early age, I abstained from putting my name—and from respect to those persons from whom I bear it. I have therefore kept it concealed except from a few friends.
>
> (*MWS Letters* I, 71)

If her name names notable others, as it so famously does, then her refusal to name herself is a way of not naming those others, shielding them from blame in matters that are her own individual responsibility. That, at least, is how she wants Scott to see the matter. But she had left clues one might almost suspect were designed to lead a reader into just such a mistake as she reproaches Scott for making. Although perhaps at the last minute her enthusiastic desire to honor her father overcame all other considerations, one would think that a writer in earnest about shielding her father from whatever mud might be slung in the course of the book's reviewing would probably not have written such a dedication as this:

To
WILLIAM GODWIN,
Author of Political Justice, Caleb Williams, &C.
These Volumes
Are respectfully inscribed
By
The Author[32]

The dedication by "The Author" to the "Author" ("of Political Justice, Caleb Williams, &C.") claims equality and may even hint (mischievously) at identity: the form of a writer addressing his doubled self, claiming a name through address. It also alludes to Mary Shelley's other "Author," Mary Wollstonecraft, whose tombstone Godwin had inscribed thus:

MARY WOLLSTONECRAFT GODWIN,
Author of
A VINDICATION
OF THE RIGHTS OF WOMAN:
Born 27 April 1759;
DIED 10 September, 1797[33]

And of course the dedication sounds—would have sounded to those almost but not quite enough in the know—like something that other author, Percy Shelley, Godwin's ambivalent and unappreciated benefactor, could have composed. By writing the dedication as she does, Mary Shelley puts herself in the position of one who knows Godwin not as a daughter knows her father (by way of an involuntary, even passive relation) but rather as one writer (the author of *Queen Mab*, say) might know another. The dedication may be read as an impersonation, though a secret, almost a joking one.[34] Percy Shelley, after all, had not only made it possible for her to protect her anonymity by dealing with her publishers himself, but also in ghostwriting the novel's Preface impersonated her. In effect, she frames her father and her husband.

The dedication—a "double-edged" one, U. C. Knoepflmacher remarks[35]—thus inscribes the blank on the title page with the very names Mary Shelley professed to be protecting. But it inscribes them not so much in the form of authors or owners of the name "Mary Wollstonecraft Godwin Shelley" as in the form of recognized positions of literary authority she could play at inhabiting. The blank on the title page reclaims the name as her own and provides her with another, "the author of *Frankenstein*," which, after some years of critical confusion, would be hers and no one else's.[36]

But Mary Shelley was unable to reclaim the work merely by putting her name to it (as she did in 1823). It has shown itself to be an essentially anonymous text, its story adapted and revised and parodied almost out of recognition, a tale most powerful (as Christopher Small points out) "where the book hasn't been read" (Small, *MS's Frankenstein*, 15).[37] Most importantly, the monster—the figure to whom the common non-reader thinks the name "Frankenstein" refers—is anonymous, and his anonymity, unlike his author's in 1818, is involuntary and unredeemed.[38] The blank on the title page acknowledges an anonymity whose most devastating effects lie elsewhere.

★ ★ ★ ★ ★

As Peter McInerney points out, *Frankenstein* is a "story about story-telling," "a re-constructed text of tissues grafted from the bodies of European books about the creation of man," a book whose central figure is a "blot," a "filthy type" that leaves black "prints" on his victims and is promised a "sequel" to marry.[39] Instead of a discussion of the processes of his physical generation, about which Frankenstein is vague, we are offered a curiously complicated narrative about the production and transmission of his story, a displacement of the sexual or technological onto the narratological. Words and bodies seem composed of the same substance. Mary Shelley herself makes the parallel between the origin of the monster and that of her "hideous progeny" the novel, "the offspring of happy days," in her 1831 Introduction (*Frankenstein*, 228, 229).[40]

In this perversely text-obsessed and literalminded text, where words share the nature of things, to lack a name is to lack full, indubitable reality. Nameless, the monster—though almost absurdly verbal, the evidence of his wordly origin and nature as plain as Nobody's ever is—tends to disappear from view, perceptible often only by way of borrowed language and analogical structure, by way of the pull he exerts upon the language around him. His power does not lie in his rhetoric. To those who meet him his words matter less than his material body; the effect of his eloquence is largely undone by the horror of his face and form.[41] Nor is it only the monster's words whose power to communicate or persuade is compromised. The novel's three principal narrators all behave as though they expected, even hoped, that their words might not be received or understood. Frankenstein in particular, exploiting the unreliability of words, issues a series of confessions carefully designed to be unintelligible, and, though motivated differently, the monster and Walton engage in similar behavior, the monster telling Walton the end of the story whose "very remembrance" he declares "will speedily vanish" (*Frankenstein*, 220), Walton writing the whole in letters to his sister that he believes will perish with him before he or his words can reach her. The verbal gesture is what they focus on, their addresses seemingly designed for (or resigned to) blockage or opacity, or oblivion. Wordly substance marks the absence of intended reference and the anticipated failure of reception.

The earliest adaptors of Mary Shelley's tale felt the importance of the monster's anonymity, as the author herself recognized when she attended a performance of H.M. Milner's *Frankenstein or, The Man and the Monster. A Romantic Melodrama, in Two Acts* in August, 1826, soon after its opening. The *dramatis personae* contained no name for the monster, not even "the monster," but instead marked the place where a name might have been expected with a row of asterisks (Mellor, *Mary Shelley*, 133).[42] Mary Shelley was pleased:"The play bill amused me extremely, for in the list of dramatis personae came, ——by Mr T. Cooke: this nameless mode of naming the un{n}ameable is rather good" (*MWS Letters*, I, 378).[43]

Mary Shelley's own "mode of naming the un{n}nameable" is subtler. Instead of asterisks, which make a clear (perhaps excessively clear) point about the absence of a name, she supplies a series of name-substitutes: "my work" (so Frankenstein calls him), "my creation," "the accomplishment of my toils," "the creature," "the wretch," "one who fled from me," "the demoniacal corpse," "dreaded spectre," "the filthy daemon to whom I had given life," and so on. These terms are useless for naming as opposed to reviling. They fail to supply the materials for constructing an answer to "Who are you?" Common rather than proper nouns, they point towards the monster as (or as within) a category or species rather than as an individual.[44] Particularization comes through modifiers derived from Frankenstein's sense of implication in what he describes: not just the monster but the monster that he made; not just any demon but the demon who is his enemy. Such descriptions locate the monster upon the coordinates of Frankenstein's intentions, projects, perceptions, and revulsions; they allow for neither unprejudiced evaluation nor independence; they subordinate the monster to Frankenstein's fantasies and intentions—turn the monster into a symptom, or double, or unacknowledged fraction of his maker. A story that names a character "the miserable daemon whom I had sent abroad into the world for my destruction" cannot diverge far from a particular kind of story unless it comes up with some other, less powerfully determining way of indicating that character, a mode of reference that does not already imply the story in which it figures.

★ ★ ★ ★ ★

The monster inhabits the divide that the grammar of Nobody opens. Though he rebels against his nonentity and tries without success to enter into the relations that would be available to him as somebody, he is helpless to escape the ugliness, the unreality, the guilty confusion of persons, the problems and paradoxes that attend embodied Nobodiliness. If the classic Nobody's adventures are structured by the excess of name to body, the monster's are motivated by the excess of body to name. Yet that physical excess seems oddly insubstantial. Considered in the mass, his body is that uncanny thing, the negation of a negation, the materials of his making having been drawn from corrupt and decayed matter that, though reanimated, never quite redeems itself from waste. If death is an emptying out of life from the body, what Frankenstein does in creating his monster is not so much to restore life as to vacate the effect of that emptying, and the monster inherits the consequences: the conditions of his being are established by the terrible uncertainty of his ontological status. To the eye of the beholder he seems not so much alive as undead.

The novel does not require us to confront the monster's ugliness directly. Although we are given a few details of the face and to a lesser extent the figure, Mary Shelley was either uninterested in or incapable of making the horror of his physical being vivid to us. The result is that the ugliness is something we infer from the monstrous reactions he draws from the other characters. To judge by these reactions ("Never did I behold a vision so horrible as his face, of such loathsome, yet appalling hideousness. I shut my eyes involuntarily") (*Frankenstein*, 216), his hideousness must indeed be overwhelming, threatening in a way that has nothing to do with any menace he offers. He is simply impossible to look upon. And so, one after another, characters cover their eyes. Thus they deprive him temporarily of visibility. It is an odd gesture, and it becomes odder in the repetition. Those who cover their faces—always their own, never his—behave as though acting upon an unwilling and unowned identification. They behave as though it were their own faces that were the problem, or as though covering theirs were somehow equivalent to covering his,[45] or else perhaps as though they hoped or believed that he might somehow exist only as a creation or reflex of the eye or the mind. The gesture suggests the monster is for them a function of visibility, belief, or identification rather than a being in his own right.

Frankenstein too behaves as if he were just slightly unsure of the monster's independent reality. From the earliest moments of his creature's life, Frankenstein treats him like a trick of the eyes, a nightmare vision that ought to be capable of being annihilated by the mere refusal to countenance it. To make the newly created monster go away, Frankenstein goes to sleep; when that fails (he wakes up and there the monster is again), he runs out of the house.[46] As far as Frankenstein is concerned, a monster he does not have to look at is a monster that does not exist.

The novel treats the monster, grossly and obtrusively material though he is, as if he were not just unbearable to behold or hard to see but as if he were not quite certainly there. Were he a conventional novelistic character, a normal avenger or murderer, he would leave traces of himself in the stories told about his actions; the countryside would be filled with complaints. At the very least, there would be a sense of some agency left unaccounted for, evidence of the monster in the form of gaps or holes in the accounts others give of their lives, and efforts to find the meaning of these gaps.[47]

It is not that the monster's actions fail entirely to register. He leaves a trail of terror and death, and sometimes, though less frequently than one would expect, those who encounter him speak of these encounters.

But the impressions the monster leaves fade fast; the gaps seal themselves behind him.[48] The monster's charitable deeds—the cutting of the DeLacys' firewood, "always replenished by an invisible hand," the leaving of refreshments for the furiously pursuing Frankenstein—are wondered at a little and then credited to some "*good spirit*" (by the briefly puzzled DeLacys [*Frankenstein*, 108, 110]) or (by the more strangely naive Frankenstein) to "the spirits that I had invoked to aid me" (*Frankenstein*, 201). That ends the matter. It is not much different with deeds of violence.[49] The story expels the monster's unassimilable agency as a healing wound expels a splinter. For the incuriosity about the first two murders there is perhaps an explanation: the monster's success in framing the second victim as the killer of the first has satisfied the townspeople that the mystery has been solved. Frankenstein, Elizabeth, and Justine know that this is not the case, but Frankenstein will not tell what he knows and neither Elizabeth nor Justine seems particularly curious about the mystery. About none of the other murders is there any curiosity at all. At Clerval's death, Frankenstein is arrested; coincidence and his own sense of responsibility contrive to make him look guilty, as indeed on some level he is. But when he provides an alibi charges are dismissed and that is the end of the matter.[50] There is no serious pursuit of Elizabeth's killer, "most of my companions," says Frankenstein, "believing it to have been a form conjured by my fancy." The dead body with the "murderous mark of the fiend's grasp ... on her neck" (*Frankenstein*, 193) requires no explanation.

If the novel tends partially to erase the monster, it also renders him extraneous through multiplication.[51] Having begun life as a replacement, or possibly instead of a replacement,[52] he comes to resemble a multiple, a crowd, or (inhabiting what he calls "the series of my being," "the miserable series of my being" [*Frankenstein*, 220, 217]),[53] a family (but an ambiguous, unnatural family—perhaps one like that in which Mary Shelley grew up)[54] of those generations that will never be born to him, even his own entire synecdochic species. Certainly his physical form, containing a liver from one corpse, a kidney from another, a lung from a third, and so on, implies an entire population, a horrific confusion of persons, a monstrous Everybody. Not only the monster himself but also the scenes in which he appears have a way of overlapping their near-doubles in ways that redistribute meanings and responsibilities. Why should the terms of Frankenstein's creation of the monster recur in the scenes of Clerval's arrival at Ingolstadt, for instance, and in Frankenstein's subsequent illness and restoration to life? It is as if the elements of his story did not actually require his existence, or as if his story were a way of organizing other stories.

The *as if*ness of these "as if"s is prominent and contagious. Fleeing the monster, Frankenstein flees "as if I sought to avoid the wretch whom I feared"; he goes to the inn where the carriages stop and waits there "with my eyes fixed on a coach that was coming towards me from the other end of the street," "I knew not why," but as if he knew his friend were arriving, as indeed his friend does (*Frankenstein*, 54, 55); and so on. The indistinguishability of the *as if* from the straight indicative pulls the (fictional) fact towards the contrary to fact. The effect, brief but recurrent and cumulative, suggests a seepage of Nobodily unreality from the monster's presence.

★ ★ ★ ★ ★

The monster inhabits the logically impossible body Frankenstein has created for him as though it were a horrible inconvenience and as a grotesque frame. Implicated in appearances that seem to accuse him of crimes before he has yet a motive to commit them, imprisoned in a body that seems to tell its own slanderous tales about him, he has been effectively, if inadvertently, set up.[55]

Although bound to his creator and from our perspective seeming to act as an agent of the violent wishes his creator cannot admit to, it never occurs to the monster that he does not possess his own individual meaning. The ideals of resurrection and redemption that brought him into being have nothing to do with his sense of himself; nor do Frankenstein's motives, conscious or not, color his own.[56] Not even common experience binds them together. The two scenes that make such an enormous impression upon Frankenstein, the moment when first the monster opens his eyes and the slightly belated repetition of it when Frankenstein opens his eyes upon the monster, scenes that fill the man with horror and a conviction of his creature's evil, make no lasting impression upon the monster at all. He has his own reasons for what he does. If others, particularly Frankenstein, cannot see this, he must make them see.

So the monster sets about trying to make himself visible. At first, as if either for emphasis or for the elimination of distracting ambiguities, he points to (and destroys) those he doubles or thinks he doubles: William, whose careless words lead the monster to believe he has found his more favored brother; and Justine, a victim (like the monster) of appearances, her story (like his) disregarded, but (unlike the monster) attractive in her distress (*Frankenstein*, 139). But if the monster is hoping to generate through his victims an excess of pity in which he may share, a funnelled and displaced compassion that he may receive in default of any other living candidate, or a more sympathetic reflection of his own suffering, he is disappointed. Although Frankenstein pities Justine (and pitied William) as he does not pity the monster, he does no more to aid her in her helplessness than he did for his own creature and has none even of his ineffectual pity to spare for him. The guilt he feels about his role in her judicial murder has about it a fictional quality, as though to entertain it required a suspension of his disbelief; it no more leads him to act than would an emotionally affecting novel. Then, the doubling of the monster's plight in that of Frankenstein's family having failed, the monster goes to work in a different direction. Through the murders of Clerval and Elizabeth he reconstructs Frankenstein as his double in emotional devastation. If Frankenstein cannot see the reality of the monster reflected in the glass of William or Justine, perhaps he can be made to recognize the reality of the monster's pain when it is his own.

Frankenstein never does achieve this recognition. But he now learns what the monster has long known: what it is like to use a powerful rhetoric to no practical effect. When at last, all his family dead, he goes to a magistrate to lay a charge against the monster, he finds his impassioned oration received as though it were merely a brilliant piece of oratory—a Polyphemus's tale, a tale of Nobody—and disbelieved (*Frankenstein*, 197). It is as if he were himself infected with the monster's implausibility.

Frankenstein has never wanted to make either an intelligible confession of his responsibility for what has happened or an intelligible accusation of the monster. But even if he had wanted to point the finger and say, "X is the killer," he could not. He himself has made it impossible. There is no name to put in the place of X; nor is there a narrative gap where an X might go—no place and no placeholder, either. There is Nobody. Until Frankenstein meets a man who has seen the monster for himself, he cannot speak more intelligibly than could Homer's blinded, complaining cyclops; until the monster appears before the eyes of a witness and provides the bodily foundation for reference, Frankenstein's tale of a body at once obtrusive and elusive, nearly invisible in its anonymity, signifying everybody and Nobody, can find no footing for itself.

The hunt that brings the novel to its conclusion is what the failure of naming, which means in part the failure of narrative, gives way to: there being no sign by which to apprehend the monster, the monster himself must be apprehended. The monster connives at his own apprehension—connives at least at his own hunting or seeking, leading Frankenstein on. That in doing so he can torment him, can make his maker feel the misery that he has felt, must add to his pleasure. But he does so primarily to open a place for himself in what he has called "the chain of existence and events from which I am now excluded" (*Frankenstein*, 143).[57] Luring Frankenstein on, he turns Frankenstein, now a reflection of himself, a reflection moreover with a name, into a pointer or sign that points at or signifies him. Hunted because he cannot be named, he colludes with his hunter for the sake of the signifying structure that that hunting enacts. What he is trying to escape is not Frankenstein but nonentity.

★ ★ ★ ★ ★

Only once in this novel is the monster asked his name, at a point at which all the violence of the story might yet have been averted. The question, put to him by blind old De Lacy, a weak and sentimental Polyphemus whose home and serenity are about to be destroyed, draws from the monster a story at once conventional and manipulative, intended to present him as similar to his auditor and thus worthy of his interest and aid (*Frankenstein*, 129–31). In response to the old man's gentle questioning, the monster represents himself as a lonely figure, "an unfortunate and deserted creature" who fears that the "amiable people" to whom he is about to apply for help may refuse him their sympathy. "A fatal prejudice clouds their eyes," he tells the blind man, "and where they ought to see a feeling and kind friend, they behold only a detestable monster." His creator's true creature, he speaks so as not to be understood.

Failing at first to recognize the monster's replication of his own family's rhetorical and narrative conventions as a replication, the old man, who cannot see the face of the creature speaking to him, thinks he has encountered a *Landsman* ("By your language, stranger, I suppose you are my countryman"). He takes the coincidences of the monster's experience with his own family's to be interesting accidents to be listened to with sympathetic complacency. So if the monster is "unfortunate and deserted," De Lacy is "poor, and an exile"; if the monster has "unknown to [his friends], been for many months in the habits of daily kindness towards them," De Lacy charitably declares "it will afford [him] true pleasure to be in any way serviceable to a human creature."

The reason De Lacy responds to the story is that it is more or less his own; his sympathy is innocent, unwitting self-love. The reason he does not know it is his own story is that the monster has so fractured and confused his personal referents that it has become impossible for the naively trusting De Lacy to follow who it is that the monster is talking about. The monster's first person, his represented "I," is modelled upon the object of his second person, his "you," De Lacy himself, while his second person is divided between the second person and the third ("they"), and the third is itself shattered and shared between the French family who have educated him and the perhaps nonexistent friends to whom he is now going. De Lacy fails to recognize himself or his family in the monster's third-personal allusions, in the references to the mysteriously ill-judging, malevolent, and improbable friends. He does not see himself as implicated in the blindness (the clouded eyes) of these "friends" who, in spite of never having seen the figure who now speaks of them, nevertheless "behold" this interlocutor who has been "for many months in the habits of daily kindness towards them," although what they behold in him (when they behold him) is not the "feeling and kind friend" he truly is but "only a detestable monster" who "wish[es] to injure them." In his blindness, De Lacy can neither literally nor figuratively see any monster either literal or figurative. He is unaware of having been unknowingly in receipt of "daily kindnesses" from any kind but invisible friends, nor does he, who has just been preaching the essential goodness of man ("when unprejudiced by any obvious self-interest"), believe that he believes anyone wishes to injure him. How could he possibly think these strange friends have anything to do with him? What he feels instead is an identification with the monster: "I also am unfortunate; I and my family have been condemned, although innocent; judge, therefore, if I do not feel for your misfortunes." Then he asks, "May I know the names and residence of those friends?"

This is the crisis. Hearing the sound of the children's approach, the monster seizes the old man's hand and cries aloud.

> "Now is the time!—save and protect me! You and your family are the friends whom I seek. Do not you desert me in the hour of trial!"
>
> "Great God" exclaimed the old man, "who are you?"
>
> At that instant the cottage door was opened, and Felix, Safie, and Agatha entered. Who can describe their horror and consternation on beholding me? Agatha fainted; and Safie, unable to attend to her friend, rushed out of the cottage. Felix darted forward, and with supernatural force tore me from his father, to whose knees I clung: in a transport of fury, he dashed me to the ground, and struck me violently with a stick. I could have torn him limb from limb, as the lion rends the antelope. But my heart sunk within me as with bitter sickness, and I refrained.

The bursting in of the family may be read in terms of the shock the old man must have felt at the monster's conversion of the third person into the second, his "they" ("they behold only a detestable monster") into "you" ("You and your family are the friends whom I seek"). The morally comfortable difference between the clouded eyes and the blind ones, the friend and the stranger, vanishes. Touching plaint becomes accusation and demand ("Do not you desert me in the hour of trial!"). Abruptly, De Lacy is in the position of the magistrate Frankenstein goes to when all his friends are dead, who "heard my story with that half kind of belief that is given to a tale of spirits and supernatural events; but when he was called upon to act officially in consequence, the whole tide of his incredulity returned" (*Frankenstein*, 197). He is in the position of Frankenstein, who, long absorbed in his fiction of immortality, finds it at last alive, a fiction no longer but a real creature who horrifyingly sees him. He is in the position of the monster, who inhabits a body that is a frame-up and a frame tale. The old man is framed, trapped, implicated, made responsible by the appealing little tale that had touched his self-approving heart.[58]

The safe line between story and vital demand or accusation is down. The collapse of the ordinality of persons—begun when the monster's first person began to exert a tidal pull upon his splitting, self-abandoning second, now turned menacing as his second person absorbs his third— requires De Lacy to recognize himself in the fiction of the hostile and prejudiced third person, requires him to occupy the place of what he is not (or not yet). There is no way out: not to answer the accusation, not to admit he is the one being addressed, is to become guilty of what would otherwise be a false accusation. The monster's "you" has cast De Lacy into the uninhabitable space of paradoxical Nobodiliness, where one exists fractured, doubled, guilty, indistinguishable from one's own opposite and negation.

"Who are you?" Lacking a name, what answer could the monster have given even had the children not arrived? The entrance of Felix, Agatha, and Safie figures the answer—the unimaginable answer—that it interrupts.

"Who can describe their horror and consternation on beholding me?" the monster exclaims. Who can describe the horror and consternation of each at the indescribable horror and consternation of the other? For a moment of terrifying confrontation, the monster and the family exchange places. As David Punter remarks, "to be the monster is also to be the monster's victim, to be the monster as a victim" (Punter, *Gothic Pathologies*, 45). The monster's "supernatural force" appears now in the son, who "tore me from his father, to whose knees I clung: in a transport of fury, he dashed me to the ground, and struck me violently with a stick." The specular chaos, the confusion of persons—which is implicit in the monster's physical incoherence, in the tale that is the rhetorical equivalent of that incoherence, in the relations of crossed and fractured sympathies and identifications he constructs from De Lacy's audience, and in the attack that speaks for the old man's attempt to refuse implication—this is the monster's unspeakable reply, and he escapes, like Nobody, like Οὖτίς, blinder of the monstrous Polyphemus who is his other form, "unperceived."

Notes

1. Letter of April 6, 1819 in Mary Wollstonecraft Shelley, *The Letters of Mary Wollstonecraft Shelley*, vol. 1, ed. by Betty T. Bennett (Baltimore: The Johns Hopkins University Press, 1980), 91.
2. Homer, *The Odyssey*, trans. Robert Fagles (New York: Viking, 1996), 224.
3. Letter of June 11, 1835, in Mary Wollstonecraft Shelley, *The Letters of Mary Wollstonecraft Shelley*, vol. 2, edited by Betty T. Bennett (Baltimore: The Johns Hopkins University Press, 1983), 246.
4. Mary Wollstonecraft Shelley, *Frankenstein, or, The Modern Prometheus. The 1818 Text*, ed. by James Rieger, reprint, 1974 (Chicago: The University of Chicago Press, 1982), 226.
5. Charles Mitchell, ed., *Hogarth's Peregrination* (Oxford: Clarendon Press, 1952), xxiv.
6. Thus, the story of Nobody is the story of "people who never actually lived." Catherine Gallagher, *Nobody's Story: The Vanishing Acts of Women Writers in the Marketplace, 1670–1820* (Berkeley: University of California Press, 1994), 165, 203–4.
7. Gerta Calmann, "The Picture of Nobody," *Journal of the Warburg and Courtauld Institutes* XXIII (1960), 91.
8. Homer, *The Odyssey of Homer*, W.B. Stanford, trans. and ed., 2nd ed. (London: Macmillan, 1964), vol. I, Book IX, 144, line 408.
9. Polyphemus's name forms an additional link between the two figures. Though the name belongs to the cyclops, it better describes his adversary: "speaking much" or "much storied."
10. Robert Gittings and Jo Manton, *Claire Clairmont and the Shelleys 1798–1879* (Oxford: Oxford University Press, 1992), 3, 4, 52, 61–2, 68, 70, 197; *The Clairmont Correspondence: Letters of Claire Clairmont, Charles Clairmont, and Fanny Imlay Godwin*, vol. 1, ed. by Marion Kingston Stocking (Baltimore: The Johns Hopkins University Press, 1995), 26 n. 4, 42–3 n. 2, 134–5 n. 9; Rosalie Glynn Grylls, *William Godwin and His World* (London: Odhams Press, 1953), 64; Don Locke, *A Fantasy of Reason: The Life and Thought of William Godwin* (London: Routledge & Kegan Paul, 1980), 214.
11. See also letter to Teresa Guiccioli, August 20, 1827, in *MWS Letters* I, 565. She was not equally attached to, or careful of other people's names. She tended, like many others in a hurry, to abbreviate names to initials, turning "Claire" into "C____," "The Godwins" into "the G____'s," and so forth, and when she did not abbreviate she often misspelled the names of friends. But then she was never very strong on spelling—and one must remember that this was a time when women (poor Harriet Shelley, e.g.) were capable of spelling even their own names wrong ("Harriett").
12. It flourished despite the frowns. See Gaye Tuchman and Nina E. Fortin, *Edging Women Out: Victorian Novelists, Publishers, and Social Change* (New Haven: Yale University Press, 1989), 45, 53.
13. James Raven finds that between 1810 and the late 1820s anonymous novels accounted for between roughly fifty and eighty percent of all new novelistic production. See James Raven, "The Anonymous Novel in Britain and Ireland, 1750–1830," in this volume.
14. So a frustrated John Wilson described the unknown author of *The Doctor & C.* (Robert Southey) in his review of that work in *Blackwood's Edinburgh Magazine* 38 (1835). See Michael

Shortland, "Robert Southey's *The Doctor & C.*: Anonymity and Authorship," *English Language Notes* 31, no. 4 (June 1994), 60.

15. See Newman Ivey White, *Shelley*, vol. I (New York: Knopf, 1940), 291. Even so, a reviewer of the poem for *The Beacon* (Edinburgh) declared, "It is to be hoped that no such person as *Percy Bysshe Shelley* the author, exists, and that the atrocious poetry committed in his name is but the well-intended device of some fiery moralist, who employs the name of Lord Byron's friend and pupil to show, by a species of *reductio ad absurdum*, the infernal portal to which his Lordship's system pushed to its limit will necessarily lead." *The Romantics Reviewed: Contemporary Reviews of British Romantic Writers*, vol. I, Part C: Shelley, Keats, and London Radical Writers, ed. Donald H. Reiman (New York: Garland, 1972), 39.

16. Letter to Edward Fergus Graham, 14 February 1811, in Percy Bysshe Shelley, *The Letters of Percy Bysshe Shelley*, vol. 1, ed. Frederick L. Jones (Oxford: Clarendon Press, 1964), 402.

17. Letter to Charles Ollier, 16 February 1821, in *PBS Letters* II, 262–3.

18. *The Wrongs of Woman*, left incomplete at her death, was published by Godwin in his edition of the *Posthumous Works of the Author of A Vindication of the Rights of Woman*.

19. Like many others, Godwin's surname had been subject to change down the centuries, "variously spelled," as he himself remarked, "Godden, Godwyn, Godwin, Godwine, and Goodwin." William Godwin, "Autobiography," in *Collected Novels and Memoirs of William Godwin*, vol. 1, ed. Mark Philp (London: William Pickering, 1992), 3.

20. *Jane Grey* performed the unusual feat of managing to appear under one pseudonym in one edition and then under the other pseudonym in another edition.

21. The first edition to name her—more or less—was the Paris edition of 1821, the novel's first translation, which introduced her on the title page as "Mme. Shelly." An 1823 London reprint of the 1818 original gave her name properly. The evidence of the New York Public Library CATNYP contradicts or at least augments W.H. Lyles, *Mary Shelley: An Annotated Bibliography* (New York: Garland, 1975), 6.

22. Even this title can be unreliable. "The Pole" was published as the work of "the Author of 'Frankenstein' " but is in fact the work of Claire Clairmont. See Elizabeth Nitchie, *Mary Shelley: Author of "Frankenstein"* (New Brunswick, N.J.: Rutgers University Press, 1953), 29.

23. "As a professional writer, [Mary] Shelley masters appearing other than herself... [she] even masters appearing invisible." Sonia Hofkosh, *Sexual Politics and the Romantic Author* (Cambridge: Cambridge University Press, 1998), 103.

24. Mary Poovey, *The Proper Lady and the Woman Writer: Ideology as Style in the Works of Mary Wollstonecraft, Mary Shelley, and Jane Austen* (Chicago: University of Chicago Press, 1984), 114–71.

25. James P. Carson, "Bringing the Author Forward: *Frankenstein* Through Mary Shelley's Letters," *Criticism* 30, no. 4 (1988), 436, 446.

26. Anne K. Mellor, *Mary Shelley: Her Life, Her Fiction, Her Monsters* (New York: Routledge, 1988), 54.

27. Peter McInerney, "*Frankenstein* and the Godlike Science of Letters," *Genre* 13 (1980), 456. See also Joan Copjec, "Vampires, Breast-Feeding, and Anxiety," *October* 58 (Fall 1991), 43.

28. Beth Newman notes that "within what one might call the framework of the text, story and character turn out to be separable, even opposing elements, which do not fuse in the creation of narrative discourse." Beth Newman, "Narratives of Seduction and the Seductions of Narrative: The Frame Structure of Frankenstein," *ELH* 53 (1986), 143.

29. On her editorial attitudes, see Mary Favret, "Mary Shelley's Sympathy and Irony: The Editor and Her Corpus," in *The Other Mary Shelley: Beyond Frankenstein*, ed. Audrey A. Fisch, Anne K. Mellor, and Esther H. Schor (New York: Oxford University Press, 1993), 17–38, and Susan J. Wolfston, "Editorial Privilege: Mary Shelley and Percy Shelley's Audiences," in *The Other Mary Shelley*, 39–72.

30. After their little daughter's death, Byron directed his publisher John Murray to oversee the funeral arrangements in his stead, excluding Claire from any share in the matter, indeed directing that Allegra's memorial tablet include no mention of Claire. The intended malice

hardly mattered: the tablet itself was disallowed by the church wardens and the body buried in an unmarked grave. Half a century passed before Claire managed to learn the name of the churchyard where her daughter's body had been mislaid. Gittings and Manton, *Claire Clairmont*, 69–70.

31. Mary Shelley, *Mary Shelley's Journal*, ed. Frederick L. Jones (Norman, Oklahoma: University of Oklahoma Press, 1947), 180.

32. *Frankenstein*, 5.

33. William Godwin, *Memoirs of the Author of A Vindication of the Rights of Woman*, in *"A Short Residence in Sweden, Norway, and Denmark," by Mary Wollstonecraft; and "Memoirs of the Author of the Rights of Woman," by William Godwin*, edited by Richard Holmes (Harmondsworth: Penguin Books, 1987), 271.

34. Christopher Small contends that not only Scott but also the reviewers for the *Quarterly Review* and for the *Edinburgh Magazine* were convinced the writer was Percy Shelley. See Christopher Small, *Mary Shelley's Frankenstein: Tracing the Myth* (Pittsburgh: University of Pittsburgh Press, 1973) 19, 21.

35. U.C. Knoepflmacher, "Thoughts on the Aggression of Daughters," in *The Endurance of Frankenstein: Essays on Mary Shelley's Novel*, ed. George Levine and U.C. Knoepflmacher (Berkeley and Los Angeles: University of California Press, 1979), 97.

36. Her anonymity was resolved gradually, a critic at a time. In 1823 a reviewer of *Valperga* in *Blackwood's* identified her as an "authoress"; in 1826 several reviewers of *The Last Man* referred to the author as "she"; in 1830 a number of reviewers of *Perkin Warbeck* named the author as "Mrs. Shelley," though one of them (for the *Monthly Magazine, or British Register of Literature, Sciences, and the Belles Lettres*) did so with hesitation; in 1833 another reviewer of *The Last Man* for *The Knickerbocker Magazine* was sufficiently uncertain to write merely that he "suppose[d] this lady to be the widow of the far famed poet and atheist Shelly [*sic*]"; and in 1835 a reviewer of *Lodore* for *Fraser's Magazine for Town and Country* felt almost sure that Mary Shelley must have been the author of *Frankenstein*. See Lyles, *Mary Shelley: An Annotated Bibliography*, 172, 173, 174, 175, 178, 179.

37. Playwrights and filmmakers have even sometimes inexplicably renamed the characters as though they too (like their author) were fundamentally anonymous and thus available for the application of whatever name anybody might want to apply to them. See Albert J. Lavalley, "The Stage and Film Children of *Frankenstein*: A Survey," in *The Endurance of Frankenstein*, 243–89; Small, *Shelley's Frankenstein*, 16–18; Johanna M. Smith, " 'Hideous Progenies': Texts of *Frankenstein*," in *Texts and Textuality: Textual Instability, Theory, and Interpretation*, edited by Phillip Cohen (New York: Garland, 1997), 121–40.

38. Bouriana Zakharieva notes that in Kenneth Branagh's film *Mary Shelley's Frankenstein* the monster's reply to "Who are you?" is "He never gave me a name." See Bouriana Zakharieva, "Frankenstein of the Nineties: The Composite Body," in *Frankenstein: Complete, Authoritative Text with Biographical, Historical, and Cultural Contexts, Critical History, and Essays from Contemporary Critical Perspectives*, 2nd ed., ed. Johanna M. Smith (Boston, Bedford: St. Martin's Press, 2000), 425.

39. Peter McInerney, "*Frankenstein* and the Godlike Science of Letters," *Genre* 13 (1980), 455–75. On the monster as a materialization or literalization, see Michael Fried, "Impressionist Monsters: H. G. Wells's 'The Island of Dr Moreau,' " in *Frankenstein: Creation and Monstrosity*, ed. Stephen Bann (London: Reaktion Books, 1994), 95–112; Margaret Homans, *Bearing the Word: Language and Female Experience in Nineteenth-Century Women's Writing* (Chicago: University of Chicago Press, 1986), 115; and David Marshall, *The Surprising Effects of Sympathy: Marivaux, Diderot, Rousseau, and Mary Shelley* (Chicago: University of Chicago Press, 1988), 206–9.

40. The monster's resemblance both to the novel that contains him and the author of that novel has been well studied. See, among others, Sandra M. Gilbert and Susan Gubar, *The Madwoman in the Attic: The Woman Writer and the Nineteenth-Century Literary Imagination* (New Haven: Yale University Press, 1979), 237, 239; Knoepflmacher, "Thoughts," 97; Homans, *Bearing the Word*,

108; Barbara Johnson, " 'My Monster/My Self,' " in *A World of Difference* (Baltimore: The Johns Hopkins University Press, 1987), 144–54; Robert Olorenshaw, "Narrating the Monster: From Mary Shelley to Bram Stoker," in *Frankenstein: Creation and Monstrosity*, 169; Jasia Reichardt, "Artificial Life and the Myth of Frankenstein," in *Frankenstein: Creation and Monstrosity*, 137.

41. The seminal reading of the split between the monster's body and his voice is Peter Brooks, " 'Godlike Science/Unhallowed Arts': Language, Nature, and Monstrosity," in *The Endurance of Frankenstein*, 205–20.

42. James Whale's 1931 film of *Frankenstein* repeated the gesture towards anonymity, omitting Boris Karloff's name from the opening credits, attributing the part of the monster to "?" Karloff's name (such as it was; he was born William Henry Pratt) was given, with those of the rest of the cast, at the end of the film. For these facts, to which my attention was happily directed by the (anonymous) reader of this volume for the press, see Donald F. Glut, *The Frankenstein Legend: A Tribute to Mary Shelley and Boris Karloff* (Metuchen, N.J.: The Scarecrow Press, 1973), 97, 99.

43. Later adaptors' transformation of the monster, originally a masterly rhetorician, into a grunting mute may be a cruder but no less interesting way of conveying the same thing, the figuration of one form of linguistic alienation by another.

44. Bernard Duyfhuizen, "Periphrastic Naming in Mary Shelley's *Frankenstein*," *Studies in the Novel* 27 (1995), 487–8; David Seed, "*Frankenstein*—Parable of Spectacle?" *Criticism* 24 (1982), 333.

45. This is not a matter of blocking sight at the least dangerous point, not a matter of reluctance to approach the monster, as we see when the monster responds to Frankenstein's command, "Begone! relieve me from the sight of your detested form," by putting his hands before Frankenstein's eyes and telling him, "thus I take from thee a sight which you abhor." *Frankenstein*, 96.

46. Andrew Griffin remarks that instead of "*undoing*" the monster, Frankenstein "get[s] it out of his sight." Andrew Griffin, "Fire and Ice In *Frankenstein*," in *The Endurance of Frankenstein*, 64.

47. The obliviousness of most of the novel's characters seemed an absurdity to Scott, who wondered how "the monster, how tall, agile, and strong however, could have perpetrated so much mischief undiscovered; or passed through so many countries without being secured, either on account of his crimes, or for the benefit of some such speculator as Mr Polito, who would have been happy to have added to his museum so curious a specimen of natural history." *The Romantics Reviewed*, vol. I, Part C, 79. That the mutation of ugliness and anonymity into invisibility begins during the monster's strangely inconspicuous departure through the daylit and public streets of Ingolstadt suggests it must be something other than a symptom of Frankenstein's craziness.

48. As one critic notes, "the creature is unnarratable." Robert Olorenshaw, "Narrating the Monster: From Mary Shelley to Bram Stoker," in *Frankenstein: Creation and Monstrosity*, ed. Stephen Bann (London: Reaktion Books, 1994), 167.

49. It is so for the monster himself. When, the morning after his terrible confrontation with the DeLacys, he creeps back to the cottage and finds it deserted, he "apprehend[s] some dreadful misfortune." That the "dreadful misfortune" is himself seems not to occur to him. *Frankenstein*, 133.

50. The production of the alibi is so far subordinated to the appearance of Frankenstein's father that it may seem it is the father's appearance that is needed to free the son, as though the true charge were not murder but fatherlessness.

51. The monster's doubled relation to Frankenstein is itself doubled in his doubled relations with other figures within the novel. But the novel supplies an abundance of monsterless analogical pairings, including the pairings of Elizabeth with Caroline, of Elizabeth with Justine, of Frankenstein with Walton. Gilbert and Gubar suggest that "the likenesses among all these characters … imply relationships of redundancy between them like the solipsistic relationships among artfully placed mirrors." Gilbert and Gubar, *The Madwoman in the Attic*, 228.

52. Frankenstein makes the monster as if to recover his mother from death, but he also animates the monster as if in spiteful or perhaps merely neglectful stead of her, substituting mummy ("a mummy again endued with animation") for mother. *Frankenstein*, 53.

53. Frankenstein describes his life in similar terms on p. 175.

54. Frances Ferguson points out that "His skin is too tight," "stretched too thin, as if [it] represented an unsuccessful effort to impose unity on his various disparate parts" that are like the members of this family that tries to assimilate too many unrelated people. See Frances Ferguson, "The Nuclear Sublime," *Diacritics* 14, no. 2 (Summer 1984), 8, 9.

55. The split between his experience of himself and everyone else's experience of him is analogous to the split between his voice, which expresses his sense of who he is and what he wants, and his face, which, though he will grow into it, expresses initially nothing he recognizes as his own.

56. Several critics have commented upon the absence of relation between the monster and his creator's spiritual ambitions. See George Levine, "The Ambiguous Heritage of *Frankenstein*," in *The Endurance of Frankenstein*, 6–7, 11, 17; Judith Wilt, "*Frankenstein* as Mystery Play," in *The Endurance of Frankenstein*, 32; Baldick, *In Frankenstein's Shadow*, 4; David Punter, *Gothic Pathologies: The Text, the Body and the Law* (New York: St. Martin's, 1998), 50.

57. For a reading of this chain in terms of signification see Brooks, "Godlike Science/Unhallowed Arts."

58. The conversion of "he" to "you" is a threat to devour the independence of the auditor—a seduction. For an illuminating parallel between the monster's "seduction" of Delaney and Rosario/Matilda's seductive autobiographical displacements in M. G. Lewis's *The Monk*, see Newman, "Narratives of Seduction," 151–2.

CHAPTER EIGHT

The Coauthored Pseudonym: Two Women Named Michael Field

Holly A. Laird

Women's struggle for a credible identity in print, a name as author, and public signatures of their own has frequently been mediated through a pseudonym. As the compiler of an index of women's pen names puts it, "until well into the nineteenth century, a woman had a special reason for wrapping herself in a nomme de plume [sic]: to escape the stigma of being branded a 'bluestocking,' 'she-writer,' 'female quill-driver,' 'half-Man,' 'scribbling dame' or other epithet for a woman who ventured into overwhelmingly patriarchal literary culture."[1] For two women writing together as a single author, the pseudonym could be both a weapon and a shelter in a fight to achieve authorship and authority in print, the primary medium of intellectual and ethical disputation. Print itself afforded a seemingly inexhaustible series of "noms" which women used to infiltrate the worlds of business and of men.

For women and men writing collaboratively, however, the battle for recognition and authority as authors has rarely been won. Among the approximately 100 women coauthors in Alice Kahler Marshall's list of 2,650 pen names from 1600 to 1984, none is canonical and the vast majority are utterly forgotten. This may not be accidental. Coauthorship stands in a vexed relation to our ideas about authorship, giving the lie both to the Romantic myth of solitary genius and to the postmodern myth of the author's death.[2] It seems as unlikely as ever today—and as undesirable—that those involved in publication (editors, agents, publishers, book-dealers) and reading (patrons of bookstores, public libraries, archives, Amazon.com) or writers themselves (of biographies, histories, memoirs, autobiographies) will soon stop wondering and digging up information about authors. But if they are reluctant to set the author-function to zero, they appear equally reluctant to imagine that the literary author can be two or more. Moreover, cloaking their doubleness in a single pseudonym has rarely succeeded in gaining for coauthors a lasting reputation. The transition from a writer's choice of a pseudonym, through disclosure of the pseudonym's occupant, to inclusion of the pseudonymous author in the lists of the great—such as occurred, for example, for George Eliot—has faltered and failed for dual authors.

Required, and perhaps on its way, for dual authorship to catch hold in the modern marketplace is yet another mythos of writing. Such a mythos emerges in the self-descriptions of the most famous women coauthors. A myth they offer is that of romance: of two people in love. While the process of collaboration is typically characterized by collaborative scholars as well as by coauthors as occurring both literally and figuratively through and as "conversation," that conversation is further imagined by the best-known collaborative novelists and poets as a love union,[3] and the enactment of this romance is nowhere more obviously performed than in the construction of their authorial name(s). In the late nineteenth and early twentieth centuries, coauthors represented their writing as romantic friendship, a love affair, and a companionate marriage, joining their names together in the romance of married authorship.

Some writers, perhaps increasingly so in the twentieth century, sign their coauthorships by joining their names (whether pseudonymic or not) with the copulative "and"—as do E. Œ. Somerville and Martin Ross (the latter the pseudonym for Violet Martin), Daphne Marlatt and Betsy Warland, Sara Maitland and Michelene Wandor, Joyce Elbrecht and Lydia Fakundiny—but most have combined and transformed their names into one. Many women even now, of course, grow up with the assumption that one of their primary destinies will be to marry and undergo transfiguration of their names, as their family name becomes their maiden name, and their husband's surname takes the place of their father's. Women authors who espouse each other's writing enact that espousal by imagining a new name for themselves and, often, by linking either their patronymic surnames or their first names in the new signature. Eva Balfour and Beryl Hearndon became Balfour Hearndon; Marjorie Barnard and Flora Sydney Eldershaw became M. Barnard Eldershaw; Jeannette Hyde Eyerly and Valerie Winkler Griffith became Jeannette Griffith; Dorothy Blair and Evelyn Page became Roger Scarlett; Margaret Wise Brown and Edith Thatcher Hurd became Juniper Sage;

Margot Goyder and Anne Neville Goyder Joske became Margot Neville; Margot Glyn and Winnaretta Singer became Marwin Delcarol. The unions thus effected at times created the impression, moreover, of a *ménage à trois*, as the demanding new author wedged himself or herself deeply into the workings of these coauthors' households and imaginative lives.[4]

I focus here on the comparatively widely known turn-of-the-century couple who called themselves Michael Field, coauthors of thirty plays (most of them in verse) and eleven books of poems. "Field" may finally be finding their way to canonicity—to the lasting place in the annals of literature that they devoutly wished and worked for.[5] Michael Field is among the very few coauthors listed in Marshall's index whose reputations grew large enough to be widely noticed by writers and critics in their own day—though Field was unevenly admired by these contemporaries. The history of their reception is marked, in particular, by confrontation between the norm of solitariness in authorship and the counter-norm of authorial marriage. Writing to Edith Cooper (the younger of the two coauthors united as Michael Field), Robert Browning wondered who had written what, and he affirmed, "Dear Miss Cooper .... It is long since I have been so thoroughly impressed by indubitable poetic *genius*; a word I consider while I wrote, only to repeat it, 'genius.' "[6] Cooper responded, "This happy union of two in work and aspiration is sheltered and expressed by 'Michael Field.' Please regard him as the author" (*Works and Days*, 3). Browning then returned, "Dear Michael Field .... I read both poems again, only to confirm my opinion of the extraordinary clearness of the evidence, that genius runs through it all, like your 'starry serpent of torchlight,' now fully emerging, now sufficiently divined" (*Works and Days*, 4). Having once "divined" genius in the new poet, Browning talks himself into reapplying it to Michael Field, but not without some struggle, some (re)consideration. If there is genius, however, it is not solitary, as Bradley and Cooper themselves both insist. Instead, in an oft-cited later moment in their journals, Bradley compares "Michael Field" to Elizabeth Barrett and Robert Browning in terms of marriage: "those two poets, man and wife, wrote alone; each wrote, but did not bless or quicken one another at their work; *we are closer married*" (*Works and Days*, 16).

Their name continued to receive eclectic recognition after their deaths in a variety of early twentieth-century books of critical essays and anthologies, which attempted to place them, variously, as a poet of the "sculpturesque," a poet comparable to Landor, a poet of the 1890s[7]— thus, without challenging the myth of single authorship, these compilers made an exception of Field in lists that otherwise exclude coauthors. Theodore Maynard featured Michael Field as his sole subject in an essay entitled "The Drama of Dramatists," but does so in rhetoric that insists not only on their singularity, but more surprisingly on their "loneliness": "there is a great and lonely name which, passing from among us, has left a heritage not only of poetry but of paradox. There had been successful literary collaborations before, though rarely in metrical drama, but no collaboration in which the identity of the artists was so completely sunk as in the case of the two ladies who are known to their readers by the name of 'Michael Field.'"[8] Pushing against the tide, Mary Sturgeon, their first biographer, endeavored without much immediate success to counteract the assumption of solitary writing through standard detailed explanation and justification of their career, but also through citation of a number of poems and passages in their plays where their writing's love union is figured—as in the following lines:

> It was deep April, and the morn
>   Shakespere was born;
> The world was on us, pressing sore;
> My love and I took hands and swore,
>   Against the world, to be
> Poets and lovers evermore.[9]

Sturgeon quotes these lines also in a chapter on Field in *Studies of Contemporary Poets*, calling them "a precious record, being nothing less than the marriage testament of these two souls."[10]

If in the 1980s and 1990s, Michael Field has slowly begun to receive more serious attention from scholars, this is thanks largely to the escalating acceptance of and interest in lesbianism. Abruptly the fact that these writers (an aunt and a niece) chose each other as soul- and bedmates (when Cooper became a young woman) made them worth attending to, if still exceptional. Treated briefly in two surveys, Jeannette Foster's *Sex Variant Women in Literature* and Lillian Faderman's *Surpassing the Love of Men*, and considered seriously and at length in the articles and chapters of Chris White, Angela Leighton, Yopie Prins, and Bette London,[11] Michael Field as a Sapphist couple has received new life as a "name" to be reckoned with. Prins was the first critic to recognize the extent to which Field might have preferred to be recovered from within a cultural context that values myths and texts rather than biographies.[12] But Field would probably also have seen a Foucaultian preoccupation with discourse as having gone too far, having removed itself from both the etherality and palpability of the worlds of poetry, of nature, and of their own erotic relationship. In the dual trajectories of recent scholarship—emphasizing either the romantic lesbian "nature" or the denatured, highly cultured textuality of Field—critics have said less than they might have about the name itself of Michael Field. This name, in which the two women's given names were "sunk," represents (in their terms) not only a "shelter" but an "expression" of their coauthorship (*Works and Days*, 3): in this name, female is transformed into male, plural into singular, but paradoxically also, one author's name is doubled by the other; two nicknames are yoked in marriage; in this marriage is figured the further yoking of heaven and earth; and a third thing infuses all these various dualities, polymorphously called "love," "nature," "God," "song."

★ ★ ★

Katherine Bradley—fifteen years older than Edith Cooper—first published a volume of poetry, titled *The New Minnesinger and Other Poems*, in 1875 (when Cooper was 13 years old) under the pseudonym "Arran Leigh." Bradley did not publish again until she had joined her writer's life with Cooper; six years later in 1881, they published a play, *Bellerophôn*, under the signature of a couple: "Arran and Isla Leigh." If one employs the alternate spelling of "Katharine Bradley" used by Mary Sturgeon and others, "Arran Leigh" is simply "Kath-*aran* Brad-*ley's*" own name with the initial syllables lopped off. It is also reminiscent of the eponymous protagonist of Elizabeth Barrett Browning's epic *Aurora Leigh*; both the name Arran Leigh and epithet "the new minnesinger" hint of the dawn of a new woman love poet, and Bradley's first volume includes verse in defense of new women poet-singers. In *Aurora Leigh*, the name "Leigh"—somewhat like "Browning" itself, shared by Elizabeth and Robert—is a patronymic belonging both to the semi-autobiographical character Aurora and her proud cousin Romney, whom she eventually marries after he has been humbled by blindness and failure and by her contrasting success as a visionary woman poet.[13] The cousin-love of the two Leighs registers both the Brownings' intimacy as man and wife and their twinning as one seer with another. But at the same time, like Mary Ann Evans, who chose in "George Eliot" the name of her husband "George Lewes" ("To L I owe it"),[14] Elizabeth Barrett in fact veils and replays her actual name change and legal (eventually also poetic) absorption by the name Browning when she created the cousins "Leigh." Bradley was perhaps not far wrong when she remarked to Cooper in the privacy of their diaries that the two women poets were "closer married" than the Brownings because they not only lived, but also wrote together. Even their pseudonym, though not a natal name for either of them, was created by joining their two names together: their nicknames of Michael (for Bradley) and Field (for Cooper).

When Bradley made this remark about the Brownings, Cooper and she were already writing as Michael Field, and "Field" as successor to "Leigh" points to an important, anterior meaning of "Leigh," beyond reference to Browning and the Brownings. A "leigh" is, of course, a synonym for "field"—a meadow, a pasture, any uncultivated, open land. "Arran" and "Isla," both of which denote islands, are brought together (rather unlike the Arran Islands) in a single fertile "leigh."[15] While a leigh yields a more accessible, less bounded enclosure than that of an island, "Arran and Isla Leigh" also produces a repetition of assonantal names with merely musical, fluid differences. This is thus a set of names taken in part from nature, in part from song, and in part from the relationship itself of names rather than from father or husband.

In a short, recent biography of Field, Emma Donoghue explains their shift from "Leigh" to "Field" in this way: the work of Arran and Isla Leigh

> got little critical attention. Therefore, like a rock group which keeps changing its name to shake off its reputation, three years later, in 1884, Katherine and Edith chose themselves a brand new pseudonym to mark the fusion of their talents: Michael Field. "Field," with all its associations of nature and open spaces, is said to come from a childhood nickname of Edith's, and "Michael" may come from the archangel. In an age when male pronouns were considered generic, and femininity and ambition were widely considered incompatible, adopting a man's name seemed the best way for a woman writer to get her work noticed and to be taken seriously as a speaker on universal themes.[16]

Certainly, Field was concerned with these benefits when they were in danger of being lost.[17] Thus, when Robert Browning broke confidentiality and disclosed the fact, not that they were coauthors, but that Field was female, Bradley admonished him in these terms:

> Spinoza with his fine grasp of unity says: "If two individuals of exactly the same nature are joined together, they make up a single individual, doubly stronger than each alone," i.e., Edith and I make up a *veritable Michael*. And we humbly fear you are destroying this philosophic truth: it is said the *Athenaeum* was taught by you to use

the feminine pronoun. Again, someone named Andre Raffalovich, whose earnest young praise gave me genuine pleasure, now writes in ruffled distress .... I am writing to assure him the best authority is my work .... We each know that you mean good to us: and we are persuaded you thought that by "our secret" we meant the dual authorship. The revelation of that would indeed be utter ruin to us; but the report of lady authorship will dwarf and enfeeble our work at every turn .... We must be free as dramatists to work out in the open air of nature.

(*Works and Days*, 6)

But there were also more intimate reasons and meanings for the name Michael Field (as Donoghue also notes); it functioned not so much to deny or negate identity as to multiply and increase identities. When the further secret of their dual authorship leaked, this further undermined their reputation, yet (quite unlike the rock stars suggested by Donoghue), they stuck by Michael Field throughout most of their career.[18] Late in their career, the name Michael Field had become enough to doom their plays; they then published them, not under another name, but anonymously—and their work was once again well received: *Borgia* was published anonymously, then *Queen Mariamne, The Tragedy of Pardon*, and *Diane. The Accuser, Tristan de Léonois*, and *A Messiah* appeared "by the author of Borgia."

Yopie Prins has written brilliantly about the way in which, to phrase this more crudely than she does, not nature, but culture "produces" the name of Field.[19] Much as Browning's epic "wrote" the surname of Arran Leigh, prior texts "write" the name of Field and link (or "double") it with a woman's signature: that of Sappho of Lesbos. Again and again in their volume of Sapphics, *Long Ago* (their sixth published volume, though their first volume of verse), Sapphic fragments provide the frames for Field's poems; moreover, the figuration of the meadow and its inhabitant maidens suggests a metonymic linkage—previously found in Sappho's fragments and name—of place and person, which thus "writes" the "Lesb-ian." I would add to Prins's arguments that the island thereby is transposed into the meadow, the single woman or writer transposed into the "doubled" writer and bevy of women singers. The woman writer is, indeed, first, tripled by Sappho, then indefinitely multiplied by the other Sapphic women singers. The further dual meanings that have increasingly accrued around the term "field"—"field" as in area of knowledge or scholarly endeavor and "field" as in the space of a poem— seem also prefigured by Field's poems, as they allude to Field dually as a scholar, who reconstructed a lost Sappho (as well as many other Greek personages in Field's verse dramas),[20] and as an inventor of a seemingly new kind of literature, a singularly coauthored poetry—"our songs" (as they often referred to them in letters to Robert Browning).

But why "Michael"—that "veritable" first name which unlike any surname, whether Leigh or Field, establishes their gender as indubitably (or, at least, veritably or virtually) male? In focusing on Field's first volume of poems rather than on their previous eight plays (nine if one includes the single work published under the names "Arran and Isla Leigh") or their subsequent books of poems and plays, Prins emphasizes Field's connections with Sappho and Lesbos over any of her other associations, including, of course, with Michael. What is most obvious about the name "Michael Field" is its blatant Anglo-Saxon maleness. Unlike the vaguely androgynous, heterosexually paired names of Arran and Isla Leigh, and quite unlike the name of Sappho, "Michael Field" is both a single, male name and, again, a doubled one, since both "Michael" and "Field" are strongly marked masculine names.

So common is "Michael" and so simple the monosyllabic "Field" (also an extremely common English name, ultimately from Old English) that "Michael Field" can seem extraordinarily unnoteworthy—a plain Jane of a name. It is a name designed perhaps to establish instant recognition as male and to attract no further notice, subordinated to the great and resonant names which repeatedly title Field's plays, male and female: William Rufus, Brutus Ultor, "Canute the Great," "Attila, my Attila!" as well as Callirhoë, "Fair Rosamund," "The Tragic Mary," Stephania, Anna Ruina, and Julia Domna. Nonetheless, Michael is the name of the highest angel; he is the chief warrior angel—victor over Satan; and thanks to his beauty of face and form, he is known also as the Catholic Apollo.[21] So named, a poet is armed to write about tragic warriors like Canute the Great and to transcribe forgotten battle scenes from ancient legends and myths.

While highly popular, especially among English knightly and military families (rather unlike Bradley and Cooper's own mercantile families), Michael is also a name next to God: ultimately derived from the Hebrew, it means "Who is like God?"[22] Critics glide over this name probably both because it is unremarkably common and because it is uncommonly arrogant in its deliberate association with the archangel. Occasionally called "Master" by Cooper, Michael was, however, the elder and in some residual sense the superior in their cross-generational relationship. As Cooper told Browning when first explaining their coauthorship, "[My Aunt] is my senior, by but fifteen years. She has lived with me, taught me, encouraged me and joined me to her poetic life" (*Works and Days*, 3).

In gliding over "Michael" without much mention of its meanings, critics may also underestimate the role of the divine and the spiritual in Field's thought and work—particularly, of course, in association with charismatic mythic visionary men as well as women, figures like Tiresias, Bacchus, and Apollo. As Donoghue's biography shows, Bradley and Cooper felt close to death and to its other life at quite an early time in their lives. Long before they converted to Catholicism, in quest in part for union in the afterlife, they felt their lives participated in a mystic (if usually pagan) spirituality. (That "Michael" actually died on Michaelmas Day would have seemed more than poetic justice to her.) Thus, in Michael Field, Bradley and Cooper combined not only nicknames, but also two of the most basic names for divinity and earth, for the celestial and the natural. They combined the archetypal fighting angel with the typical place of arcadian retreat.

As seriously as Bradley and Cooper wished friends, acquaintances, and, above all, readers, to take their name, they were equally playful with their names when at home and with their closest friends. Thus they called themselves and were called "the Fields" and also "the Michaels"—household names focusing on their coupledom and turning both names into mock-patronymics. In addition, Edith Cooper went by the nickname "Henry," so that their complete couple's name became—as we would think of it now—very gay: "Michael and Henry Field." Or, in a manner to which women are deeply accustomed, their names could be simply joined: Michael Henry Field. As common a name as Michael, Henry is of course more regal in English usage; only Edward rivals Henry as a name for English kings. So their names linked royalty from below as well as on high.

But there was nothing fixed about the positions these names implied, Michael above and Henry below, in the couple's toying with them. While Prins emphasizes the production of the name of "Field" through their writing, their other names are as likely to be found at play in their texts: for example, in the first volume ever published under the name of Michael Field, in the play *Fair Rosamund*, the titular character Rosamund is the foster daughter (the Edith) of a character named Michael, who in turn is forester for King Henry of England, who (completing the circle) has taken Rosamund as his mistress.[23] Michael has been employed, after all, as a pastoral name as well as an angelic one—as the shepherd in Wordsworth's well-known poem, for example. In this reversed and combinatory set of relations, Michael is foster parent, but he also serves the king.

Using names to tease, caress, and taunt each other, their names redu-
plicated and multiplied over time. As Donoghue summarizes some of
their self-naming practices, "Over the years Edith called Katherine
'Michael,' 'Mick,' 'Sim' or 'S' (from Simiorg, a fabulous wise Eastern
bird), 'the all-wise bird or fowl,' and even (slightly tongue in cheek)
'Master.' Katherine called Edith 'Field,' 'the Blue Bird,' 'the Persian' (cat),
'Puss,' 'Pussie,' or 'P,' and later 'my Boy,' 'Henry,' 'Hennery,' 'Henny,' and
'Hennie-boy.' "[24] In addition to the divine and the regal, the spiritual
and the earthly, the master and the boy, their names thus also linked them
as mythic and mundane, exotic and domestic, artful and ordinary, bird
and cat—the latter hinting perhaps not merely at their love of and identification with animals, but also at those moments when they stalked
each other, fled, and fought like (female) birds and cats.

★ ★ ★

In constructing the name of Michael Field, however, Bradley
and Cooper did not see themselves only as playing a language game but
as creating a name capable of expressing themselves, and its multiple
meanings in fact correspond to the several worlds they inhabited: nature,
the supernatural, and poetry (or song). "Michael Field" succeeds not
merely in reproducing fragments of Sappho, but in indicating the con-
vergence of discrete, yet parallel and overlapping spheres: nature, divinity, song, and their own lives and bodies. Thus "Michael Field"
"expresses" two earthly women whose writing, like lightning rods, seeks
to attract divine inspiration. While the notion of "expression" as a central function of poetry was attacked by objectivists and new critics earlier in this century and is now assiduously avoided by poststructuralist
theorists, for Field—as for many others in the late nineteenth century,
one of poetry's highest functions was to express visionary perception.
Interestingly, however, Field extended this term to convey poetry's
capacity for translating other poets and the external world as well as
themselves. One finds in Field—as John Guillory suggests in his analysis
of the evolution of poetics in the Renaissance from an emphasis on
"inspiration" and "enthusiasm" to "imagination"—a "further remystifi-
cation" of imagination. Indeed, "inspiration" also is not "dead" (as it is to
Guillory's "post-Miltonic imagination"), but instead necessary to both
"enthusiasm" and "imagination" for Field.[25] Field-the-poet becomes
the point of intersection between the inner and the outer when a third
thing (love, nature, God) intervenes with its fiercely illuminating and
connective joy.

The nature/culture debate that emerges between Leighton and Prins thus strikes me as not complex enough, on either side, to convey Field's sense of their name or of their writing. Prins has argued thoughtfully against Leighton's view of the "naturalness" of Field's poetry.[26] Field's love poetry seems to Leighton to belong, as Field herself phrased it, "out in the open air of nature" (*Works and Days*, 6). Prins points out, however, that "even the journals of Bradley and Cooper, where we might expect glimpses of life, are self-consciously mediated by the many texts they read and write together."[27] In one example, Prins cites an entry in which Bradley "discovers hyacinths growing in a metaphorical field associated with Sappho: 'In Edith's Valley the other evening we found a bank of hyacinths. Above them, overlooking low oaks, was a full, pale moon, not shining, not yet an influence—a steady dominating presence'" (142). Having earlier noted the association between hyacinths and Sappho, Prins proceeds here to connect the moonlit scene with a Sapphic lyric in Field's *Long Ago*:

> The moon rose full: the women stood
> As though within a sacred wood
> Around an altar—thus with awe
> The perfect, virgin orb they saw
> Supreme above them.[28]

As Prins explains, "The opening lines are based on Sappho's description of a full moon, and indeed in this lyric Sappho herself is figured as the moon, shining down on a circle of women who are awaiting 'Sappho's word'" (142).

The allusions are striking ones, and indeed it is unlikely an adult woman poet would look at such a scene without expressing it (as Field "expresses" Sappho—a term they also use in their preface to *Long Ago*)[29] in language employing previously translated tropes, phrases, and rhetorical devices learned from the poetry in which they were immersed. Still, there was something sensually primal and literally natural in scenes of this sort for Bradley and Cooper, which may warrant Leighton's "naturalized" vocabulary, though it should also not be limited to that. Donoghue alerts us, for example, to an incident recorded by Bradley on 12 January 1862 when "Katherine was walking through a meadow in the moonlight," and James Cooper (her brother-in-law) "came up to her, shouting, 'There is a dear little baby'"—her niece Edith.[30] "Nature" probably seemed to Field not subordinate to art or language, nor vice versa; rather, nature was productive of a language of its own—self-multiplying, self-repeating, and self-differentiating, in an erotic (re)productivity Field desired for herself.

Thus, Field writes often of meadows (both in the moonlight and at other times of day and night) as sites of song. In "Cowslip-Gathering," the third poem of Book Three of *Underneath the Bough* (in an autobiographical sequence, attributed by Sturgeon to Bradley),[31] Field writes:

> Twain cannot mingle: we went hand in hand,
> Yearning, divided, through the fair spring land,
> Nor knew, twin maiden spirits, there must be
> In all true marriage perfect trinity.
> But lo! dear Nature spied us, in a copse
> Filling with chirps of song and hazel-drops,
> And smiled: "These children will I straight espouse,
> While the blue cuckoo thrills the alder-boughs."
> So led us to a tender, marshy nook
> Of meadow-verdure, where by twos and threes
> The cowslips grew, down-nodding toward a brook;
> And left us there to pluck them at our ease
> In the moist quiet, till the rich content
> Of the bee humming in the cherry-trees
> Filled us; in one our very being blent.[32]

Revising Christina Rossetti here, whose springtime lovers in *Monna Innominata* were perpetually yearning and divided, Field argues that three, not two, are necessary for marriage. That third thing both extends from and intrudes from beyond each self. Then again, not only does a third thing emerge, but also indefinitely self-multiplying things, as "by twos and threes," the cowslips and the bees multiply, the bees "filling" the "twin maiden spirits" like cowslips with their punningly "rich content," their conventionally poetic "humming."

For Bradley and Cooper, not only is language or, rather, "song" interlaced with nature (and vice versa), but it is interlaced also with the supernatural—the great, if clichéd abstractions: "Nature" with its position as central divinity (a female Jehovah) in a trinity of "spirits." Though they began their lives imbued with the religions of their parents—dissenter for Bradley, Anglican for Cooper—as adult poets, they embraced a pagan sense of nature's spirits and Bacchic enthusiasm. This is a direction in their writing that distinguishes them, as Leighton also argues, from other decadent and *fin-de-siècle* poets—*ennui* and exhaustion are hard to find in Field:[33]

> Ye women, greet it!
>   Light hath called you, come!
>   Love, sing, no more be cold and dumb;
>   Light calls you, meet it!
>   O women, be ye drunk with that
>   Kindling the wine that brims the autumn vat![34]

In all but this stanza (stanza eight) and the last stanza of the ten-stanza poem "Sunshine is calling," the phrase "O Bacchus" occupies the position held by "O women." Women—here likened to "Love"—thus too may be invoked for inspiration even as they are urged to turn to the "Light" and to Bacchus for "kindling."

In their play "The Tragedy of Pardon," the third thing is love, and love is God:

> There is love
> Of woman unto woman, in its fibre
> Stronger than knits a mother to her child.
> There is no lack in it, and no defect;
> It looks nor up nor down,
> But loves from plenitude to plenitude,
> With level eyes, as in the Trinity
> God looks across and worships.[35]

Cited by Sturgeon as "the ultimate expression of the love which held these two lives in union,"[36] this passage insists yet again on the repetition or doubling of "plenitude" as the unfixable place or person through which love expresses itself. Not capitalized here, "love" is nonetheless a "fibre"—a visceral sinew or aesthetic thread—that moves from "woman unto woman," "knitting" them, and "looks nor up nor down" but with "level eyes." This form of equity, where not only women, but nature, craft, and divinity itself have equivalent statuses and at the same time cannot be extricated from each other, bears analogy only to divinity, "in the Trinity/God."

In "The Sleeping Venus," this reciprocity and *entrelacement* of women, art, nature, divinity, and of all this with "F/field" are even more pronounced than in "Cowslip-Gathering":

> Here is Venus by our homes
> And resting on the verdant swell

Of a soft country flanked with mountain domes:
She has left her archèd shell,
Has left the barren wave that foams,
Amid earth's fruitful tilths to dwell.

...

And her body has the curves,
The same extensive smoothness seen
In yonder breadths of pasture, in the swerves
Of the grassy mountain-green
That for her propping pillow serves:
There is a sympathy between
    Her and Earth of largest reach,
    For the sex that forms them each
    Is a bond, a holiness,
    That unconsciously must bless
    And unite them, as they lie
    Shameless underneath the sky
    A long, opal cloud
    Doth in noontide haze enshroud.[37]

In this poem, an "expression" of a painting by Giorgione, Venus and Earth are each alike formed by "the sex" (potentially meaning both the gender "female" and the more profound erotic fertility of "nature"); and in their similarity, their twinning, they become "bonded" in a "holiness" that is "shameless." That they are also "enshrouded" at high noon, allows even death its visitation rights (and rites) in the midst of life. (Commentators often note that Bradley and Cooper were so "twinned" that they died—each of cancer—within nine months of each other.)

I have focused in this essay on a few of the more enthusiastic, self-mythologizing moments in Michael Field's writing, but I do so in order to describe the ways they imagined their relationship as coauthors when it worked, as it did work for more than three decades prior to their deaths in 1913 and 1914. If we describe this coauthorship only in terms of contemporary categories of the lesbian author or of a reiterative *l'écriture*, of solitary genius or of an author function, we will fail to grasp what coauthorship—and Michael Field's coauthorship in particular—distinctively has to tell us about authoring poetry. The name Michael Field, deceptively simple, innocuously male, was produced through a complex imagining of paired, seemingly antithetical worlds—of women and language, nature and the supernatural—which married and bore fruit, not when one was subordinated to the other, but rather when all entered into intimate, fertile conjunction with one another.

Notes

1. Alice Kahler Marshall, *Pen Names of Women Writers: From 1600 to the Present* (Camp Hill, PA: Alice Kahler Marshall, 1985), vii.
2. For the most exhaustive discussion, to date, of the myth of "solitary genius" as opposed to multiple authorship, see Jack Stillinger, *Multiple Authorship and the Myth of Solitary Genius* (Oxford: Oxford University Press, 1991); the classic essay on the death of the author is, of course, by Roland Barthes, "The Death of the Author," *Image—Music—Text*, trans. Stephen Heath (New York: Hill and Wang, 1977), 142–8; see also Michel Foucault's famous essay, "What is an Author?" *Language, Counter-Memory, Practice*, trans. Donald F. Bouchard and Sherry Simon, ed. Bouchard (Ithaca, NY: Cornell University Press, 1977).
3. Elsewhere I discuss this phenomenon of "conversation" and present a more detailed discussion of women's coauthorships from 1850 to the present: see *Women Coauthors* (Champaign, IL: University of Illinois Press, 2000).
4. See especially the interesting contemporary case of Joyce Elbrecht and Lydia Fakundiny, who sign themselves also as Jael B. Juba and give Jael B. Juba a leading role as author-character in their novel: *The Restorationist: Text One—A Collaborative Fiction by Jael B. Juba* (Albany, New York: SUNY Press, 1993); "Scenes from a Collaboration: or Becoming Jael B. Juba," *Tulsa Studies in Women's Literature* 13 (Fall 1994), 241–57.
5. I use the pronoun "they" for Field in this essay.
6. Quoted in Michael Field, *Works and Days: From the Journal of Michael Field*, ed. T. and D. C. Sturge Moore (London: John Murray, 1933), 2. Subsequent citations appear parenthetically in the text.
7. For these evaluations, respectively, see H. J. Massingham, *Letters to X* (London: Constable and Company, 1919), 264–5; W. B. Yeats, ed., *The Oxford Book of Modern Verse: 1892–1935* (New York: Oxford University Press, 1937), xvii; A. J. A. Symons, ed., *An Anthology of 'Nineties' Verse* (London: Elkin Matthews and Marrot, 1928; rpt. St. Clair Shores, MI: Scholarly Press, 1971), 55–70.
8. Theodore Maynard, *Carven from the Laurel Tree: Essays* (Oxford: B. H. Blackwell, 1918?), 45.
9. Quoted in Mary Sturgeon, *Michael Field* (London: George G. Harrap & Co., 1922), 79.
10. Sturgeon, *Studies of Contemporary Poets* (New York: Dodd, Mead and Company, 1920), 351.
11. Jeannette Foster, *Sex Variant Women in Literature* (1956; Baltimore, MD: Diana Press, 1975); Lillian Faderman, *Surpassing the Love of Men: Romantic Friendship and Love Between Women from the Renaissance to the Present* (New York: William Morrow, 1981); Chris White, "'Poets and Lovers Evermore': Interpreting Female Love in the Poetry and Journals of Michael Field," *Textual Practice* 4, no. 2 (1990), 197–212, rpt. in *Sexual Sameness: Textual Differences in Lesbian and Gay Writing*, ed. Joseph Bristow (London: Routledge, 1992), 26–43; White, "The Tiresian Poet: Michael Field," in *Victorian Women Poets: A Critical Reader*, ed. Angela Leighton (Cambridge, MA: Blackwell, 1996), 148–61; Angela Leighton, *Victorian Women Poets: Writing Against the Heart* (Charlottesville: University Press of Virginia, 1992); Yopie Prins, "A Metaphorical Field: Katherine Bradley and Edith Cooper," *Victorian Poetry* 33, no. 1 (1995), 129–48; Prins, "Sappho Doubled: Michael Field," *The Yale Journal of Criticism* 8, no. 1 (1995), 165–86; Bette London, *Writing Double: Women's Literary Partnerships* (Ithaca, NY: Cornell University Press, 1999). See also Prins's incorporation of her essays into a chapter of *Victorian Sappho* (Princeton, NJ: Princeton University Press, 1999); my discussions of Field in *Women Coauthors*; and, for an assessment of Field's career and reception, David Moriarty, "'Michael Field' (Edith Cooper and Katherine Bradley) and Their Male Critics," in *Nineteenth-Century Women Writers of the English-Speaking World*, ed. Rhoda B. Nathan (New York: Greenwood, 1986).

12. London's chapter on Field in *Writing Double*, which appeared after this article was complete, is another important exception in this scholarship since it focuses not on Field's lesbianism *per se*, nor on Field's texts, but rather on Field's collaboration as in itself a notable cultural phenomenon, if also a problematic one: see London both for a discussion of the sexualizing of Field's collaboration and for a critique of Field's occasional evocation of their "union" as "seamless" (63–74). London does not comment extensively on Field's pseudonym. See also Ana Parejo Vadillo's recent article for a discussion of "visuality" in Field's poetry: "*Sight and Song*: Transparent Translations and a Manifesto for the Observer," *Victorian Poetry* 38, no. 1 (2000), 15–34.

13. Elizabeth Barrett Browning, *Aurora Leigh*, ed. Margaret Reynolds (New York: Norton, 1996).

14. For a useful discussion of George Eliot's pseudonym, see Michal Peled Ginsburg, "Pseudonym, Epigraphs, and Narrative Voice: *Middlemarch* and the Problem of Authorship," *ELH* 47 (1980), 542–58.

15. *The New Century Cyclopedia of Names*, ed. Clarence L. Barnhart (New York: Appleton-Century-Crofts, 1954), 193, 227, 2143.

16. Emma Donoghue, *We Are Michael Field* (Bath, England: Absolute, 1998), 36.

17. Note, however, as I suggested above in my abbreviated list of collaborative pseudonyms, that women coauthors frequently adopted female pseudonyms; in addition, they wrote under epithets, like that of "The Two Sisters," and anonymously. Women writers of this period did not universally find the male pseudonym an essential strategy for success in publication.

18. The analogy to the rock star (and starring actors more generally) does make sense, however, when we realize that in both cases, names have been seen as crucial to making or breaking a star's fame. For the importance of an authorial name's "aura," see Leroy C. Breunig, "For a Poetic of the Pseudonym," *Romanic Review* 75, no. 2 (1984), 256–62; and for the turn-of-the-century woman writer's interest in the pseudonym as "a name of power," see Sandra Gilbert and Susan Gubar, "Ceremonies of the Alphabet: Female Grandmatologies and the Female Authorgraph," in *The Female Autograph*, ed. Domna C. Stanton (New York: New York Literary Forum, 1984), 28–33.

19. Prins, "A Metaphoric Field" and "Sappho Doubled."

20. See Prins, "Sappho Doubled," for Field's challenge by and to the "'scholarly conscience as male,'" 170–1.

21. *New Century*, 2735. For further details, see *The Interpreter's Dictionary of the Bible*, ed. George Arthur Buttrick, vol. 3 (New York: Abingdon Press, 1962), 372–3.

22. Patrick Hanks, *A Dictionary of Surnames* (Oxford: Oxford University Press, 1988), 366.

23. Field, "*Callirhoë*," and "*Fair Rosamund*," (London: George Bell & Sons, 1884).

24. Donoghue, 37.

25. John Guillory, *Poetic Authority: Spenser, Milton, and Literary History* (New York: Columbia University Press, 1983), viii, ix. Nor does this aesthetic exclude the representational function, though I would not emphasize the latter over "inspiration" and "imagination" in Field's poetry. As Ana Parejo Vadillo stresses, Field learned from Ruskin and Berenson to value the "translation" of "objects" (16–17 ff.).

26. Leighton, 130.

27. Prins, "A Metaphorical Field," 141. Subsequent citations will appear parenthetically in the text.

28. Field, *Long Ago* (1889; Portland, Maine: Thomas B. Mosher, 1897), xxix.

29. Field, preface, *Long Ago*, n.p.

30. Donoghue, 15.

31. Sturgeon, *Michael Field*, 74. Although Donoghue writes that Bradley and Cooper misled friends about their coauthorship and that they wrote poems and some plays separately, the process of collaboration occurs for such writers also through conversation and through openness to editing, and these various phases of composition are impossible to recover for Field as for many other coauthors. Critics' recurrent effort to separate coauthors' hands and to attribute texts to one coauthor or the other is testimony to the tenacity of the myth that a poem can only be

written in solitude or only understood when written in that way. After *The New Minnesinger* and *Bellerophôn*, Bradley and Cooper published their work under the name of Field and asked friends and acquaintance to see them as that "one" poet.

32. Field, *Underneath the Bough* (London: George Bell, 1893), 67–8.
33. Leighton, 217–19.
34. Field, *Underneath the Bough*, 134.
35. Anonymous [Field], *The Tragedy of Pardon*, in *"The Tragedy of Pardon," and "Diane"* (London: Sidgwick and Jackson, 1911), III. iii.
36. Sturgeon, *Studies*, 352–3.
37. Field, *Sight and Song* (London: Elkin Matthews and John Lane, 1892), 98–9.

CHAPTER NINE

From Ghostwriter to Typewriter: Delegating Authority at Fin de Siècle

Leah Price

In 1894, *Cassell's Family Magazine* began an article on "New Paid Occupations for Women" on a platitudinous note. "There are hundreds—even thousands—of girls and women to whom the earning of money is a necessity," Elizabeth Banks lamented, "belonging to that class known as 'gentlewomen.' " Her solutions were less predictable. Ranging from dog-walking to "scientific dusting" to personal shopping to breaking in other people's new boots, Banks's club of queer trades also features a ladylike consultant at the dressmaker's shop.

> On inquiring why this girl was in the fitting-room, I was told that she was a "suggester." The dress-maker informed me that she was unable to do so much as sew a straight seam ... but that her little head was full of valuable ideas .... It occurred to me that here was another occupation for which some women are specially adapted: that is, the furnishing of ideas for other people to use .... There are women in the world whose minds are brimful of ideas, whose brains are continually conceiving plans which their hands are unable to carry out. "Why don't you write about so-and-so, or invent such and such a thing?" is a question such women are constantly asking. They have ideas for stories, plots for novels, subjects for journalistic "write-ups." ... The gift for writing is one that many people possess, but the gift of originality does not always go with it. It is the same in nearly every line of work; and I would

suggest that the woman with ideas take the "children of her brain" to people who can dress them up and give them to the world.[1]

Why ladies should be specially adapted to furnish ideas remains unclear, but the reasoning seems to be that acting as a surrogate is more ladylike than producing goods. Where walking one's own dog or wearing one's own new shoes can be dismissed as pleasure but walking or wearing someone else's counts as work, publishing in one's own name veers on trade but suggesting plots to someone else can pass for a genteel profession. Yet Banks's mixed metaphor betrays some doubt about whether breaking in new shoes can in fact save women from breaking into new careers. The "suggester" paid to give fashion advice has metamorphosed, by the end of the paragraph, into a mother who delegates the task of clothing her brainchildren to a hired dressmaker. In an article designed to make creative "suggesters" out of suggestible readers, the decorous veil drawn over any distinction between lady professionals and their customers masks a more fundamental confusion about which commands a higher price, the "gift of originality" (embodied in the girl whose gentility forbids her to sew straight) or the skill to "carry out."

Banks's coinage "suggester" names a job for which a neologism was already available: the *Oxford English Dictionary* dates to 1884 the first instance of "ghost" being used to mean "one who secretly does artistic or literary work for another person, the latter taking the credit." Oddly, though, her confidence that ladies can sell their "ideas for stories, plots for novels, subjects for journalistic 'write-ups'" reverses the flow of cash from the person who performs the work to the one who commissions it. Just as ladies are in fact more likely to pay for the privilege of wearing new shoes than to be paid for it, ghostwriters are normally hired to execute an idea conceived by wealthier employers, not to assign topics to one of the "many people" (as Banks airily puts it) who have the technical skill to produce the final text. The impracticability of Banks's career advice betrays her desperation to distract readers from the knowledge that far from allowing women to give ideas, the most common "New Paid Occupation for Women" in 1893 required them to take dictation. Although the division of labor in which one writer implemented what another conceived was indeed gendered, it took place in precisely a job that Banks labels unfeminine. "The uncombative, retiring, modest, home-loving woman," she postulates, "cannot type" (585).[2]

Banks's swerve from typewriting to ghostwriting dramatizes a displacement accomplished more subtly by other fin-de-siècle genres. Literary fantasy allowed career advisors like her to test, at a safe remove, how to make sense of the less glamorous mode of textual production emerging in the modern office. Conversely, a startlingly wide range of contemporary fictions (children's books, feminist polemics, ghost stories, and temperance tracts) deployed debates about women's work to resolve whether a text owes its value to the "mind" that designs it or the "hands" that produce it. Yet that attempt to translate interpretive dilemmas into social problems raised more questions than it answered, for at the very moment when employers were enlisting gender to underpin the division of textual labor, the balance of power between those who tangibly produced documents and those to whom ultimate responsibility for their content was assigned became more disputed, not less.

I have found no evidence that the coinage of "ghostwriting" at the end of the century coincided with an increase in the practice it names. What it did coincide with was an increase in the number of female office workers—a group that multiplied more than eighty times between 1850 and 1914, going in the same period from 2 to 20 percent of the total number of British clerical workers.[3] In its most literal form, the ghostwriter exorcized the typewriter. As the spread of stenographic typing substituted a male voice dictating to a female hand for the feminine Muse who had traditionally inspired male writers, a wave of misogynistic ghost stories salvaged the older allegory by transposing the hitherto realist genre of the *künstlerroman* into a fantastic mode.[4] Their realist contemporaries who represented ghostwriting rather than punning on it, however, were less unanimous about the gender of anonymity. Co-opted successively by exponents of women's influence, critics of women's exploitation, and satirists of women's writing, the figure of the ghostwriter was pressed into service by almost every camp in the fin-de-siècle gender wars. From Mabel Wotton's feminist denunciation of men who subcontracted their writing to cheap female labor, to Elinor Adams's anti-suffragist celebration of modest secretarial anonymity, to John Strange Winter's misogynistic accusation that society authoresses simply provided photogenic figureheads for hardworking hacks, texts that agreed on nothing else uniformly replicated personnel managers' optimism that textual credit could be mapped onto sexual difference. Yet the same representations of ghostwriting that, taken individually, can help us understand why late nineteenth-century employers suddenly turned to women to fill the office jobs formerly monopolized by men can also, if read together, reveal what problems new bureaucratic practices raised for old literary theories. The sheer range of incompatible positions into which plots slotted the ghostwriter—alternately exposing and reversing the more mundane dynamic in which male bosses signed what female

secretaries wrote—caused gender to threaten the very system of delegation that it had promised to naturalize.

That occupational question correlates in turn with a more narrowly
literary riddle. Why, at a time when institutions from the gossip column
to the *Dictionary of National Biography* (1882–) were investing authors'
lives with unprecedented importance, should a neologism pair "writing"
with death? The first generation of typists were trained at a moment
when longstanding debates about the ethics of anonymous publication
had finally been resolved (at least outside the daily press) in favor of signature. In 1877, the newly founded *Nineteenth Century* still provoked
outrage by putting authors' names on the cover; by 1907 even the conservative *Quarterly* had begun to attribute its articles.[5] Between those
two dates, the collapse of the circulating libraries' monopoly on current
fiction spurred publishers to invent new marketing gimmicks that ostentatiously violated not just the social distinction between the public and
the private, but the interpretive distinction between word and flesh:
autographed photographs, illustrated interviews, house tours, even direc-
tories listing home addresses of pseudonymous writers.[6] Yet the fall of
anonymity and the rise of the New Journalism coincided with a coinage
that disjoined writing from visibility, and a wave of fiction that literal-
ized the death of the author. As it spilled outside the dictionary, the
figure of the ghostwriter tested readers' power to trace works to lives.

Some forms of anonymity remain nameless. Although the transaction
to which it refers was anything but new, "ghostwriting" does not appear
in the *Oxford English Dictionary* until 1927. Even adumbrations of
the metaphor—"a sculptor's ghost" in 1884, a secretary as "ghost" to the
millionaire whose speeches he composes in 1889—emerge over a century after its French equivalent. Traditionally too common to require
comment, the practice of selling the right to sign a text along with
the right to publish it acquired a name only once it became a crime. The
greater the power of signature to determine texts' financial and esthetic
value, the less the practice of passing off a low-paid author's labor as the
full-priced article could be differentiated from fraud. The disreputable
trace of an anonymity finally driven underground, ghostwriting can
also be seen, on the contrary, as the apotheosis of the star system. If
approached via the production of texts, ghostwriting appears a subset (or
even a limit case) of anonymity: it erases the writer's identity more firmly
than does either anonymous publication or pseudonymous publication in
which the *nom de plume* lacks a legal referent. From the reader's and publisher's point of view, though, ghostwritten texts are anything but anonymous: the high proportion of autobiographies among ghostwritten

books, and of celebrities among their signatories, suggests ghostwriters' stake in the cult of authorial authenticity. Ghostwriting precludes anonymous publication as absolutely as it requires anonymous composition. Far from undermining the author-function, the coinage of "ghostwriting" displaced anonymity from books to persons.

The stigma of pseudonymity replaced the stigma of print. Once anonymity began to connote the powerlessness of hacks rather than the reticence of gentlemen, the ghostwriter's earnings came to be understood less as payment for producing a text than as a payoff for not producing a signature. A century after Boswell compared "the casuistry by which the productions of one person are passed upon the world for the productions of another" to "the ancient Jewish mode of a wife having children born to her upon her knees, by the handmaid," ghostwriting began to arouse some of the same anxieties that surround surrogate motherhood today.[7] Like the prostitutes whom many of the texts discussed below invoke, ghostwriters were compensated for commodifying what was now (in theory at least) an inalienable part of the self. As what ghostwriters sold was redefined from labor to discretion—from textual expression to paratextual self-suppression—a transaction that had formerly been assimilable to other kinds of hackwork became associated instead with blackmail.

Indeed, the first novel I have found, in which the term appears, makes "ghostwriting" at once an occasion and an analog for blackmailing. *Confessions of a Publisher*, published in 1888 under the name of John Strange Winter—the pseudonym of a woman named Henrietta Stannard with a double career in proprietary anti-wrinkle creams and tales of regimental life—is narrated by a publisher who has laid himself open to extortion by brokering a deal between a wealthy would-be authoress and an impoverished male hack. The plausibility of the plot depends on the shamefulness of ghostwriting: the publisher's fear of exposure reveals how scandalous a gap between producer and signatory becomes in a literary market where the signature carries so much commercial value that its falsification amounts to fraud. Yet the currency of the blackmail turns out to be less financial than bibliographical. The runaway success of the novel published under the society lady's name leads its unacknowledged author to demand that his previous novels—whose unsaleability had driven him to ghostwriting in the first place—be published not only at an extortionate price, but under his own name. The plot's vagueness about where ghostwriting stops and blackmailing begins makes clear that the connection between the transactions depends on resemblance even more than causality, because each involves payment for refraining from revealing something—one's own authorship or another's crime.

Confessions of a Publisher internalizes that criminalization of ghost-writing, for the uncanny ability of characters within the novel to guess the real author from stylistic evidence alone makes misattribution not just difficult to get away with, but impossible to represent. When the ghostwriter goes on to publish under his own name the second novel brought out as the price of his silence, "one review simply took for granted that it was by the same author; ... another spoke of the marked similarity between the two books as far as style went—said it seemed almost incredible that it could be the work of a different hand."[8] Winter's faith that every text will sooner or later reveal its true origins, as inexorably as a foundling in romance, presumes that signature permeates the text rather than being affixed from without. Even in a plot that hinges on ghostwriting, the implications of its feasibility remain too disturbing to face. Like crime, ghostwriting never pays—no matter what the mechanism of punishment.

Winter's assumption that truth will out has a more specific corollary: what looks like a woman's writing will sooner or later be unmasked as the work of a man. The photogenic authoress is reduced to a front for the unpresentable male hack. In the novels published under the name of John Strange Winter—a cross-gendered signature that owed its value to boys' books but was used in facsimile to caption frontispiece photographs of a lady in furs—the writing that appears to be produced by women always turns out to have a less reputable source. Winter's temperance tract *A Name to Conjure With* (1899) charts the decline of a best-selling authoress driven by the pressure of supporting her invalid husband into a writer's block that prevents her from capitalizing any longer on the "name" referred to in the novel's title. After even therapeutic tricycle-riding fails to refresh the heroine's exhausted brain, she discovers that the still less womanly recourse of drink makes writing "as easy to her as if some one else had been sitting there quietly dictating to her." Something, not someone: the bottles of green chartreuse hidden in the cupboard of her study replace not only the inspiration that the authoress lacks, but the "dozen ghosts" whom her husband urges her in vain to hire. "She is too utterly conscientious, and will not even try dictating to a stenographer," he complains, as if delegating to a secretary were the first step on the slippery slope toward depending on a ghost-writer; but we know, with dramatic irony, that dictation by the bottle has already rendered dictation to a typist superfluous.[9] Like *Confessions of a Publisher, A Name to Conjure With* traces women's writing to a guilty secret. The only difference is that one personifies inspiration in the shape of a masculine ghost while the other puns on it in the equally immoral form of spirits.

Indeed, the fashionable authoress who employs a male ghostwriter in *Confessions of a Publisher* could be seen as the evil double of the secretary who fails to appear in *A Name to Conjure With*: where one's wealth enables her to affix her name brazenly to the texts that she has hired men to write, poverty forces the other to produce documents for a male employer to sign. M. Mostyn Bird's 1911 handbook *Woman at Work* warned the anonymous writer to beware the society authoress, interrupting its practical advice to would-be typists and journalists with an oddly digressive attack on the "artificial and unfair competition of the idle woman who does not want money, but desires to see her name in print. There is little drudgery entailed in scribbling off a short story or an article upon some pretty scene or national custom she has noticed in the course of her luxurious travels abroad, while a typewriting agency will copy and punctuate it for her. It is not unlikely that she will send it in to an editor with a hint that she requires no payment; a temptation that all editors are not proof against, especially when the material is good and some struggling sub-editor can be found to correct what is left lacking by my lady's own somewhat inadequate education."[10] In a portrait where Elizabeth Banks's ladylike "suggester" takes on a less flattering guise, the figure of ghostwriting provides an analytical tool to distinguish the social from the textual—not just to remind readers that writing has no necessary connection with signing but also, more radically, to dismiss the apparent coincidence of the two as a fraud. Living becomes incompatible with writing: while the typist and subeditor presumably cannot afford vacations from the jobs for which Bird coaches them, the woman who travels, by definition, is too lazy to write. Or, more precisely, to typewrite—for she is happy to "scribble," a verb that connotes not just writing sloppily, but writing by hand. Like signatures, autograph manuscripts have traditionally connoted an authenticity defined in contradistinction to print or typing. Here, on the contrary, the autobiographical "scribbler" 's literary imposture stands opposite the honest labor situated in the impersonal typewriting agency. The same reversal that reduces the woman who reports her own experiences to a fraud transfers authenticity to the woman who copies another's words.

However counterintuitive, this paradox has its precedents. In studies of mid-Victorian authorship, Elaine Showalter and Mary Poovey have shown that the moral significance of hackwork varied according to gender. Where male writers were concerned, predictably enough, writing for money was assumed to entail artistic as well as moral disaster. Personal greed precluded artistic genius. For women, surprisingly, the opposite was true. To write for fame laid one open to charges of unwomanly vanity; to support "the invalid mother, the bankrupt father, the tubercular husband, and the errant son" connoted modest self-sacrifice, not selfish greed.[11] The model of authorship described by Poovey and Showalter can provide a clue to the riddle of why employers at the end of the nineteenth century suddenly began to recruit women for the clerical work previously monopolized by men. The deskilling and unmanning of secretarial work has traditionally been explained by factors as various as turn-of-the century corporate mergers, the 1870 Education Act, and the commercialization of the typewriter and the phonograph along with lower-tech inventions such as the filing cabinet and the index card. But in a society where women's labor is almost invariably cheaper and where employers always want cheaper labor, economic factors alone can never suffice to explain why one field becomes feminized at a particular time rather than another. A more convincing cultural explanation can be found in the mid-Victorian models of literary writing against which copying, typing, and stenography were defined. In spreading from authorship itself to more populous occupations, the double standard that made commercialism a vice for men and a virtue for women sharpened. By flanking the secretary with a manly boss and the authoress with an emasculated hireling, fin-de-siècle fiction widened the gulf separating the right kind of feminine writing—instrumental and anonymous—from the wrong.

In fiction at least, the Edwardian typewriter girl who worked for money rather than signature inherited the moral credentials of the mid-Victorian female hack who worked for money rather than fame. Elinor Davenport Adams's *Miss Secretary Ethel: A Story for Girls of To-Day* (1898) pits a teenaged private secretary against a boss so humiliated by his growing dependence on her skills that he eventually fires her—and one can see why. Not content with alternately drafting, editing, and delivering his speeches, or even with saving him from a runaway hansom cab, Ethel puts herself in Sir Edgar's place with an intrusiveness that suggests how easily feminine empathy can shade into ventriloquistic insubordination: " 'While you're reading it, may I just go and tell Lady Allesley you want her to sit out with you? You do want her, don't you?' Sir Edgar made no reply. His eyes and thoughts were already occupied with the papers in front of him. 'Very well,' said Ethel, in a still, undisturbing voice. 'Then I'll tell her.' "[12] Ethel's voice may well be "still," for she has no need of her own mouth when she can put words into her boss's. Although the term "ghostwriter" never appears in a text which distrusts new coinages as much as New Women, *Miss Secretary Ethel* helps one understand why the *OED* gives the secretary who composes a millionaire's speeches as an example of a "ghost" (1889) forty years before applying that prefix to a professional author. The stenographer, no less than the ghostwriter, is paid not simply to write letters or documents, but to refrain from writing one thing—her name—so that her boss can affix his to the texts which, in the most literal sense of the word, she has manifestly written. In fact, the meddling of an officious Girtonian feminist, who urges Ethel to sign her own name to the articles she composes rather than publishing them under Sir Edgar's, gives Ethel the occasion to explain that her job makes professionalism incompatible with signature: "It wouldn't seem a bit like being a secretary if I put my own name and not my Chief's!" (123). Far from allowing Ethel to find an identity, as in more overtly feminist fictions of women's work, Ethel's career requires her to efface it.

Why would a novel so priggishly didactic invite girls to emulate a role model who not only lies but defends her lying? Exemplary where *Confessions of a Publisher* is satirical, *Miss Secretary Ethel* contrasts the secretary's modesty not with the society authoress's self-importance (as does Bird) but with a fee-paying student's feminist self-assertion. The presence of a Girton girl, in fact, is all that allows Adams to differentiate the secretary from the otherwise dangerously similar figure for women's writing, the New Woman. At first, on learning that the secretary "won't be a 'he,'" Lady Allesley braces herself to meet "a typewriting female with spectacles, and short gowns, and pocket editions of the classics" (17). Readers can appreciate the dramatic irony of that scene only in retrospect, once a feminist classicist does appear in the person not of the modest working girl, but of her arrogant, leisured friend. Ethel earns the privilege of being a heroine only by renouncing the right to be an author: a logic of moral compensation is all that allows Adams to flout the convention forbidding a secretary to become a major character, or a major character to remain a secretary. Her career takes to its logical conclusion the anti-suffragist doctrine that women should influence electoral politics only through the intermediary of men. "Isn't this a clear case of woman's influence?" Ethel protests when her employer chafes at her eagerness to write (and, on one occasion, to deliver) his campaign speeches (207). The foundational theorist of separate spheres, Sarah Stickney Ellis, had explained that England's prosperity depended on "those exemplary women who pass to and fro upon the earth with a noiseless step, whose names are never heard."[13] Where the typewriter industry joined New Woman fiction in offering secretaryship as an escape from older models of femininity, Ethel's job description makes the former an extension of the latter. ("It is one of the disadvantages of private secretarial work," explains one how-to manual, "that the better it is done the less it is in evidence."[14]) Most powerful where least visible, women's influence shares not only the anonymity of the ghostwriter but the disembodiment of the ghost.

Yet the self-effacement that absolves Ethel from the posturing with which Winter charges authoresses becomes more sinister once the metaphorical female ghostwriter gives way to a literal feminine ghost. Long before the term itself was coined, spectrality had provided a traditional image for anonymous publication, a theme on which the unnamed Author of Waverley already elaborated endless variations. But only at the end of the century did the English language come to equate the lack of a signature with the absence of a body—rather than, like the older French term, *nègre*, with the withholding of a wage. That shift from an economic to a supernatural analogy may help explain why in turn-of-the-century Britain, the traditionally realist genre of the *künstlerroman* suddenly took over the ghost story. From Vernon Lee's tale "A Wicked Voice" (1890), in which a modern composer finds his own music drowned out by the melodies of an effeminate eighteenth-century predecessor which he has no choice but to publish under his name, to George Du Maurier's *The Martian* (1897), in which a novelist takes dictation from a female extraterrestrial whose words will later be transcribed by his wife, to Oliver Onions's "The Beckoning Fair One" (1911), in which the move to a haunted house forces a novelist to rewrite and eventually destroy his magnum opus at the dictate of a feminine ghost, a new subgenre of short fiction began to trace textual production to supernatural agents.

However disembodied, those agents were rarely unsexed. On the contrary, in the process of personifying the Muse, the fantastic mode came to offer a refuge for the feminine authorship which realist satire like Winter's had dismissed more literally as a fantasy. The social implications of that generic shift form the subject of Algernon Blackwood's horror story "A Psychical Invasion" (1908), which chronicles a male writer's degeneration from dictating to a female stenographer to taking dictation from a feminine ghost. As the story opens, John Silence, the "psychic doctor" who lays spirits with the help of a cat, a dog, a secretary, and a Watsonian sidekick, is called in to cure a comic author of the writer's block brought on by his move to a haunted house. Hypothesizing that "something in the house ... prevented his feeling funny," Mr. Pender's wife wrests the word "funny" back from its colloquial meaning, but the psychic sleuth has more trouble reversing the spell which has displaced the comic by the uncanny.[15] All that Silence succeeds in learning about the dead tenant is her gender. No less than Winter's satire on ghostwriting, Blackwood's parable of a ghost writing relies on sexual difference to lend moral consequences to literary misattribution.

The nature of that moral, however, is less clear. Haunting makes Pender's work not just unsaleable but inscrutable—even to readers of "A Psychical Invasion," for Blackwood's refusal to supply any information about the subject of the ghost's compositions forces us to decide for ourselves whether the horror they cause characters is moral or esthetic. On the one hand, Pender's complaint that his writings have ceased to be funny is called into doubt by a description of what sounds suspiciously like a dirty joke: "Dreadful innuendos had managed to creep into the phrases.... And shocking! Yet most damnably clever in the consummate way the vile suggestions are insinuated under cover of a kind of high drollery. My stenographer left me of course—and I've been afraid to take another—" (18). On the other, the unrepresentability of the texts inspired by the ghost suggests that their depravity lies less in their content than in their lack of it. Although she drives him to produce one sketch after another of her face ("a talent not normally mine"), Pender can give Silence no clue to the woman's identity, for the drawing consists of "nothing but a few scrawly lines. That's all I found the next morning. I had really drawn no heads at all—nothing but those lines and blots and wriggles" (17). Like Pender's ungrammatical text, his nonrepresentational images betray a proto-modernist esthetic haunted less by the dead than by the future.

Blackwood ultimately resolves the tension between too much and too little content by mapping those alternatives onto sexual difference—which turns out to be synonymous with the difference between authors and scribes. While Pender experiences what the ghost inspired him to sketch as incomprehensible, the stenographer takes what Pender orders her to write as indecent. "My stenographer left me of course": the exit of Pender's lady typist, a moment before Silence's male secretary comes on the scene, reduces him from dictating to a woman's hands to writing at the command of a woman's spirit. This is not to say that Pender ever confesses to dictating. Instead he reserves for his own speech the misnomer "writing," which would more logically be reserved for the stenographer's actions. "All that day I wrote and wrote and wrote," he tells Silence, "but when the stenographer had taken her departure and I came to read over the pages she had typed out.... I was amazed at what I read and could hardly believe I had uttered it.... The words, indeed, were mine so far as I could remember, but the meanings seemed strange" (14–15). Pender's inability to recognize the typescript as his owes as much to the stenographer as to the ghost. For the first genera- tion with access to typists' services, the estrangement of seeing one's voice set instantaneously into print must have approached the shock of hearing one's voice recorded. But Pender's unease at feeling the phan- tom's evil thoughts in his mouth does not mimic the discomfort of watching his own voice materialize under the typist's fingers so much as, on the contrary, the stenographer's experience of finding another's dirty words emerging from under her own hand.

"All day I wrote and wrote": in making himself the grammatical sub- ject of the stenographer's action, Pender elides her agency as brutally as the ghost will override his. With poetic justice, the female ghost teaches the male author what his stenographer already knows: what it feels like to find onself reduced to a conduit for another's words. But although gender underpins the division of labor between ghost and author as much as between author and typist, each cancels out the other. The woman's hand transmitting a man's thoughts gives way to a man's voice conducting a woman's spirit. (Pender's attempt to describe the "psychi- cal invasion" insinuates rape into the language of electric conductivity, explaining that the spirit has penetrated his "thought-stream" "so as to switch off the usual current and inject her own" [13].) Pender becomes to the ghost what the stenographer is to Pender. Or not even, for the haunted author still depends on his typist, and by extension on the machine upon which she relies in turn. Not content with subjecting the author to a woman's orders, Blackwood reduces him to the conductor linking two women: one, fleshless, who conceives texts but needs an embodied medium to sign them; another, mindless, who produces mate- rial documents but is incapable of originating them. Squeezed between a ghost whose disembodiment renders her inescapable and a stenogra- pher whose manual dexterity makes her indispensable, Pender finds himself able neither to disclaim his words or to control them.[16]

In measuring Pender's own writer's block by his stenographer's resig- nation, Blackwood evokes the danger of dependence on a woman's eso- teric skill. Once the invasive ghost has replaced the stenographer too well trained to express her outrage in anything more than raised eyebrows, not only Pender but Silence find themselves surrounded by women who refuse to let men do the talking. The story begins with Silence silencing the would-be lady expert who first brought Pender's case to his attention, "obviously trying," as the narrator remarks sardonically, "to explain herself very intelligently." "John Silence stopped her tirade with a gesture .... She thanked him elaborately, effusively, with many words, and he, with much difficulty, kept the conversation thenceforward strictly to the teapot" (3). The woman whose babble prevents Silence from thinking straight foreshadows the "woman of consummate wicked- ness and great personal power of... intellect" who takes over Pender's brain (20). The male author who dictates to a silent stenographer has no place in a story that contrasts feminine babble with manly Silence.

Women's voices, in fact, are what drive Silence to diagnose writer's block as a symptom of too much inspiration, not too little. The epony- mous doctor's self-containment matches the brutality with which he shuts up first his garrulous informant, next Pender's "breathless" wife, and finally the ghost. Even before we learn the gender of the ghost, Mrs. Pender's "incoherent rush of words stop[ped] sharp when she saw his face in the gaslight. There was something in John Silence's look that did not encourage mere talk .... 'Good evening, Mrs Pender,' he said, with a quiet smile that won confidence, yet deprecated unnecessary words .... He did not finish the sentence, for the men exchanged a look of sympathy that rendered it unnecessary." (6) The two men immediately disappear to the smoking room where they can remain safe not only from the wife's babble, but from the feminine spirit that haunts the study (where the stenographer works) and the sitting room (where Mrs. Pender receives). Silence's exorcism restores on a domestic scale the sexual division of space which the "invasion" of typists has by 1908 made impossible to map onto the boundary between home and office.

Yet although the first sign of the ghost's invasion had been Pender's urge to move his work from "the library, as we call it" (7) to the less pro- fessional and more feminine space of the sitting room, "A Psychical Invasion" does not import worries about the gendered delegation of writing from the businessman's office to the self-employed professional's home, so much as overlay those new anxieties about stenographers writ- ing to men's dictation on top of older fears about wives telling authors what to write. Blackwood at first tempts readers to situate his story within the long line of Victorian plots about artists' worldly wives that stretches from Browning's "Andrea del Sarto" (1855) to Gissing's *New Grub Street* (1891). On being told of Pender's problem, Silence's first reflex is to ask "And is [Mrs. Pender] a cause, perhaps?" The answer, of course, is "not in the least": "she is a devoted; a woman very well edu- cated, though without being really intelligent, and with so little sense of humour herself that she always laughs at the wrong places. But she has nothing to do with the cause of his distress" (5). The problem lies not with a wife who is devoted "without being really intelligent," but with a seductress of "great ... intellect" (even if both share a fondness for verbiage). Yet by raising the possibility of Mrs. Pender's guilt only to rule it out a sentence later, Blackwood calls attention to his departure from the fiction of a generation before, where materialistic wives had seduced authors from "serious" work—leading, in *New Grub Street* at least, to the same writer's block from which Pender suffers. Here, in contrast, an immaterial woman seduces Pender into producing serious work: literally, work that isn't funny.

A disembodied mind that makes the man's art unmarketable replaces the mindless women who traditionally nagged men to prostitute their art. Far from urging Pender to sacrifice the spirit to the body, the feminine spirit of "A Psychical Invasion" forces him to give up a vulgar and profitable literary career. A ghost replaces inspiration as that which saves—or in this case, prevents—a man from producing popular art. Ultimately, Blackwood appropriates Gissing's warning against women's influence on men's writing for opposite ideological ends. Where Gissing's misogyny affirms high art, Blackwood's instead affirms the middlebrow esthetic that the ghost story not only represents (in the form of Pender's jokes) but exemplifies. In saving Pender from the dangerous depths of the spirit world, Blackwood vindicates his own shallowness. The traditional cult of the male genius gives way to an even more misogynistic fear of the muse.[17] Inspiration threatens to reduce the author to a woman's stenographer, but luckily no one could call a joke-writer inspired.

Yet "A Psychical Invasion" doesn't just invert the male writer's traditional relation to a materialistic wife: it extends that process into the workplace by reversing the businessman's newer dependence on his secretary's manual labor. Like Ethel's angelic ethereality, the evil spirit's ghostliness overcompensates for the radically new gender dynamic that shifts businessmen's corporeality onto business girls. Typed correspondence now bears the (lowercase) initials of the woman whose hands directly produced a material letter beside the (uppercase) initials of the man who takes ultimate responsibility for its textual content. In small letters, manual labor; in capitals, an absent voice. The prime mover looms literally larger than the proximate cause.

What Pender's secretarial role means for the status of actual secretaries, however, remains an open question. Although the stenographer's departure coincides with the ghost's "invasion," the happy ending says nothing about the former's return to work. The story's silence about whether the exorcism has cured Pender's fear of stenographers—"I've been afraid to take another"—leaves open whether the walkout of the prudish stenographer reverses, or on the contrary foreshadows, the expulsion of the dictatorial and oversexed ghost. By extension, the ending fails to resolve whether the threat posed by the stenographer lies in the professional invisibility that she shares with the ghost, or in the moment when she sheds that automatism long enough to show her shocked comprehension of the words that she has typed. On the one hand, the coincidence of the stenographer's departure with the ghost's "invasion" structures "A Psychical Invasion" as a decline from masculine authority to feminine power. From the mundane bureaucratic transaction in which the text visibly produced by a female stenographer's hands is credited to a man's mind, the story progresses to the fantastic hypothesis that the work of a man's hands can be traced to the disembodied agency of a female spirit. On the other, what makes "A Psychical Invasion" horrific is the climate of retrospective suspicion which forces us to read backwards to find presages of the *femme fatale*'s seizure of language in the wife and the secretary who at first had appeared respectively inarticulate and silent. Over the course of the story, the "home-loving" "suggester" whom Elizabeth Banks had contrasted with the unfeminine office worker becomes indistinguishable from the androgynous spirit that haunts Pender's house.

By the same token, the resemblance of the exorcist's motives for ridding the house of the ghost to the anxiety of (woman's) influence that causes Sir Edgar Allesley to turn his ghostwriter out of doors makes it difficult to distinguish the malevolent spirit of "A Psychical Invasion" from the modest secretary of *Miss Secretary Ethel*. When Sir Edgar fires Ethel after spilling ink all over his desk because she has overfilled the well which he always leaves to run dry, even the reassuring echo of a more domestic scene, in which Ethel had shown the same eagerness to replenish the water in the teapot, fails to counterbalance the heavy symbolism (*Ethel*, 69–71). No less than Pender (whose ideas have less literally dried up), Sir Edgar finds himself unmanned by a woman who forces inspiration upon him. Indeed, Sir Edgar's irritation at stumbling over an invisible secretary whenever he retreats to his study anticipates Pender's discomfort at finding a woman's spirit lurking in his (*Ethel*, 98). While women's influence makes up for their lack of brute bodily strength, disembodiment (or invisibility) lends ghosts (or ghostwriters) a more insidious power. "Mind you don't use undue influence, and make the election void," Sir Edgar warns Ethel when she campaigns overzealously on his behalf (187); but if Ethel's ostensible secretarial function requires her to influence his constituents, her real job—ghostwriting—exerts an even more questionable influence upon her boss himself. "A Psychical Invasion" reveals the danger of what Banks had termed more flatteringly modest women's power of "suggestion." Women's influence upon men turns out to have not just more power for good than do women speaking in their own names (as conservatives such as Ellis had argued), but also for evil.

"A Psychical Invasion" suggests, in other words, that not only the invisibility but the domesticity that *Miss Secretary Ethel* had deployed to resolve the tensions created by middle-class women's entrance into the workforce can exacerbate them instead. As a result, paradoxically, Blackwood's misogynistic parable of inspiration has less in common with Adams's fantasy of feminine subordination than with New Woman fictions devoted to denouncing men who subcontract writing to cheap feminine labor. If Winter's parable of a society lady signing the work of a male hack forms an imaginary counterweight to the real division of labor emerging between male bosses and their female secretaries—as does, more obliquely, Blackwood's allegory of male hands taking dictation from feminine spirits—contemporary feminist fiction used ghostwriting instead to expose, by analogy, the ethical dangers of the more socially accepted form of subcontracting that allowed well-paid men to sign the texts produced by badly paid women.

Witness Mabel Wotton's short story "The Fifth Edition" (1896), in which a successful author named Leyden manipulates his fan Miss Suttaby into inviting him first to correct, and then to publish under his own name, her autobiographical novel. By turning the writer quite literally into a ghost (Leyden postpones paying Miss Suttaby until she dies of malnutrition), the story's ending fulfils the fantasy that had justified Leyden's plagiarism in the first place: "he would have another look at the story, he decided, and amuse himself by arranging in his own mind what he would have done with it if Miss Suttaby had died and bequeathed it to him for his personal property."[18] More disturbingly, by timing Miss Suttaby's death before she can be paid, Wotton avoids acknowledging that on its own (commercial) terms, ghostwriting might work—in fact, might work to the advantage of both parties. Bibliographical crime must be compounded by financial fraud. A false signature on the title page cannot be exchanged for a valid one on a check. Like Winter's faith that stylistic evidence will always give the ghostwriter away, Wotton's gratuitous plot twist of broken bargains suggests that the sale of signing rights is too unsettling to be represented.

Yet although "The Fifth Edition" brands as unthinkable the same transaction which *Miss Secretary Ethel* presents as exemplary, and although one uses ghostwriting to discredit masculine arrogance while the other uses feminine modesty to legitimize ghostwriting, the effect of both plots is oddly similar. In *Miss Secretary Ethel*, the boss's initial ingratitude serves to point up the secretarial self-abnegation which female readers must strive to emulate; Wotton, too, can establish her heroine's artistic disinterest only by making the plagiarist a selfish cad. In the same way that, as I suggested earlier, Sir Edgar's motives for firing Ethel inscribe within *Miss Secretary Ethel* the logic that comes to dominate the narrator's own perspective in "A Psychical Invasion," Wotton's condemnation of the man who accepts Miss Suttaby's offer to ghostwrite for him bears an uncanny resemblance to the arguments of Ethel's Girtonian friend. The only difference is that the point of view that Adams relegates to a misguided minor character is here transposed to the narrator's own voice. Despite Ethel's generically imposed function as a role model for young readers, in other words, Adams puts into the mouths of her own characters both of the same—apparently incompatible—condemnations of women writing in men's names that dominate the narrator's perspective in New Woman novels on the one hand and in misogynistic ghost stories on the other. Conversely, the plagiarist in "The Fifth Edition" celebrates that sexual division of labor in a tone closer to Adams's than to Wotton's own. Retouched by him, he exults, the novel will become "the joint work of a woman dealing with the subtleties a man could not divine, and of a man writing what a woman never notices" (161). Wotton's irony never entirely discredits his claim, for "The Fifth Edition" makes selflessness as fundamental to literary genius as *Miss Secretary Ethel* makes it to feminine modesty.

Wotton criminalizes ghostwriting not only by compounding textual with monetary fraud and switched identities with reversed genders, but also, more importantly, by making the stolen text autobiographical. "There was no art about it at all," the narrator observes in a free indirect discourse which makes the villain's exploitation of the heroine's defencelessness indistinguishable from the story's endorsement of it: "She had looked into her own heart, and written of what she found there .... It was a powerful book, because it bore so plainly the impress of truth" (154–5). Combined with the sexual difference between the ghostwriter and the signatory, the content of the manuscript doubly overdetermines the criminality of Leyden's appropriation: first, because royalties will now go not only to someone who has not expended the labor needed to produce the text, but to someone who has not suffered the harrowing experiences that it describes; and second, because once the narrative appears under a name whose gender differs from the narrator's, the text will no

longer be read as autobiography, but on the contrary will be taken as
"art." Conversely, the scholar's wife through whose consciousness
Beatrice Harraden's novel *The Guiding Thread* (1916) is focalized no
sooner ceases to do his research than she begins to dream of writing
about herself: "now she could write down other things—her own
thoughts and feelings—things that belonged to her—to her own self-
experiences."[19] The slippage from "things that belonged to her" to
"her own self-experiences" implies that only autobiography can guarantee literary property.

In practice, of course, it does no such thing. The fact that memoirs are
more routinely ghostwritten than any other genre makes clear that the
importance with which they invest signature invites rather than deters
its falsification. Misattribution functions not simply to grant brand
recognition to autobiographies (by making the signatory a celebrity) but
also, ironically, to increase their authority (by making the signatory's
name coincide with the narrator's, even at the price of unmooring the
signatory's from the author's). In contrast, Wotton's and Harraden's
definition of ghostwriting as the opposite of autobiography makes
authenticity depend on a threeway equation of author, signatory, and
narrator—on the naming of the author not simply on the title page, but
throughout the work.[20] "Art" becomes synonymous with plagiarism,
solipsism with "the impress of truth." Once autobiography has been
declared the precondition of honesty, ghostwriting can be no worse than
third-person narration.

Yet in both fictions, sincerity depends just as crucially on the author's
gender. Where Winter opposes men's honest toil to leisured ladies'
manipulation of a corrupt marketplace, Wotton and Harraden contrast
women's intransitive urge to express themselves with men's calculated
pursuit of readers—a model that has left its mark on twentieth-century
criticism well beyond Sandra Gilbert and Susan Gubar's *The Madwoman
in the Attic* (1979).[21] Little evidence is available to establish which scenario was more common in practice, men's ghosting for women or
women's for men. (In any case, no evidence at all suggests that either was
more frequent than the permutation rarely mentioned at all in fiction:
signing a text written by someone of one's own gender.) Although the
cheapness of women's labor may well have made female ghostwriters a
bargain, Wotton's and Harraden's interest in men taking credit for (and
profits from) women's writing can be explained less directly as a displacement of bureaucratic practice. Only by transposing from a clerical
to a literary context well-paid men's ability to sign what ill-paid women
write, can "The Fifth Edition" reconcile the celebration of women's

textual power with a denial—not very different from that found in proponents of separate spheres like Adams—that women, or indeed writers, should work for money.

If Wotton's contrast between the real female ghostwriter and the fraudulent male celebrity looks forward to Gilbert and Gubar, however, it also looks back to an already outdated ideal of artistic creativity that stands opposite the model of hackwork described above. As Poovey argues, writers earlier in the century invoked women's domestic work as an analogy for the disinterested nature of masculine authorship: "The construction of literary labor as the exception that mitigated the rule of alienated labor had as one of its critical components the reinforcement and appropriation of another representation of nonalienated labor—the image of women's domestic labor as a nonalienated expression of a selfless self" (13–14). Yet by 1896, the influx of women into the new profession of typewriting made it increasingly difficult to align literary works of genius with feminine labors of love, for the women most visibly associated with textual production—typists—now yoked writing with commerce far more tightly than even the most mercenary hackwriter could do. As a generation of women (and characters) moved from unpaid housework to typing paid by the word, feminine labor became a rather less flattering analog for literary work. Blackwood consigns that comparison to the past by exorcising the domestic woman's influence that prevents a male hack from pandering to the taste of the book-buying masses.

That these plots seem forced, even improbable, suggests just how much contrivance was needed to substitute anonymity for signature as the mark of genius. The self-effacing ghostwriter provides a mirror image for the self-promoting celebrity called into being by the new literary marketplace. One's inability to take credit counterbalances the other's obligation to grant autographs. Plots that represent (or literalize) the compound joining "writer" to "ghost" make textual production incompatible not only with recognition but with visibility, not only with materialism but with materiality. In Henry James's "The Death of the Lion," a New Journalist atones for his past invasions of privacy by bullying a famous author to "be as dead as you can" and his voyeuristic fans to "succeed in never seeing him at all."[22] Miss Suttaby's refusal to eat or sign, too, expiates Mrs. Deane-Pitt's voracity for sex, money, and bylines. Anorexia conspires with anonymity to purify word from flesh. By overlaying the topos of the starving artist with the metaphor of the ghostwriter, "The Fifth Edition" reaffirms the independence of work from life that the new star system threatened to undermine. Once the division of labor between writer and signatory absolves self-expression of self-interest, sexual difference allows textual production to stake out a separate sphere. Yet the plot twists that make readers privy to information unavailable to characters within the text undercut each story's ambition to quarantine the literary from the social. Moving from the cover of a book to the interiority of a writer, from paratextual surface to psychological depth, their idealism replicates the intrusiveness for which they satirize the New Journalism. Both trace texts to selves that in turn become coextensive with secrets. In training readers to trust inferences about invisible subjects over evidences of tangible objects, they stage the surrender of bibliography to biography.

Notes

1. Elizabeth L. Banks, "New Paid Occupations for Women," *Cassell's Family Magazine* (1894), 585–88.
2. Ironically, Banks's *Autobiography of a "Newspaper Girl"* (New York: Dodd, Mead, 1902) traces the beginning of her own journalistic career to her own secretarial experience, which she writes up in an article called "All about Typewriter Girls."
3. Zimmeck estimates that between 1850 and 1914 the number of women clerks rose from 2,000 to 16,600 (and from 2 to 20 percent of the total number of clerical workers). See Meta Zimmeck, "Jobs for Girls," in *Unequal Opportunities: Women's Employment in England, 1800–1918*, ed. Angela John (Oxford: Blackwell, 1986), 153–78. Using slightly different methods, Lockwood calculates that between 1851 and 1901—a period when the number of office workers was climbing exponentially—women went from one-tenth of a percent of the clerical workforce in Britain to 13.4 percent. See David Lockwood, *The Black-Coated Worker: A Study in Class Consciousness* (Oxford: Clarendon Press, 1989).
4. On the replacement of the muse by the typist, see Friedrich A. Kittler, *Discourse Networks 1800/1900*, trans. Michael Metteer (Stanford: Stanford University Press, 1990).
5. On the debates about anonymous journalism, see Dallas Liddle, "Salesmen, Sportsmen, Mentors: Anonymity and Mid-Victorian Theories of Journalism," *Victorian Studies* 41 (Autumn 1997): 31–68; Oscar Maurer, "Anonymity vs. signature in Victorian reviewing," *University of Texas Studies in English* 27 (1948), 1–27; Mary Ruth Hiller, "The Identification of Authors: The Great Victorian Enigma," in *Victorian Periodicals: A Guide to Research*, ed. J. Don Vann and Rosemary T. VanArsdel (New York: Modern Language Association, 1978), 123–48; Christopher Kent, "Introduction," in *British Literary Magazines: The Victorian and Edwardian Age, 1837–1913*, ed. Alvin Sullivan (Westport: Greenwood, 1984), xiii–xxvi; David Vincent, *The Culture of Secrecy* (Oxford: Oxford University Press, 1998); Leslie Marchand, *The Athenaeum* (New York: Octagon Books, 1971); and Joanne Shattock, *Politics and Reviewers: The Edinburgh and the Quarterly in the Early Victorian Age* (Leicester: Leicester University Press, 1989). On the relation between anonymity and pseudonymity more generally, I'm indebted to Robert Griffin, "Anonymity and Authorship," *NLH* 30 (1999), 877–95.
6. Margaret Diane Stetz, "Life's 'Half-profits': Writers and their Readers in Fiction of the 1890s," in *Nineteenth-Century Lives*, ed. Laurence S. Lockridge, John Maynard, and Donald D. Stone (Cambridge: Cambridge University Press, 1989), 169–87. On the conventions invented by the New Journalists to represent the author's private life, see also Joel Wiener, ed., *Papers for the Millions: The New Journalism in Britain* (Westport: Greenwood, 1988); Nigel Cross, *The Common Writer: Life in Nineteenth-Century Grub Street* (Cambridge: Cambridge University Press, 1985); and Peter McDonald, *British Literary Culture and Publishing Practice, 1880–1914* (Cambridge: Cambridge University Press, 1997).

7. James Boswell, *The Life of Samuel Johnson*, ed. R.W. Chapman (Oxford: Oxford University Press, 1980), 179.

8. John Strange Winter [Henrietta Stannard, pseud.], *Confessions of a Publisher, Being the Autobiography of Abel Drinkwater* (London: F. V. White, 1888), 91. The best source on Winter's nomenclature is Oliver Bainbridge's hagiographic *John Stranger Winter: A Volume of Personal Record* (London: East and West, 1916); for a brief but acute analysis of the novel, see Margaret Diane Stetz, "*New Grub Street* and the Woman Writer of the 1890s," in *Transforming Genre: New Approaches to British Fiction of the 1890s*, ed. Nikki Lee Manos and Meri-Jane Rochelson (New York: St. Martin's Press, 1994), 21–46.

9. John Strange Winter [Henrietta Stannard, pseud.], *A Name to Conjure With* (London, 1899), 99, 232.

10. M. Mostyn Bird, *Woman at Work: A Study of the Different Ways of Earning a Living Open to Women* (London: Chapman and Hall, 1911), 231.

11. Elaine Showalter, *A Literature of their Own: British Women Novelists from Bronte to Lessing* (1977; reprint, London: Virago, 1978), 55; Mary Poovey, *Uneven Developments: The Ideological Work of Gender in Mid-Victorian England* (Chicago: University of Chicago Press, 1988), 125.

12. Elinor Davenport Adams, *Miss Secretary Ethel: A Story for Girls of To-Day* (London: Hurst and Blackett, 1898), 116. Thanks to Helen Bittel for calling this novel to my attention.

13. Mrs. Ellis, *The Women of England. Their Social Duties, and Domestic Habits* (London: Fisher, 1838), 49.

14. Herbert Blain, *Pitman's Secretarial Handbook* (London: Isaac Pitman, 1908), 67.

15. Algernon Blackwood, "A Psychical Invasion," in *The Complete John Silence Stories*, ed. S. T. Joshi (Minneola: Dover, 1979), 5; see also Geoffrey Gilbert, "Intestinal Violence: Wyndham Lewis and the Critical Poetics of the Modernist Career," *Critical Quarterly* 36 (Autumn 1994), 86–125.

16. On the relation between secretaries and mediums (literal ghostwriters) in this period, see Pamela Thurschwell, "Henry James and Theodora Bosanquet: On the Typewriter, *In the Cage*, at the Ouija board," *Textual Practice* 13 (1999), 5–23; Bette London, *Writing Double: Women's Literary Partnerships* (Ithaca: Cornell University Press, 1999), 150–78; and Lisa Gitelman, *Scripts, Grooves, and Writing Machines: Representing Technology in the Edison Era* (Stanford: Stanford University Press, 1999), 184–218.

17. See also Elaine Showalter's argument that *fin-de-siècle* male writers attempted to do away with the feminine Muse altogether by substituting male inspiration (*Sexual Anarchy: Gender and Culture at Fin-de-siècle* [1990; reprint, London: Virago, 1992], 78).

18. Mabel E. Wotton, "The Fifth Edition," in *Daughters of Decadence: Women Writers of the Fin-de-siècle*, ed. Elaine Showalter (New Brunswick: Rutgers University Press, 1993), 139–65. In still a third New Woman novel, Mary Cholmondeley's *Red Pottage*, a clergyman whose sister rewrites his newspaper article credits her only for help with "the stops and grammar and spelling" ([n.p., 1899], 84). On Wotton, see Margaret Diane Stetz, "Turning Points: Mabel E. Wotton," *Turn-of-the-Century Women* 3 (Winter 1986), 2–3; on the figure of the starving artist more generally, see Maud Ellmann, *The Hunger Artists: Starving, Writing, and Imprisonment* (London: Virago, 1993), 25–7.

19. Beatrice Harraden, *The Guiding Thread* (London: Methuen, 1916), 116.

20. See Philippe Lejeune's argument that autobiography represents a limit-case of the confusion between person and author which structures literary interpretation more generally (*Le pacte autobiographique* [Paris: Seuil, 1975], 33).

21. Stetz, for example, pairs fictions like "The Fifth Edition" with contemporary woman writers' autobiographies to establish women's writing as "something that occurs spontaneously and unbidden" ("*New Grub Street*," 28).

22. Henry James, "The Death of the Lion," in "*The Figure in the Carpet*" and Other Stories, ed. Frank Kermode (Harmondsworth: Penguin, 1986), 268, 285. For an acute analysis of James's relation to the New Journalism, see Richard Salmon, *Henry James and the Culture of Publicity* (Cambridge: Cambridge University Press, 1997).

CHAPTER TEN

"A Poet May Not Exist": Mock-Hoaxes and the Construction of National Identity

In memory of Armand Schwerner (1927–99)

Brian McHale

1

Let me begin by describing two recent acts of literary impersonation, and their respective receptions.

First, in 1997, a book appeared from a major publishing house, purporting to be the first-person memoirs of a Japanese woman born in the 1920s, a successful and prominent geisha. Entitled *Memoirs of a Geisha*, the book was in fact written by a white American male, Arthur Golden.[1] Golden's impersonation of a geisha was critically well-received, and spent over a year on the New York *Times* best-seller list. As I write, it is being developed as a movie project by Steven Spielberg.

Second, throughout the mid-1990s, there appeared in a number of distinguished American literary journals, including *Grand Street, Conjunctions* and *The American Poetry Review*, a series of poems and related prose texts purportedly written by a Japanese poet and survivor of the Hiroshima bombing named Araki Yasusada. In fact, no such person as Araki Yasusada ever existed, and the poems published under his name were written by someone else—perhaps "Tosa Motokiyu," itself a pseudonym for a person or persons as yet unidentified; perhaps Kent Johnson or Javier Alvarez, both real people; perhaps some combination of these three, or some other person entirely. Initial responses to this act of impersonation were violently negative. *The American Poetry Review* ran a disclaimer in a subsequent issue, repudiating the Yasusada texts, and the *APR*'s editor, Arthur Vogelsang, characterized the Yasusada imperson-ation as "an essentially criminal act."[2] Wesleyan University Press reneged on its plans to publish the Yasusada manuscript,[3] and Pierre Joris and Jerome Rothenberg changed their minds about including a selection of Yasusada writings in the second volume of their *Poems for the Millennium* anthology. A few critics rose to Yasusada's defense, notably Eliot Weinberger and Marjorie Perloff, but for the most part the literary insti-tution was, if not unanimous, certainly emphatic in its condemnation.

What accounts for the disparity in response to these two acts of impersonation? A number of contributing factors need to be considered. One might be lack of fidelity in representing Japanese culture. A profes-sor of Japanese culture has been quoted as dismissing the Yasusada texts as "just Japanized crap. It plays into the American idea of what is inter-esting about Japanese culture—Zen, haiku, anything seen as exotic—and gets it all wrong."[4] But the same "Japanized crap," the same heavy dosage of exoticism—indeed a much heavier dosage—is present in Golden's *Memoirs*, without anyone's finding it illegitimate or exploitative. Instead, critics praise *Memoirs of a Geisha* for "indubitable authenticity of voice and period detail."[5]

Alternatively, the disparity of response might be explicable in terms of the Yasusada poet's bad faith in assuming the persona of a victim and sur-vivor, without possessing the proper credentials. By this criterion of "wit-ness" (about which Weinberger has written tellingly[6]), only someone who actually experienced the Hiroshima bombing has the right to speak as a survivor of it. Yet, by this criterion, Golden too, should be subject to cen-sure, since he too impersonates a victim. A male writer, he dares to speak as a female victim of child sexual abuse; he speaks, moreover, as a survivor of the American bombing campaign in Japan in the last years of the Second World War, and even indirectly as a survivor of the atomic bomb-ings, since one of the geisha's close acquaintances is reported to have per-ished at Nagasaki. Yet, no one has accused Golden of bad faith, as they have the Yasusada poet. Moreover, the criterion of witness is a slippery one, and has hardly been applied consistently in recent cases of survivor imperson-ations. Thus, on the one hand, Binjamin Wilkomirski's dubious Holocaust memoir, *Fragments: Memories of a Wartime Childhood*, is denounced as a hoax, though the evidence suggests that Wilkomirski is likely deluding himself rather than seeking to delude others;[7] while other conspicuous Holocaust impersonators, such as Roberto Benigni or indeed Steven Spielberg, are praised and rewarded. The criterion of witness can be waived, evidently, if one wields sufficient culture-industry clout.

A more adequate explanation of the disparity of reception between Golden's *Geisha* and the Yasusada texts begins to emerge when we take into account the difference of genre. A text marketed as a "novel" engages different expectations from one marketed as "poetry;" crucially, poetry is held to a different criterion of "authenticity." One lingering legacy of the Romantic movement in the West is the assumption that the "I" of a poem is to be identified with the "I" of the poet. This assumption has survived the modernists' invention (or discovery) of the *persona*, and persists despite the best efforts of several generations of New-Critically trained teachers to persuade us that every lyric poem (and in our time all poetry belongs, in effect, to the sub-genre of lyric) amounts to a kind of dramatic monologue, that the lyric speaker is always a fictional character, even when the poem's subject matter is autobiographical. While we may endorse these modernist and New Critical precepts in theory and in our own pedagogy, in our collective practice as readers and agents of the literary institution we evidently persist in expecting that the lyric poem will express the poet's subjective truth and reflect his or her true identity, unless there are overriding reasons to assume otherwise. No reader would make such an assumption about a first-person novel, of course, for novels are exempt from any such expectations of authenticity. Prose fiction is licensed to impersonate.

Or, to put it differently, the assumption of autobiographical authenticity, of an identity between the poem's "I" and the poet's self, is something like the "default setting" for lyric poems. It is the preferred reading, except in cases when some conspicuous anomaly makes it necessary to posit a fictional *persona* (e.g. when the speaker appears to be a duke of the Italian Renaissance while the poet is known to be a middle-class Englishman of the nineteenth century). For first-person prose narratives, by contrast, the "default setting" is impersonation, that is, fictionality, rather than authenticity.[8] Poetry, in other words, in practice if not in theory, is generally denied the privilege of fictionality that we routinely extend to novels. The literary institution justifies celebrating Arthur Golden's impersonation of a geisha on the grounds that *Memoirs of a Geisha* is a novel; conversely, it condemns the Yasusada impersonation as an "essentially criminal act" at least in part because the Yasusada texts are poems, and so *ought not* to be fictional.

I am being disingenuous here, for in emphasizing the difference in generic expectations I obviously misrepresent the true grounds for objecting to Yasusada. *Memoirs of a Geisha* is acceptable and the Yasusada texts unacceptable not, after all, because the latter is held to different criteria of authenticity than the former, but because the Yasusada poetry is a hoax. The Yasusada texts were foisted on unsuspecting editors under flagrantly false pretenses, as the work of a non-existent poet and Hiroshima survivor, when it is really the work of someone else, whether the person or persons masquerading under the pseudonym "Tosa Motokiyu," or Kent Johnson, or whomever—in any case, anyone *but* "Araki Yasusada." It is *this*, surely, that makes the Yasusada impersonation "an essentially criminal act" in most people's eyes. Golden's book, by contrast, never tries to pass itself off as an authentic memoir; it is labeled a novel on its title page, and its author is openly acknowledged to be Arthur Golden, never the geisha Nitta Sayuri.[9] One author lies about his (or her, or their) identity, while the other does not; this much, surely, is obvious.

Or is it? The objections to the Yasusada impersonation would be more compelling, and the accusation of hoax more damaging, if we could be sure that, in using the term "hoax," we were all talking about the same thing. It would be convenient if literary hoaxing were a unitary phenomenon, a single thing that we might unequivocally identify as, say, "hoax poetry;" unfortunately, it is not. We need to distinguish among at least three types of literary hoax. First, there are the "genuine" hoaxes, perpetrated with no intention of their ever being exposed. The classic instance of genuine hoax poetry is James Macpherson's "Ossian" poems, beginning with his *Fragments of Ancient Poetry* (1760). Hoaxes of this type belong to the same general category of phenomena as non-literary forgeries such as the Piltdown Man forgery, the art-forgeries of Hans van Meegeren, Clifford Irving's fake biography of Howard Hughes, or Konrad Kujau's forged Hitler Diaries.[10]

Second, there are "entrapments" or "trap-hoaxes," designed with didactic and punitive purposes in mind. The intention here is for the hoax to be exposed by the hoaxer himself or herself when the time is right, to the discomfiture of the gullible. A classic case of poetic entrapment is the Ern Malley hoax, perpetrated by James McAuley and Harold Stewart on Australian avant-garde poetry circles in 1944, with the intention of exposing modernist poetry to ridicule. McAuley and Stewart jointly composed a set of sixteen modernist poems, derivative of Eliot and Dylan Thomas, fabricated a poet to whom they could be ascribed—one Ern Malley, conveniently deceased—and then palmed them off on the editors of the poetry journal *Angry Penguins* as authentic productions. Once the poems had been published and praised, McAuley and Stewart went to the newspapers with their story, and the trap was sprung, with damaging long-term consequences for the Australian avant-garde.[11] Related to trap-hoaxes of the Ern Malley type are such non-poetic forms of entrapment as the one recently (1996) perpetrated by Alan Sokal on the editors of *Social Text*, and possibly Tom Keating's art-forgeries, which Keating himself alleged were intended to expose the venal practices of the art-world establishment.[12]

Finally, there is the class of phenomena that I propose to call "mock-hoaxes." The deception here, as with trap-hoaxes, is temporary, but where trap-hoaxes depend for their effect on the dramatic moment of exposure ("gotcha!"), mock-hoaxes are meant eventually to be seen through without any traps being sprung. To that end, they typically refer in a more or less veiled manner to their own double nature, leaving it to their readers to draw the relevant inferences. Classic examples include the poems that Fernando Pessoa published under his "heteronyms" of Alberto Caeiro, Alvaro de Campos, and Ricardo Reis and, at a somewhat lower level of ambition, closer to light verse, Kenneth Koch's sequence "Some South American Poets," from *The Pleasures of Peace* (1969).

Mock-hoaxes differ most markedly from trap-hoaxes in lacking any intention to edify, remediate, or punish—which is to say that the primary purpose of a mock-hoax is aesthetic. Whereas in trap-hoaxes, deliberate inauthenticity always serves some ulterior extra-aesthetic purpose—for example, in the Ern Malley hoax, that of a stick with which to beat the avant-garde—in mock-hoaxes it serves no such purpose, but rather tends to be absorbed into the very poetics of the work. That is, in mock-hoaxes, issues of authenticity and inauthenticity are elevated to the level of literary "raw materials." Mock-hoax poems, a special case of literary mock-hoaxes, are "about" these issues, not necessarily in the sense of making authenticity and inauthenticity an explicit theme or topic (though that is one possibility), but rather in the sense of foregrounding their own raw materials, much as other poems might foreground poetic conventions or poetic language itself, or indeed language in general. Mock-hoax poems are *made out of* inauthenticity, and out of inauthenticity they make self-reflective art.

On the strength of what I have said so far, it might be inferred that the distinction among types of hoax—genuine hoax, trap-hoax, mock-hoax—is entirely determined by the poet's motives or intention: an intention to deceive yields a genuine hoax; to punish, a trap-hoax; to make art, a mock-hoax. If this were the case, then the typology would rest on the shakiest of epistemological grounds, for how often would we be in a position to verify a poet's "true" motives, even if (a very big "if" indeed) these were transparent to the poet himself or herself? Intention does play a determining role—not, however, the poet's "actual" intention (whatever that might mean), but rather the intentions that readers, in the process of reception, *ascribe to* the author. Intention, in this sense, amounts to an interpretative hypothesis about the text—a readerly reconstruction, not a point of origin or ultimate source of meaning. In other words, a hoax poem, like every other kind of poem, exists as a "social text," and its significance, far from being under its author's exclusive control, is collectively and dialogically negotiated.[13]

This approach to intention accommodates the disparities that often arise between what hoaxers appear to have intended and public responses beyond their control, for instance in the Ern Malley case, as we will shortly see. It also allows for multiple receptions—one and the same text being taken as a trap-hoax by one constituency among its readership, as a mock-hoax by another constituency, for instance—and for shifts in classification over time. Texts initially perceived as belonging to one category are apt to migrate to another as subsequent generations of readers come to construe them differently, sometimes clean against the intentions of the original hoaxers. The changing reception of Thomas Chatterton is an example. Traditionally grouped with the disreputable Macpherson as a genuine hoaxer for his literary crime of forging pseudo-medieval poetry and ascribing it to a nonexistent monkish poet, Chatterton has recently been reinterpreted as a kind of historical novelist before the fact.[14] Once they have been reconstrued in this way as no longer "essentially criminal" but rather aesthetic acts, Chatterton's forgeries become candidates for inclusion in the mock-hoax category. Even the Ern Malley poems have achieved the status, for readers distant in time or space from their original context, of something akin to a mock-hoax, contrary to the hoaxers' own undeniably malicious intentions.[15]

The Yasusada writings serve as an example of a hoax construed differently by different constituencies. Yasusada's power to deceive has proved short-lived, and his self-exposure seems to have been programmed in advance, so, despite the wronged editors' outrage, it seems hard to assimilate him to the "essentially criminal" category of genuine hoax. Some readers, however, have construed the Yasusada impersonation as a trap-hoax, while others have construed it as a mock-hoax; I belong to the latter constituency. Not only can both constituencies adduce good evidence in support of their readings, but each can adduce the very same evidence to different effect. Thus, for example, Marjorie Perloff has demonstrated that the Yasusada texts are full of anachronisms, anomalies and errors too flagrant not to have been intended, suggesting to her that the hoax was designed to be seen through almost immediately.[16] Charles Bernstein, however, interprets those very same anomalies and deliberate errors as part of a design to humiliate the editors inattentive enough to be taken in by the con. For Bernstein, the Yasusada hoax reflects resentment (specifically, "white male rage") toward poetry-publishing institutions that appear to favor works by women and people of color, particularly when these latter can claim the status of "victim." On this reading, the intention of the hoaxer or hoaxers was simply to expose the non-literary criteria observed by literary editors. Having sprung the trap, moreover, the Yasusada poet would be in a position to seize the moral high ground, as a defender of "literary" values against "extra-literary" considerations, and thus would have succeeded in perpetrating a *secondary* hoax on those (including, presumably, Perloff and myself) who read his poems as aesthetic texts (i.e. mock-hoaxes) rather than what they really were, devious expressions of white male resentment.[17]

Bernstein's reading is persuasive enough, as far as it goes, and it certainly captures a dimension of the Yasusada hoax's significance as "social text."[18] But it fails to account for the foregrounded *artifactuality* of the Yasusada text—its formal heterogeneity and complexity, its multiple framings and proliferation of ancillary texts, its mix of genres and styles, its intertextual play, its conspicuous visuality and materiality, and so on. If the hoax's sole or main purpose was entrapping unwary editors, what explains this formal excess, which seems wildly disproportionate to any debunking function the text might conceivably serve?[19] Once we concede the essentially aesthetic purpose of this excess of form over function, then it is only a short step to entertaining the possibility that the Yasusada impersonator's inauthenticity, too, is essentially aesthetic in purpose, that his (or her, or their) deceptive doubleness is less a means to an end than an end in itself—in other words, that this is a mock-hoax rather than a trap.

2

However, the controversy over which type of hoax it belongs to—mock-hoax or trap-hoax?—does not fully explain the violence of the reaction to the Yasusada impersonation, or to other notorious twentieth-century poetic hoaxes, for that matter. For instance, once the Ern Malley perpetrators had sprung their trap, and the deceived editors had been duly humiliated, matters did not end there. No doubt responding to the furor surrounding the hoax, but quite independently of the hoaxers, a zealous police detective initiated proceedings against the publishers of the Ern Malley poems on the grounds of indecency—and this, despite the fact that the poems were generally conceded to make no "sense" at all, indecent or otherwise! Mere hoaxing does not seem sufficient to inspire repression of this intensity, even when (or especially when) it has so transparently mistaken its target. Something more must be at stake in hoax poetry. I propose to spend the remainder of this paper exploring that "something more," the *surplus* anxiety and outrage that hoax poetry seems to inspire compared to other genres of hoax.

Genre, I suggested earlier, seems to hold the key here: because poetry is expected to faithfully reflect the poet's identity and experience, hoax poetry inspires disproportionate revulsion and repression. But the expectation of authenticity is not the whole story. We need also to take into account hoax poetry's long and troubled entanglement with issues of national (or more generally ethnic) identity-construction. Beginning with Macpherson's Ossian poems, hoax poetry has been implicated in the formation and reformation of national identities, sometimes on the side of constructing or reinforcing such identities, at other times on the side of critiquing or deconstructing them; but in either case, the hoax poem is likely to attract the kinds of anxieties and passions that questions of national identity typically arouse.

Anthony Grafton observes that the emergent nations of medieval Europe sought to buttress their sense of national identity by recourse to forged histories that lent these nations-in-the-making the dignity and legitimacy of descent from ancient heroes, for example, the heroes of Troy (*Forgers and Critics*, 23). In the early modern period, the task of consolidating and reinforcing national identity shifted from prose fabricators to the poets, who were charged with reproducing the identity-conferring functions of the Imperial Roman *Aeneid* in new national epics composed in the European vernaculars; Camoes's *Lusiads* is one case in point, Spenser's *Faerie Queene* another. These two traditions—the venerable tradition of fabricating history and the somewhat more recent one that regarded poetry as privileged bearer of national identity—reemerged and converged in the later eighteenth century in James Macpherson's practice of hoax poetry.[20]

The problem for Macpherson was the reassertion of a separate Scottish identity in the context of Scotland's political absorption into the United Kingdom. His solution was to fabricate a cycle of ancient Scottish epics—the so-called "Ossian" poems, purportedly translated from the original Scots Gaelic—that would serve to consolidate Scotland's national identity. Macpherson's hoax poetry became a model for the fabrication of national identity, not only in the British Isles but ultimately throughout Europe. Bishop Percy, and after him Sir Walter Scott, undertook to reconstruct national culture in much the same way Macpherson had, recovering lost border ballads but also "restoring" and "improving" them, so that the project always involved a certain degree of "forging anew"—a certain finite amount of hoaxing and inauthenticity mixed in with the authentic scholarship. Susan Stewart writes of Scott in particular that his "role becomes more and more that of an archivist charged with the invention of the archive."[21]

This characterization applies not just to outright hoaxers like Macpherson, or ambiguous "improvers" like Percy and Scott, but to the whole project of Romantic nationalism, which invariably presented itself as a project of *recovery*—the recovery and reconstruction of a former national identity that over the course of time, and through illegitimate coercion, had become submerged, effaced, dispersed. National identity, in former times whole (or so it was supposed), had been reduced to mere fragments, and some of those fragments were literal: ruined archaeological sites of former greatness; fragmentary texts attesting to a lost cultural unity—Macpherson's *Fragments of Ancient Poetry*, for instance. Out of these fragments, a renewed national identity would have to be forged—"forged" in both of its relevant senses (*Forgers and Critics*, 32, 34).

In the course of the nineteenth century, Romantic-nationalist folklorists recovered one after another the submerged folk cultures of Europe, thereby setting in place the cornerstones of one "new" (that is, "restored") national identity after another. A case in point is Elias Lönnrot's reconstruction of the Finnish national epic, *The Kalevala* (1835, 1849). Like Macpherson's Ossian, *The Kalevala* is a patchwork of fragments—the surviving remnants, it is alleged, of a lost folk epic, at one time whole and complete. Unlike Macpherson, Lönnrot actually did collect his "fragments of ancient poetry" from folk bards (or rune-singers) in the field, rather than composing them himself, as Macpherson had done, and passing them off as folk productions; or at any rate, Lönnrot didn't himself compose very much of the poem—evidently not more than about 2 percent of the total lines.[22] But it is an open question whether any such epic whole as Lönnrot imagined ever really existed, or whether in fact the fragments he assembled had not originated quite separately of one another, so that, even if the parts were individually authentic, the whole was a fabrication, a kind of collage—a hoax, if you will. However, there can be no question whatsoever of the efficacy of Lönnrot's "forgery," for his *Kalevala* has served as the foundation upon which Finnish national culture came to be erected.

National identity is always, to some more or less substantial degree, a fabrication—a fiction—so it can hardly come as a surprise to learn that projects of national identity-construction have relied so often on hoaxes and forgeries of various kinds, and in particular on hoax poetry. One might assume that "national" or "ethnic" motives for hoax poetry would have faded away once the great nineteenth-century projects of national identity-building had been brought to more or less successful conclusions, but this appears not to be the case. National identities, it turns out, require regular maintenance, refurbishment and defense and hoax poems are apt to be implicated, on one side or the other, in such identity-maintenance. If, as appears to be the case, "national" and "ethnic" hoaxes have tended, in the course of the twentieth century, increasingly to resort to prose genres instead of poetry, this is not because identity-maintenance has any less need of inauthenticity, but merely reflects poetry's increasing cultural marginalization. As the cultural functions that were once the privileged preserve of poetry have tended to migrate to prose genres, so too have "national" and "ethnic" hoaxes.[23] From this perspective, poetic hoaxes such as the Ern Malley and Yasusada hoaxes seem almost old-fashioned, reflecting a residual privileging of poetry as cultural medium.

In the case of Ern Malley, an unmistakable nationalistic subtext runs like a thread right through the hoax. Ern Malley, one critic writes, is "a site of conflict," pitting "the modern against the traditional, [and] internationalism against nationalism" ("Australian Hoax," 95). The documents in the Malley case offer ample confirmation. For instance, there is an unmistakable tone of xenophobia, anti-internationalism, and defensive–reactive Australian provincialism in the letter to the press wherein the hoaxers, McAuley and Stewart, exposed their hoax. The victims of the hoax, Max Harris and other *Angry Penguins* editors and contributors, represent, according to McAuley and Stewart, "an Australian outcrop of a literary fashion which has become prominent in England and America."Their hoax, they write, is aimed at debunking the literary movement that "began with the Dadaist movement in France during the last war, which gave birth to the Surrealist movement, which was followed in England by the New Apocalypse school, whose Australian counterparts are the *Angry Penguins*" (quoted in *Ern Malley Affair*, 137, 139). One does not even need to read between the lines to see that the danger being fended off by means of the hoax is a threatening cosmopolitanism—poetry that is French, English, American, in short, anything but Australian. A minor protagonist in the Ern Malley hoax, writing at the time, exults, "I don't think anything could have happened so salutary—so completely prophylactic!"[24] National prophylaxis: one begins to understand now where that benighted police detective picked up the idea that the Ern Malley poems must somehow be indecent!

The Yasusada case raises national-identity issues in a different way. Where the Ern Malley hoax constituted a kind of rear-guard defense of national identity against a threatening internationalism, the Yasusada hoax has been read as an act of aggressive cultural imperialism, an illegitimate misappropriation of identity. The issue is not so much one of external imperialism—the misappropriation of a Japanese identity by a non-Japanese—as internal colonialism, the miming of Asian identity by (presumably) a poet who is not himself an Asian–American (though, strictly speaking, that has yet to be established). This reading of the case has been advanced most forcefully in a collective contribution to the *Boston Review* Yasusada forum by a group of Asian–American intellectuals (Juliana Chang, Walter K. Lew, Tan Lin, Eileen Tabios, and John Yau), who charge the Yasusada hoaxer with performing in "yellowface," on analogy with the demeaning blackface performances in which certain white American entertainers once specialized.[25]

But there is also a more positive approach to reading the national-identity issues engaged by the Yasusada impersonation. It is possible, I would argue, to see the Yasusada notebooks as a kind of experimental laboratory for identifying and analyzing forms of cross-cultural misprision—the ways that cultures mutually construe, and misconstrue, one another. Far from seeking to con us into believing in a fictitious Japanese poet, the Yasusada experiment compels us to see that this poet, constructed in this particular way, could only be the product of a North American cultural imagination, just as the "America" that this imagined poet in turn imagines reflects a Japanese construction of American culture. Each construction—the American construction of an imagined Japan, the imagined Japanese construction of America—is "wrong," in a sense, but by juxtaposing their respective "wrongnesses" about each other we perhaps achieve something like a scale model of cross-cultural assimilation and resistance, cross-pollination and contamination, difference and sameness.

It is possible, in other words, to place a more positive construction on the indulgence in inauthentic *japonoiserie* with which some experts (as I noted at the outset) have charged the Yasusada impersonator. If the Japan of *Doubled Flowering* is a North American's projection of Japan, the "japaneseness" it projects is not an arbitrary invention, but one rooted in certain concrete historical tendencies in American poetry, which the hoax serves to bring to light. Eliot Weinberger rightly observes that the Yasusada poems rely on "the style, not of Japanese poetry, but of American translations of Japanese poetry," in particular the translation conventions popularized by Hiroaki Sato, and he concludes that "Yasusada, regardless of authorship, is very much an American Japanese poet: a product of the specifically American tradition of translating Japanese poetry."[26] Elaborating on Weinberger's point, we might go on to specify all the ways the Yasusada texts evoke, sometimes against the grain, the entire history of Japanese poetry's "presence" in North American poetry, back to Pound's *Cathay*, Imagist aesthetics, turn-of-the-century *japonoiserie* of the Lafcadio Hearn and *Madama Butterfly* type, and beyond. In short, viewed in this light, the Yasusada texts appear less as a (flawed, uninformed, stereotyped, and the like) representation of Japanese culture, then as a reflection *on* the representation of Japanese culture. We are being invited, not so much to look through a North American lens at Japan, but rather to examine the lens itself.

Moreover, what we see when we do look through the lens is a Japanese poet looking back at us. One of the more striking anomalies of the Yasusada texts, as detailed by Marjorie Perloff, is the presence in them of North American (and more generally "Western") writers who could not possibly have been available to a Japanese poet at the time these poems were allegedly written. This is conspicuously the case with the San Francisco poet Jack Spicer, who is evoked in several of the texts.[27] Not only do the Spicer allusions serve to alert us to the flagrant "inauthenticity" of the notebooks—Spicer, at that time (the Sixties) a thoroughly obscure figure even in his homeland, would surely not have been noticed in Japan—but they also inaugurate a kind of thought-experiment, in which we are invited to speculate, if a Japanese poet did have access to American avant-garde poetry of the Sixties, which poet might he have found attractive, and why? Well, perhaps Jack Spicer, and perhaps because Spicer, apart from anything else, figures among the postmodern heirs of the "japanized" or orientalist tendencies in the poetry of earlier modernists such as Pound.[28] The same pattern may be discerned in Yasusada's reading of Roland Barthes's *Empire of Signs*—a reading that, as Perloff observes, is strictly impossible, given the date ("Authentic Other," 150). Barthes, the "Westerner," misconstrues Japan; Yasusada, the Japanese, in turn misconstrues Barthes's misconstruction. It is through such loops, such back-and-forth traffic of mutual misprision, that the Yasusada impersonator stages and engages issues of national cultural identity.

But surely, in staging such misprisions, any Japanese poet would serve; why imagine one who is specifically identified as a Hiroshima survivor? The motives for introducing Hiroshima into the Yasusada back-story are too many and too complex for me to enumerate here, but one reason, at least, must be to avoid minimizing the obstacles to cross-cultural exchange. Impeding all the avenues to free, unhindered trafficking in cultural models and values between Japan and the United States is the looming fact of the atomic bombings and their aftermath. The fact of Hiroshima endlessly complicates Japanese perception of America and American perception of Japan; so, rather than wish away this major barrier to mutual cultural exchange, the Yasusada impersonator factors it in by imagining a poet who is situated right astride that barrier, who *embodies* that barrier in his own person and his own life-story: Araki Yasusada, survivor.

3

The "something more," then, that helps explain the violence of the negative reaction to the Yasusada impersonation is its venturing to tamper with constructions of national or ethnic identity. By exploring identity issues with the tools of inauthenticity, the Yasusada impersonator joins the long historical sequence of (to recall Susan Stewart's phrase) "archivists charged with the invention of the archive," beginning with Macpherson and Chatterton in the eighteenth century and continuing right down to Pessoa, the Ern Malley hoaxers and Kenneth Koch in the twentieth. But Yasusada has more immediate precursors as well, some acknowledged and others left unacknowledged, and some brief consideration of one of these precursors may serve to place the "essentially criminal act" of the Yasusada impersonation in sharper perspective.

The principle unacknowledged precursor of *The Notebooks of Araki Yasusada* is *The Tablets*, a book-length poem by Armand Schwerner.[29] Begun in 1968, and continued in irregular instalments down to Schwerner's death in February 1999, *The Tablets* comprises twenty-seven sections, some no longer than a page, the last ones twenty or more pages long, purporting to be scholarly translations of Sumerian pictographic texts incised in clay tablets some 5,000 years ago. The Sumerian originals of which *The Tablets* are a translation don't exist, of course; like Macpherson's pseudo-translations of ancient Scottish poetry, *The Tablets* are a kind of hoax. Unlike the "Ossian" poems, however, but similar to the notebooks of Araki Yasusada, the hoax is designed to be seen through almost immediately. *The Tablets*, in other words, constitute a mock-hoax.

Armand Schwerner openly acknowledged his authorship of *The Tablets*, signaling it unambiguously by placing his own name on the title page; while the ultimate authorship of the Yasusada poems (if such a concept even makes sense) is multiply veiled, placing Yasusada (as Kent

Johnson puts it) "in a different attributional state altogether and therefore in a considerably different conceptual field" from The Tablets.[30] In
this sense, if in no other, The Notebooks is much more fully and uncom-
promisingly a mock-hoax poem than The Tablets.[31] But, granted this crucial difference between the Yasusada notebooks and their precursor, what
can The Tablets tell us about the nature of "national" or "ethnic" motives
in The Notebooks, or in contemporary hoax-poetry generally? First, in
what sense, if any, do The Tablets tamper with national identity?

The answer is not immediately obvious. After all, Schwerner is not
projecting a contemporary ethnic "other," as the Yasusada author does,
but rather a temporally remote one, poised at the very limit of recorded
history. How can national identity categories of any relevance to a contemporary poet possibly figure in a poetic world displaced so far from
the world of the poet's immediate experience?

More than once, in comments made late in his life, Schwerner seems
to suggest that his motives for entering into the elaborate fiction of The
Tablets included experimenting with alternative forms of Jewish identity.
Born in Antwerp, a non-observant American Jew—in fact a practicing
Buddhist—Schwerner had no interest in any of the available models of
American Jewish identity. Instead, he sought to construct an alternative
model by identifying imaginatively with the temporally distant Semites
of the ancient Middle East. In a piece prepared for the Australian journal Boxkite, Schwerner wrote, "Invested in the wonder about my beginnings, I went to the Sumerians, the first Everything in high civilization,
and thence to the Akkadians my Semitic relatives." "My profound disinterest in almost any manifestation of 'Jewish' Americana," he wrote in the
same vein to Norman Finkelstein, "is one of the factors that led me
5,000 years back to find, represent and embody my relatives the
Akkadians."[32] How seriously are we to take these professions of a
"national" or "ethnic" motive behind The Tablets? Schwerner was, after
all, a hoaxer—a trickster, not to be trusted. Nevertheless, our confidence
in Schwerner's (half-) seriousness here may receive a boost if we pause
to reflect for a moment on some of the historical fabrications endorsed
by Schwerner's own poetic precursors—in particular, Pound and Olson.

Pound, as one hardly needs to be reminded, regularly relied on
"authorities" of the most dubious kind to shore up the historical infra-
structure of his long "poem including history," The Cantos. In particular,
he relied in at least two of the late Cantos—Canto 94 from Rock-
drill and Canto 97 from Thrones—on the historical fabrications of one
L. A. Waddell.[33] Waddell (1854–1938), a retired British army officer and
colonial administrator, and an amateur orientalist, asserted, in a series of

(highly repetitious) books published from the mid-1920s through the late 1930s, that the ancient Sumerians, Egyptians, Phoenicians, and the city-dwellers of the Indus Valley were one and the same people, that they were all racially Aryans, that these Aryans were responsible for all the advances attained in this earliest phase of civilization-building, and that, as seafaring people, they disseminated civilized values throughout the world, as far as ancient Britain and perhaps even to the Americas. The motives animating Waddell's extraordinary reconfiguration of ancient history were barely veiled, if at all: he intended to exclude the Semites (including Schwerner's "relatives," the Akkadians) from any credit for the founding or development of civilization. Nor was Waddell's anti-Semitism restricted to the ancient world. The British, according to Waddell, are descended from "the Phoenician sea-going branch of the Early Aryans or 'Sumerians,'" and it is their Sumerian racial heritage which may, he writes, "give the British an advantage over non-Aryan and non-seafaring people, the Jews for example and the Chinese, in the contest for the future control and development of Civilization."[34]

It is all too easy to imagine why Pound would have found Waddell's historical fabrications so attractive. Charles Olson, too, was attracted to Waddell's Herodotean scope and "poetic" boldness of speculation. He more than once recommended Waddell to his readers, students, and proteges.[35] But Olson also recognized and deplored, as his own mentor Pound did not, Waddell's anti-Semitic agenda. Referring to Waddell, Olson wrote to the younger poet Robert Creeley from Yucatan, "... I balk ... or at least resist, simply because I take it, racism has to be kept at the end of a stick.... ((As you know, this whole intellectual demarche, has, at its roots, a negative impulse, deeper, even, than the anti-Asia colonialism of Europe: at root, the search is, to unload, to disburden themselves, of Judaism, of Semitism.))"[36]

Schwerner would surely have been aware of both Pound's and Olson's interest in Waddell. When we return to *The Tablets*, we detect there not only the expected echoes of Schwerner's precursors Pound and Olson, but also of Waddell himself. The Scholar–Translator of the Tablets, Schwerner's fictional alter ego, seems to entertain historical fantasies resembling Waddell's. Seeking, in Tablet XXVI, to decode a pictographic script that seems to belong to the very earliest strata of the history of writing, he speculates on the existence of a scribe in touch with the archaic beginnings of human consciousness whom he calls, out of the blue, the "Ur-Aryan" (*Tablets*, 77). Schwerner, in one of the entries in the "Journals/Divagations" appended to *The Tablets*, clearly reflecting on these strange late developments in the Scholar–Translator's thinking,

offers this telegraphic annotation: "S/T's [i.e., Scholar/Translator's] anti
'Semitism' " (*Tablets*, 145). So, whether Schwerner knew of Waddell's historical fabrications directly, or only inferred them, or something resembling them, from his readings in Pound and Olson, he certainly appears
to have woven Waddell's anti-Semitic revisionism into the fabric of the
late *Tablets*.

Having detected the presence of Waddell, or a position akin to his, in
the ironic, dialogic structure of *The Tablets*, we are now able to return to
the question of whether Schwerner had any serious purpose in constructing a simulacral "Semitic" identity. The ancient Semitic ethnic
identity constructed in *The Tablets* now appears to have had a polemical
purpose: it answered and rebutted Waddell's construction of a history of
civilization devoid of Semites.

We have to do here with more than one kind of inauthenticity, of
course. On the one hand, there is Waddell's and Pound's variety, which I
suppose involved a large measure of self-delusion. Waddell may well have
believed in his own fabrications (as perhaps Binjamin Wilkomirski, the
present-day Holocaust-survivor impersonator, does in his), while Pound,
whether or not he fully believed in Waddell, certainly found the latter's
fabrications opportune. On the other hand, there is Schwerner's variety
of inauthenticity, which is clearly intentional and tendentious—strategic.
Think of Schwerner's strategy here as a kind of "counter-inauthenticity."
Instead of answering the manifest inauthenticity of Waddell's fabricated
history with "authentic" history—the "truth" of the distant past, to the
limited degree that that truth is recoverable at all—Schwerner opted
to answer one inauthenticity with another: to fabricate a collection of
documents, a cast of characters, a quasi-fictional world to counter
Waddell's fabrications. By countering inauthenticity with an alternative
inauthenticity—a mock-hoax—Schwerner exposes the fictiveness of all
identity-construction. It is, *mutatis mutandis*, the same strategy that the
Yasusada impersonator adopts in *The Notebooks*: mobilizing the counter-
authenticity of a knowingly fabricated "Japan" to counter all the national
identity-constructions, all the "Americanisms" and "Japanese-nesses,"
that are the common counterfeit currency of culture.

Coda

So much depends on the maintenance, in good working order, of these
constructs—Americanism, Japanese-ness—or for that matter Scottishness,
Finnishness, Australianness, Jewishness, Aryanness. From time to time,
hoax poets have been called on to lend a hand in the maintenance of such

constructs. At other times, however, they have sought treacherously to undo these identity-constructs, to trope upon them, and then other kinds of cultural agents have had to be called in to police the hoax poets and prevent unsanctioned tampering with national identity. Literary journals and their editors have sometimes served such police functions. This is the function that Arthur Vogelsang, editor of *The American Poetry Review*, was performing, whether consciously or not, when he (reportedly) denounced the Yasusada impersonation as an "essentially criminal act."

Perhaps the editor of *The American Poetry Review* is not so different, except in his methods, from the Australian police detective who, responding to public outrage, initiated a criminal prosecution, on the implausible grounds of indecency, of the Ern Malley poems. Known locally around Adelaide by the nickname of "Dutchie" (*Ern Malley Affair*, 186), this police detective's full given name (I'm not making this up) was Jacobus Andries Vogelesang.

Notes

I was privileged to be able to present versions of this paper on three different occasions, to three different audiences. The first occasion was a panel with Kent Johnson and Chiaki Sekiguchi at the Festival of Postmodern Piracy at Kent State University—Salem on 16 April 1999; the second, the Eighth Tampere Conference on North American Studies, University of Tampere, Finland, 22–25 April 1999; and the third, a panel on "Poetry and the Inauthentic" at the 115th MLA Annual Convention, Chicago, 29 December 1999. My thanks to the organizers of all three events, especially Doug Rice at Salem, Ralf Norrman at Tampere, and Peter Quartermain at Chicago, and to my fellow panelists at Salem. Special thanks to the panelists and audience at Chicago, including Charles Bernstein, Philip Mead (unable to attend in person, his paper was read for him by Bob Perelman), Hank Lazer, Michael Davidson, Norman Finkelstein, Tyrus Miller, and Aldon Nielsen; far from clarifying matters for me, they only complicated them!

1. Arthur Golden, *Memoirs of a Geisha* (New York: Random House, 1997).
2. In a curious contribution to the *Boston Review* forum on the Yasusada case, Vogelsang claimed that the words "essentially criminal act" were not his, but had been placed in his mouth by the *Lingua Franca* interviewer, Emily Nussbaum. On the other hand, in a follow-up letter he repudiates as a fraud the letter in which he denies the words were his ... which leaves us where, exactly? See "Lessons from a Hoax: Responses to the Araki Yasusada Affair," *Boston Review* 22 (Summer 1997), 3. http://bostonreview.mit.edu/BR22.3.
3. The Yasusada texts were subsequently published in book form by a small press; see Tosa Motokiyu, Ojiu Norinaga, and Okura Kyojin (trans. and eds.), *Doubled Flowering: From the Notebooks of Araki Yasusada* (New York: Roof Books, 1997).
4. John Solt, professor of Japanese culture at Amherst College, quoted by Emily Nussbaum, "Turning Japanese: The Hiroshima Poetry Hoax," *Lingua Franca* 6(7) (November 1996), 1.
5. John Burnham Schwartz, "Masked Memoir," *The New Yorker* (29 September 1997), 82.
6. Eliot Weinberger, "On Yasusada: Can I Get a Witness?" and "Postscript: I Found a Witness," *Jacket* 5 (1998), http://www.jacket.zip.com.au/jacket05/yasu-weinberger.html; repr. in part from *The Village Voice Literary Supplement* (July 1996).

7. On the Wilkomirski case, see Philip Gourevitch, "The Memory Thief," *The New Yorker* (14 June 1999), 48–68.

8. A case in point: if the Wilkomirski "memoirs" are ultimately judged to be fabrications, then they will be reclassified as a "novel," and merely shifted from one shelf of the bookstore to another; see Gourevitch, "Memory Thief," 52. But once Yasusada was revealed to have been an impersonation, how could the Yasusada texts be reclassified? What shelf could they be shifted to?

9. Actually, the situation is slightly more complicated, since Golden interposes an intermediary, a fictitious translator named Jakob Haarhuis, between himself and his memoirist; the book professes to be Sayuri's memoirs "as told to" Haarhuis. But this intermediary figure, who might be seen as veiling the fictionality of the memoirs themselves, never reappears after the opening "Translator's Notes." Moreover, in the acknowledgments at the novel's end Golden dispels any lingering ambiguities by declaring outright that "the character of Sayuri and her story are completely invented."

10. On these and other forgeries, literary and non-literary, see Ian Haywood, *Faking It: Art and the Politics of Forgery* (New York: St. Martin's Press, 1987). On the history of textual forgery, and its symbiotic relationship with the development of philology, see Anthony Grafton, *Forgers and Critics: Creativity and Duplicity in Western Scholarship* (Princeton, NJ: Princeton University Press, 1990). Grafton usefully distinguishes forgery proper from, on the one hand, pseudepigrapha, that is, misattributed works, and mystification, "the production of literary works meant to deceive for a short time only, as practical jokes" (5). His category of forgery proper corresponds to my category of "genuine" hoax, while my other two categories fall under his rubric of mystification (though his attribution of only one motive, that of practical joking, to such productions seems to me too limiting). I am indebted to Bob Griffin for calling this book to my attention.

11. On the Ern Malley case, see David Lehman, "The Ern Malley Hoax: Australia's 'National Poet,' " *Shenandoah* 34(4) (1983), 47–73; Paul Kane, "An Australian Hoax," *Raritan* 11(2) (Fall 1991), 82–98; and especially Michael Heyward, *The Ern Malley Affair* (London and Boston: Faber and Faber, 1993). The Ern Malley case is also a touchstone of K. K. Ruthven's *Faking Literature* (Cambridge: Cambridge University Press, 2001), which appeared too late for me to be able to take it fully into account here.

12. For Sokal's hoax, see Alan D. Sokal, "Transgressing the Boundaries: Toward a Transformative Hermeneutics of Quantum Gravity," *Social Text* 46/47(1–2) (Spring/Summer 1996), 217–52; for the hoax's exposure and its repercussions, see Alan Sokal, "A Physicist Experiments with Cultural Studies," *Lingua Franca* (May/June 1996), 62–4, and "Forum: Mystery Science Theater," *Lingua Franca* (July/August 1996), 54–64. See also Steven Weinberg, "Sokal's Hoax," *The New York Review of Books* 43(13) (8 August 1996), 11–15. On the ambiguous Tom Keating case, see Haywood, *Faking It*, 118–27.

13. I am indebted to Charles Bernstein for this perspective on the "social text" character of hoax poetry.

14. See Ian Haywood, *The Making of History: A Study of the Literary Forgeries of James Macpherson and Thomas Chatterton in Relation to Eighteenth-Century Ideas of History and Fiction* (Rutherford, Madison and Teaneck, NJ: Fairleigh Dickinson University Press/London and Toronto: Associated University Presses, 1986).

15. For later generations of Australian poets, as for the New York School poets John Ashbery and Kenneth Koch, Ern Malley's poetry came to be seen as a model for emulation rather than, as the hoaxers McAuley and Stewart intended, an admonition and warning; see Heyward, *The Ern Malley Affair*, 229–34.

16. See Marjorie Perloff, "In Search of the Authentic Other: The Araki Yasusada 'hoax' and what it reveals about the politics of poetic identity," *Boston Review* 22(2) (April 1997), http://bostonreviewi.mit.edu/BR22.2/Perloff.html; repr. as "In Search of the Authentic Other: The Poetry of Araki Yasusada," in Motokiyu *et al.*, *Doubled Flowering*, 148–68.

The Ern Malley poems, too, were salted with clues to their own inauthenticity; one of them even reads, "It is necessary to understand/That a poet may not exist"; "Sybilline," in *Ern Malley: Collected Poems* (Pymble, NSW: Angus and Robertson, 1993), 30. Their advertising of their own inauthenticity enhances these poems' susceptibility to being reclassified retrospectively as a mock-hoax, instead of the trap they were intended to be; on the other hand, for the hoaxers' original victims failure to pick up these clues served only to sharpen their humiliation.

17. I am paraphrasing Bernstein's unpublished paper, "Fraud's Phantoms: A Brief Yet Unreliable Account of Fighting Fraud with Fraud (No Pun on Freud Intended), with Special Reference to White Male Resentment," delivered on the panel, "Poetry and the Inauthentic," MLA 115th Annual Conference, Chicago, 29 December 1999.

18. Bernstein's reading finds corroboration in some of the other responses to Yasuda; for instance, many of the contributors to the *Boston Review* forum on the Yasusada case ("Lessons from a Hoax"), including those most sympathetic to Yasusada, seem to take it for granted that the hoax's intention was to unmask poetry editors' extra-literary agendas; see the contributions by Charles Simic, John Bradley, Greg Glazner, and Jon Davis.

19. Bernstein could counter (as he did on the occasion of our MLA panel) that the formal interest of the Yasusada text is only a kind of decoy, designed to give readers such as myself grounds for justifying Yasusada in aesthetic terms. In doing so, we make ourselves accomplices in the primary hoax, and victims of the secondary hoax. Bernstein's catch-22 is hard to escape, for the more reasons one gives for *not* reading Yasusada as a trap-hoax, the more one exposes one's gullibility with respect to the secondary hoax.

20. On Macpherson, see Robert Folkenflik, "Macpherson, Chatterton, Blake and the Great Age of Literary Forgeries," *Centennial Review* 15(4) (Fall 1974), 378–91; Haywood, *The Making of History*, 73–100 passim; and especially Hugh Trevor-Roper, "The Invention of Tradition: The Highland Tradition of Scotland," in *The Invention of Tradition*, ed. Eric Hobsbawm and Terence Ranger (Cambridge and London: Cambridge University Press, 1983), 15–41. It is painful to recall that Trevor-Roper, skeptical debunker of the cherished myths of Scottish national identity, was himself duped in the case of the forged Hitler diaries.

21. Susan Stewart, "Scandals of the Ballad," in *Crimes of Writing: Problems in the Containment of Representation* (New York and Oxford: Oxford University Press, 1991), 131.

22. See Juha Y. Pentikäinen, *Kalevala Mythology*, trans. and ed. by Ritva Poom (Bloomington and Indianapolis: Indiana University Press, 1989), xv.

23. Contemporary "ethnic" hoaxes tend to favor the prose memoir; Wilkomirski's *Fragments* is a case in point, as are a number of other recent hoax "ethnic" memoirs, purportedly by Native Americans, Australian Aboriginals, and others. Note, too, that even the poetic hoaxes under discussion here are actually mixed poetry and prose: the forged letter from Ern's sister Ethel is an integral part of the Ern Malley hoax, as are the interpolated letters and prose appendices (interviews with Kent Johnson and Javier Alvarez, commentary by Mikhail Epstein, afterword by Perloff, and others) in the Yasusada case.

24. Brian Elliott, letter to Clem Christesen, 23 June 1944, quoted in *Ern Malley Affair*, 135.

25. Juliana Chang, et al., "Displacements," in "Lessons from a Hoax." The charges leveled in this letter are all the more telling in view of the fact that at least three of the five signatories (Lew, Lin, and Yau) are themselves avant-garde poets with strong track-records of refusing to pander to simplistic (nostalgic, essentialist, and other) constructions of Asian–American identity.

26. Weinberger, "Postscript: I Found a Witness," *Jacket* 5. See also his "Three Footnotes," in "Lessons from a Hoax."

27. For example, the letters to Ozaki Kusatao and Akutagawa Fusei, dated 17 November 1965 and 7 November 1967, respectively; the untitled and undated poem dedicated to Spicer; and the poem entitled only "6," which the editors' note identifies as "a transformation of poem #6 in Jack Spicer's 1965 collection *Language*"; *Doubled Flowering*, 62, 78, 80, 81.

28. On Spicer's relation to Pound's orientalism, see his rewriting of Pound's paradigmatically "Japanese" (and Imagist) poem, "In a Station of the Metro": "Ghosts drip/And then they

leap/The boy sang and the singing that I heard:/Wet shadows on a stick"; "Who Knew," from *The Heads of the Town Up to the Aether* (1960–61), in *The Collected Books of Jack Spicer*, ed. Robin Blaser (Santa Rose: Black Sparrow Press, 1989), 131.

29. Previously available only in partial editions, *The Tablets* appeared in a complete edition in 1999 (Orono, ME: National Poetry Foundation).

30. "An interview with Kent Johnson, conducted by Norbert Francis," *Jacket* 5 (1998), http://www.jacket.zip.com.au/jacket05/yasu-larsen.html.

31. We mustn't exaggerate, however: despite the name on the title page, Schwerner's authorship is neither unambiguous nor absolute. Throughout the "Divagations" appended to the text, and even more so in his last interviews (e.g. Willard Gingerich, "Armand Schwerner: An Interview," *The American Poetry Review* 24(5) [September–October 1995], 27–32), Schwerner tended to distance himself from the Scholar–Translator, his fictional alter-ego, who is alleged to be responsible for the translations and their idiosyncratic, sometimes downright loony annotations. Nevertheless, it is often unclear where "Armand Schwerner" leaves off and the "Scholar Translator" persona begins. The situation is further complicated by the proliferation of other authors and sub-authors upon whom responsibility for parts of the texts or their translations are occasionally off-loaded: ancient scribes, nineteenth-century scholarly precursors, contemporary collaborators, and so on. How can we be certain, given this complicated Chinese-box structure, when we are hearing Schwerner's "own" voice, rather than that of some subordinate figure or ventriloquist's dummy? Nor does it clarify matters that one of the tablets (Tablet XII) proves not to be a fake but an "authentic" translation of an actual clay-tablet text: a pseudo-pseudo-translation! In view of all these complications and mystifications, the claim that *The Notebooks* belong to "a different attributional state altogether" from *The Tablets* seems less tenable.

32. Quoted in Finkelstein's *Not One of Them in Place: Modern Poetry and Jewish American Identity* (Albany: SUNY Press, 2001), 115–16.

33. See Boris de Rachewiltz, "Pagan and Magic Elements in Ezra Pound's Works," in *New Approaches to Ezra Pound: A Co-Ordinated Investigation of Pound's Poetry and Ideas*, ed. Eva Hesse (Berkeley and Los Angeles: University of California Press, 1969), 187–9.

34. L.A. Waddell, *The Makers of Civilization in Race and History: Showing the Rise of the Aryans or Sumerians, Their Origination and Propagation of Civilization, Their Extensions of It to Egypt and Crete, Personalities and Achievements of Their Kings, Historical Originals of Mythic Gods and Heroes with Dates from the Rise of Civilization about 3380 B.C., Reconstructed from Babylonian, Egyptian, Hittite, Indian and Gothic Sources* (London: Luzac & Co., 1929), 517.

35. See, for example, "The Gate and the Center" and "Proprioception" in *Charles Olson: Collected Prose*, ed. Donald Allen and Benjamin Friedlander (Berkeley, Los Angeles, London: University of California Press, 1997), 170, 188.

36. Charles Olson, "Mayan Letters," in *Selected Writings*, ed. Robert Creeley (New York: New Directions, 1966), 97–8; double parentheses are Olson's.

INDEX

Lackington, James, 157–8
Laertius, Diogenes, 50
Lamb, Jonathan, 62n45
Lamb, Susan, 89, 92–5, 96, 98, 102n18,
    102n19, 102n20
Langhorne, John, 155
Lavalley, Albert J., 190n37
Lawes, Henry, 31, 34
Lawrence, D. H., 81, 83, 100n3
Lazer, Hank, 249
Lee, Vernon, 220
Lehman, David, 250n11
Leighton, Angela, 196, 203, 207n11,
    209n33
Lejeune, Philippe, 231n20
Lennox, Charlotte, 9, 91, 92, 152, 153
Lessing, Doris, 8, 17n24
Lester, Elizabeth, 13, 152
Levine, George, 190n35, 192n56
Levine, Joseph M., 58n3, 58n5, 58n6,
    58n7, 61n35
Lew, Walter K., 243
Lewes, George, 197
Lewis, M. G., 192n58
Liddle, Dallas, 11, 15n2, 17n20,
    230n5
Lilliat, John, 38n34
Lin, Tan, 243
Lintot, Bernard, 70
Locke, Don, 188n10
Locke, John, 67
Lockridge, Laurence S., 230n6
Lockwood, David, 230n3
London, Bette, 196, 207n11, 208n12,
    231n16
Loewenstein, Joseph, 37n28
Lönrot, Elias, 241
Love, Harold, 36n5
Lucas, Charles Reid, 158
Lucian, 43
Luke, Hugh J., Jr., 17n15
Lyles, W. H., 189n21

Mackenzie, Anna Maria, 146, 148,
    151, 152, 158
Macnamara, Matthias, 104
Macpherson, James, 236,
    240–1, 245
Maitland, Sara, 194

Malley, Ern, 14, 236–7, 238, 239, 242–3,
    245, 249, 250n11, 251n16, 251n23
Manley, Delariviere, 71, 92
Manning, Peter, 15n2
Manton, Jo, 188n7
March, John, 109
Marcus, Sharon, 15n2
Marlatt, Daphne, 194
Marlborough, Duke of, 119
Marlowe, Christopher, 19
Marotti, Arthur, 20–1, 24, 36n5,
    36n7, 36n8, 36n13, 37n19, 37n24,
    37n30, 38n32
Marshall, Alice Kahler, 193, 207n1
Marshall, David, 190n39
Martin, Violet, 194
Mason, Mrs., 170
Massingham, H. J., 207n7
Masten, Jeffrey, 37n22
Matthews, Eliza Kirkham, 153
Matthews, Elizabeth, 165n6
Maturin, Charles, 159
Maurer, Oscar, 230n5
May, Steven, 38n34
Maynard, John, 230n6
Maynard, Theodore, 196, 207n8
McAuley, James, 236, 242, 245
McBurney, W. H., 165n3
McCuaig, William, 59n17
McDonald, Peter, 230n6
McGann, Jerome, 15n2, 36n8
McGovern, Barbara, 66, 69, 71, 78n5,
    78n15, 79n18
McInerney, Peter, 173, 178, 189n27,
    190n39
McKenzie, D. F., 16n12, 38n8
McKeon, Michael, 58n7
McWhir, Anne, 78n12
McWhirter, David, 79n24
Mead, Philip, 249
Meegeren, Hans van, 236
Meeke, Mary, 158
Meerhoff, Kees, 59n17
Mellor, Anne, 173, 179, 189n26, 189n29
Meres, Francis, 24, 38n31
Mermin, Dorothy, 67, 78n8
Messenger, Ann, 69, 78n14
Miller, Jacqueline, 37n28
Miller, Tyrus, 249